COUPLE

is about falling in love . . . almost falling out of love . . .

Franny

Feisty, funny, smart-alecky, and scared to death underneath, she never even *hoped* anybody as gorgeous as Michael would ask her out. Or insist on taking care of her. Or tell her he wanted to marry her . . . and have children with her. Loving Michael was like a fairytale come true . . . until it all came apart.

Michael

Strong, sexy, and mature, with a face that belonged on a magazine cover, he was drawn to Franny's childlike wonder and innocence, the two things he no longer felt after Vietnam. All he wanted was a wife and children, so he reinvented himself to fit into Franny's life. Accepting her family. Her religion. Her home. He just wasn't prepared to accept himself . . . or what was going to happen to him.

. . . AND DISCOVERING THE IMPORTANCE OF LOVE

Such A Lovely Couple

Linda Yellin

WARNER BOOKS

A Time Warner Company

WARNER BOOKS EDITION

Cover photo by Herman Estevez
Cover lettering by Carl Dellacroce

Warner Books, Inc.
666 Fifth Avenue
New York, N.Y. 10103

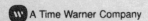 A Time Warner Company

Printed in the United States of America

First Printing: November, 1991

10 9 8 7 6 5 4 3 2 1

For Rick Cadwell
who's in my heart

People I am grateful to, owe favors to, and would be willing to loan money to:

Jennie Fields for all her butt-kicking and hand holding; Susan Spano Wells for wrangling me into kick-off position and making me laugh; Rita Parpan and Jack Hetherington for all the repeated attacks on their corporate laser printer; Bruce Beach for dog tag lessons and perspective; Debbie Purcell for all her long distance cheerleading; my editor, Jamie Rabb, one gracious lady; and the mystique-laden, ever-cheery Lisa Bankoff, my agent. Stay healthy. Bernadette, Stephanie, Dahlink, Joel, and Colleen, well shucks, you *knowwww*. And FCB, Chicago, for all the 3M yellow Post-its I stole out of your supply cabinet while freelancing on No Nonsense Pantyhose in 1988.

❧ *Chapter 1* ❧

He called me up and told me this whole long story about meeting me at a party and seeing me in the library and being in the same English class as my roommate Piper. By then I was too embarrassed to tell him I didn't know who the hell he was, so I said, yeah, sure, lunch would be fine.

When I interrogated Piper about him, she said, "Michael Wedlan? Oh yeah. Real cute. Real smart. Nice guy. But not your type."

"Why isn't my type cute, smart, and nice?" I asked.

"I think Michael was in Vietnam," Piper said. "All his English compositions are about jungles and mutilated bodies."

"Oh," I said, the corners of my mouth turning downwards. "Not my type."

It was 1972, and in the interest of school spirit, I'd done my share of protest marching and candle lighting and banner drawing, but I could never quite work myself into the proper

1

frenzy. I descended from a long line of mild-mannered, extremely pleasant people who, having successfully escaped the pogroms of Czarist Russia, promptly dedicated their lives to avoiding anything smacking of politics. Other students were so *passionate* about hating Vietnam. But I didn't want to hate anyone. I was having a good time.

Michael suggested we meet at the YMCA cafeteria. In my three years at the University of Illinois, I had dined in many of the finer culinary establishments in town: McDonald's, Burger King, the dorm, but never the YMCA. I stood in front of the TODAY'S SPECIAL CREAM OF MUSHROOM sign, surrounded by sounds of scraping chairs and clinking silverware, waiting for someone who might have been a soldier in Vietnam, someone who might actually have napalmed babies and burned a few villages.

What if the guy was *insane*? The papers were filled with tales of crazy Vietnam vets. What if I was about to have lunch with a *crazy man*?

The more I thought about it, the more the idea appealed to me. Plenty of women knew men who would kill for them. But I was about to meet one who knew *how*.

Piper had instructed me to look for a sort of tall guy with sort of dark hair and maybe green eyes.

"That's it? Nothing more specific?" I said.

"If you mean will he be wearing fatigues and have a jagged scar across his face—no, Franny, probably not."

As I was checking my watch and thinking maybe soldier boy was standing me up, a tall, dark-haired man with green eyes walked up, radiating confidence with his straight posture and his held-back shoulders, like someone had stuck a yardstick down his shirt. I promptly projected upon him all sorts of wondrous attributes: strong, tough fighter; masterful in bed; someone I could fall wildly in love with and who would fall even more wildly in love with me and care for me and protect me and seriously maim anyone who ever looked at me cross-eyed.

My imagination had a way of conjuring up glorious imaginary futures.

"Oh good, you waited," he said, immediately taking charge and guiding me toward the cafeteria line. "Do you know what you want to eat?" This was a man who got right down to business.

"Not really." I stared at rows of little dishes filled with balls of egg salad. "It all looks so healthy."

"You're not into health food?"

"Not unless I can wash it down with a Twinkie."

Michael paid for his tuna fish sandwich and glass of milk, and the red Jell-O, Coke, and french fries on my tray, after saying hello to the salad lady and hi to the cashier. He was awfully friendly for a killer.

"I haven't eaten here before," I said, sliding into a green vinyl booth underneath a picture of Jesus.

"My dad used to run this place when I was a kid." Michael smiled.

"Really?" I pointed at the wall above us. "So this must be his picture!" Michael stopped smiling. "Sorry," I said. "Dumb joke." I couldn't decide if I should eat my Jell-O with a spoon or a fork so I decided not to eat it. "Was your dad the owner or something?"

"He was the director."

"The son of a director. That sounds very glamorous."

Michael handed me half of his tuna sandwich. "Here. You better eat this. Pretend it's a Hostess Ding Dong."

I thanked him for the sandwich, politely took a bite, then placed the sandwich on my tray. Michael stared at me with such bemusement that I wondered if I had something stuck in my teeth. I scrambled for some dazzling conversation-grabber, one that would leave him thinking I had a brilliant and discerning mind.

"So," I ventured, "where do you live on campus?"

"In a house on Tenth Street."

"With your parents?"

"Are you *kidding*?"

Apparently I had offended him. "Yes, I'm kidding." I pounded on the bottom of an upturned ketchup bottle, aiming for my fries.

"My folks live in Springfield now," Michael said. "My father's retired from the Y. He's teaching Sunday school at the Baptist church."

"That's one wholesome background," I remarked, setting down the ketchup bottle and busily dumping salt on top of the ketchup I'd just dumped on top of my fries.

"What about you?" he asked.

I hate answering what-about-you questions. My answers always come out boring, like one of those obituaries that leaves you feeling all depressed because the person led such an uneventful life. But I plunged ahead with various vital statistics. "We're Jewish. We live in Chicago. My mom's a mom and my dad makes plastic terrariums—those things that look like see-through plastic space saucers that people stick plants in. They're very big now. You've probably seen them in hardware stores and floral shops and K-Mart carries them. Dad got a huge order from K-Mart. Before that he used to make pet supplies, but somebody sued him for stealing some top-secret dog-bowl design so he had to quit. Have you ever owned a dog? I always wanted a dog but my mom worries about her carpets so we never got one."

I slowly became aware that one of us was chattering and it was me. I had a bad habit of getting all nervous and hyper, resulting in my rambling about ridiculous subjects when talking to guys who looked like they belonged on magazine covers. And at the moment I was sitting across from a Greek god candidate. Even then, I could usually perceive the former boy in the man or the onetime girl in the woman, but there was nothing soft or childlike about Michael's features. It was as if he'd been *born* looking like an adult. His thick dark hair kept falling onto his forehead in a way that made me want to reach over and touch it. And his eyes were the most intriguing combination of tenderness and wariness. But the funny thing was, he wasn't intimidating gorgeous. He was sort of *approachable* gorgeous. I rarely got a shot at gorgeous. Gorgeous rarely asked me out. Not that my looks were totally hopeless or anything. A lot of guys liked girls with dark curls, brown eyes, and slight potbellies. People often told me I was pretty. But it was usually people like my mother or my aunts.

"Tell me about yourself," I said in what I hoped was a sophisticated voice. "I want to know absolutely everything." I couldn't remember just which movie I'd heard that line in, but I was pretty sure it was Lauren Bacall who had said it, and she always seemed to say the right thing.

"I'm twenty-six years old," Michael said.

"Yow!" I blurted. I was twenty years old. To me, anyone twenty-six was a Social Security candidate.

"Yow what?"

"Yow nothing. Please continue." I pushed back my plate of Del-Monted-to-death fries and asked about his major. In college, majors were considered key personality traits.

Michael looked momentarily perplexed. "I'm an advertising major, Franny. I'm working on my master's. I told you that when we met at the department Christmas party."

"Oh, of course!" I cried, like silly me, how could I forget?

"You were standing in the corner with your girlfriend drinking punch and singing all twelve choruses of 'The Twelve Days of Christmas.' "

That was not an event I particularly wanted to be remembered for. And I certainly couldn't believe it was the basis for someone wanting to ask me out on a *date*.

Michael smiled at me. "You were quite charming."

He thought I was charming.

"Do you want something different?" he asked, eyeing my abandoned fries and untouched Jell-O. "Maybe there's something else you'd like. How about a hot dog? I could get you a hot dog. They have good ones here." He was so eager to please that I was beginning to wonder what was wrong with him. I wasn't used to any guy being that nice to me.

"No, thanks," I said. "I read this article, maybe you saw it, on how hot dogs have pig intestines and cow eyeballs and chicken toenails and all sorts of disgusting things in them. Really, they're the worst. I try to avoid hot dogs."

"Thank you for sharing that with me." Michael sat quietly for a moment. I could practically feel him watching my face. "What kind of music do you like?" he asked.

I twirled my straw around in my Coke, making the ice cubes spin. "Oh, just regular music. The kind you hear on the radio."

"Jazz is on the radio. Classical music is on the radio. Do you like classical?"

"It so happens I might be listening to a great deal of classical music and several select operas this summer," I informed him, pausing for effect. "Piper and I are traveling to Europe to become worldly and cultivated."

Michael looked properly impressed. "Have you heard *Madame Butterfly*?" he asked.

"No." I leaned forward across the table. "Have you heard *Iron* Butterfly?"

After that we hit one of those first-date conversational snags. Michael took a bite of tuna. I sipped my Coke. Michael wiped his mouth with his napkin. I hate awkward silences. I always feel obligated to fix them, like they're all my fault. I sat and thought how grateful I'd be if I could possibly meet someone, fall in love, get married, and have children without ever having to go on one more date.

I'd spent the past six months nuts about a junior named Donny Marlowe, who was not the sort of guy any sane, self-respecting woman was supposed to be nuts about. We'd been dating long enough for me to walk up to the second floor of the Kappa Omega house without anyone screaming, "Girl on the floor!" At the time, Donny was rooming with a guy named Richard Waxler, who was a nice enough guy except for a rather distasteful habit of locking Donny out of their room, disappearing with various girls, and throwing used condoms behind Donny's waterbed. But usually Richard wasn't with a girl. Usually Richard hung out with Donny and smoked dope. It was their hobby. So most of my dates with Donny were spent watching Richard and him get stoned. Unfortunately, I didn't know how to get stoned. Donny theorized that there must be some major defect in my DNA or something, because all I ever did was fall asleep. Mortified by my shortcomings, I contented myself with watching Donny and Richard attempt what they called their death-defying drug experiments. Like the night they opened up five Contact capsules and carefully divided hundreds of tiny time pills into little piles of red balls and white balls. Richard swallowed all the red balls and Donny swallowed all the white balls and then we all sat around staring at the walls and waited to see what happened, while I wondered why I wasn't happier.

"I'm glad we got together," Michael was saying.

I told him thank you. "Piper said you were in the service."

"Yes," he said. "I dropped out of Southern and joined the Marines."

"You joined on *purpose*? In the middle of an undeclared war?" I didn't mean to sound appalled, because sounding appalled sounded kind of rude, so I quickly added, "That was very brave."

"No. It was stupid," he said. "When I was growing up my father gave nightly lectures at the dinner table about values and honor and gratitude for the opportunities this country offers us. He'd speak reverently about each citizen's debt and each citizen's duty." Michael shrugged. "So I became a Marine to make my father proud of me."

"Was he pleased?"

Michael picked up his milk glass, drank from it, then soundlessly replaced the glass on the table. "He said I was stupid."

"Oh." I rearranged the folds in my paper napkin.

"My father's devoted his life to staying on an even keel, but the day I enlisted he really lost it, stomping around the living room crying, 'Don't you realize there's a war on!' Like I wasn't intelligent enough to know that. But he adjusted to the idea. He would have been embarrassed *not* to. By the time I left for overseas he just chucked me on the shoulder and told me to keep my wits about me."

I looked at Michael. "And did you?"

"Well, I'm still here," he said softly. He kept slipping back and forth between Mr. Warm, Open, and Friendly, and Mr. Tough, Pensive Marine. "You learn a lot about yourself in a war," he said. "Sometimes it's pretty surprising."

Jesus, I thought, this guy must have done something *terrible*. I was dying to know what it was, but I couldn't think of a polite way to ask. Were you scared? Did you kill anybody? Were you afraid of *dying*? There are still questions I want to ask and answers I need to know. I wish I could call him up so we could talk. But I do know one answer: Michael was scared of dying.

❦ *Chapter 2* ❦

I'd walk out of a classroom and he'd be standing in the hallway waving a Frisbee.

I'd come home from the library and he'd be hovering outside my apartment door balancing two melting ice cream cones.

But after one jazz concert date, one movie date, one Frisbee date, one ice cream cone date, and several evenings spent sitting in smoke-filled coffeeshops holding hands, Michael had still not made love to me. We were in an era of anything goes, and so far nothing had gone. I thought: maybe he's shy, maybe he's not attracted to me, or *maybe it got shot off in the war*! I later found out he was just being extra careful not to make me feel like some one-night stand, sexual revolution aside. But that was much later, when I was also finding out things like the price of a blow job in Vietnam.

Michael had asked me to help him buy a tie that would look nice for job interviews. It was a Friday night and I was wearing the trashiest blouse I owned, a rose-colored, see-through nylon concoction with two huge pockets strategically positioned for decency's sake.

"That's some blouse," Michael said when I met him in the lobby of my apartment building.

"You think so?" I asked, trying to sound seductive.

Michael held open the lobby door as I glided past, my hips slightly thrust forward. "You look lovely," he said. I was

9

sorry Piper was off at a Women Against Psychosis rally. I would have liked for her to hear that.

. Our walk across campus was enhanced by the usual someone's-bombing-something-somewhere-and-fuck-you-Dow-Chemical protest marches, complete with wild-eyed students and terrified campus police. As we wove our way across the quadrangle, Michael gently reached down and laced his fingers through mine, the way my father had when I was a child and he didn't want me running against the red light. We stopped at a corner in Campustown, waiting for a traffic signal. Green Street was surprisingly calm and quiet, its rows of stores usually a favorite target for politically committed window smashers. Michael suddenly let go of my hand and turned his head as he fixated on the crackling sound of static sputtering from a small military radio held by a baby-faced student standing tenuously off to the side in an ill-fitting ROTC uniform. The student was clearly frustrated as he held the radio up to his ear, then out at arm's length, looking at it accusingly as he fiddled with the controls. Michael walked over to the boy and, without saying a word, and with no protest from its owner, removed the radio from the boy's hands and expertly adjusted two knobs, deftly tuning in to a clear frequency. He handed back the radio, the boy now looking both surprised and appreciative as Michael held up two fingers and flashed him a peace sign. Then Michael turned and walked back to me and quietly took my hand. "Former job of mine," he explained, as we proceeded down the street.

We entered Morrie's Men's and Boy's, the largest men's and boy's store in downtown Champaign. Michael headed directly to the section he wanted, his every movement self-assured and focused. I could have ripped off his clothes and ravished him right there on the floor, right in front of the madras sports coats.

"Okay, so what image do you want to project?" I asked.

We were standing in front of a big table that had tons of ties carefully lined up the same way my mother lines up forks for luncheons. "Do you want to look dependable? Reliable?"

"I am dependable and reliable."

"Well then, maybe we should throw in a new aspect to your personality." I held up a handpainted tie obviously inspired by Peter Max. "This one looks creative."

"Too creative," Michael said. "I'll be interviewing for these ad agencies' research departments. I should look like a researcher."

"Perhaps something in a pipe and deerstalker would be nice." I ran my finger along the rows of ties like I was flipping through an index file. It's not easy to match the personality of a tie to the personality of a man who is strong and confident and considerate and vaguely scary all at the same time. "Now I know why I never buy my dad ties," I said. "Now I know why he has twenty bottles of Old Spice."

Michael plucked a burgundy paisley tie from the table. "This is the one," he said.

"That's it? You look at it? You pick it up? You buy it? No holding it up to a shirt or deliberating over how it'll match your suit?"

"Franny, it's just a tie."

"Fine. But there is such a thing as being *too* decisive."

Michael looked at me. "I've decided it's time you came home with me."

"Excellent decision," I said, as he headed toward the cash register, with me in hot pursuit.

When Michael had first told me he lived in a house on Tenth Street, he neglected to say that his apartment was in the basement. And it wasn't one of those garden basement apartments where the windows look out on the street; it was one of those *basement* basement apartments where the windows looked out on people's feet. A laundry room had been revamped into a makeshift kitchen, and a furnace room converted into a living room, which Michael had furnished with bookcases, a pole lamp, and two red bean-bag chairs. A blue plastic bowl sat in the corner of the room next to a water dish, spilling over with uneaten cat food.

"It's very nice," I said.

"It's cheap," Michael said.

"The yellow walls help."

"The landlord's a nice guy," Michael said.

I didn't think there was such a thing as a nice slum lord, but I refrained from saying so. Michael told me that the abandoned food in the corner was for his cat. "He ran away several weeks ago, but I'm still hoping he'll come back." He shook his head. "My cats always run away."

"So why own a cat?"

"I love cats."

Before I could ask why Michael would love a cat that didn't love him back, he opened a door revealing the Taj Mahal of basement bedrooms, a dark seductive room with French blue walls, a cream-colored shag carpet, an Indian madras bedspread, and tiny votive candles, *already lit*, flickering in little holders that looked like miniature jelly jars. Within seconds we had our arms around each other and we were kissing and touching and pressing and feeling and moving our hips in unison. I didn't even stop to worry about will he like my body? Will he hate my thighs? I just wanted all clothes off and I wanted them off *fast*. "There's no rush," Michael gently told me, as I fumbled with one of his buttons. "I want to enjoy every part of making love to you."

Michael treated me like I was fragile and precious. He'd stroke my hair and kiss my neck and glide his hands over my body and look at me like he was afraid I wasn't real. "Does this make you happy? Is this what you want?" he'd ask. I loved touching him and he loved to be touched. His body was strong and beautiful and healthy, except for one small scarred area on his right calf, the size of a penny, the result of a shrapnel wound that tickled and felt sensitive to him if anything rubbed against it. A war wound, I thought. *How incredibly sexy*. I was crazy with the joy of him. And I learned what it was like to feel cherished and safe and connected.

We must have fallen asleep for a while, and when I awoke I was alone, and the air felt cold on my chest. Michael walked into the bedroom wearing only a clean pair of jeans slung low on his hips. I couldn't believe anything that beautiful had just made love to me. His flat stomach and wide shoulders and strong arms were strictly Charles Atlas material. All those push-ups in the Marines had sure paid off.

"Hi," he said, padding over to the bed in his bare feet and leaning over to kiss me. "Are you hungry?"

"Sort of," I said. It must have been after midnight.

"Keep sleeping." He pulled the covers back over me. I stayed in bed and dozed some more, waking when Michael returned carrying a large plate with an omelet and two forks in one hand, and two napkins and an opened bottle of Mateus in the other.

"Dinner is served!" he announced grandly.

"I'm sorry," I said, "but only naked people are invited to this dinner party." Michael removed his jeans.

We sat Indian-style on the madras bedspread, devouring the omelet and taking turns drinking from the bottle of wine. It was a cheese omelet with mushrooms and green peppers and little rivers of melted butter.

"Michael, have you been in love a lot?" I asked, between bites of food.

"That's an odd question," he said.

I didn't think there was anything odd about it. But considering we were both naked, maybe the timing was a bit odd. "I'm just curious," I said.

Michael took a deep breath. "Well, there was *one* girl. Her name was Marianne." I immediately felt jealous of all girls named Marianne. "But it was right before I went overseas. And she got bored with my being gone. So it didn't work out."

"She sent you one of those *Dear John* letters?" That struck me as totally improbable.

"No. She just stopped writing."

"Too bad you didn't know me. I'd have written you tons of letters."

"I know. And I would have been so busy reading them, I would have gotten myself shot."

I popped a sliver of green pepper into Michael's mouth. "I used to sit in algebra and write my high school boyfriend letters and leave them in his locker. He barely had enough room for his books or coats, he had so many of my letters stored in there. Then one day he made me watch him clean out his locker. He threw out my letters and told me he was seeing someone else."

"He was young," Michael said. "He didn't appreciate you."

"What an excellent explanation. Did you have a girlfriend in high school?"

"I thought I did," Michael said. He stopped to wipe the bottom of my chin with a napkin. "But I was wrong. We were supposed to go to this big Christmas formal our senior year—only I got sick with the flu and had to cancel our date at the last minute. She was upset, but we kept dating and everything seemed fine and I asked her to the prom. On the night of the dance I show up at her door in my rented tux with this fancy corsage and the two tickets to the dance and my dad's Chevy, which I borrowed, and she tells me she's not going with me, that the only reason she'd *said* she was going with me was so she could back out, just like I did to her for the Christmas dance.''

"What did you do?"

"I went home and watched television," he said matter-of-factly. "My mother wore the corsage to church on Sunday."

"Here's to all those stupid people who didn't properly love us!" I said, waving the Mateus bottle over my head. I reached for a napkin with my other hand. "And here's to all the omelet butter I've managed to dribble over me."

"I know the perfect solution to that," Michael said, taking away the wine bottle and pulling me up from the bed.

I had never showered with a man before. Michael and I took turns soaping each other and scrubbing his back and scrubbing my back and standing under the spout to rinse off, the process considerably slowed because Michael kept rubbing more handfuls of suds over my body. "I love showers," he said, massaging the back of my neck with a washcloth. "When Khe Sanh was under siege I went fifty-eight days without showering. Until one Sunday morning, when for no reason at all the shelling just stopped! I immediately stripped down and ran into the lake and soaped up. But a new wave of rounds suddenly hit and I had to scramble out of there before I could rinse off. Then all I could do was wait for the soap to dry and *scratch* the damn stuff off." Michael happily scrubbed behind my ears. "I love showers," he said again. "Especially showers with beautiful naked girls." I traced figure eights against his soapy chest and he leaned over and kissed my shoulder. "You have the ability to see the world through the eyes of a child, Franny. I can't do that anymore."

I slipped my arms around his neck and pressed myself against him and grinned up at him. "I bet I can outswear you." I figured that after all those months hanging around a fraternity house I had learned a thing or two. What I hadn't learned was to *never* make a bet like that with a former Marine. Michael proceeded to pleasantly ramble off a list of the most creatively degenerate words I have ever heard. And for his grand finale, he whispered something in my ear which I'm *still* trying to forget. "That's disgusting!" I said. "And not only is it disgusting—it's not even physically possible!"

"Oh *yeah!*" Michael laughed and we hurried out of the shower and raced back to bed and made love once again, in a fairly traditional manner, except for my being cautious not to rub against his shrapnel wound. "When I make love to you, I feel like I disappear," he whispered afterward, our bodies still tangled together.

"Well, don't go too far away." I pressed my lips against his neck, then looked at his beautiful face. "Maybe we should try a new subject. We've already tried sex. How about religion? Is the Sunday school teacher's son religious?"

"No," Michael said, like he was surprised I'd even ask. "I used to attend church. Before I came back from the service. Before Vietnam. But not anymore."

"Why not?"

Michael was lying on his back, staring at the ceiling. He shrugged, and it was several moments before he finally answered me. "Because now I know there's no God."

I started rubbing his inner thigh. "That's funny, I could have sworn I just *saw* him!" But Michael didn't laugh. I leaned back on one side, resting my head on one hand, so I could look at him more closely. His mood had changed so quickly.

"I witnessed a lot of bad things, Franny. Nothing you need to hear or I need to talk about."

"Are you sure?"

He twisted around in my direction, his eyes steadily fixed

on me. "I don't want to talk about them or think about them. Not with you, Franny. I want to protect you from the bad things." I wasn't certain if he meant bad things in life, or bad things in *him*. "I want to be strong for you."

I felt that was an odd, touching thing for him to say, because he was so obviously strong. I touched his face. "Do you ever see your buddies from the war?" I asked.

"Buddies?"

"In the movies guys always have war buddies."

"No," Michael said. "That's all over with."

"Come on," I persisted. "Didn't you have some friend you could borrow soap from or a can opener or bullets? You must have had some buddies."

"Within one month I had three different tent mates; all of them were good guys, 'buddies.' "

"Don't you ever *call* them?" I seemed unable to let the subject drop. "Wouldn't it be nice to get together and rehash old war stories?"

Michael spoke slowly, as if he were inventing the words as he formed them. "Franny, they're dead."

"Oh! I'm sorry. I should have—"

"Each one was killed, one right after the other. After that I stopped sharing a tent with anyone. I felt I was bad luck." A fragile hollowness had edged into Michael's voice. But at least he kept talking. "There was one guy, a big, happy, curly-haired Irish lug, Sergeant Flannagan. He had just returned to Vietnam; *volunteered* for a second tour. Both wrists had been shot through early in the morning. God, did he bleed—a whole poncho full. He wasn't in much pain because of the morphine. Just sleepy. We tried to keep him awake, fearing the sleep he wanted so badly. The med-evac helicopter arrived half an hour after he died." Michael suddenly pulled me to him and enfolded me in his arms. "It's not that we expected him to make it, but if he had lived to be loaded onto the helicopter, we would have been left with some hope.''

I didn't know what to say. I was trying my best to understand. ''I always thought men liked war, that fighting was something primal and basic and thrilling to men. The best years of your life and all that.''

''That's Hollywood bullshit, Franny. Propaganda to lure you into unnatural circumstances. It's confusing to think of yourself one way, then find out you're capable of acting another way.'' I couldn't imagine Michael being confused about *anything*. To me he was so sure of himself. He always did the right thing. Almost like he was following a script.

''I'm afraid of dying,'' I said, pulling my legs closer to me.

''Don't be,'' Michael said. ''Don't be afraid, Franny. Death is no big deal. It's not all that interesting. I've seen a hundred guys die and it's just something that happens.'' He sat up and faced me. ''I don't want you afraid of anything.'' He tenderly pushed a strand of hair off my face. ''I should never have been in Vietnam,'' he said. ''I didn't belong there. This country didn't belong there. All I want is a normal, everyday, wife-and-kids life.'' He hesitated, then said in a hushed, reverent voice, ''I want to be somebody's priority.''

We made love again, but this time Michael seemed somehow frantic and desperate.

Afterward we had Campbell's tomato rice soup and whole wheat toast for breakfast or lunch, it was hard to tell what time it was by then. We were still in bed. I held my soup bowl in two hands and drank from it like it was Chinese tea.

At night, when I can't sleep now, I try to tell myself, maybe Michael was right, maybe there's nothing to be afraid of. I try to conjure up his ersatz bravery and all the things he said that night, all the things he once believed about dying.

That's the conversation that still haunts me the most.

❦ *Chapter 3* ❦

When I was thirteen years old I saw my father's picture in the post office. And it wasn't on a stamp.

Eight months earlier he had kissed his three children good-bye, said he'd call soon, headed for the airport, and left the country. He claimed he was trying to avoid jail. My mother claimed he was trying to avoid child support.

Turns out they were both right.

But standing under those wanted posters in a Chicago post office on a hot day in 1964, I wasn't quite certain just what heinous crime Daddy had committed, what with mail fraud being sort of a new concept to me. Later, when I started asking "what did Daddy do?" questions, I was told I was too young to understand. When I asked the same questions even later, the response was, "Why bring *that* up now?"

But at the time I was thrilled to have a father who had nine—yes, nine—aliases. And he was without a doubt the handsomest man on the bulletin board.

All the rest looked like criminals.

While I was checking out my father's vital statistics, my mother was mailing a letter to her best friend, Beryl, who had moved to New York to become a career woman. Beryl was considered somewhat avant garde at the time. But Mom had known Beryl since some high school club where patriotic girls knitted mufflers for World War II. Mom and Beryl wrote letters back and forth every week. Beryl would write how lucky Mom was to be rid of my father. Mom would write how lucky Beryl was to not have three children to support. As for how I knew what was in my mother's letters, let's just say criminal tendencies were obviously in my genes.

My mother walked over to tell me she was ready to leave and immediately went into apoplectic shock. I guess she wasn't too delighted seeing her former husband's picture plastered on a bulletin board next to killers and thugs. I took her arm and led her outside, where she stood on the sidewalk just sort of slowly shaking her head in the sun. Four months later she married Paul, whom she met on a blind date, and who adopted my brother and sister and me, changed our last names, and moved us all to the suburbs.

Suddenly, I was a woman with a past.

Paul had a son named Eddie, who didn't live with us but occasionally hung around on weekends with his head stuck in the refrigerator. Paul would always ask how Eddie's mother was and what her health was like and whether she was dating anyone she might like enough to marry real soon. This was back when men had to pay lifelong sentences of alimony to ex-wives who didn't remarry. Except, of course, men who skipped the country.

I immediately fell madly in love with Eddie.

He was a senior in high school with green eyes and smelly feet. I didn't care about the feet. He was the only seventeen-year-old boy who'd actually *talk* to me. I'd lie awake in bed at night and wonder if there was some incest-through-adoption law that would prevent me from marrying Eddie. I'd worry about how we'd word the wedding invitations and whether we'd have unhealthy babies.

My sister, Madelyn, was four years younger than me. Her goal in life was to become a game-show hostess. Billy was seven years younger. His current goal was to learn to fart on cue. I tried my best to avoid Billy.

The counselor at my new suburban school, who had apparently read my records or read the newspapers, called my mother and suggested I see a school psychologist, just in case I was traumatized by my father's deserting me. But my mother said I looked perfectly fine, my color was good, and she was sure that wouldn't be necessary. It was an unwritten rule in our family that we were all supposed to pretend we'd led no life previous to our current respectable one. Any mention of Jerry quickly became tantamount to mentioning nun-raping Nazis, gun-toting Vietcong, Nixon-loving Republicans, and other undesirables. Sporadic letters would arrive with the flap unglued, preopened, preread. I wasn't certain just what it was the government was looking for from my father, but it must have been exciting. It's not like they didn't know where to find Jerry. All they had to do was look at his exotic postmarks. The letters were always signed, "Daddy loves you. Daddy misses you. You were not the reasons why I left." I knew that. But I also knew we weren't reason enough for him to stay. My father had never particularly liked me. He just liked me as some glorious reflection of his own manhood. His *daughter*. I suspected he managed to have a wonderful relationship with me over the years despite my physical absence, as if the thought of me mattered more than the actual me.

In the meantime, my mother worked very hard to make us into One Big Happy Family. She did this mainly by cooking gourmet meals and making us all eat them in the same room at the same time. Fortunately, she was a pretty good cook. A regular Betty Crocker.

When Michael started pressing for me to meet his parents,

and him to meet mine, I felt tiny crazy flips in my stomach, but I didn't know if they were from happiness or panic. How likely was it that a gorgeous wonderful guy like Michael would ever show up in my life again?—wanting to marry me and take care of me and buy a home and start making babies. He was everything I wanted, only sooner than I wanted. I was overwhelmed that he had chosen me. If I were someone else, and I knew him and I knew me, I wouldn't even have thought to fix us up. He was so much stronger and self-assured and decisive. I envied him his certainty. And felt guilty that I could experience even remote qualms about marriage and commitment, things that he seemed so positive about.

I once asked him, "Michael, how do you know? You're so *sure*—together forever and ever and all that—it's such a long time. Things do get screwed up. My father left my mother and that was after twenty years."

"I wouldn't leave you, Franny," he said.

I felt enormous comfort in his words. *"Really?"*

"Never."

"Me either," I said. "I would never leave you." I felt safe with him, which was odd to me, because I wasn't aware of having felt unsafe before.

Michael's game plan—our game plan—consisted of Michael finishing his master's while Piper and I spent the summer in Europe, then me finishing my senior year while Michael established himself with a job and an apartment in Chicago. We would marry as soon as I graduated.

"That sounds perfect, doesn't it?" he asked.

"Yes," I said. "Almost too perfect."

So there we were driving to Chicago in Michael's blue Volkswagen, me vaguely nervous, him genuinely excited that his life was going according to plan.

I'd suggested we meet my family first. Piper strongly urged

me to go to Springfield to check out Michael's family first. "You better be careful," she said. "They say you don't marry the man, you marry the whole package." But I wanted to start out with a package I was familiar with. I wanted to start out on friendly turf. I had put off telling my folks about Michael for reasons that weren't all that clear to me, but I knew it had something to do with the fact that once my mother was involved, my engagement would take on a life force all its own.

After all, I was her oldest daughter.

"A wedding!" she squealed. I had called home in the evening because that's when she's the calmest. My mother's always at her best during that one hour each night after the dinner dishes have been cleared away and she's Ajaxed the sink, and she hasn't started worrying yet about what to make for tomorrow's dinner.

"You've got plenty of time, Mom. I've still got another year of school."

"Do you know how hard it is to get a hotel room?" she said. "I can't believe you're marrying somebody nobody knows." I could picture her twisting her index finger through her hair. She had a way of doing that when her thoughts were moving too fast.

"I know him, Mom. That's what counts."

"You never really know a man," she said. "They don't let you know them. You can't rush into these things."

"You married Daddy after only six weeks."

"That was different. We were older."

"You were nineteen."

"The war made everyone older."

"Well, you married Paul after knowing him only three months.

"That was also different," she replied. "I was mature.

I'd been divorced. I'd learned from my mistakes. Believe me. What you want in the beginning of a relationship is not necessarily what you want in the middle.''

She called three times to ask what she should cook for Michael and whether he had any food allergies. Then she called to ask if she should shake his hand when he arrived, or kiss him on the cheek.

On the drive to Chicago, I filled Michael in with a few of the better highlights from my family history.

"This is a fine time to tell me you have the blood of a crook coursing through your veins," he said.

"Well, I was kind of hoping we could name our children Bonnie and Clyde." Michael was steering with his left hand while resting his right hand on my leg. Except when he had to shift. I was holding his shoulders while rubbing my thumb along the back of his neck. Except when he had to shift. Then I'd place my hand on his crotch and also shift. Michael pretended he didn't notice, but he sure seemed to shift gears a lot for a guy who was driving down a straight empty highway surrounded by corn fields. "My new name will take some getting used to. Frances Wedlan. It has a rather nice Christian ring to it, don't you think? If you'd stayed in the service, I could have been Mrs. Lance Corporal Wedlan. That certainly sounds authoritative."

"I wish I could take your last name," Michael said. "Baskin is much nicer than Wedlan."

"I think Wedlan sounds classy."

"Maybe. But I'd rather have your name." Michael concentrated on the road, and inched his foot down on the accelerator. "I'm going to need a flow chart to keep your relatives straight. Paul's your dad and Jerry's your father?"

"Something like that."

"But Paul will give you away when we get married?"

"Definitely. My father already got rid of me once. He's

fulfilled his quota. Besides, if dear old Dad popped up for the wedding, we'd probably have instant FBI agents crawling around." I leaned over and kissed Michael's ear. I couldn't keep from touching him. "Paul'll probably want to talk to you. About your honorable intentions and all that. He can be kind of old-fashioned at times."

"Good," Michael said. "Because I'll be wanting to talk to *him* about your dowry. I'm setting a minimum of ten chickens and twelve goats. And of course I'll be requesting a fine piece of bottomland."

"Any complaints about my bottom?"

"None at all."

I started playing with Michael's hair. It was long enough to weave around my fingers.

"Maybe we should elope," he said.

"That might be nice. That might make a whole lot more sense than anything. If you don't mind my mother hounding you to your grave."

"It's our wedding, Franny. It has to be what we want."

"Our wedding." I was trying on the phrase for size, trying to make it feel real. I leaned over to kiss the back of Michael's neck even though the stick shift jabbed into my hip. "One more thing," I said.

"Let me guess. Your great aunt's an abortionist."

"No. She's a kaluke player. It's about the house we live in."

"It's haunted?"

"It's big. Kind of. Seventeen rooms, not counting the bathrooms."

I think Michael swerved the car a little. I wasn't sure, but I think he definitely might have.

"That's *obscene*," he said.

"I know. Those plastic terrariums really rake in the dough."

"And what happens if people get tired of terrariums?"

"No problem. Paul will invent something else. He's very talented."

I knew my life was radically better thanks to Paul. It scared me how much I loved him. But I'd spent my teenage years living in a huge home feeling like I never had the right to ask for anything. Everything Paul did for us felt like things I didn't deserve.

I stared out my side window, looking for a McDonald's.

Before we all married Paul, my mother and brother and sister and I lived in a scrawny narrow townhouse with four floors, which meant we were always walking up and down stairs. The hardest part was vacuuming the stairs. We'd all fight over whose turn it was to lug the Hoover up those stairs, then compromise by not vacuuming them. There were two tiny bedrooms on the top floor, one for Billy and one shared by Madelyn and me. Mom slept on a day bed in what was supposed to be the family room. Assuming anyone had a family that small. We moved into the townhouse right after my father cut out, right after we had to sell our *twelve*-room house and all the down-filled sofas and silk damask chairs and the antique ivory chess set and half the paintings (no one wanted the portraits of Madelyn and Billy and me), and use the money to pay our bills until Mom retook all the tests she needed to update her teaching certificate, so she could get a job in a life-threatening Chicago neighborhood.

But that was before she met Paul on that blind date set up by his sister, now my aunt Shirley, rescuing and redeeming my mother to the life of a suburban housewife, the job she enjoys the most.

Housing developments were beginning to dot the horizon. We were getting closer to the city.

"We have to live by mountains," Michael said.

"But my parents are here."

"There aren't mountains in Chicago. We should live by mountains."

"Parents are more important than mountains. We have to stay here."

"Okay," Michael said. "If that's what you want."

My mother shook Michael's hand at the door. Later she whispered to me, "If things go well, I'll kiss him when he leaves." I knew she'd have a plan. Her short dark hair was perfectly buffed and coifed. Her makeup was shining. And she was wearing her red silk go-to-luncheons dress and black patent heels. She had dressed up for my future husband.

We were wearing blue jeans.

"I bet you're both starving," she said hopefully.

"No," I told her, "we stopped for Big Macs."

"But I cooked."

"Don't worry," I said. "We'll be starving again soon."

I took Michael on a tour of the house. Our home was so ridiculously big that guests were always walking in and commenting on the size and how they'd never seen such a place and how they'd *like* to see such a place, and eventually it became an automatic reflex to hang up someone's coat and take them on a tour, whether they requested one or not. When we first moved into the house, I was afraid to invite my girlfriends over from my old neighborhood. I was afraid they'd think I'd turned into a snob or a brat, or someone they'd no longer want as a friend.

Our family held long debates over which room got called the den and which the family room and which the TV room. This was especially difficult since all three rooms had televisions. The house had been built in 1927 and hadn't been redecorated since the early forties, so we originally lived there surrounded by claustrophobic floral prints plastered all over the walls and carpets. My mother spent six months and a lot of Paul's money running around the Merchandise Mart with her decorator friend Elaine. The end result was a lot of golds and reds and dramatic touches of black in something that looked like an *Architectural Digest* article gone mad. Plus the paintings. Paul collected modern paintings. None of us knew what we were looking at, but Paul said they were good investments. So we decided we liked them.

"Where is everyone?" I asked Mom, walking into the kitchen with Michael trailing behind me. I had just stood behind the door and mauled him so he'd have to hide a hard-on while talking to my mother. "I just gave Michael the grand tour."

"She certainly did," Michael said, his hands gracefully folded in front of him.

"That's nice, kids." Mom was forming dough balls in her hands and dropping them into boiling chicken soup, making them pop up twice their size.

"Where's Paul?" I asked.

"He'll be home soon. He had a meeting with one of his designers. Some big new idea about a plastic manger scene that also works as a planter. It's for the southern market."

"Sounds very nice," Michael said.

"Those are matzo balls," I told him, pointing to the soup pot. "They look like baseballs and they taste like baseballs."

"What's wrong with my matzo balls?" my mother asked.

"Nothing. They're just kind of heavy sometimes."

"Don't criticize unless you can do it yourself," Mom said.

"I'm suddenly starving," I said. The best way to avoid confrontation with my mother is to eat her cooking.

"Don't spoil your appetite for dinner," she said.

Paul sat at the head of the table. Mom sat at the foot. Billy and Madelyn sat on one side, Michael and me on the other. Eddie was twenty-six, like Michael, and had his own apartment in the city. Paul was hoping Eddie would go into business with him—one of those father-and-son deals—but Eddie had career plans of his own. He sold stereo equipment and dated loose women with money.

The introduction between Michael and Paul had gone quite well. Paul had walked into the kitchen after returning from his plastic-manger meeting, looked at me, and said, "Are you still living in those dungarees?" Then he turned to Michael, stuck out his hand, and said, "You must be him."

Since it was Friday night, dinner started off with Paul saying the blessings over the wine and bread. The kiddush cup was passed around the table, with everyone taking a sip of the kosher wine. Never, in the six-thousand-year history of the Jews, has there been such a miracle as a decent-tasting bottle of kosher wine. Michael was quite a trooper, though, sipping from the cup and smiling.

Mom and Madelyn were carrying in the bowls of soup. I was being treated sort of like a guest and got to keep sitting, I guess in honor of having caught a husband.

"So, Michael, what's this I hear about you in Vietnam?" my mother asked pleasantly, finally joining us at the table. We were all frantically blowing at steaming soup spoons held close to our faces. "You must feel like quite a celebrity."

"Not really," Michael said.

North Shore boys never went to Vietnam. They all hired lawyers to prove they were temporarily insane or psychiatrists to swear they had eating disorders or plastic surgeons to trash out their feet. My brother Eddie avoided the draft because someone had bitten his trigger finger in a college football game and it didn't bend right anymore. He immediately dropped out of college. That's the sort of luck North Shore boys have.

"Did you see any dead people?" Billy asked.

"Of course he saw dead people," Madelyn said. "It's a

war." Then she added, "An illegal war that this country has no business being in, but nonetheless it's a war."

"I was just *asking*," Billy said. "I've never seen any dead people."

"There were a few," Michael said softly.

"What about Grandpa Baskin?" Madelyn said to Billy. "You saw *him* dead."

"That didn't count," Billy said. "He wasn't mutilated with any good wounds. He looked like a wax mannequin."

"I thought they did a pretty good job on him," Paul said. "Real lifelike."

"Do you *mind*!" I cried.

"Has anyone else noticed how much Michael looks like Uncle Sidney?" Mom asked.

"Mom, Uncle Sidney has buck teeth and a broken nose," Madelyn said.

"It's not that," Mom said. "Something around the eyes. The way they crinkle."

"I was looking for the salt," Michael said.

Billy passed Michael the salt shaker, after sniffing it. Billy liked to sniff things. Nobody knew why.

"Sidney's my mother's brother," Mom explained to Michael. "You'll meet him someday. It's just too bad you couldn't have met him before the shock treatments." She tipped her bowl away from her, so she could spoon out the last drop of chicken soup. "His wife's a ball of fun, though."

"Who? Marlene?" Paul grumbled.

"Oh yes," Mom said. "Marlene has so much personality for someone who's married to Sidney."

"Having fun?" I asked Michael.

"It's time for the brisket," Mom announced.

I helped clear the soup bowls. Usually clearing the table and washing the dishes was Odesta's job. She'd been our maid ever since we married Paul and got rich. But Odesta was always having to take time off and travel to South Carolina or North Carolina or one of those Carolinas to take care of one of her sick sisters. Odesta had a lot of sisters. I once suggested to Mom that we eat in restaurants on the nights Odesta was away. But Paul had an unfortunate habit of going into restaurants and thinking he was still in his office—barking orders at the waitresses and constantly getting up to ask the hostess what was holding things up in the kitchen. We'd leave and Mom would say, "Well, there's another restaurant I can never show my face in again." We ate at home a lot.

"I thought you called this brisket," Michael said, biting into his overdone meat. "It tastes like roast beef."

"It is roast beef," I said. "But it attended temple as a young cow." I drenched my plate with ketchup. My mother hates when I use ketchup all over her brisket, but I can't help myself.

"So, was it love at first sight?" Madelyn asked. She was sixteen and enjoyed prying into other people's romances.

"Just about," Michael said. "It was for me." He could be so polite.

"It was plenty fast for me, too," Paul said, chasing after a boiled potato with his fork until he had sufficiently stabbed it to death. "I've been married to Joanne seven years now—"

"Eight," Mom corrected.

"Whatever," Paul said, "and she's still full of surprises."

"What surprises?" Mom asked.

"Lonnie Caswit's older sister got engaged real fast," Madelyn said, daintily biting into a piece of brisket. "She's divorced now."

"What surprises?" Mom asked.

"Well, for one thing, I'm surprised we don't have any cranberry sauce tonight," Paul said. "We always have cranberry sauce on Friday nights. And tonight we don't."

"Surprise!" I cried out.

"I hate cranberry sauce," Billy said. "It's the color of blood."

"I tried to buy cranberry sauce," Mom said, now clearly distressed, "but all the cans at the Golden Shopper were dented, and I didn't want to buy dented cans, because I was worried about us catching botulism or salmonella or whatever it is dented cans come from."

"They come from lousy stockboys!" Paul declared. He was in his I'm-at-the-office mode. "That's the problem with the minimum wage."

I had no idea what the problem was with the minimum wage, but we all nodded like that made perfectly good sense.

"I should have served sliced tomatoes," Mom said.

Michael was taking everything in stride. He had a way of fitting in, a *homines* to him, an ability to make himself comfortable in any situation. He always said the right thing and knew the right thing to do. Watching him charmingly fend off my family's various interrogations, I felt a wave of love for him, the kind that's so wonderful and intense it makes you kind of sick.

"I thought we could have a talk later," Paul said to Michael. "Get to know one another a little better."

"That'll be just fine," Michael said.

I leaned over to him and whispered, "Don't forget about the goats."

Michael never did tell me what went on with Paul, other than to mumble something about a lot of "male-bonding-type talk women wouldn't understand." When we left Sunday morning, everyone walked us out to the driveway, carrying overnight bags, opening car doors, and standing around Michael's Volkswagen giving us advice. In my family, you get a lot of help.

"Have you got enough gas?" Paul asked.

"We'll get gas," Michael said, through his rolled-down window.

"Have you got enough money?" Mom asked. She was cradling an oddly shaped parcel wrapped in aluminum foil. "If you don't have enough gas, you'll need enough money . . ."

"We're fine," Michael said.

"*I* never have enough money," Billy said.

"Don't drive too fast," Mom said. "Better to get there fifteen, twenty minutes later, than have happen to you what happened to Laverne Forbes's daughter."

Michael started to open his mouth. I told him, "Don't ask."

"Is she that girl who drools all the time?" Billy asked.

Paul was walking around the back of the car checking the tires.

"I wish I had a boyfriend with a car," Madelyn said.

"You wish you had a boyfriend," Billy said.

"Better check the air on this back left tire," Paul called out.

"Did you bring a sweater?" Mom asked me, now leaning into the car window.

"Mom, we've got everything we need," I said.

She kissed me and shoved the aluminum foil package through the window. "Cold brisket," she said. "To nibble on."

Paul was standing in front of the car. "Should we check under the hood?" he asked.

"That's the trunk," Michael said.

"Damn German cars," Paul said.

Michael started up the engine of his damn German car.

Paul walked around to the side of the car and stuck his

hand in front of Michael's face. Michael shook Paul's hand. "Welcome to the family," Paul said.

"Thank you, sir," Michael said. "It should be very interesting."

Mom, Paul, Madelyn, and Billy stood in a tight little group in the middle of the driveway, waving merrily goodbye. It would have been a touching sight if they hadn't all been wearing mismatched bathrobes.

As we began to drive off, my mother threw her hands up into the air and cried, "Wait!" as though she'd just remembered something very important. She ran up to Michael's window, poked in her head, and noisily kissed him on the cheek.

❧ *Chapter 4* ❧

Young Americans in Europe was a tour group designed for college kids whose parents wouldn't let their kids go to Europe unless they went with a tour group. This immediately eliminated all draft dodgers and hitchhikers—all the really *interesting* college kids. I had longed to be a young American in Europe ever since my ninth birthday, when I read *Junior Year Abroad*, a book about twin sisters who traveled around Europe and dabbled in lighthearted romances with French and Italian boys who respected them for their minds. But by the time Piper and I arrived on the Grand Continent, I no longer cared about French boys and Italian boys. I spent the summer waiting for letters from Michael.

Michael spent the summer taking the one last course he needed for his master's. In Heidelberg, I received a letter about his job interviews in Chicago. "Apparently everyone's eager to fulfill some government quota and 'Hire a Vet.' Or else—they can't resist my charm." In Paris, I received a letter about the offer he accepted in the research department of Crosswaite & Doran. In Rome, I learned he'd rented a two-bedroom, one-bath walk-up apartment in a fringe area of Lincoln Park, one of those areas that was dangerous one minute and filled with expensive condos the next. He'd be sharing it with another grad from the advertising department who'd been hired as an assistant account executive working on Kraft cheese at J. Walter Thompson. "I don't know Barry very well," Michael wrote in his strong, angular penmanship, scrawled in neat, even rows on yellow lined notebook paper. "But he seems to be a friendly fellow." In Vienna, I found out that Michael had applied for an extension for his term paper, which would delay getting his graduate degree, but he didn't care. He already had a job offer. He'd found an apartment. He was so excited about his new life, it was difficult to concentrate on something as meaningless as a term paper. And P.S.: America wasn't the same without me.

My senior year I no longer fit in with my college girlfriends. They were talking about boys and bars, while I was heavily involved with real-life subjects like pots and pans. On the weekends Michael didn't drive down to campus; I'd cut Friday classes and take the Thursday Greyhound local to Chicago, which made three hundred stops, as opposed to the Friday Greyhound *express*, which only made two hundred stops. But the local allowed me an extra day with the man I loved.

On a rainy Friday night two weeks before Thanksgiving, after I'd carpooled to Chicago with four freshmen boys who played Led Zeppelin tapes full blast the entire trip, Michael gently escorted me to the entrance of his apartment. A red heart cut from construction paper was taped to the outside of the front door. Another red heart was taped to the inside of the door. There were red hearts climbing up the wall, red hearts all across the ceiling, red hearts inching past Barry Salzer's bedroom door, on into Michael's bedroom, across the ceiling, and down the wall leading to the bed, where a tiny heart-shaped box rested on the pillow. Inside was a gold band with a small diamond. Michael had taken out a bank loan to buy me a ring. I didn't feel like anybody who *deserved* anything so beautiful, but I quickly slipped the ring on my finger, glad it was a little tight so that no one could easily take it away.

Michael's mother wrote my mother that she and her husband strongly believed that all wedding plans should be left up to Michael and me, whatever we wanted would be fine by them; they had no intentions of getting involved.

My mother considered this excellent news.

She dragged me on several scouting expeditions to various hotels and wedding halls, always taking copious notes in a purse-size spiral notebook so she wouldn't mix up her facts when she reported back to Paul.

"The Gold Room in the Drake has a view of the lake," she'd say, "but the ballroom in the Hyatt is newly decorated. The Continental promises a cut rate on bartenders, and the Conrad Hilton throws in a free hour's worth of canapes, but that part of town's so seedy, I'm not sure anyone will come."

"How much?" Paul would say. Paul was a bottom-line kind of a guy.

Then Mom would scurry through her notebook looking up price-per-person rates, which could get pretty complicated because the prices kept changing depending on whether you ordered chicken, beef, or threw in a fruit cup. It soon became clear to me that the easiest way to handle all wedding plans would be to just show up and follow orders. My bottom line was: I'd be married to Michael.

My mother finally stumbled upon a place called the Fountain of Gold, a big hall on Melrose Avenue with a neon sign out front that flashed: WEDDINGS, BAR MITZVAHS, AND HAPPY OCCASIONS. The Fountain of Gold was as gaudy as a whorehouse, with brass-framed mirrors and crystal chandeliers and fountains spewing water lit by pink and blue lights, but it featured a thirty-foot sweet table, three hours of a "free" open bar, and fruit cups in carved-out pineapple boats at bargain prices.

Mom turned to me, her face beaming, clearly proud of her major find, and said, "Franny, what's your opinion?"

"Well, it's not really quite what I had in mind," I said. "I was kind of hoping for something a little more understated and, uh, elegant."

"Elegant?" Mom said. "Have you seen that fountain?"

Michael chose to handle all the wedding wackiness with mild bemusement; his one insistence was that the marriage ceremony be held in a temple instead of a hotel room. None of that throw-up-a-canopy-and-call-it-a-house-of-worship stuff for *him*. His Christian roots were nagging.

"No one will come to the ceremony," my mother told me, in one of her many excuse-me-for-interrupting-your-college-studies-but-we-do-have-to-discuss-this-wedding phone calls. "You know this family. If you don't stick the rabbi right under their noses, they'll skip the entire ceremony and just show up for the food."

"Just so Michael shows up," I said. "That's all I care about."

"Do you think he might be going too far with his conversion classes?" she asked, when faced with the prospect of informing my relatives that there'd be a forty-five-minute commute between the temple and the sweet table. "Felice Naper tells me it's the converts who can really turn fanatical on you."

Michael had proposed marriage and Judaism practically all in one sentence. He had been teasing me about how nice it would be to have a wife whose body he could ravish nightly upon demand.

"Marriage isn't even fashionable," I told him. "You're supposed to just live with someone."

"That's something *children* do."

"Well, just because you're crazy about me is no reason to go rushing off to a justice of the peace."

"I figure you'll prefer a rabbi. I can convert."

I wasn't certain if Michael was still teasing me. "But you don't believe in God," I protested.

"I'm a white Anglo-Saxon Protestant from the Midwest with no cultural background, no customs, no way to define myself. Judaism has an entire heritage. That's why it appeals to me. I'll have something to grasp on to. I'll have an identity. A Jewish man knows who he is."

"Yes. And usually he's a short bald guy named Harry or Abe. Do you really think you can qualify?"

"I'll like being Jewish," Michael said. "It'll make things less complicated when we're married."

And after that we were engaged.

I felt blessed that Michael continually wanted to make things easy for me. I didn't know enough to question his constant eagerness to accommodate, his ongoing willingness to reinvent himself. He was handing over big chunks of his soul and all I could see was that he loved me so much he would do anything for me.

Having successfully navigated through Meet the Baskins weekend, I was crazy anxious nervous for Michael's parents to like me, and not be upset that their formerly Baptist son was in love with a currently Jewish girl.

Michael's parents were much older than regular parents. And his sisters were much older than regular sisters. One lived in Spokane, and one lived in Minneapolis, and both had been married and moved out of home by the time Michael entered kindergarten. During World War II, his father, Gordon, had taken a leave of absence from the YMCA and spent two years serving coffee and doughnuts for the Red Cross, and setting up variety shows for our boys overseas. Ten months after his return, Michael was born. Norma Wedlan was forty at the time, which may be kind of trendy now, but then it was considered somewhat of a medical miracle. My first visit to Springfield, I suggested we all attend church. It was my way of saying, okay, so your son's gonna be Jewish, but that doesn't mean we can't all be Christians together.

Whether from a sense of propriety or an absolute acceptance of their son as an adult who made his own decisions, the Wedlans never commented on Michael's decision to enroll in conversion classes. If I'd announced I was turning Baptist, my parents would have taken my decision as a personal insult to their value system, a defection against my birthright. They would have waged a full frontal attack to change my mind. In our nightly phone calls, Michael waxed enthusiastic about his conversion classes. He was more interested in my religion than *I* was.

"Hello, dear!" he would say, with a happy sexy lilt in his voice. I loved being called "dear." It made me feel so grown up. "What did you do today?" he would ask.

"I went to college. Did you go to your career?"

"Yeah," Michael said, without much interest.

"And was it fun?"

Michael never liked discussing his job. "I suppose. I don't know. The people are nice but the job's rather lame."

"Wait until you're chairman of the board. Then you'll have more fun," I assured him.

"I left early to go to classes," he said, the enthusiasm returning to his voice. "Tonight I learned Jews don't get heaven."

I had to stop and think about that particular piece of news. "What do you mean we don't get heaven?"

"I mean you only go around once. Eternal sleep. The black hole. Adios, amigos. This is my kind of religion."

"Jesus. Maybe we should both try Catholic."

My parents' rabbi was too heavy-duty religious for Michael. So Michael had to cough up his own rabbi. He looked in the Yellow Pages under "Temples—Reform," and there was Temple Beth Emmet Israel and Rabbi Rivke. All Rabbi Rivke insisted upon was that Michael go to conversion school for eight weeks, have a few talks, and donate three hundred dollars to Temple Beth Emmet Israel.

"Piece of sponge cake," Michael said.

For another two hundred dollars to cover "clean-up crew and donation," we could get married in the sanctuary.

Michael converted to Judaism in a simple bloodless ceremony held in Temple Beth Emmet Israel the week before Easter. He chose the Hebrew name Moishe after Moses and after my great-great-grandpa Minkovitz, who, according to my mother, was a sage back in Russia, one of those sages who never earned a dime but knew a lot about being Jewish.

"Moishe Wedlan," I said. "Very catchy."

Moishe stood on the bimah in his blue pinstripe suit with a yarmulke on his head and Torah scrolls clutched in his arms while Rabbi Rivke said a few prayers. Then Moishe sipped some wine from a kiddush cup, Rabbi Rivke said some more prayers, made a blessing, and *poof*! I was engaged to a Jewish boy.

Two weeks later I graduated college and Michael's roommate, Barry, moved out to live in sin and secret with his Kraft cheese client who claimed her career would be thoroughly destroyed if anyone at Kraft ever discovered she was living with the J. Walter Thompson assistant account executive, but she was willing to risk all for the love of Barry Salzer. Three months later she would throw him out when her name came up for a promotion, but in the meantime Barry was gone and Moishe the Marine and I got to keep the apartment in the semidangerous fringe area of Lincoln Park.

"Do you expect me to visit you in that neighborhood?" my mother asked. We were in the safe sanctity of my bedroom in suburbia. I was folding and stacking sweaters to take to the apartment. Mom was refolding and restacking them "correctly" as soon as I finished.

"Yes!" I said.

"What if your neighbors steal your wedding gifts?"

"I'll make them give them back."

"I sure hope Michael knows what he's doing," she said. "He's a man. He's safer. Things are different for him."

"He knows what he's doing, Mom."

"Well, if you insist on living there, at least you can make the place nice."

"It is nice."

"I thought this one was mine." She held up a blue cotton knit cardigan with white trim.

"No. You gave it to me."

"I thought it was mine." She refolded it and added it to the pile. "You could use some furniture. You don't have a decent dining table."

"It's okay for now."

"It's too small for dinner parties."

"What dinner parties?"

"You don't plan to invite your mother and father for dinner?"

I started rolling socks. Mom arranged them in subpiles according to color. "It's going to be a pretty expensive dinner if I have to buy a new dining-room table," I said. "But I could use the money from Grandpa Minkovitz. I have about twelve hundred dollars in savings from him."

She stopped sorting socks and sat on the one twin bed that wasn't covered with clothes. "Keep it in your own name and don't touch it, Franny. A wife should always have something tucked away for herself. Then, if something goes wrong, not that I expect something to go wrong—"

"You always expect something to go wrong," I said, shoving the pile of red socks into the pile of blue socks and sitting on the bed opposite my mother.

"I'm just being realistic!" she said. "Nowadays, any woman who's financially dependent on a man is asking for trouble. Look what happened to me with that bum."

"My father?"

"That *bum*. He didn't leave a dime." The subject of my father was always a strained one. My mother could never see past the point that he'd left more than her, that he'd also left his children.

"Michael wouldn't do that," I protested. "He would never leave."

"I'm just trying to warn you," she said. "It's wonderful when a man cares about you. But you can't *count* on it. I've *been* there, Franny. Every person has good points and bad. When we fall in love with someone we concentrate on the good; when we fall out of love we only see the bad. It's all a matter of focus."

"Are you saying Michael might not be aware of my bad points?" I asked, my voice rising.

"No, honey. I'm saying you're newly in love; everything looks rosy; neither one of you might be seeing things clearly now. And I don't want to ever see you stuck in a bad marriage because you can't take care of yourself. Or have someone leave you and you can't support yourself and you don't have any money. Not that Paul and I wouldn't do everything we could to help. But we won't always be here. You just never know.'' Mom smoothed her skirt with both hands. ''Look out for your own interests.''

''Thanks for the vote of confidence,'' I said.

''I'm sure you'll be very happy,'' she said.

❧ *Chapter 5* ❧

My mother booked Stuart Feldman and the Champagne Musicaliers seven months in advance, and even then the only reason we got him was because another bride-to-be canceled after discovering she was pregnant, and her wedding had to be moved up to a date when *Stuart wasn't even available*!

A Stuart Feldman wedding always guaranteed a good turnout.

The initial meeting of the Wedlans and the Baskins took place the night before the wedding at the rehearsal in the synagogue. In what looked like a gallant attempt at unobtrusiveness, Mrs. Wedlan stood off to one side, seeking shelter behind her husband, while alternately craning her neck and peeking around, her eyes darting about. She was wearing a brown wool suit. My mother was wearing a cocktail dress.

After exchanging all those polite pleasantries polite people exchange when they're about to be stuck together as relatives, Mom explained to her captive audience how in Jewish wedding ceremonies *both* parents give away the bride and groom. "It's easy," she said, bestowing her friendliest smile on my future in-laws. "All you have to do is walk down the aisle together, stop halfway, the best man goes by, and you wait for Michael to join you. Then link arms three across, one of you on either side of him, and head on down to home plate!"

During the run-through, Mrs. Wedlan kept saying, "Are you *sure* about this?"

"Yes," I said. "That's the way it's done."

"Okay," she'd say. Then, ten minutes later, "Are you *sure* about this? I would have worn more comfortable shoes."

The next day the sun managed to shine as though Joanne Baskin had personally arranged for it herself, the same way she'd arranged for the monogrammed matchbooks and fifteen dozen printed napkins that said "Franny and Michael."

"Honey, you've got good-omen weather!" Mom gleefully announced, as we all scurried about before our trip to the temple, loading Paul's Cadillac with dresses and shoes and rented tuxedos and spare pairs of pantyhose "just in case."

"What a waste of a great golf day!" Paul bellyached, then flashed a big smile to show me he was kidding. Sort of.

The ceremony began Jewish standard time: half an hour late. Michael's three best friends from high school, Clifford, Wes, and Benny, handled the ushering duties. Paul had a small coronary upon discovering that the ushers were all hippie intellectuals with shoulder-length hair. The bridesmaids were less controversial. Piper, Madelyn, and my cousin Debbie, who had to stand up in my wedding because I stood up in her wedding, wore full-length pink velveteen dresses sprinkled with white hearts. In the interest of coordination, my mother requested that the ushers wear pink cummerbunds with their black tuxedos, but Michael, reminding my mother that he had been in the *U.S. Marine Corps for God's sake*, put an immediate halt to that suggestion.

As I heard the first strains of the music, and my mother's excited voice hurrying the wedding party into position, my sister and I hovered behind a doorway, so nobody could see my dress, condemning me to bad luck, a miserable life, and a ruined marriage. "Your wedding gown looks *perfect*," Madelyn gushed, as she adjusted my veil for the umpteenth time, careful not to crush any of my sausage curls. "Just like Julie Andrews in *The Sound of Music*, only without the ten-foot train." I could hear my mother telling Paul to hold in his stomach. Then I heard her tell him: get ready, get set, go!

"Do I really look okay?" I asked Madelyn. "I'm afraid the only time people will say, 'Oh, how beautiful!' is when they're looking at the *groom*."

"It's my turn!" Madelyn whispered, as we both heard her musical cue. "Take a deep breath before you head out there. And don't worry about tripping." I hadn't even thought about tripping until she mentioned it. Then she added, "You're fine, Franny. You look beautiful. *Honest!*"

I was left all by myself, clutching my bouquet and concentrating on the music. I could picture my sister cruising down the aisle, with my parents flanking the halfway point like two proud bookends, as Madelyn honored the audience with one of her game-show-hostess smiles.

Slowly, finally, standing alone in the entranceway, feeling like I was about to take the first step off a high dive, I propelled myself down the aisle, unable to take my eyes off Michael, ridiculously relieved to see that he had shown up. With Paul on one side of me, and my mother on the other, the three of us marched down the remainder of the aisle while Stuart Feldman sang "We've Only Just Begun." Rabbi Rivke delivered some flowery generic speech about commitment and devotion that I could barely remind myself to pay attention to, and Michael and I exchanged our vows in Hebrew. So I never really knew what I was promising.

For our grand finale, the rabbi placed the traditional wine-glass on the floor and Michael smashed it with his foot. All the Jews in the audience cried out, "Mazel Tov!" All the Baptists turned and said, "Is it over?" Then the wedding party paraded back down the aisle, while the well-wishers stood up and moaned because they had to drive forty-five minutes to the reception.

The Fountain of Gold was even gaudier than I remembered. The room looked like a Vegas casino all glitzed up with colored lights, bold flower arrangements, rows of round ta-bles, napkins folded into fans, and plastic terrariums planted with daisies and carnations as centerpieces. That was Paul's idea. A green adhesive dot had been placed under one saucer at each table to determine which guest got to keep the ter-rarium. That was Mom's idea.

There was a table for immediate Baskins, a table for im-mediate Wedlans, a table for Paul's business friends, a table for temple friends, a table for college friends. There were three tables filled with friends of the Wedlans who had driven up from Springfield. The Tuesday night bridge group was at table ten, the Wednesday night bridge group at table twelve, and the Saturday night bridge group at table six. "If any of these people is carrying a deck of cards, we can cancel the band," Michael whispered.

Michael and I sat with the bridesmaids and ushers at the head table, which would instantly be converted into the ea-gerly awaited sweet table as soon as we swallowed our final bites of roast beef.

There was no table filled with Jerry's relatives. I had written my father with the news of my upcoming marriage. In return, he sent me an expensive card with a note written on the bottom, wishing me great happiness and assuring me how desperately sorry he was that he couldn't be there to escort his little girl down the aisle. I never showed the card to Michael, and I didn't bother to save it.

During dinner there were toasts. Paul's was the longest. It lasted throughout the entire Caesar salad. "Eight years ago," he began, "when I married Joanne—against the advice of my friends, family, and accountant, who are all gathered with us here today on this joyous occasion—I became the happiest man alive."

Wes made a toast. Barry Salzer made a toast. Piper made a toast because she was offended that no women were making toasts.

Then Mr. Wedlan walked to the microphone and all the glass clinking and chair shuffling in the room came to an eerie stop. My relatives were curious to hear what the devout Baptist would say at his son's Jewish wedding. He spoke about when Michael was a little boy and when Michael went to college; and how concerned Norma and he had been that Michael would not return from Vietnam, but today they were delighted to see their son married, and happy. Without any musical accompaniment, standing alone in a room half-filled with strangers, holding his hands against his chest, the timbre of his voice filling the air, Michael's father sang the wedding song from *Fiddler on the Roof*. Sunrise, sunset, sunrise, sunset, he sang. Then, speaking gently into the microphone, he said, "My wife and I are looking forward to our grandson's bar mitzvah." And he strode back to his chair with the same stalwart, square-shouldered posture as his son.

I must have been crying because Michael took a napkin from my hand and edged it delicately beneath each of my eyes. I looked at him like he was something I'd imagined, like he still wasn't mine.

During the roast beef, Stuart Feldman's band played background music, mainly the classics, or what amounted to ten different arrangements of "Tie a Yellow Ribbon Round the Old Oak Tree," and anything ever written by Herb Alpert.

Someone started clinking a water glass and within seconds everyone was furiously banging away at their water glasses, wildly engrossed in the strange ritual of hammering water glasses until the bride and groom kissed.

"Be grateful they aren't using our new crystal," Michael laughed, through puckered lips.

"Remind me never to invite these animals to our home," I puckered back.

"Thank you for marrying me," Michael said.

My mother signaled us that it was time to "work the tables": walk around the room, mingle with the guests, and talk to relatives, while Nick of "Photos by Nick" followed after us with his camera.

We began at the far back table, with my mother's side of the family. "You're such a beautiful bride," my aunt Rose said, clutching my hand in a clingy sweaty grip. "When I saw you walking down that aisle, I poked Herbie in the side and I said, 'Herbie, can you believe for one minute that's Franny? She is such a beautiful bride." Aunt Rose's amazement was bordering on the insulting. "I'll ask your mother for a picture," she said. "I want to remember how good you look today."

"Hey, I hear you were in Vietnam!" Uncle Herbie said, clasping Michael's hand in a hearty shake.

"Uh, yes," Michael said.

"Well, welcome to the family anyway," Herbie said.

"Let's try one of *your* tables," I told Michael as we mingled our way toward another table. As Michael and I moved through the room, the Jewish guests kept stuffing his pockets with envelopes. The Baptist guests brought toasters. We stopped to visit with Michael's two sisters, the ones who were so much older than Michael that he grew up thinking he was an only child. His sister Judith had driven down from Minneapolis with her husband, Walter, who owned a chain of hardware stores in Golden Valley. Michael's sister Diana flew in from Spokane. Diana's husband, Garry-with-two-r's, had not accompanied her. Apparently Garry never attended family functions. But Diana told me how happy she was to have a new sister-in-law, and how happy she was that Michael wouldn't be alone anymore.

We were heading toward the Tuesday night bridge group when my cousin Fern waved us over. Cousin Fern had been widowed fifteen years earlier and swore on Cousin Leo's grave she'd never even *date* another man, much less look at one, a promise that led my mother to speculate whether Cousin Fern's marriage to Cousin Leo was so good that Fern couldn't top it, or so bad that Fern would never risk marriage again.

"How's the punchbowl?" Cousin Fern asked, a big smile spreading across her face. Cousin Fern had some of the best teeth in the family. Cousin Leo had been a endodontist.

"Lovely," I said.

"Lovely," Michael said. I could tell he didn't know *what* punchbowl.

"I knew you wouldn't like it," Cousin Fern said. "Return it. I insist. I want you to be happy."

"Remind me to invite Cousin Fern over for punch and cookies in the near future," I was telling Michael, just as Stuart Feldman's brother did a drumroll announcing the official opening of the sweet table. Michael and I were practically mowed down by relatives stampeding for pastries. Even the Baptists dove right in. Stuart Feldman played a medley of cha-chas to help set the mood. Michael and I stood off to the side and watched. We had no place to sit because our chairs had been removed and replaced with a two-tier fountain spitting out cappuccino. We stood together holding hands like a small, isolated island. The celebration was happening all around us, and I felt more and more like an observer than one of the main participants.

While everyone else careened around the sweet table, stacking their plates and stuffing their faces and jamming "doggie napkins" filled with take-home goodies into their pockets, Aunt Rhoda ran around to all the dinner tables, emptying bowls of peanuts into her purse. Aunt Rhoda never left a wedding without at least four pounds of stolen peanuts.

"This is unfair," my Great-Aunt Lillian said, on her way to the sweet table, leaning on her walker. "I should have been given a half-hour lead time. By the time I get there, none of the good stuff will be left."

Then she leaned in closer and told me, "Don't worry about tonight. It'll be fine," she said, lifting her walker a step forward and continuing onto the sweet table.

I turned to Michael and said, "I think I've just been told to close my eyes and think of England." Nick of "Photos by Nick" snapped a picture.

Michael spent the next half-hour drinking at the bar with Benny, Wes, and Clifford. Paul also hovered around the bar. He doesn't drink. He just wanted to make sure he wasn't being cheated by the bartender.

I didn't want to talk to anybody. I had a mad urge to hide out in one of the toilet stalls in the bathroom. Without Michael by my side, I felt painfully self-conscious from all the constant fussing over me. Michael finally rescued me when it was time for our wedding waltz, which turned out to be more of a wedding tango, as he spun me and dipped me and strutted me across the dance floor.

Stuart Feldman played several horas until everyone got sick from dancing on stomachs full of pastries. "What is this?'' the Wednesday night bridge group asked. ''It's the Jewish hokey-pokey!'' I cried.

Uncle-Sidney-you-should-have-known-him-before-the-shock-treatments drank two vodka tonics and danced the mambo.

Paul paid Stuart Feldman and the Champagne Musicaliers for an hour of overtime.

Aunt Rhoda and her stolen peanuts left with the trombone player.

Mrs. Wedlan told me she'd had a very interesting evening.

Our marriage had begun.

❦ *Chapter 6* ❦

It was a lot like a honeymoon.

During the day we'd tramp up and down San Francisco, snapping pictures of each other posing in front of tourist attractions. At night we'd sit on our hotel-room bed and watch the Watergate hearings on TV. Michael hated for any news to happen without his knowledge.

''Now that's loyalty,'' he said, remarking on some footage of John Dean sitting behind a table, crouched over and talking into a microphone, while his wife, Maureen, sat behind him, her blond hair pulled tightly back in a bun to keep her face from crumpling.

''What's loyalty?'' Michael was lying across the bedspread on his stomach, his chin cupped in his hands; I was perched on his butt, massaging his back.

"She probably thought she was going to be the wife of an important White House staff member. Instead, she's the wife of a stool pigeon. But she's standing by him."

"Oh, come on," I said to the back of Michael's head. "Three months from now she'll write a best-seller and go on Phil Donahue."

"No. She doesn't look the type. But I feel sorry for her. Some people get married without knowing what they're getting into."

"Do you know what *you've* gotten into?" I scrunched back and lightly slapped Michael on the butt.

"So far so good!" he said. He rolled over, reached for the remote control, and clicked off the television.

In the mornings we'd eat bowls of frosted flakes in the hotel coffeeshop while Michael read the *San Franciso Chronicle*, in case anything of the utmost national importance had occurred while we were making love.

"This Watergate business will have immense ramifications," he said, a folded-over newspaper section in one hand, a pecan sweetroll in the other. "What part are you reading about?"

"I'm reading about some woman who killed herself over a guy."

"In Washington, D.C.?"

"No. In Sausalito. She swallowed weed poisoning."

Michael lowered his newspaper. "Jesus, Franny, why do you read that crap? There are countless important events going on in the world, and you get all caught up in that garbage. You ignore anything that has to do with the real world."

I leaned across the table and eyeballed my husband. "Why should I worry about a bunch of screwed-up politicians while I'm on my honeymoon? They'll be just as screwed up when we get home. Pay the check and we'll go upstairs. I want to exploit your body."

"Okay," Michael said, "but all I'm asking is that you be a little more aware."

"I'm aware of the fact that I want you naked, in our room, with a Do Not Disturb sign on the door, within ten minutes!"

"Sir, yes, sir!" my husband said, as he sprang to his feet and quickly signaled for the check.

But he brought along the newspaper.

Having brilliantly failed in my pavement-pounding efforts to obtain a beginning copywriter job in an advertising agency, followed by blazing success in my half-hearted application to be accepted into the Sears Roebuck catalog copywriter intern program, I was on the verge of my career. But I wasn't assigned to show up at Sears until early August, leaving me an entire two weeks to play housewife after Michael and I returned from our honeymoon.

"So, spouse, what do you plan to do today?" Michael asked, leaning across the bed to kiss me goodbye before he left for work. He was wearing a business suit that made him look like somebody's handsome father. I was wearing a trashy black nightgown Piper gave me as a shower gift. I sat up in bed and threw my arms around Michael's neck in some kind of romantic frontal half-nelson.

"I thought I'd take a hot bath, shop, do my nails, eat some Kraft Macaroni and Cheese, then maybe take a nap or two so I'll be refreshed before my beloved returns from his hard day of groveling at the altar of commerce."

"Are you going to make dinner? We've got all those new pots and pans. Perhaps you could try them out."

"You think? They're so nice and shiny, I hate to mess them up."

"Risk it." Michael broke loose from my neck hold.

"Maybe I'll try and figure out the Crock-Pot. It's supposed to be easy."

"Maybe I should bring home a pizza," Michael said, waving his fingers as he left our boudoir.

After a taxing morning of watching game shows, writing thank-you notes, and talking to my mother on the telephone, I decided to tackle the laundry. Our apartment building had a laundry room with only one washer and one dryer, so it was considered a major triumph to do a load of laundry at an off hour. At four o'clock, my washing efforts as complete as they were going to get, I dug through the front hall closet pulling out various Marshall Field's boxes filled with woks and chafing dishes and Corning Ware casserole sets while debating what to cook. I finally settled on the spaghetti pot from Cousin Glenda, who probably had received it as one of her own wedding gifts but couldn't return it and passed it on to me. I could tell because it was from an obscure store and the ribbon was slightly frayed. I strongly suspect that there are two or three wedding gifts that have been floating around the world for years, unused, unappreciated; they just keep getting passed along from bride to bride. But I was grateful to have Cousin Glenda's spaghetti pot. Boiling spaghetti in a pot was a job I could handle.

By the time my corporate warrior returned home, our dinette table looked like a regular Buckingham Palace. Crystal goblets. Fine china. Silver flatware. Brass candlesticks. A tablecloth from the Saturday night bridge group dragging on the floor because it was big enough for a big table and we only had a little table. And for added drama, wet shirts on hangers hung all over the living room. There were shirts hanging from lampshades. Shirts hanging from chairs. Shirts hanging from curtain rods.

"What is this, a garage sale?" Michael asked, surveying the apartment, strutting around, poking about, like he was a general growling his way through an inspection.

"I did laundry," I informed him. "But I didn't want to

leave the shirts in the dryer because then they'd get wrinkles dried into them and I'd have to iron them and I couldn't iron them because nobody gave us an iron. I think I forgot to register for one.''

"I own one."

"You own an iron? You never told me. What else haven't you told me?"

"I have four illegitimate children. Now you know everything." Michael walked around the living room smoothing and straightening his shirts. "Franny, there's a difference between damp dry and sopping wet. There are puddles forming under these things. How much time did you leave them in the dryer?"

"Well, actually I ran out of quarters. Your jockey shorts aren't too bad, though. They should be dry in a day or two, so I went ahead and stuck them in your drawer."

"From now on I'll do the laundry," he grumbled. "You didn't do it right."

"What's not right?"

"Forget it." Michael muttered something about me being lucky to have someone to take care of me. "I'm in charge of laundry."

I was about to protest, then realized that any offering of indignation would be the act of an *insane* woman. If he wanted to do the laundry, let him do the laundry. I was assigned the permanent job of sorting socks. Michael felt I could handle sock sorting.

"What's for dinner?" he asked.

"Spaghetti," I said. "And green Jell-O with marshmallows. Doesn't the table look nice?"

"I'll go change."

"Careful in the bathroom! There are shirts hanging in there."

I tugged on my two brand-new, clean, virginal cooking

mitts, regretting the possibility of messing them up, then moved my new colander that was maybe a flour sifter into the sink, and balanced Cousin Glenda's spaghetti pot over the colander to drain my wet noodles. I added a little store-bought sauce, a little Parmesan cheese, two shakes of pepper. I was some cook.

"They don't go on the same plate," Michael instructed me, standing at the table. He was wearing his blue jeans and a T-shirt. He looked more like Michael again. "The Jell-O's going to melt into the spaghetti. It's started already."

"No one gave us salad plates."

"Then you shouldn't make Jell-O."

"You like Jell-O. Sit down. Eat your Jell-O. I made it a special way. In the freezer. So it would be done in time."

"*Frozen* Jell-O?"

"It's not frozen. You just said it's melting."

Michael picked up his dinner plate. "Let's eat in the den," he said. Barry Salzer's bedroom had been turned into our den. "I don't want to miss the news."

"But what about the candlesticks?" I protested. "We've got goblets here!"

"What about Walter Cronkite?" Michael said, walking toward the den carrying his plate of soggy spaghetti and melting green Jell-O.

After that, we always ate in front of the television.

"Tell me about work. You never tell me about work. You were too busy watching news to tell me about work."

We were lying in bed and I was trying to talk to Michael before he fell asleep. My mother had told me that the secret to a good marriage was never going to sleep mad, so why should Michael get to fall asleep while I was still mad at him for trashing my dinner?

"There's nothing to talk about," he said. "It's just okay."

"Did you miss me? I missed you all day."

Michael paused before answering, his voice truly ingenuous. "You know, I was so busy today I don't think I thought about you."

I sat up. "If you were so busy, why is there nothing to talk about?!"

"I'm tired," Michael said. "We'll talk tomorrow."

I put my head down on my pillow again. I would have preferred resting my head on Michael's chest, but he hated that; he'd shift and move around and complain about my hair tickling. "Michael, are you happy being married?" I asked.

"That's a stupid question," he said, talking up into the dark. "Sure I'm happy. I think you're perfect. Even your weird Jell-Os and stupid questions are perfect. Now get some sleep."

Almost immediately Michael retreated into a deep sleep. I leaned over and kissed him on the cheek, then positioned myself on my back, lying perfectly still, staring up at the ceiling, my arms pressed against my sides, and wondered when I'd adjust to being married, even though I wasn't quite certain just what adjustments I was supposed to be making. Maybe men as husbands were automatically different than men as boyfriends; maybe I was lagging behind Michael and hadn't caught up in knowing how to feel and act *wifely*. I was looking forward to starting work because it would be something to *do*, but I was determined to hate the job for being a compromise instead of the glamorous avocation I felt I deserved. I wallowed in the fantasy of a gleaming polished office with my name stenciled in gold leaf on a frosted glass door panel, a name I wasn't even comfortable with, but one that I considered exceedingly elegant: Frances B. Wedlan, copywriter extraordinaire and woman of the world. And wife. And maybe someday mother. But not that soon a day. First I wanted my job, the one that would assuage all my mother's fears, and reassure us both, that I would never grow up to discover myself financially dependent on a man. My husband.

I was assigned to fans, batteries, fuses, lamps, and electrical appliances.

After two weeks of Sears catalog copywriter boot camp, the Class of August 2nd was parceled out to the various merchandise departments. Dwayne and Louie, my two new best friends from boot camp, were both assigned to hardware, plumbing, pet supplies, and chain-link fencing. Part of the intern program required us to sit in windowless conference rooms, listening to long-term *committed* catalog copywriters gush about Sears employee benefits. We heard about the janitors who retired after twenty years with half a million dollars; the subsidized Searsburgers in the company cafeteria; and the 10 percent discount on anything charged on a Sears employee charge card. At the end of each morale-building harangue, one of the Sears Moonies would stand in front of us indoctrinates, grinning and nodding and asking, "Any questions?" We'd hear about hospital benefits; I'd ask, what happens when you leave? We'd hear about profit sharing; I'd ask, what happens when you leave? I think my employers suspected early on that my corporate devotion was limited.

"That was a good question you asked in there," Louie said one morning as we were all piling out of a thirty-minute lecture on Sears' exceptionally generous accidental-death benefits.

"Which one?" I asked.

"The one you always ask," Dwayne said. "The one about leaving."

"Yeah," I said. "You really clean up on this place if you leave by *dying*."

I learned over some subsidized Searsburgers and fries that

Louie and Dwayne had also spent the past year banging on doors, begging for interviews, and combing the advertising community in search of beginning copywriting jobs. Dwayne had figured he had an advantage over Louie and me—he had a master's degree in communications from Northwestern University.

"Did they pay you a higher starting salary here?" Louie asked.

"No," Dwayne said.

"Did you get stuck getting a job here?" Louie asked.

"Yes," Dwayne said.

"Some big advantage," Louie said.

Louie didn't have a degree in advertising. Louie had a degree in English literature from a small college in Wisconsin. He liked to think of himself as the Truman Capote of the catalog world. Louie was short and beefy with a Jewish Afro and in love with a girl named Nadine who never returned his phone calls. Dwayne was engaged to a pretty redhead named Daisy. He kept her photo pinned up on the bulletin board in his cubicle right next to a photo of Sears complete selection of reversible-bit drills. Dwayne was so tall he could slink around the catalog department and peek over the tops of all the cubicles without standing on his toes. Really, he was about as tall as a guy could get without feeling obligated to be a professional basketball player.

"You'd think having a husband at Crosswaite & Doran would help you land a job there," Dwayne said to me during lunch one day.

"He's not sure he wants to stay there himself," I said. "He thinks it's silly."

"He oughta try this place," Louie said.

"Do either of you want to finish my Searsburger?" I asked. "It's making me sick."

"Now there's a tempting offer," Dwayne said.

"We should find some places to eat in the neighborhood," Louie said, "and get out of here during lunch."

"We could get killed in this neighborhood during lunch," Dwayne said.

"It'll be better when we move into the new building," Louie said. "At least we'll be downtown."

"Yeah," I said, "closer to the ad agencies for noontime interviews."

Sears was building the tallest building in the entire known universe. At least once a week we'd be marched in and sat down to sit through another employee slide show about how many miles of elevator cable and how many miles of telephone cable and how many miles of electrical cable it takes to build the world's tallest erection. We were supposed to leave those meetings feeling very proud and committed. I left feeling more like the Manchurian candidate.

"You know," I told the guys, on the way out of one of our pep rallies, "the more they try and shove this place down my throat, the more I can't wait to get out of here."

"You're just saying that because you aren't feeling creatively challenged," Louie said.

"How can you say that to the woman who just this morning wrote the headline FANS ON SALE?"

"Monkeys on typewriters. That's what we are," Louie said.

"Monkeys on computers is more like it," I said. "Five years from now we're all going to be phased out."

"Then what'll we do?" Dwayne said.

"If I'm still here in five years I'll kill myself," I said. "I'll jump off the world's tallest building."

My dad would get annoyed with me when I'd tell him how many resumés I'd sent out, how many phone calls I'd made, in my mad and futile attempt to get a "real" job.

"You're making a big mistake," Paul would say to me. "Sears is a fine company. A respectable company. It's good to work for a fine, respectable company."

Sears was one of Paul's biggest customers for his plastic terrariums.

"Don't be in such a rush to give up a ten percent discount," my mother warned.

"It's a classic case of displacement," Piper wrote. "You're so settled in your life, you're bored with your job. Find a hobby."

"You don't need a job," Michael said. "You have me."

❦ *Chapter 7* ❦

There was no debate over which set of parents got custody of us for Christmas. One set of parents was Christian. One set of parents was in Miami.

"This is so exciting," I kept blubbering to Michael as we drove toward Springfield through two hundred miles of snow-covered cornfields.

"What's so exciting?"

"Spending Christmas in a real house that celebrates Christmas. I don't care how much Sunday school propaganda gets shoved down Jewish kids' throats, all that 'don't forget Christmas is only one day, but Hanukkah is *eight*.' Forget it! No way! You don't have to be a rabbinical scholar to figure out Christmas is the place to be."

Michael seemed perplexed by my relentless enthusiasm. "You've never been to someone's house for Christmas?"

"Well, yes, sure, there were times friends would take pity on me and invite me over for Christmas dinner, but I'd inevitably end up staring at *their* tree, and *their* decorations, and *their* gifts strewn all over the floor, and feel like a tourist viewing Paris from the inside of a bus."

"My poor little matchgirl."

"Did you buy me something nice?" I asked. "Something sufficiently exquisite to compensate for all the deprivations I suffered as a child?"

"What makes you so sure I bought you anything?"

"The fact that I'd cry and mope and yell and scream and embarrass you in front of your parents."

"Yes," Michael conceded. "I bought you something nice."

He pulled into his parents' driveway just as the sun was setting behind my in-laws' black-shingled roof. "It's eve," I said, my heart captivated by the magic of the moment. "It's Christmas Eve." One scrawny strand of Christmas tree lights had been twisted around the outdoor lamppost, another one, an even scrawnier strand, outlined the frame of the front door. "We should have brought one of Paul's plastic outdoor manger scenes," I said. "Do you think your parents would like one?"

Before Michael could answer me, his father came scurrying out the front door, waving both arms over his head. "Hello, hello," he cried. "Do you need any help carrying things? Your mother thought you might be burdened with lots of presents."

"We can handle it," Michael said. He shook hands with his father. I thought that was strange, men who were related to each other shaking hands.

Right after our wedding, I had begun calling Michael's

mom and dad, Mom and Dad, and Michael had agreed to call my mom and dad, Mom and Paul, because everyone in my family traditionally called their in-laws Mom and Dad, which admittedly confused things and made everyone feel awkward, but that was the way we did things. "How are you, Dad?" I asked, kissing Michael's father on the cheek. He seemed flustered by any show of affection, and didn't return my kiss, but he did say thank you.

"How was traffic?" Mrs. Wedlan asked, as we piled into the house, unloading packages and suitcases and pulling off hats and gloves and parkas and boots. "Don't track in."

"Fine, Mom," I said. "Fine."

The Wedlan house was a study in green. Green walls, green carpets, green chairs with flowers. Little clay pots lined evenly along the windowsills, spitting out African violets. All the living room furniture was pushed against the walls, resulting in a ring-around-the-rosy effect with everything facing everything else, and all of it focused on the television set. A huge pine cone wreath hung over the fireplace in the place where the print of that Andrew Wyeth picture of the crippled girl in the wheatfield usually hung.

"The wreath's lovely," I said, as we all sat down in our usual seats. Mrs. Wedlan sat on the sofa under the picture window; Mr. Wedlan sat in one of the two green easy chairs across from the television; and Michael sat in the remaining easy chair, which automatically, for all future purposes, left me permanently stationed on the one end of the sofa Mrs. Wedlan was not occupying.

"Our Ladies of the King Society sells those wreaths," she said to me, "to raise money for our home for children. You know, children who have been abused or molested."

"That's lovely," I said.

From the top of the television set, three wise men made of cardboard, felt, doilies, and buttons, with pipecleaner smiles, cast benevolent grins across the room. Another strand of Christmas lights had been wrapped around the frame of the picture window behind the sofa. And one of those funny Swedish things consisting of flat wooden sticks glued together like a Christmas tree, with tiny plastic charms stuck all over it, sat perched on an end table. A small glass Santa Claus sat in the middle of the coffee table next to a framed photo of Michael in his Marine Corps uniform. Michael looked kind of mean in the photo, but I figured that was because he was a Marine and they told him to look mean.

"Where's the tree?" I asked.

"Oh, dear," Mr. Wedlan said.

I felt a rush of nervous panic. "There's no tree. There's no Christmas tree. That Swedish thing doesn't count. Where's the tree?"

Mrs. Wedlan responded matter-of-factly. "We've decided not to have a tree this year. We're really all too old for a tree, and you have to lug them in and you have to lug them out, and all the needles get dry and fall off into the carpet, and it takes days to vacuum them out and sometimes you miss one anyway and weeks later you step on it when you're barefoot and it really hurts, so we've decided not to have a tree this year."

Michael smiled at me apologetically and shrugged.

"But you have to have a tree!" My voice rose several octaves. "All my life I've wanted to wake up Christmas morning and have a tree in the living room. We have to have a tree."

"Let's get ready for dinner," Mrs. Wedlan said, standing up and turning toward the kitchen. "Then you can unpack."

"Where will we put the presents?" I said. "There's no tree."

"Under the coffee table will be fine," Mrs. Wedlan said, in a voice clearly meant to imply *subject closed.* "We eat late on Christmas Eve, and then we go to the midnight service. Were you planning on going to church with us?''

"Yes," I said.

"No," Michael said.

"Yes," I said, trying to compensate for feeling so blatantly Jewish whenever I set foot into my in-laws' home. I might as well have had cloven feet and horns.

I set the table, a nondenominational chore I could handle.

Mrs. Wedlan arranged three red Christmas ornaments in a glass candy dish, then placed the dish on a doilie in the center of the dining table. She instructed me to use the official Christmas placemats, pictures of Santa Claus and his reindeer flying through the sky, and the official Spode Christmas china, white plates with green Christmas trees, a gift two years ago from Judith and Walter in Minneapolis, which Mrs. Wedlan explained she liked very much even though the plates took up room and collected dust in the attic fifty-one weeks of the year.

While the women slaved in the kitchen, Michael and his father officially disappeared. They actually upped and left the premises, the slamming of the front door the only announcement of their departure. My mother-in-law made no acknowledgment of the men's retreat. She was far too absorbed with the task of siphoning and spewing juices through a gravy baster held over a meat pan on the stove, while making absentminded conversation.

"We always have lamb on Christmas Eve," she said, her chatting directed as much to herself as to me. "A lot of families have ham, but we always have lamb. At least they rhyme."

"The table's set," I said. "What else can I do?"

"You can whip the Potato Buds," Mrs. Wedlan said. "The beater is under the cabinet next to the stove. Put butter in but not too much butter because too much butter can kill you."

I beat Potato Buds while Mrs. Wedlan boiled peas. "Are your parents away for the holidays?" she asked.

"Yes, they're down at their condo."

"Is it pretty?" she asked, a resonant gurgle emanating from her gravy baster.

"It's nice," I said.

"Did your sister and brother go with?"

"Yes," I said.

"And your father's oldest boy? Eddie, yes?"

"Yes. Uh, no. He didn't." I threw an extra slap of butter into my Potato Buds. "I think these are done."

"Did you add salt?"

I added salt.

The sound of stomping feet interspersed with muffled laughter and an odd swishing noise filtered through the back door as Michael and his father tramped into the kitchen carrying the most endearingly pathetic three-foot Christmas tree I'd ever seen.

"Merry Christmas!" Michael announced.

"Ho ho ho!" his father said.

"Watch those needles," his mother said, spinning around from the stove and doggedly eyeing her kitchen floor for any prickly green offenders.

Michael kissed me on the cheek, his face feeling cold against mine. "Now you can wake up Christmas morning with a tree."

"We were lucky to find a place still open," Mr. Wedlan said. "Most of the trees were picked over, but this little fellow looks pretty good."

"You can decorate it before dinner," Michael told me.

"*After*," Mrs. Wedlan said. "Now get that thing out of here and into the living room and everybody wash up and sit down! It's Christmas!"

"Thank you for my tree," I said. "I love it."

After a Christmas Eve meal spent discussing Patty Hearst, the Simbionese Liberation Army, Nixon, Watergate, Pat Nixon's taste in shoes (Mrs. Wedlan's contribution), and whether the lamb needed cooking another ten minutes or so, I suppressed a mad urge to climb up on my chair and belt out: "Hey, everybody! Lighten up!" Instead, I quietly helped Mrs. Wedlan clear the dishes and clean the kitchen, while the men disappeared again.

"I'll finish up with the counters and drying the rest of the dishes," my mother-in-law said, wrapping a long sheet of Saran Wrap around a bowl of leftover peas. "Go do your tree."

"Are you sure?" I asked. Heavy footsteps were creaking along the wooden planks of the attic. An Andy Williams special was blaring from the television set in the living room.

"Yes," she said. "Otherwise I wouldn't offer." I had a guilty feeling that she wasn't saying what she really meant, that she was waiting for me to *insist* on staying to help, but I was much too eager to dash into the other room to adorn my awaiting tree, and too excited to put any energy into deciphering my mother-in-law's hidden thoughts.

"Are you sure?" I asked again, but spun out of the room before waiting for a response.

Michael's father emerged through the attic door off the living room, his arms loaded with several overflowing boxes of ornaments, lights, and tinsel. "There's enough here for an eight-foot tree," he announced. "That should be plenty to pick from."

Not one ornament, not one strand of lights, not one single piece of tinsel escaped my perusal or remained unused.

"Well, what do you think?" I finally asked Michael and his dad, as I proudly stepped back to admire my efforts. Andy

Williams and every relative he'd ever met joyously sang "White Christmas" in the background. "Worthy of the front lawn of the White House, yes?"

"Kind of gaudy, don't you think?" Michael said.

"It's very festive," Mr. Wedlan said.

Mrs. Wedlan walked into the room drying her hands on a dishtowel. "That's your idea of a Christmas tree?" she said, crossing the room to pull her drapes closed. "It's very nice."

"I like it," I said.

"It's time to get ready for church," she said. "I don't want to miss the preservice chime concert. So wash up and get ready."

"Mom, we haven't gotten dirty since the last time we washed up," Michael laughed. Then added, "We'll be ready whenever you want."

"Suit yourself." Mrs. Wedlan twirled around, tossed the dishtowel over her shoulder like Isadora Duncan's red scarf, and headed toward her bedroom.

The songs and prayers of the Christmas service floated through the church, creating a soft, peaceful, majestic atmosphere. The deacons who usually passed around the give-us-money baskets, passed out short, fat white candles wearing fist-sized rings of white cardboard. As Dr. Regan led the congregation in a few sweet-voiced choruses of "It Came Upon a Midnight Clear," the church lights were dimmed and, one by one, like a gentle relay race working its way down the pews, each congregation member turned to the person next to him and lit a candle.

"This is just like in the movies," I said to Michael. "I feel like Heidi." An old man in the row in front of us turned around and hissed at me.

"Merry Christmas," I hissed back.

Mrs. Wedlan nodded politely to a woman across the aisle

and two pews down from us who was waving her candle at us.

"Who's that?" I asked, half under my breath.

"Charlotte Leckenby," Mrs. Wedlan said. "She and her husband used to play bridge with us Tuesday nights."

"What happened?" I asked.

"He died."

"So she doesn't play bridge with you anymore?"

"Oh, she tried for a while," Mrs. Wedlan said, wrinkling her nose. "But she never really fit in after that."

"That's the Christmas spirit, Mother," Michael whispered.

"Shhhhh," the old man in front of us hissed.

After three rounds of "O Little Star of Bethlehem," and much to my major disappointment, absolutely no rounds of "The Twelve Days of Christmas," we gladhanded, greeted, stumbled, and wove our way out of the church, along with all the other quickly retreating worshippers. Out in the cold night air the congregation members seemed to linger just a moment longer, silently pausing at the top of the church steps before hastily dispersing to their automobiles.

"Don't you find Christmas just a *little* bit exciting?" I later asked Michael, lying on my side of his former, fortunately double, childhood bed, with a green wool blanket wrapped around the two of us. It still felt weird and somehow far too *public* to be sleeping with Michael in a bed that was only one thin plaster wall away from his parents' bedroom.

"It's not my holiday anymore," he said.

"How can you say that? It's your background. Your family."

"Well, yes, sure, of course. Maybe. I don't know." He reached over and squeezed my hand under the covers. "Christmas is a holiday for children. That's why it's fun to see you having so much fun. But we're someone else now."

I looked at Michael, barely able to make out his face in the dark. "We're someone else?"

"Yes," he said. "We're Jewish! Doesn't that make you happy?"

"I guess. I'm happy. But you can't ignore who you are and make yourself into a new person, right?"

This time Michael sounded impatient. "I try to respond to your questions, Franny. I just don't always have the answers. If Christmas makes you happy, then it makes me happy." He pulled me to him, his way of saying, let's get off this subject.

"Michael, do you think your parents think it's strange having me in here with you, with them right next door?" I whispered, my face pressed against his chest.

"They'd probably think it was stranger if you were up here and I was sleeping down in the basement," he whispered back. He was kissing my neck and rolling on top of me.

"Merry Christmas, Michael," I said.

"Merry Christmas, Franny," he said.

I wrapped my arms around him and clasped the muscles in his back. "Oh dear," I said. "I hope we can do this without making noise."

The next morning I was the first Wedlan out of bed.

"I thought everyone's supposed to wake up at the crack of dawn and dash into the living room to rip open their presents," I said to my semialert husband, shaking his shoulder to joggle him out of his slumber. Michael mumbled at me to go back to sleep.

By 9:00 A.M. the family finally, casually, *strolled* into the living room, fully dressed, coifed, chatting about what to have for breakfast and how skinny the morning newspaper was, while I paced around the room and cried, "*Now* do we get to open the gifts?" My first Christmas morning was so unlike what I had wanted it to be, what I'd expected it to be. But I was the newcomer, the intruder. I asked myself: What right did I have to try and turn the day into a scene from *Miracle on Thirty-fourth Street*? PLENTY! a part of me screamed.

"What are you expecting?" Michael asked. "A diamond tiara?"

"I'm just trying to get into the spirit of things."

"We approach our gift giving in an orderly fashion," Mrs. Wedlan said.

"Yes, we have a system," her husband said.

"A tradition," my husband said.

I was being given how-to-be-a-Wedlan lessons. I had married into a small gathering of calm, unflappable souls. No madcap, spontaneous catch-as-catch-can grabbing and ripping apart of presents for this crowd. Mr. Wedlan served as "deliveryman," carefully sorting and dividing each person's pile of presents, then instructing us to take turns going around the room opening gifts one by one.

I got to go first, probably due to the fact that I was panting by then, and I opened a box of blue-colored talcum powder from my in-laws, for which I thanked them profusely. Then it was Michael's turn. I had made him a half-and-half Christmas stocking out of colored felt and Elmer's glue. One side, the Christian side, was green and red and said: MERRY CHRISTMAS. The other side was blue and white and said: HAPPY HANUKKAH. Michael and his father laughed and applauded. Mrs. Wedlan waited impatiently. She opened her first gift next, an automatic drip coffeemaker from Judith and Walter and their kids.

"It's perfect," she said. "The exact make and model number, too."

Michael and I exchanged a *lucky break* look, one I liked to think of as a secret code between two people who were intimately linked through marriage. We had nearly bought his mother the exact same automatic drip coffeemaker, guided by several letters she had written right before Christmas, filled with heartfelt paragraphs relaying how much better life would be if only she had an automatic drip coffeemaker, make and model number included. Before her birthday she had written three times to tell us how difficult it was to find a stylish brown pantsuit, size ten.

Next Mr. Wedlan opened the navy blue cardigan we'd bought him.

"This is very interesting," he said. "And it looks like it might fit."

"It will fit," Michael said. "You wear the same size I do and it fits me."

"You wore it already?" Mrs. Wedlan asked.

"No, Mother," Michael said. "It's new."

Michael surprised me with my first ever silk blouse, and shocked me with a see-through blue negligee.

"It matches my talcum powder," I said, hoping to mask my total embarrassment in front of his parents.

"She'll freeze to death in that," Mrs. Wedlan said.

"I'm still saving for the diamond tiara," Michael said to me, anchoring a kiss on my forehead. I promptly handed him an ornately wrapped package containing a new plaid sports jacket, something I knew he would never buy for himself, probably for good reason. I also gave him a red metal box from Sears with a handle on top and little compartments inside for holding screwdrivers and nails, or fishing tackle and bait, whichever he wanted.

Mrs. Wedlan bestowed upon her husband brown socks and a Weedeater. He'd bought her a matching pin-and-earrings set that looked like Christmas trees made out of sparkling red and green stones, a bottle of hand lotion, and a Chicago Cubs coffee mug, because Mrs. Wedlan worshipped the Cubs.

"These are all very useful gifts," I commented.

"Of course," Mrs. Wedlan said. She opened the can opener we gave her in Sears newest designer color. Celery green. "Very nice," she said. "Did you get a discount?" We'd also bought her a beige cardigan with green trim around the cuffs and neckline. She hunted for the label. "Wool," she said. "Wool scratches. But at least the color's cheery." The last gift of the day was a big box sent from Spokane by Diana and Garry-with-two-r's, an automatic drip coffeepot.

"Have you been hinting again, Norma?" Mr. Wedlan asked. "You ought to vary your hints."

"Oh, Diana never gets anything right," Mrs. Wedlan sputtered.

"It's the same make and model as the one Judith sent," Michael said.

"Well, I don't need two of them!" Mrs. Wedlan said.

The doorbell rang before anyone could respond. Michael opened the front door to three grinning faces, and the Benny, Wes, and Cliff brigade filed into the living room, just like the three wise men, amid a chorus of ho ho ho's and Happy Holidays.

"Who wants coffee?" Mr. Wedlan asked. "Everyone can have their own pot." He scooped up an armful of presents, including Judith and Walter's version of the new coffeemaker.

"We might as well figure this new contraption out," Mrs. Wedlan said, following after her husband toward the kitchen. As soon as Michael's parents left the room, Cliff and Wes sat down on the sofa, Michael sat in his usual chair, Benny sat on my father-in-law's usual chair, and I sat Indian-style on the floor amid colorful scraps of wrapping paper. Benny immediately produced a pack of Camels and a matchbook from his shirt pocket and lit a cigarette. He took a long drag, exhaled a thin trail of smoke, and asked, "Anyone mind if I smoke?" Benny was classified as some sort of conscientious objector, the kind whose main objection was to getting shot. Benny was obligated to teach school in East St. Louis in order to avoid the draft. His students were all gang members and drug addicts. Consequently, Benny smoked three packs a day and drank two.

"Who decorated this Christmas tree?" Clifford asked, eyeing it curiously.

"I did," I piped in. "Do you like it?"

"It looks like something out of Elton John's closet."

"Did you guys get some good gifts?" I asked.

"Shirts and socks," Benny said.

"Three new ties," Wes said.

"Christmas sucks," Clifford said. Clifford was built like a bagful of Lincoln logs, tall and uncoordinated. He was working on his doctorate in philosophy at Ohio State, even though there were absolutely no jobs available for doctors of philosophy. "So what if I can't get a job?" Clifford liked to say. "At least I can be philosophical about it." Wes was a short, bulldoglike combination football-running-swimming coach and driver's-ed teacher for a small high school in a blink of a town right outside of Springfield. When Clifford stood next to Wes, they looked like the letter *b*.

Benny picked up a candy dish, dumped a handful of Brach's peppermint candies into his lap, and flicked a cigarette ash into the empty candy dish.

"So, why don't you gentlemen have any women with you this holiday season?" Michael asked good-naturedly. There was an obvious affection between the four men. The kind that comes from knowing one another for so long, nobody ever bothers to get judgmental.

"Didn't we tell you?" Clifford said. "We're in love, too." He leaned across the sofa and put his arm around Wes. "With each other."

"It's been very sudden." Wes clutched his hand against his heart. "Even the newspapers don't know about it yet."

Then Wes and Cliff immediately disengaged from each other. Midwest boys can only joke like that for so long.

"The last time I had a halfway decent woman with me, you scared her off!" Clifford said.

"Who, *me*?" Michael grinned.

"The one in the restaurant," Clifford said.

"That was ages ago. You haven't had a date since?"

Clifford turned his full attention on me. "This is a tragic tale." He leaned forward with his elbows on his knees and his hands clasped. "I had this new girlfriend," he said, "a good one, one I really liked. Her name was Barbara. A name I really like. And she was plenty good-looking, too."

"You don't mind if I doze off while you tell this story, do you?" Benny asked, shaping a cigarette ash against the candy dish.

Clifford pointedly ignored him. "I take Barbara out to dinner and we're sitting in this restaurant eating steaks."

"You took a girl for *steaks*?" Wes interjected.

"Maybe it was hamburgers," Clifford said. "Let's not equivocate. I was feeding her, okay? And we're sitting by a window overlooking the parking lot."

"How romantic," Benny said.

"I see Michael across the room eating with his parents. This was right after he came back from Vietnam. Right after. And he comes over to our table to say hello."

"A rather friendly gesture on my part," Michael complimented himself.

"You were hitting on my girlfriend," Clifford said. Then he smiled at me for effect, the same way hit men in the movies smile right before they plug you full of bullets. "All of a sudden a car backfires in the parking lot, and your hubby here takes a *nosedive* under the table. It took me through dinner and an extra dessert to convince my date that Michael was a crazy Vietnam vet, and not some guy trying to look up her skirt.''

"*You* were some guy trying to look up her skirt," Michael laughed.

"That took some convincing, too," Clifford said.

"That's a funny story," I said, but I was having a hard time imagining Michael so geared up and on alert that he would have behaved like that.

"And there was another time, before you, Franny," Clifford said, plainly warming to his subject now, "when we're all at this party at someone's house, and some older guy is bragging about his brother being a minister in Vietnam. He was really being a pain in the ass about it. Real patronizing, going on and on about the daily body count and the government lying about it and things being much worse than anyone back here knew, but how *he* knew because he had this brother over there with the inside scoop. Michael's not saying anything. Just drinking his beer. And then this old guy says in this real condescending voice, looking at us, 'Of course, all of you were probably safely tucked away in college at the time.' Well, you could hear Michael's teeth starting to grind. As we all know, he does not suffer fools lightly. Wes and I look at each other, wondering if Michael's gonna punch the guy out, and instead Michael says, in this really stiff, formal voice: 'No, sir. I was in the Marine Corps at the time.' Then there's this real awkward pause and the guy says—waffling now—'Oh really? Where were you stationed?' And Michael answers him, with the words practically spitting out through his teeth: About three miles south of the DMZ.'' Clifford hooted in laughter but Michael didn't join in.

"Why are we talking about all this?" Michael said. He was smiling, but it wasn't what you'd call a sincere smile.

Mr. Wedlan appeared in the entryway wearing his new navy blue cardigan and carrying a tray filled with china coffee cups and a sugar bowl and creamer. "Here comes Mr. Coffee!" he announced. Mrs. Wedlan was wearing her new Christmas tree pin and earrings and holding napkins. Benny stubbed out his cigarette. Mrs. Wedlan didn't acknowledge any cigarette smoke. She just silently fanned herself with the napkins.

After all of us had finally scooted and slid and rearranged our seating so the Wedlans could comfortably sit down among us; when all of us were adroitly balancing coffeecups on our laps, I said to Clifford, "So tell me more stories about Michael right after Vietnam. Did he come back any different?"

"Different?" Clifford said.

"He grew that silly ponytail," Mrs. Wedlan said.

"He cut it off," Mr. Wedlan said to his wife. "He looks fine now. The service gave him direction and helped him grow up."

"Yeah! Before that he was headed for Joliet prison!" Clifford laughed at his own joke.

"No, he wasn't headed *any*where," Mr. Wedlan said.

"He was headed toward bars every weekend and partying his way right out of school," Wes said.

"Let's change the subject," Michael said. "It's Christmas."

❧ *Chapter 8* ❧

Michael, slave to fashion that he was, caught the Asian flu. And maybe it was my imagination, maybe I had a few flu bugs in my own brain, but I could swear Mr. Halls of Montezuma immediately regressed to a five-year-old who needed Mommy.

"It must have been Gregory Fletcher," he said, pacing around the bedroom in his Jockey shorts and an undershirt, reading a thermometer with the same respect and attention he'd normally give to the editorial page.

"It must have been Gregory Fletcher's what?"

"He came to work Tuesday, coughing, sneezing, spreading germs all over the place, and hasn't been back to work since."

"He's probably too terrified to face you. Get in bed," I ordered, taking the thermometer from Michael and reading it. "This only says a hundred. You aren't so sick."

"Franny, people die from this flu." Michael headed for the bed, eager to follow my instructions.

"What can I do for you? You can read the Sunday papers. I can bring you some juice. I can turn on the radio."

Michael crawled under the covers, after reassessing, rearranging, and repositioning the Kleenex box on the nightstand so it was at least an inch closer to the bed. "I should be taking medicine," he said. "What medicine should I be taking?"

"Take aspirin. It's supposed to be a miracle drug."

"Will you get it for me?"

"You're too weak?" I tucked the covers into the side of the bed and smiled my best Florence Nightingale smile. "I'll get aspirin for you."

"And some water?"

I rummaged through the bathroom medicine cabinet. Found some Anacin. Rinsed out a glass. Then detoured through the living room to pick up the Sunday paper, pulling out the TV guide, the movie section, the real estate section, and the fashion section, and tossing all of them onto the sofa. I carried the remaining *boring* parts of the paper into the bedroom along with Michael's aspirin and the drinking glass.

"What if I can't go to work tomorrow?" he asked, his arms lying straight out on top of the covers, like he was awaiting some horrid fate.

"So what? You hate work."

"I've got a big report on the target market analysis of bug-spray users due next week. I'm expected to present it."

"Maybe that's why you're sick." I turned Michael's hand over and dropped two aspirin into it. He lifted his head off the pillow, stuck both aspirins onto his tongue, grimaced, and swallowed a big gulp of water.

"Maybe what's why I'm sick?" he asked, dramatically plopping his head back down on his pillow.

I sat on the edge of the bed. "When I had a book report I didn't want to do in school, I'd get sick. Usually it was my stomach. We'd get an assignment. I'd know what day it was due. And right on schedule I'd start getting nauseous and queasy and want to throw up. People get psychologically sick. It's psychosomatic if it's psychological."

"That's psychological bullshit," Michael said impatiently. "People catch germs."

"I think you'll live." I smoothed his cheek and handed him something that would make him happy. "Here's the newspaper. Unless you want to borrow my book."

"You only read junk."

I stood up and frowned. "I didn't ask you to insult my taste in reading. I just made a nice gesture."

"Can you make me toast?" Michael asked sweetly. "I like toast when I'm sick."

"Sure, okay," I said, turning toward the kitchen. "I certainly hope you never got sick in the Marine Corps. This would not have been impressive behavior in a barracks."

For the rest of the day Michael dozed, ate toast, and read newspapers. I read my trashy novel. And of course we watched television. The TV had become a third member of the family.

The next day Michael stayed home from work. He was sitting up in bed, the covers scrunched down, the pillows propped behind him, contentedly polishing off a bowl of butter pecan ice cream, when I returned from a grueling day of writing headlines for twelve-volt batteries. I placed the mail on the nightstand on top of a crumpled heap of used Kleenexes, and rested my hand against my husband's forehead.

"Fever's gone. How was your day?"

"I'm been thinking about quitting work," Michael said, "and I started reading your trashy novel."

"You *are*?"

"It's not bad. That Lorraine is one slutty nurse."

"You're thinking of quitting?"

"It's not a real job."

"It pays a real paycheck."

"Yes. But it's stupid. Who cares what percentage of male heads of households like some bug spray commercial?"

I picked up the mail pile and crawled over Michael's legs

to the other side of the bed. "Let's concentrate on the day's events. Starting with a big day in correspondence: A letter from across the golden seas from my father, Jerry, the crook, including a picture of him with his new—and decidedly young—wife." Since receiving Jerry's congratulatory wedding card, complete with grave remorse over not attending my marriage ceremony, I had received sporadic chatty letters informing me that he had met someone he liked, then later that he loved the someone he liked. I'd always answer his letters, but more out of politeness or habit or filial duty than anything else. I kicked off my shoes and held the photo of my new stepmother in front of Michael. "She looks young enough to be my older sister."

"Looks good to me!" Michael said, checking out the photograph and sounding notably healthier.

"Her name's Cindy." I dropped the photo in my lap and scanned the accompanying letter. "I thought women in Europe were too sophisticated to be named Cindy."

"Three more months," Michael said, sliding back down under the covers and lying against his pillows. "If I still hate my job in three months, I'll quit."

"And do what?" I redirected my attention to him. Maybe he was *serious* about this job-quitting business.

"Something else. Maybe somewhere else. Chicago's crowded and expensive and has lousy weather. I'd much rather live out west. We'll be happier there."

I stuck Jerry's letter under a *Ladies Home Journal* on my nightstand. "My parents are here. My friends are here. I don't want to leave Chicago."

"Franny, you're my wife! That's supposed to mean more now than being somebody's *daughter*."

I stared at Michael angrily. "We aren't talking about a couple of *some*bodies. We're talking about my mom and dad."

Michael sat up like something in the sheets had just burned him. "You can't expect me to live someplace I *hate* because you can't move away from your parents."

"Oh! So now you hate Chicago?"

"I've *never* liked this city!" His face turned a feverish red, except I knew it wasn't from fever. "I'm here because you wanted to be here."

"And I still want to be here. You hate Chicago. You hate your job. What *do* you like?"

Michael sank back down on the bed and gripped the edge of his blanket. He spoke in a low, funny, weary voice. "You, Franny. I love you. I'm just not so sure about me."

"What are you *talking* about?" My heart pounded against my chest and I was growing increasingly confused. "You don't even sound like you. Are you feeling weird from being sick? What's going on?" I was trying to make sense of how a normal everyday husband-and-wife conversation could twist and turn around so easily.

But Michael's eyes were closed and he didn't respond.

Two days later I came home from work with a sore throat and a fever. Michael happily tucked me into bed, made me hot tea, and read aloud to me from my trashy book. My Marine was back in charge.

One month after our first anniversary, Louie and President Nixon quit their jobs. For the president it began with Watergate; for Louie it began with a clown.

A catalog copywriter in the children's clothing department—ages infants to preschoolers; polyester, wash and wear, and mixed blends—named Kenny Rooney had ripped out the clown from the inside of a jack-in-the-box. When questioned about his action, Kenny shrugged and said it seemed like a good idea at the time. Kenny Scotchtaped his clown to the side of his gray metal typewriting table, and three weeks later he was offered a beginning copywriting job with an up-and-coming ad agency in Ohio. Before packing up his pencils, notepads, and Playboy Playmate of the Month calendar, Kenny bequested what was now officially dubbed the Good Luck Clown to Louie. The day of Nixon's resignation speech, Louie was offered a copywriting job with an insurance company in the suburbs. He dashed down to personnel and quit his job *immediately*, admitting that, yeah, sure, the new job wasn't perfect, but it certainly was a stepping stone. For his last official act he passed the Good Luck Clown along to Dwayne. One month later, following in Louie's stepping-stone steps, Dwayne accepted a second opening at the insurance company. And I inherited the good-luck clown.

In November I was fired.

"I think that clown had a malfunction," I wailed to Louie, when I called him at home that night. The clown had been recently relocated to a garbage can. "Can you believe it? They made me sit there while they droned on and on about the recession of 1974 and the cutbacks they'll need for 1975 and how they had to look around at all their employees in the department and once they looked around they concluded that perhaps I was not as *dedicated* as some of their other employees. Jesus, just because I detested the place doesn't mean I didn't do a good job! For my final humiliation they made me hand in my employee charge card."

"At least you have a husband," Louie said.

After one week of making phone calls and waiting for phone calls, and making the most of a healthy dose of self-pity, I started taking the bus downtown at the end of the day to wait for Michael. I needed a goal, a destination, somebody to play with. I'd stand in the lobby of his office building, within spitting distance of the bronze-plated Crosswaite & Doran sign that hung between the building's two elevator banks, secretly hoping, praying, who knows, these things happen, that some honcho from the agency's creative department would spot me standing there, looking unquestionably talented and creative, and cry out: Sign that girl up!

I also prayed that none of the creative directors who had previously rejected me would walk by and make clucking noises. See that little nobody cringing in the corner, they'd whisper. She wasn't even qualified to be—can you believe it?—*a catalog copywriter*. At which point some security guard would be ordered to escort me off the hallowed premises.

On a cold Thursday night after I'd spent a divinely paranoid twenty minutes warming my hands and cooling my heels hiding behind a potted ficus tree, peeking through the sparse leaves, I spotted Michael among a happy cluster of men and women emerging from an elevator, laughing and talking like they all belonged to some exclusive wonderful club. I had never noticed before how much more employed people laughed and smiled than unemployed people. Michael waved goodbye to a few of his co-workers, and looking unattainably handsome in his navy wool coat with the squared-off shoulders, a burgundy muffler draped elegantly around his neck, he walked over to where I was hovering.

"Hello, gorgeous wife," he said, leaning over to kiss me. "What are you doing back here?" His kiss was perfunctory, the kind that said: I don't believe in public displays of affection. He reached into his pockets and pulled out his black leather gloves, slipping them onto his hands as he guided me out of the building, pushing the revolving door around for me. When our faces were attacked by the first rush of frigid winter air, he instructed me to button the top button on my overcoat and questioned why I wasn't wearing my heavier boots. We walked down Michigan Avenue glove in glove, until Michael stopped at a corner newsstand to buy a paper and chat with a small grizzly proprietor he addressed by name. I wandered on ahead to study the fashions in the Saks Fifth Avenue windows, while jumping up and down to warm my toes. A wiry, unshaven man, with foul-smelling breath and a slimy smile suddenly pressed his red, chapped face in front of mine. The man's lips curled up as he breathed at me. "Hey, baby, you're looking fine tonight, baby. I bet I could make you feel even finer tonight, baby." High-brow, stimulating type conversation like that. I knew he wasn't going to *rape* me. It was too damn cold for any halfway-thinking man to want to whip his *thing* out. But still, I felt my stomach knot up in fear as I reflexively stepped back. And then I heard Michael's strong steady voice behind me, his words clipped and authoritative: "Leave the young lady alone. Do not hassle her. Kindly be on your way." The man retreated, backing away and disappearing into the shadows without saying another word. Michael casually slid his arm around my shoulders, a newspaper tucked in the crook of his other arm, and we proceeded down the street. "I leave you alone for one minute and you start picking up strangers, huh?"

"Thank you," I said. "For showing up and all."

Michael squeezed my shoulder. "How'd today go?"

"Dismally. I couldn't set up one interview. I'm bored. And worried about getting another job. And afraid to spend any money shopping or entertaining myself because I'm not making any money, and my severance pay runs out next week."

"Don't worry about money," Michael said. "I'll take care of you. I want to take care of you."

And I didn't understand why my stomach still felt knotted up.

The next day I doubled my job-hunting efforts, sending out twice as many résumés, making twice as many calls, and two weeks later, partly through persistence, but mainly through a fluke, I was offered a beginning copywriter job at Ethan King and Partners. Not a major name in the advertising business. Not even a big name in the business. But *in* the business. Missy Purcell, a former classmate of mine and a media planner at Ethan King, set up an interview for me with Mr. King himself, and all because I once loaned her four quarters for the college dorm washing machines.

When I told Michael my fantastic news, he claimed he was happy for me. We celebrated by watching *Little House on the Prairie* and going to sleep early.

Michael had one of his nightmares.

The bad dreams didn't occur often, but they always frightened me, starting with the moans; forbidding moans that would wake me up, eerie and haunting, like the sounds of a wounded animal wailing in pain, an animal afraid of dying. I hated listening to those baleful noises, those muffled short cries of anguish. I felt scared and confused, positive Michael had experienced traumas totally alien to anything I could possibly imagine. That night, I wrapped my arms around him and gently rocked him awake. "You're okay. It's okay. It's only a dream." He opened his eyes and stared into space for a split second, as though the dream were being rerun for him on some invisible screen. Then, like every other time, he blinked and came awake and claimed in a dispassionate voice that he didn't know what I was talking about. "I wasn't having nightmares," he said. "I wasn't dreaming at all."

I'd seen the reports on TV about Vietnam vets and their assimilation problems, and I'd quiz Michael, asking him what I hoped were the right questions. Honey, do you ever think about the war? Are you ever bothered by the war? He'd tell me no, quit worrying about the past, quit dramatizing ancient history. Another night, lying in bed, neither of us really talking, I asked, "But what was it *really* like?"

He rolled over, his back toward me, and answered. "Hot. Humid. Lonely. And scary. Now let's get some sleep."

And the conversations ended.

Two days after I started my advertising job, Michael quit his advertising job, declaring advertising pointless and moronic. It wasn't him, he said. He'd never liked it, he said. He enrolled in the University of Illinois, Circle campus, on the near West Side of Chicago, and declared a major in oceanography. He had always been interested in the ocean, he said. Oceans were nature. They were life. They were *real*. Of course, what with there not being any local oceans within a thousand-mile radius, the university did not have an oceanography program. But the administration permitted Michael to work out his own curriculum, letting him sign up for ecology, geology, whatever nature-ology classes he was interested in. I figured if he wanted to take a bunch of courses about seaweed, fine, that was his business; the Veterans Administration was covering his tuition. I simply assumed responsibility for our finances, as though my handling the checkbook and paying the bills were the natural order of things. After all, my mother had prepared me.

Michael would go to the library. I'd go to New York on business. Whenever I returned he'd be waiting for me at the airport, standing at the gate, smiling and happy to see me again.

"I just spent three days in a city where people mug you in the street for looking at them sideways, and you're worried about me taking a cab home?" I once told him, kissing him on the cheek and handing him my suitcase.

"Gotta keep my girl safe."

"Afraid I'll be whisked away by the Krishnas?"

"No," he said softly. "Just afraid you'll be whisked away."

We'd stop for dinner at a neighborhood restaurant—usually Chinese, sometimes Italian—and I'd pay the check with the expense-account money I would have spent on a taxi.

We were married almost two years before the money fight over the clock.

"Where'd that come from?" Michael asked, walking in from school one evening and throwing his books on the sofa. The clock was a contemporary version of a grandfather version of a wall clock. Two feet high. Golden oak. Brass pendulum. I'd hung it over the sofa, right next to the genuine batik painting we'd bought at a neighborhood art fair.

"Do you like it?" I asked.

"How much?" Michael asked.

"How much do you like it?"

"How much did you *pay* for it?"

I debated whether I should tell him. For the first two or three years after my mother married Paul, whenever he asked her the price of a new dress, she'd look at him all wide-eyed and innocent and say in a sweet voice, "What? This old thing? I pulled it out of the back of my closet." Then she'd pay the charge bill out of her household account. But I told Michael the truth. "A hundred twenty dollars."

My honesty was not well received.

"We don't need it," Michael said, in a voice meant to convey that he'd made up his mind and that's that. "You have to take it back."

"No, I don't!" As soon as I spoke the words, I realized they were true. No, I didn't have to take the clock back and I didn't plan to. "I don't need your permission to spend my own money," I said. "I earned it! And I can spend it. What right have you to tell me what to do?"

Michael didn't say a word. He picked up his books and headed into the bedroom, slamming the door behind him.

The clock stayed.

* * *

I didn't know what I was doing wrong. I'd tell him I loved him. I'd make a point of reassuring him all the time. I'd pass him on my way to the refrigerator and say I love you. I'd pass him on my way to the bathroom and say I love you. He'd smile or nod and go back to his books or reading the paper or watching the news. I told him what gift I wanted for my twenty-fifth birthday. I figured it would be easier for him if he knew exactly what would make me happy. I'd seen a picture of a gold bracelet in the magazine section of the Sunday paper, so I circled it and drew big red arrows pointing to it, and taped the picture to the top of Michael's nightstand. He acknowledged my helpful gesture by sticking the picture in his drawer.

"I like that particular bracelet," I said, three days before the big event, "the way the two bands are twisted around together like a dainty braid. I think that's really different, don't you? A lot of gold bracelets are just plain old gold bracelets but I think that one's really special."

Michael agreed with me. Or maybe he just grunted. It was difficult to tell.

On the night of my birthday I arrived home late, as usual, but Michael came home even later, which was not so usual. At seven o'clock he strode in with just the right size box, wrapped in silver foil paper with a big blue bow. "Surprise!" he said, looking quite pleased with himself. "I know you're going to like it."

"Yes, I know so, too," I said, with a big, happy, expectant grin on my face. I was sitting on the living room couch where I'd been reading an article in *Cosmopolitan* about orgasms for careerwomen. Michael sat down next to me, clearly excited, as I proceeded to open a box holding the wrong gold bracelet, a wider and fussier one with filigreed flowers etched all over the place.

"What do you think?!" Michael asked. "Pretty, isn't it?"

"Sure," I said. "It's okay."

"I hope you don't mind that I charged it."

"But then I have to pay for it. It's like *I'm* buying it. I'm buying my own birthday present. And it's not the right one! You knew what I wanted. You knew which store. Why couldn't you take the time to get the one I wanted? How come? And especially since I have to pay for it."

The color drained from Michael's face. "I can't help that you have to pay for it. I don't have a lot of cash. And what you wanted was expensive."

"We can afford it."

"*You* can afford it," Michael said quietly. "I can't."

The next day I returned the bracelet for the one I wanted.

After that, Michael increasingly spent his evenings studying in the second bedroom while I sat in the living room watching television with the sound turned real low, so I wouldn't disturb him or get him mad at me. He'd never *tell* me if he was annoyed at me, but I could feel his anger by the way he'd look at me, his eyes filled with disappointment, often for reasons I couldn't fix, or fathom.

He passed his exams in spring, then promptly signed up for summer school. He passed his exams in summer, then promptly signed up for courses in fall. My father couldn't understand how Michael could quit a decent-paying job and go back to school to take what Paul considered a series of dead-end courses. I countered by becoming as supportive as possible.

For Michael's birthday I bought him his own Sea World. I looked up the name of an aquarium store in the Yellow Pages and purchased a fish tank along with all the extras: an air filter, fake plastic plants, a metal tank cover, cardboard shakers of food that looked like Accent meat tenderizer; and several Baggies filled with water containing different varieties of fish, and two teeny African frogs the man behind the counter told me were a must item.

But Michael was pleased.

"See," I said, "you'll have an ocean right here in the living room. You don't even have to leave Chicago."

❦ *Chapter 9* ❦

The following spring he stopped attending classes and began spending his days in bed.

"I love you," I'd say, as I kissed him goodbye each morning, leaving for work. "Try and get up and do something today. You'll feel better."

I'd come home and he'd tell me what the winning-door number was on *Let's Make a Deal*, or the question to some answer he figured out on *Jeopardy*, but he'd still be lying around in his shorts, with the blinds pulled down and the lights turned off, his hair uncombed, his face unshaven. He hadn't gained any noticeable weight, but his face had grown perceptively fleshier, subtly altering his appearance with lines of self-criticism etched in his features, reflecting the hollowness in his spirit. Michael was legitimately hurting, and I ached for him, but I didn't understand the pain; I felt embarrassed for his pain, and embarrassed with myself for feeling embarrassed. I kept telling myself that Michael's visceral malaise, his incessant need to continue moldering in the apartment, was simply not permanent. It was an experiment. A letting go of responsibility. Just something he needed to do.

"Maybe you should go talk to someone," I suggested one day. I hadn't returned from work until after seven. A half-eaten sandwich on an overturned plate had been discarded on the bedroom floor. The room smelled of stale bed linen and unwashed dishes. I bent over to pick up the plate, then stopped, squelching an impulse to pick up after him, to condone his misery.

"Talk to who?" Michael said.

"Someone. Anyone. Don't depressed people usually go talk to someone?"

"I'm not depressed. Just because you're earning a paycheck doesn't make you an expert on my mental health. I don't need to pay some stranger to pry into my private life."

"Your private life sucks right now!" I cried, my voice rigidly strident. "It consists of wasting away your days in this bedroom and rejecting your wife at night. I love you. I care about you. I'm not telling you you're crazy. I'm just saying this isn't normal behavior. It's not healthy behavior." Michael's only response was the sound of him busily puffing up and rearranging his pillows, making quite a project of the whole affair. I kept talking, compelled to fill the vacuum between us. "All this energy that you're using to be miserable could be channeled into something constructive, something to make you happier. Maybe you can go back and finish that term paper and get your master's degree."

"Why the hell would I need a master's in advertising?"

"Well, at least it's *some*thing. You're substituting any productivity with self-imposed wretchedness. You need help. We need—" I broke off in midsentence, suddenly feeling exhausted and emotionally beat up. I sidestepped a pair of Michael's cotton shorts on the floor, and moved toward the bed, moved toward Michael, and held out my hand as he looked up at me. We wordlessly laced our fingers together, me still angry at him because I didn't know how to help him.

He started talking about the Alaskan pipeline. I was dressing for work, he was lying in bed, the covers pulled up to his chin even though the room was heavy with summer heat.

"A lot of guys go up there, work a few months, and make a fortune," he said. "They pay a ton to get you up there, but there's nothing to spend your money on once you're there, so you can stash away a fortune. And it's beautiful. The pictures look so beautiful. Clean. Pristine. Unmarred. It's the last place in this country that hasn't been screwed up."

"So what is it you're saying here?" I asked, sitting on the edge of the bed and tugging on some pantyhose. "Do you want to *go* there? Is that what you want? I've been paying the rent and paying the bills and now you want to just leave so you can play Jack London? What's this all about?"

"Nothing," Michael said. "It's about nothing."

"Then why are we talking about it?"

I stood up and pulled a blue and white seersucker dress over my head.

"Don't you think your butt's getting kind of big for that?"

"What?" I said, poking my head through the top of the dress.

"That outfit. You look huge in it."

"Huge?"

"I don't like it," Michael announced.

"I didn't ask you," I said, fumbling with the buttons.

"How much weight have you gained?"

"I'm still the same size." I slipped a red belt around my waist. "Sort of. And what right have you got to criticize me? Do I criticize you for sitting around all day, isolated, refusing to remove yourself from the bed? At least I get *off* this butt and *do* something."

Michael retreated once again. "What time will you be home?"

"The same," I said.

"Late?"

I looked at my wristwatch. "The same," I said.

I came home one evening to find him dressed in cutoffs and a clean T-shirt, the curtains pulled back, the windows open, Michael scooting around the kitchen making a salad for dinner. "There's lots of good stuff in here," he said. "Tomatoes, green peppers, sliced carrots. I thought we should eat something healthy. Do you feel like a salad? A salad's a good idea, don't you think?"

"Fine," I said, surprised to find him so chipper. He was brimming with energy, happily pulling vegetables out of the refrigerator and arranging them in neat piles next to the cutting board. "A salad would be good."

"Oh," he added, "and I got a job."

"A job job?" I sat down on the wooden stool we kept pushed beneath the kitchen wall phone and watched Michael scooting around the kitchen.

"Yes!" he said, carefully laying leaves of wet lettuce on top of paper towels spread across the countertop. "I saw a notice up on the bulletin board at the grocery. For this job I got. A nice guy. A young guy. I met him today. He has a landscaping business, does a lot of the bigger homes in Evanston and Wilmette; I'm going to work for him."

"He needs advertising?"

"No. He needs guys who mow lawns." Michael blotted the tops of his lettuce leaves with a second piece of paper toweling.

"And that's what you are?"

"Just for now." Michael turned to me. "It's outdoors! It's physical! I'll be able to see what I've *accomplished* at the end of the day and use my body." He paused. "And I don't have to think."

"Think about what?"

"Sometimes I think too much," Michael said quietly. But he immediately brightened when he informed me, "Six bucks an hour. Not bad, huh?" He smiled.

"Well, I guess it's better than working at McDonald's." I walked out of the kitchen, going nowhere in particular.

"What kind of dressing do you want?" Michael called after me.

"Thousand Island," I said, turning back to him. "I think we've only got Thousand Island."

"No," Michael said, opening the refrigerator door again and staring inside. "We've got lots of them. We needed some, so I bought lots of them. I thought they'd make you happy." I was uncomfortable and confused by his efforts to please me.

"I'll take Thousand Island."

"Oh, okay." Michael sounded disappointed.

"Michael?" I was still standing in the living room, uncertain how to approach, whether to trust his "return" to his regular self. "I'm glad you got the job. It'll be good for you."

"Thank you," I heard him say. "Are you sure you don't want to try one of my new salad dressings?"

I hated to admit the delight I felt when flying off to New York or California to make a television commercial, grateful to be disappearing into a different life for two weeks, attired in my standard copywriter's ensemble of blue jeans and silk blouse, my idea of the perfect balance between creative spirit and glamorous careerwoman. Inevitably there would be some Brooks Brothers–clad gentleman in the adjoining seat on the airplane. "So, little lady," Mr. Brooks Brothers would ask, "off on a vacation?"

"No, indeed," I would respond grandly. "It so happens I'm traveling on *business*."

I adored traveling on business.

There were casting sessions where I'd get to reject blond, blue-eyed models and make up for a lifetime of not looking like a blond, blue-eyed model. There were meetings with set designers and meetings with directors and expense-account lunches where I could order à la carte appetizers without any guilt. I'd call Michael every night, but he never wanted to talk beyond the basic exchanges of marital pleasantries. How was your day, dear? How was work? What did you have for dinner? There was always some baseball game he was in the middle of watching, or some book he was in the middle of reading. He seemed content just to have me check in, touch base, let him know I was thinking of him, let him know that I loved him.

On a Saturday in early fall, right after returning home from one of my business trips, I arranged to meet my mother for lunch in a restaurant in a nearby shopping mall. But I was late because I spent too much time standing in front of a store window wondering if I liked the red plaid pantsuit on the mannequin enough to go inside, search for my size, get all undressed, and face one of those horrid three-way mirrors. By the time I dashed into the restaurant—one of those California-style eateries groaning with macrame hangings and Swedish ivy plants—my mother was already seated and chatting with an elderly couple at an adjoining table. Mom liked to do that, engage in immediate camaraderie with strangers sitting at adjoining tables in restaurants. As a teenager, I considered her friendly overtures mortifying, as if I were the daughter of a politician constantly running for office. But by the time I graduated college, I accepted the fact that lunch with Mom automatically included the opportunity to Make New Friends.

"Here she is now," Mom said, holding out her arm and flapping her hand as I approached the table. I felt like a guest star being introduced on the *Tonight Show*. I could tell that I'd been the topic of conversation. I kissed my mother on the cheek and nodded to her new buddies as I sat down.

"Show them your ring," Mom said, with no further introduction.

"My ring? My wedding ring?"

"Yes, your ring."

I pulled out a chair, sat down, and obediently stuck out my left hand.

"It's very sweet," the woman said.

"Of course it's just a starter ring," my mother said. "But you know how it is; a few years down the road you upgrade."

"Or you find a second husband with more money." I smiled sweetly at my mother.

"Maybe we should look at the menus," she said, turning away from her friends the strangers.

I opened my menu. "I'm not all that hungry."

"Why not? Are you on a diet?"

"No. I just don't feel that good. And no, I'm not pregnant."

"Are you trying?"

"No!" I retorted, apparently rather loudly because our new best friends at the next table turned and smiled at us inquisitively. I smiled back to demonstrate that I was in full control of my emotions, then returned my attention to my mother. "No," I said to her, lowering my voice. "Not at the moment."

I ordered a cheeseburger medium rare, fries, baked beans, cole slaw, and a Coke. Mom ordered a spinach salad without the Bac-Os.

"I had an idea for Michael," she said, when our food arrived. "A good idea. I'm really proud of it."

"What's that?" I asked, salting my fries.

"Michael should start a landscaping business. If what he wants to do is cut grass, he should own the company. All he'll need is a truck, some clippers, some mowers, and several illegal aliens. But he could be the boss."

"I don't think he wants a business," I said, picking up a fry. "He wants to mow lawns."

"In winter he can have a driveway-shoveling business. All he'll have to add is a plow."

"You're trying to make him more respectable, Mom. Something fancier to tell your friends."

"Felice Hyman knows someone whose podiatrist has a cousin with a son-in-law in the landscaping business and she says he makes a very decent living."

"Well, at least you got that information from a reliable source."

"It's a blessing you've got your own money." My mother selected a roll from the bread basket, ripped it in half, then threw the second half back in the basket. "And us."

"What's that supposed to mean?"

"I'm talking about security, a backup plan, a safety cushion," she said. "Are you happy?"

"*Yes.*" I was weary of constant inquiries regarding the state of my marital happiness. Of course I was happy, I was supposed to be happy. But I still managed to feel that something somewhere was my fault; somehow, I was screwing up.

Mom sat back in her chair, absently tapping her fingers on the edge of the table. "Mothers know things, Franny. Are you happy?"

"*Very,*" I insisted. After that declaration, Michael could have been a fall-down drunk, wife-beating psychopath, and I would still have refused my mother the satisfaction of saying: Ah-ha! I knew it! You're having troubles! Hearing me divulge innuendos of even the slightest tensions between Michael and me would have set her into full force. Mighty Mom to the rescue! She was incapable of unearthing a *hint* of a problem without immediately responding with a major solution. Fixing her children's various dilemmas was Mom's self-declared area of expertise in life. For better or worse? I strongly feared that my mother, all maternal instincts aside, preferred to hear the worst.

"Honey, there's an unwritten contract between every husband and wife. You expect things from him. He expects certain things from you. If those understandings change without anyone discussing them, you head into trouble." My mother momentarily examined her roll, as if looking for some hidden flaw in the dough. "Michael loves you *deeply*," she said. "It *shows*. But he's made a lot of concessions for you. The religion. Putting up with our admittedly crazy brood."

"Those are things he *wants* to do," I insisted.

"Franny, he does them for *you*. Don't be too disappointed if he can't make all the changes fit."

"So why are you so eager for him to own a lawnmowing business?"

"He needs something that's *his*," my mother said. "Men do. They're funny that way. He'll settle down." She was slapping butter on her bread with a knife. "In the meantime, be careful. Sometimes people threaten divorce in the middle of an argument and it becomes a reality without their ever meaning it to."

"Divorce?" I said. "Where the hell did *that* come from? What kind of a word is *divorce*?"

My mother leaned forward and stared at me from across the table, her eyes boring into my soul. "A powerful one." She leaned back. "Look at Eddie. He was married to that girl for what? Three months? Four months? It didn't work out."

"He's happy," I said.

"He's a bum," my mother said.

"Do you think Michael's a bum?" I asked, feeling simultaneously hurt, indignant, and defensive.

"No," she said. "He's just going through a stage." She stabbed at a spinach leaf with her fork, then focused her eyes on me. "You *act* supportive of him, Franny. But you always look so disenchanted. Take care of him. Figure out what he needs from you. And don't lose sight of how much you care about each other. It's not good to go through life not knowing what's important to you."

I shook my head and wondered what it was I wasn't figuring out. The couple at the next table stood up to leave. I waved goodbye with my hand with the ring, the ring that symbolized I was married for life.

❧ *Chapter 10* ❧

The Alaskan pipeline conversations began again in January of 1978. That same month, Alabama Governor George Wallace divorced his wife, Cornelia; Hubert Humphrey's body lay in state in the Capitol; President Carter delivered his State of the Union address; and the state of *our* union drifted into the comfort and familiarity of daily routines, with neither of us fully realizing we were experiencing totally separate marriages. Oh, sure, flashes of discord and occasional butting of goals would occur, but we would always back off, avoiding the Big Fight, the one we feared might be the Last Fight.

Far easier to live side by side in separate orbits, foraging our individual paths, caring for each other and genuinely loving each other while still refusing to make way or compromise. Michael talked mountain ranges. I campaigned for a condo.

Every Sunday morning, while Michael sat on the living-room sofa reading his parts of the newspaper, I'd sprawl out on the living-room floor, divebombing through the real estate section in search of my American Dream—which I interpreted as a two-bedroom condo in the suburbs. I'd draw big, red, enthusiastic Magic Marker circles around anything that sounded halfway plausible.

"How's this strike you?" I'd ask

"Not interested," Michael would say.

"You didn't let me read it yet."

"Not interested," Michael would say.

"You don't like *anything*."

Michael put down his paper. "I don't like the idea of spending money on an *apartment*. I want a garage and a workroom and a place to grow some vegetables. I'd like to renovate a place; use my *hands*. We can wait until we save enough for a house."

"But we'll never save enough. Every time we save a little more, the price of the houses gets higher and we can't catch up. We've lived here almost five years. You didn't want to live with me. You wanted to marry me. I don't want to rent. I want to own. I hate this place. I'm tired of this place. I want a place where we can pick out our own wallpaper."

"Wallpaper wouldn't be such a big deal if you lived someplace where you could look out the window and see a decent view."

"What's wrong with our view?"

"There are some people who live in places where you can look outside and see water or a mountain range."

"I'll buy you a picture of mountains," I sniffed. "You can stick it in the window."

Michael was silent. I thought he wasn't going to talk at all, that he'd go back to burying his face in his newspaper. But then he started speaking, calmly, almost too calmly, clipping each word. To me, an overly controlled Michael could be far more ominous than an out-of-control anyone else. "Why the big need to get all tied down to an apartment now? Why not travel? Drive around the country? There are other ways to live out there. I want to see Alaska. I'll show you Alaska, Franny."

"You mean quit my job?" I jammed the red Magic Marker cap back on the red Magic Marker.

"Why not?"

"Why *now*?"

Michael folded his arms across his chest. "If you want to be so settled, then why don't we start a family? We could have a baby."

I picked at a scab on my elbow. "We will," I said. "But it doesn't have to be this minute. I won't be able to afford anything; I mean we won't be able to afford anything. I want a home first. I don't always want to be catching up or resenting a child because I can't buy a new sofa."

"You care more about a stupid piece of furniture than a *baby*?"

"I'm just saying we can have *both*."

Michael's eyes hardened into a censorious stare. "I've always wanted to go to Alaska. I would have gone up there right after college, but I stayed here because of you."

"And now you're *leaving* because of me?"

"No. It has nothing to do with you."

"But your decisions should have something to do with me," I said, and then, in a far more tenuous voice: "We're married."

Once again we reached an unspoken danger point in the conversation, one from which we both automatically retreated.

I went back to reading the real estate section. Michael resumed reading the travel section.

In May I told him I was going to buy a condo and he was invited to come live with me, but I was going to buy one. Two days later he told me he was going to drive to Alaska and I was invited to join him, but he was definitely going to go.

Michael toweled off from his morning shower while I stood in a robe at the bathroom sink with my back to him, rolling my hair in electric curlers. I watched his body in the mirror: his long hairy legs; his full, developed chest; and his small, perfect behind. He was in beautiful shape from a year of mowing lawns and shoveling heavy snow.

"I don't understand what's there. Why Alaska?" I asked.

"Come with me and find out," he said. I didn't respond. I couldn't imagine picking up without the security of a job. "It's a place where you have to survive day by day." Michael bent one foot up along the edge of the tub, and then the other, and briskly dried his legs, then looked up at me and said in a voice filled with self-assurance, "I know how to do that."

"But you can do lots of things! You can do anything!" I protested. I must have looked scared because Michael dropped his towel and walked over and stood behind me and held my shoulders. I looked at our two reflections in the mirror. Him with his strong, handsome, excited face. Me in my rollers.

"It's only temporary," he said.

On weekends we'd alternate between condo sightseeing with a real estate agent and trips to Harris O'Neil's World's Largest Sporting Goods. Michael was searching for a new camping tent. At night we would sit in front of the television and discuss our future during the commercials.

"I can't believe people live like such slobs," I'd say.

"I better get a tune-up," Michael would say. "I don't want to get stuck in the wilderness with car trouble."

"They know strangers are going to be trooping through their home and they don't even bother to make the beds or put away the laundry."

"And I'll need film. Lots of film. I'll be taking the camera."

"Do you think a storage shed is necessary?"

"Not now. The show's back on."

Our realtor's name was Wanda.

Wanda looked like someone named Wanda. Too much jewelry. Too much hair. Too much bright red lipstick. Wanda wasn't a relative, but she was recommended by a sort-of relative. Aunt Marlene's neighbor's son used to date Wanda's sister when he was in high school.

Wanda would set up appointments for us and then immediately cancel them because the condos had been sold before we could dash over there. Buyers were out of control, offering more than the asking prices to be sure of snapping up some can't-be-missed property before it was too late.

"This is ridiculous," I told Wanda one day after a condo had been put under contract ten minutes before we were supposed to see it. "The most expensive decision of our life and we have to make it with no time for thinking."

"You don't have to think," Wanda said, jangling three bracelets and smiling through her bright red lips. "I'm your realtor. All you have to do is trust your realtor."

Each time we walked through a condo Michael would pound walls and flush toilets, while I planned where we'd put the sofa, and Wanda stalked around saying things like,

"Put in a bid! Put in a bid!" Finally we found something that fit our criteria: Two bedrooms. Two baths. Close to transportation. Affordable on the salary of the one person who wasn't leaving for Alaska.

And it was only three blocks away from the lake if you didn't mind cutting through a cemetery.

Wanda said to trust her. Offer the full asking price. Two hours later we signed a contract. And after weeks of angst and apprehension (on my part), we got approval for a mortgage. The day we received the official okay, I celebrated by opening a bottle of wine. Michael celebrated by buying a camping tent.

Our closing was handled by my sister Madelyn's new fiancé, Marty, the new lawyer. We were Marty's first ever clients. He had passed the bar one week earlier. While Michael and I signed papers, Marty sweated.

Barry, Louie, Dwayne, and Dwayne's wife, Daisy, were our movers, proving what some people will do for a free six-pack.

Two days later Michael quit his job and wallpapered the kitchen. At night I would unpack cartons while Michael packed up camping gear. I bought him a reversible blue and gray nylon windbreaker with a zip-on, zip-off hood for a fifth anniversary gift. He brought home a tall bouquet of pink roses.

"They're beautiful," I said.

"Watch out for the stems. The thorns."

"Okay."

"You aren't watching."

I looked at the stems. Poked through like two sparkling little thorns were two tiny diamond earrings.

"How'd you afford these?" I asked.

"I've saved some money. Do you like them?" He looked so hopeful, and eager to please.

"I love them." I pulled the earring stems out of the flower stems and ran to the bathroom mirror to try on my new diamond earrings. Michael followed after me.

"When I asked the florist to stick the earrings through the flowers he thought it was a really creative idea," Michael said. "Do you think it was creative? I thought it was." I wondered what the florist would think if he knew Michael was leaving me.

"I love them," I said, smiling at my husband. I wrapped my arms around him and pressed my head against his shoulder, clinging to as much as hugging him. "I really do."

The next day Michael left for Alaska. I finished unpacking, sold the fish tank, and flushed all the fish and two African frogs straight down to Goldfish Heaven.

❧ *Chapter 11* ❧

I'd lie alone in bed, on my side of the bed, next to the cold side of the bed, the unoccupied side of the bed, and think: How did this *happen*? But somehow, having Michael gone was better than having Michael unhappy. At least now I could imagine him navigating his way down open stretches of highway toward the mountains and streams he craved. I visualized him joyfully singing, like a railroad builder in an Old West movie, as he swung a mallet through the air, his muscles happily aching as the heavy tool arched over his head and thwacked into a long metal pipe. I had no conception what it was Alaskan pipeline workers actually did. I just figured it involved a great deal of pounding, hoisting and sweating. I could picture Michael reveling in the camaraderie of fellow Paul Bunyuns, laughing, belching, farting, performing manly acts that would make him happy. At night he would sit around the campfire with his comrades and long for me. In the grand tradition of men working in the wilderness, he would miss his woman. I tried not to think: How long will he be gone? And I couldn't think: What will I do if he wants to *stay* there? I assured myself he'd return soon; he'd come back strong and hopeful, like he was when we were first together, and we would proceed with the normal marriage we were supposed to have. He was simply getting the Wild West—or North— out of his system. I refused to take his absence personally.

At least twice a week I ate dinner at my parents'.

I became Michael's greatest defender.

"Does he write?" my mother asked.

"He will," I said.

"Heh!" my mother said.

"What's that supposed to mean?" I asked. Any loyalty she'd felt toward Michael had reversed itself. She had once had a husband leave her, and she couldn't tolerate any husband leaving me.

"Nothing," she said, "just heh."

Madelyn and Marty the fiancé were usually there, discussing wedding plans. I tuned all that out. Billy was away at college trying to convince everyone that his name was really William.

"Eat some brisket. You'll feel better," my mother insisted.

"I feel fine," I insisted right back.

"How's the condo coming?" Madelyn asked, trying to eat brisket with one hand while rubbing Marty's thigh under the table with the other.

"Fine," I said. "I just can't decide where to put the wall clock. It looks best by the bedroom hall but the ticking's too loud."

"Oh," Madelyn said. "We were going to register for a wall clock. But maybe we shouldn't if they tick too loud. What do you think, Marty?"

"We better discuss it further," Marty said, trying to eat brisket with one hand while rubbing Madelyn's back with the other.

"Pass the ketchup," Paul said.

"What's wrong with the meat?" my mother asked.

"Nothing. Pass the ketchup," Paul said.

"You know, he stopped here on his way out of town," my mother told me.

"Who?" I said.

"Michael."

"He was heading north," Paul said, unscrewing the ketchup bottle cap.

"What did he say?"

My mother answered me, shaking her head sadly. "He said he couldn't imagine living his life without you."

"Oh, that's so romantic," Madelyn said. "Marty, don't you think that's romantic?"

"That's very romantic," Marty said.

"Then he went and left anyway," my mother said.

"I thought he was a very nice fellow," Marty said.

"He said that?" I said.

"What?" my mother said.

"I'm sorry I didn't get to know him better," Marty said.

"That thing about not living with me."

"Forget it," Paul said, pounding on the bottom of the ketchup bottle. "He's not settling down."

"You were too easy on him," my mother said, "not complaining when he quit a good job to go back to school and then quit another not-so-good-but-paying job to go running around the Yukon, for God's sake. I feel terrible for you. I know how upset you are."

"Let me know if you need a good lawyer," Marty said.

"I'm not upset!" I said, wildly slicing through a piece of meat. "Why should I be upset? Michael loves me. His leaving has nothing to do with me. He'll come home. It's just something he needs to do."

"Heh!" my mother said.

"Heh!" Paul said, a huge glob of ketchup flying out onto his brisket.

"Hey!" Marty said. "Is there any gravy?"

Paul handed him the ketchup bottle.

"Don't worry," Madelyn told Marty. "We'll register for a gravy boat."

"Forget him," Paul told me. "Face reality."

I stopped having dinner at my parents' twice a week.

I had never lived alone before. Once I realized I could wolf down an entire tin of frozen Sara Lee brownies without anyone else around to watch and be appalled, Sara Lee brownies stopped tasting quite as good, and I began losing weight. I skipped dinners. I'd stay at work even later than usual, or necessary. I'd come home and paint bathrooms, shove furniture around, line cabinets with washable shelving paper. I'd write Piper long letters about all the exciting things I was doing and she'd write back short letters about how she was too crazed with her dissertation to write back long letters. I told everyone I knew that Michael had gone to Alaska. Somehow talking about it made it seem more real, but once I talked about it, I felt embarrassed and uncomfortable and stopped going to movies or having drinks or doing anything with the friends I had told.

At night I couldn't sleep. I felt small and abandoned in

my own bed. I'd lie on my back and stare at the ceiling. During the day I thought I was acting fine, and handling things in a mature, casual way, one that said to the world: I'm okay. I can deal with this. But my mother and her sixth sense started dropping off tuna noodle casseroles and home-made sweet-and-sour meatballs, the same comforting foods she usually brought to funerals.

I received my annual phone call from Jerry. He was living in the Canary Islands at the time, still married to Cindy the child bride. I told him about Michael leaving for Alaska and then fell silent. I never had actual conversations with my father. Mainly, I just listened to his soliloquies.

"Doesn't sound good, kiddo," he said. I hated when he called me kiddo. "Sounds like my pumpkin has a big problem." Pumpkin I didn't mind so much. "Cindy and I, we do everything together. Your mother and I, we didn't do a thing together, other than have you three children. But if you don't do everything together, the marriage stinks on an important level. You know what I mean? You better ask yourself if your marriage stinks. And why didn't he bring you with? If he loved you, he would have brought you with. And if he asked to bring you with but you didn't go with, then why didn't you go with? Too bad I can't be there now. If I could I would but I can't. Give my love to your sister and brother. They never write but give them my love. And, pumpkin, don't forget! Daddy loves you! I pray you never took it personally that I left."

Love letters started arriving with the bills.

In the first letter Michael wrote about a flat tire in Montana, missing me, and wanting to live by mountains and water.

In the second letter he wrote about losing his waders in Canada, missing me more than he realized, and how it would be okay not to live by mountains and water as long as he had a job that paid enough so he could visit mountains and water whenever he wanted.

In the third letter he wrote he didn't care where he lived as long as it was with me. Besides, there were no jobs left on the Alaskan pipeline; it was done being built; and what he really wanted was to get a good-paying job and start making babies.

He was romancing me again. Maybe I'd done something right.

The fourth letter arrived from Prudhoe Bay. He was coming home. He loved me. He wanted to be an accountant.

If I'd known he was going to be gone such a short time, I'd never have told anyone he left. I would have just spent five weeks saying things like, "I'm sorry. Michael can't come to the phone right now. He's in the bathroom."

In September, Michael started how-to-be-an-accountant classes two nights a week.

"Are you sure about this?" I asked, when he first spelled out his master plan.

"Sure," he said. "I like numbers. And I like people."

"Since when do you like numbers?"

"They're okay," Michael said. "I like them just fine. Accounting's a good stable position."

"I suppose. It just doesn't sound very exciting."

"Accounting's a good choice," he said.

During the day Michael was a banker. He had opened the newspaper and picked out a job and got hired at the Bank of Chicago. His entry-level position cost more in new suits than it paid in salary, but Michael claimed he liked it because it involved numbers. He sat at a desk in the main lobby of the bank behind a nameplate with an important sounding title: Assistant Customer Service Executive. Michael helped little old ladies balance their checkbooks and post their quarterly interest right there in their passbooks where they could see it; and he sold them C.D.s when the rates rose a quarter of a percentage point in the right direction. The little old ladies wrote letters on monogrammed stationery to Michael's manager all about how kind Michael was, and how patient Michael was, and why couldn't that bank be smart enough to hire more Michael Wedlans?

He talked about a few new friends. Dodi in secretarial. And LeeAnn in marketing. Dodi wanted to improve herself and go to night school. LeeAnn had a bad habit of dating rotten men who treated her like dirt and was always asking Michael for advice. Michael advised her to quit dating rotten men who treated her like dirt.

I started traveling to Los Angeles for two weeks at a time with Holly Booker, my art director, to produce TV commercials for Dunkin' Donuts, our big account. Michael didn't complain about my being away; he was busy studying. On the nights I was home and he wasn't in classes, he'd sit in front of the television with a textbook spread open across his knees and pore over it during commercials. The letters from little old ladies must have started adding up, because Michael was promoted at the bank in some sort of record time. He was no longer an assistant customer service executive. He was a full-fledged regular one.

We upgraded our lifestyle and purchased a second television for the bedroom. A portable one with genuine wood-grainlike finish and a remote control. Now Michael could watch his basketball games and his news shows and animal shows in the den, while I watched miniseries in the bedroom. I'd be en route to the kitchen or the bathroom and poke my head in the den and tell Michael I loved him. He'd say, ''I love you, too,'' without looking up from his textbook.

At night I'd lie in bed as close to him as possible without

getting so close he'd complain about my hair tickling, and I'd ask him questions.

"Michael, are you happy now?"

"Sure. I'm happy."

"And it's okay wanting to be an accountant? You still like your classes?"

"I'm not so sure," he said.

"Oh."

"I'm thinking maybe I just want to be a banker. I kind of like being a banker." He was lying on his back, the position secure people sleep in.

"So you're going to quit accounting school?"

"Banking pays better. And I want to earn some money so I can take care of you and have some babies. And if my parents ever need helping out, be able to take care of them, too." He rolled away from me and sat up and squished his pillow into a new shape and lay back down again. I rolled up against him. "You must really love me to have stuck with me while I was gone," he said.

I stretched my arm around his chest. "I hated it."

"I know."

I inched in closer to him, until our bodies were so tightly pressed together that it was no longer possible to tell where he stopped and I began. "Michael, don't die before me."

"Huh?"

"Promise me you won't, okay? I don't want to be the one who's left behind, okay? I hated being alone."

"Okay. I promise." Michael adjusted his pillow one more time. "The wall clock's too close to the bedroom. It's noisy at night."

"I was going to buy you a ham today," I said. "The kind your mother always talks about but never makes in front of me. I thought I'd march into the grocery and buy my husband a ham. But I just couldn't do it. I guess my kosher roots are more rooted than I thought.''

"Maybe we could make some babies,'' Michael said. "I think it's time.''

"Just about. Probably next year for sure, okay? We just don't seem ready enough to have kids yet.''

Michael lifted his head and looked down at me in the dark. "We've been married over five years.''

"But not settled for five years,'' I said.

"We own a place. We both have jobs. What else do I have to do to be settled enough?''

"I just want my promotion to associate creative director first. Louie's one already. That should be real soon, and then I can stop and have a baby. Okay? Next year. Definitely next year.''

❦ *Chapter 12* ❦

I celebrated my sixth anniversary by toasting Michael with a glass of Zinfandel. Or maybe it was Chardonnay. I can never keep those two straight. All I know is that it was pricey; I was dining on expense account, so I ordered it.

Holly and I were canvassing the country in search of a Shimmer Shampoo girl. For three weeks we sat in small, interchangeable casting rooms, while hundreds of beautiful, pert-nosed, long-leggy, interchangeable hopefuls paraded before us, and we rejected them right and left.

"This makes up for every dance I ever went to as a wallflower," Holly said, beaming with good cheer. "These girls may have looks, but *we* have power." Holly was short with a bad perm and a worse nose, and not much of a chin, and perpetually ten pounds overweight, but she spent a lot of money on her clothes, so she always looked stylish in an artistic overdone kind of a way.

Holly had broken up with her last boyfriend a year and a half earlier.

"Michael's so jealous," I said. "I kept calling him last night, and when he finally got home he said he was too jealous to talk to me. I guess he thinks *he* should be sitting here looking at blondes strut around a little room while I sit in the bank and talk to old ladies."

"He's probably just upset about your being gone so long."

We waited for our next model while munching on Oreos and grapes.

"So what's the latest love-life problem Michael's friend from the bank is immersed in?" Holly asked, splitting her Oreo in two and scraping off the frosting with her teeth. "I adore hearing about other people's love-life problems. It makes me feel so much better about my own love-life problem."

"What's your love-life problem?"

"Not having a love life." Holly picked at some chocolate crumbs stuck under her fingernail. "I'm positively grateful this decade is almost over. Socially, the seventies sucked, don't you think?" She looked up at me like I was a specimen in a petri dish. "No, you wouldn't think so. You have a husband. But me, I need a fresh start. And I think 1980 is going to be my year. Now tell me about Michael's friend, something truly pathetic to reassure me there's another woman in the world who actually gets dumped on more than me."

"I didn't hear any new details last night."

"Michael and you are so sophisticated. You're the only couple I know where you both have friends of the opposite sex. You have Louie and Dwayne. He has the girl with the screwed-up love life. A lot of couples don't do that. They don't have opposite-sex friends."

"Why not? It seems normal to me."

The next bombshell walked into the room.

Her name was Gina.

Holly rejected her for having a freckle.

I brought home a black and white photo of Gina to give Michael as a souvenir of my business trip.

"Well, what do you think?" I asked. "Would this woman inspire you to shampoo your hair?"

"You're better-looking," he said.

"You mean it?"

"Sure," Michael said, studying Gina's upturned nose, luminous eyes, and full pouty lips. We were lying in bed watching the ten o'clock news after making love. Michael was clutching Gina's photo so close to his face that he was practically licking it.

"Listen, if I'm so much better-looking, how come you're staring at Gina's photo instead of me?"

"I'm not staring at Gina," Michael protested. "I'm watching the news."

"Sure you are."

In the interest of setting a good example, I pretended to be thoroughly engrossed in every news items delivered by my favorite anchor, the handsome one with the voice like ice cream and the strong jawline. World catastrophes seemed a little more manageable when reported by a handsome man. After relaying the standard stories about the latest muggings on the south side and which alderman got stuck with which hand in which cookie jar that week, he switched to one of his special reports. The kind news anchors like to do in hopes of winning Pulitzers.

A class-action suit had been filed by Vietnam vets against the U.S. government—for its use of a toxic defoliant sprayed during the war to expose areas in the jungle where the Vietcong were hiding. Apparently the spray planes often flew directly over the American troops, exposing them to poisonous chemicals. And now there were increasing reports of Vietnam vets dying of cancer, and producing children with birth defects.

I bolted upright. "Have you ever heard about that stuff?" I asked Michael. "Were you sprayed with it?"

"Sure. Three or four times." He didn't sound particularly interested or concerned.

"So isn't that bad? Aren't you worried? They said there are birth defects."

"You can't worry about things like that." Michael pulled me back down. "You are married to a healthy, gorgeous specimen of manhood. Feel free to examine my God-like body at any time. Allow my bulging biceps, my rippling pectorals, my sublime ass, and massive male organ to assuage your fears. I assure you, little woman, we and all our offspring will be fine."

"This could be serious," I said. "Maybe we should ask somebody."

"Ask somebody what?"

"What we should do because you were sprayed."

"We don't have to do *anything*." Michael sounded impatient now. "I'm perfectly fine. All we have to do is watch the sports."

Okay, I told myself, so Michael was in perfect health, but what if he could pass along some horrid disgusting thing to a child? I couldn't handle having an unhealthy child. I didn't want to be that strong or that good of a person.

The next time I went to the gynecologist, while lying on my back, my knees flailing in the air, trying to think of some pleasantries to exchange during a Pap smear, I asked Dr. Gepperman how I could know in advance if my children would have birth defects, on account my husband had been sprayed with chemicals in Vietnam. Dr. Gepperman didn't know from chemicals in Vietnam, but he assured me there were plenty of tests pregnant women took to determine if their fetuses were healthy. Then he told me I could sit up and relax.

It's not like it was his birthday or our anniversary or Christmas. I just wanted any husband of mine to own a gold watch.

The one I finally selected—after agonizing debates worthy of an exceptionally dimwitted rabbinical scholar—was shaped like a rectangle with white face and tiny gold dots instead of numbers. The watch had three narrow ridges of gold surrounding its face like a delicate picture frame, a black lizard band, and a genuine sapphire knob for setting the time. The day I purchased it I proudly paraded it before Holly, who admitted, yes, it was a singularly beautiful watch. "The gift of time," she said. "What everybody wants."

I carefully carried my gold offering home, wrapped in a skinny black box with a royal blue velveteen lining, but Michael arrived home late that night, skipped dinner, and went cross-country skiing in the park two blocks from our condo. He returned really tired, showered, and went directly to bed. And there was never a right time to give him the watch.

In the morning, I woke before he did and I watched him sleep. His lips were parted in a contented half-smile; his dark hair was tousled around his extraordinary face. I could still be amazed that anyone so handsome had wanted to marry me. But sometimes, no matter how hard I wished I was wrong, I'd look at Michael and feel lonely. I didn't know how I could be so connected to him without feeling attached to him.

We dressed in our separate bathrooms.

"Good morning, you handsome devil!" I heard him say to his mirror.

My face was made up and my hair combed, but I was still in my flannel nightgown when Michael pulled on his navy blue banker's overcoat.

"I have something for you," I said, stopping him at the front door, the skinny watch box hidden behind my back.

"I'm late. I have to go."

"Not yet! You have to have this!" I shoved the box in his hands.

"What is it?" He opened it up. "It's a watch. Why? I have a watch."

"Don't you like it?"

"It's beautiful," Michael said. "But what's it for?"

"For you. You don't have a dressy watch and I wanted you to have one. It's for you."

Michael slipped the watch out of the two elastic loops holding it against the blue box lining. He removed his old watch with its stainless steel stretchy band, and fastened the new watch around his wrist.

"Thank you," he said. "Nobody's ever given me anything this nice. I don't deserve anything this nice." He gathered me in his arms and pressed his face against the top of my head. "I love you," he said.

"I love you, Michael."

At that moment it seemed as if everything would be all right.

❦ *Chapter 13* ❦

In 1980, Piper was married.

In 1980, Piper was divorced.

She packed up her matching set of Harttman luggage, loaded up the trunk of her new Toyota, and moved back to Chicago, taking a job as a staff psychologist working with geriatric patients at Northwestern Memorial Hospital. Piper preferred old people. She felt safer with them.

Michael had just dragged two loads of dirty clothes and a newspaper off to the building laundry room, while I concocted a tuna noodle casserole in Piper's honor, and she paced around our kitchen lamenting her taste in husbands.

"It'll serve me right to spend the rest of my life as a *nun*. My track record with men is appalling. My picture should be in the Guinness Book of Records above the caption: 'Dated Most Assholes.' I am the worst judge of character."

"That's probably not a good trait in a psychologist," I said, jamming a can of Campbell's Cream of Mushroom soup under the electric can opener. "I don't see how anyone can be good enough to marry in January and rotten enough to divorce in March. He can't have changed *that* much."

For a woe-is-me divorcee, Piper managed to look composed and unfettered with her chin-length cropped hair and varnished blond looks. No matter what circumstances were currently befalling her life, Piper always looked like she descended from old money.

I opened the freezer door and dug out a box of Bird's Eye peas hidden behind a box of Eskimo bars.

"He was always rotten," Piper rumbled. "I was just too stupid to notice. Hell, he was constantly talking about his ex-wife. What could be more rotten than that?"

"Well, if he was all that rotten, why did his ex-wife want him back?" I asked, standing in front of a whirring can of Chicken of the Sea.

"She didn't want him back until he was married to me. Then she started with the phone calls. Honey, I can't figure out how to run the disposal. Honey, there's something wrong with the air conditioner. And ol' honey went running over there. So I finally told him to just *stay* there! I don't see what other choice I had." Piper shuddered. "What is it with men and needy women?"

"Do you still love him?"

Piper collapsed on the white vinyl stool under the kitchen wall phone. She looked small and defeated, in a somehow elegant kind of way. "Right now I don't feel a thing for him. Which is either a good sign because I'm over him, or a bad sign because I'm not in touch with my feelings."

"Hmm," I said, smashing a bag of potato chips before sprinkling the chips on top of my raw and naked casserole. "I could have sworn that called for a yes or no answer."

Piper sighed. "I'll be okay. I'm good at moving on."

"Not me!" I used two hands to lift one of those ridiculously heavy glass covers over my casserole dish and shove the whole shebang in the oven. "I'm terrible at letting go."

"There's nothing you have to let go of. Everything in your life's settled. Michael's great. You like your job. You've got a nice place to live in with all your new furniture." She waved her arm toward the doorway to the living room. "Your home looks so grown-up. Like real people live here."

"Yeah, it came out nice."

"It looks like you," Piper said admiringly. "Except for the poster with the big trout, and that carved wooden duck."

"Those were Michael's contributions." I opened the cabinet under the sink and tossed the empty soup and tuna cans into the garbage. "He never cared about the decorating. I'd ask him what he thought, but he didn't want to spend the money, so I just went ahead and used my own money."

"Did that bother him?"

"No. He never said so." I pulled myself up on the kitchen counter and sat with my legs dangling down, banging against the cabinet doors. "We never talk about money. We each have our own bills. I pay the mortgage. He pays the maintenance and utilities. I pay the groceries. He pays for restaurants and movies. It works fine."

Piper cocked her head and said in an accusing voice, "Don't you have *anything* joint?"

I couldn't understand what was bothering her. "No. Not really," I said, still flopping my legs. "Nothing other than the condo. It's too confusing that other way, too hard to keep track. This works better."

"Jesus, Franny, the way you've got things set up, you've still got one foot out the door. You've been married almost what, seven years? Quit trying so hard to protect yourself. Michael's not your father; he's not going to leave you."

Before I could respond, we heard a tangle of keys and Michael pushed his way through the front door carrying a laundry basket stacked high with neatly folded clothes.

"I've gotta go!" he cried.

"I stand corrected," Piper said.

I jumped off my perch on the kitchen counter and followed Michael through the apartment and into the bedroom, Piper right behind me. He set the laundry basket down in the middle of the bed.

"Go where? Go *now*?" I said. "What about dinner? I'm

cooking dinner. Will you be gone late? I'm leaving for L.A. early tomorrow and wanted to spend time with you.''

"LeeAnn called," Michael said.

"In the laundry room? She called you in the laundry room?"

"Well, actually I called her," Michael said. "There's a pay phone in there. You probably don't know that because you never go there, but there's a pay phone in there. She was having a bad day, her boyfriend dumped her again, and I called to see how she was doing." He selected a pair of freshly washed socks from the laundry basket. "I folded the socks. You won't have to fold them."

"Thank you," I said.

"Who's LeeAnn?" Piper said.

"Is she okay?" I asked.

"She'll be okay," Michael said. "But she sounded really bad. I told her I'd go over there." He kicked off his loafers, slipped off the socks he was wearing, and pulled on a pair of clean socks. "She was muttering something about killing herself."

"Killing herself!" I said.

"*Killing* herself?" Piper said. "Maybe I should go over there. I'm a professional."

"She'll be okay," Michael said. "I'll just run over there, talk to her, and make sure she's fine."

"Okay," I said. "But how long are you going to be gone?"

"Just until she's feeling better."

"Okay," I said. "Okay."

Michael kissed me on the cheek and scooted out the bedroom door. "'Bye, Piper! Sorry! See you soon!" he called back at us. "Franny, don't forget to put the laundry away!"

"Who's LeeAnn?" Piper asked, as soon as we heard the front door slam.

"One of his friends from the bank. I've never even met

her, but he's like her big brother." Piper sat on the edge of the bed, her hands resting on her knees. I opened Michael's underwear drawer and stood behind the laundry basket tossing socks across the room like little basketballs. "She has really shitty luck with men."

"Who doesn't?" Piper said. One of my flying socks missed its target, bounced off the wooden box on the dresser top where Michael kept his loose change and two Purple Hearts, landed on the floor, and rolled under the dresser. Piper scrunched down on her knees and crawled after it. I pelted her with two more pairs of socks. "Don't you think it's a little strange that your husband calls some woman at seven o'clock at night and goes running off to see her?" she asked. "Doesn't that bug you?"

"No. I thought it was nice of him. He's being a good friend." I decided to leave the rest of the laundry sorting for later.

"You're either the most sophisticated wife I know," Piper said, standing up, "or the stupidest."

"We better check the oven," I said, not wanting to pursue the subject of LeeAnn any further. "Those tuna things don't have to cook too long." I figured Piper was just going through a stage, one of those I-don't-trust-men stages divorced women are famous for.

She left by nine o'clock. At nine-thirty I packed my suitcase for California. At ten o'clock I began to get edgy. It couldn't have taken Michael *that* long to talk to LeeAnn. He never spent that much time talking to *me*. But she *was* in trouble, and Michael cared about his friends; he hated to see anyone feeling troubled. He had such a good heart. He'd be home any minute.

At eleven o'clock I called Information for LeeAnn's phone number. At eleven-fifteen I stopped being understanding. At eleven-thirty I dialed her number.

I counted the rings. It took four rings. A woman's voice answered after one two three four rings.

"Hello?" it said.

"Hello," mine said. "Is my husband there?" I made a special point to emphasize the word *husband*.

There was a long pause, and then—"Uh, no," LeeAnn said. "He left about ten minutes ago. Uh, thank you for letting him come over here. He was, uh, very helpful."

"Fine," I said. "Thank you," I said. "Goodbye," I said. And hung up.

I finished sorting the laundry and crawled into bed. A few minutes later, I heard Michael's key in the front door. He walked into the bedroom softly, very softly.

"I'm up," I said, my face still buried in my pillow, my legs curled up against my chest. "Quit creeping around."

"You didn't have to wait up."

"I didn't wait up. I'm in bed. *Our* bed—where you should be. You didn't have to stay there all night."

"I wasn't gone all night. You're exaggerating." Suddenly the problem was *my* fault. "It took a long time to calm her down."

"I just called her. She sounded plenty calm."

"Called her?" I could hear Michael take a deep breath, but I still wasn't looking at him. "What do you mean you called her?"

"I called to ask her where the hell my husband was!" My voice was cold and resentful. It didn't sound like me, more like some other—much angrier—girl was doing the talking. I sat up and watched Michael kick off his shoes and pull off his pants. He unbuttoned his shirt. Slowly, methodically, he unbuttoned it one button after another, and threw it into the hamper.

"Go back to sleep," he said. "Everything's fine. Everything's okay." He walked over to the bed and straightened the covers so I'd lie back down again. "I just want to get some juice from the kitchen and then I'll come to bed, okay?" I crawled back into my curled-up position; Michael straightened the covers again and he kissed me on the cheek. "I'll be right back," he said.

Moments later I could hear his muffled voice coming from the kitchen. I picked up the bedroom phone.

"Michael, hang up," I said angrily. "Hang up right now."

She hung up. He hung up. I hung up.

Michael returned to the bedroom and finished undressing, quietly opening and closing dresser drawers. "I just wanted to see if she was upset from your phone call," he said. "I thought you might have upset her." He started softly chatting about traffic or the weather—I don't know what—his voice a hypnotic lull of soothing, patronizing tones. I clutched my pillow closer to me, tighter against my chest, and focused on a faded area on the rug in front of the closet door. Someone must have spilled something there. It wasn't me. It must have been Michael, Michael with his entreating chatter. It suddenly seemed absolutely imperative that I keep staring at that faded spot on the rug. Something was terribly wrong between Michael and me, but I felt too confused, upset, and tired to figure it out. All I wanted to do was get some sleep, wake up, leave for Los Angeles, and stop thinking.

❦ *Chapter 14* ❦

I called home only once. Yes, the flight was fine. Yes, the commercial's going fine. Michael informed me he'd be driving to Wisconsin to go fishing with Benny over the weekend. I notified him that a movie would be nice; perhaps the night I returned from California we could see a movie. A dark crowded theater left no opportunities for portentous confrontations.

Michael had long since stopped meeting me at the airport after my business trips. We fell out of the habit. And we no longer needed the expense account cab money to eat in a decent restaurant. I was pleased to be home in my own living room on my new white sofa with my new peach pillows. I sat curled in a corner, thumbing through back issues of *Vogue*, calmly waiting for my husband to get home from work so we could go to the movies.

Two hours later I heard the keys jangling in the front door. I sat, still waiting on the sofa, my hands folded in my lap, knees together with both feet on the floor, like a nervous wallflower on the sidelines at a dance.

"I just had the best talk!" Michael breezed into the room, loosened his tie, and plopped down on the sofa next to me. He leaned over and kissed me. "Hi! How was your trip? How was your day?"

"Better than my night," I said crossly. "We were supposed to go to the movies. You were supposed to come home. Who were you talking to?''

Michael seemed oblivious to my anger. ''Well, LeeAnn and I started walking home from the bank—the weather's really perfect today—did you get out today?—it's perfect today—and we just kept walking and talking, and enjoying the weather and . . . you know how that is.''

''Wait a moment. You were walking around talking to LeeAnn while I was *sitting* here waiting for you all night? What about the movies?''

''I forgot.'' He shrugged good-naturedly. ''We'll go tomorrow night.''

I exploded. ''We *can't* go tomorrow night! I'll be in New York tomorrow night. I'm leaving for my music session tomorrow night.''

''You're always leaving for New York,'' Michael said, sounding both hurt and accusatory.

''That's not true.''

''Yes, it is true. You're gone all the time.'' He stood up and walked around the coffee table to sit in the armchair across from the sofa, as if we were suddenly two opponents in a debate about to square off.

''You never seem to care,'' I countered. ''When I call, you talk to me for two seconds. You're always busy watching a basketball game or reading the paper or out with your banking friends.''

''Well, they'd be your friends, too, if you ever wanted to spend any time with them. At least when I talk to LeeAnn, I can do something for her, I can help her, I feel like she *needs* to talk to me.''

I looked at him in disbelief with my mouth open. ''And I don't?''

''No. You don't need me,'' Michael snapped, his face a dark red now. ''You take care of yourself just fine. Anything you want you go out and buy for yourself." He sliced his hands through the air. "This stupid condo. And all this stupid new furniture. Whatever you want you get. You don't need anyone."

I couldn't imagine how he could think that. "Just because I don't need you to put food in my mouth and clothes on my back doesn't mean I don't need you. Someone doesn't have to blatantly need someone to still need them!"

"Blatantly?" Michael said.

"What?" I said.

We glared at each other.

"Franny, your thinking is so screwy. Half the time I can't follow you; I don't know what you're saying. At least LeeAnn makes sense."

"So you'd rather be with her than *me*?" I cried.

"Of course not," Michael said, all in one rush of words. "I don't think so. You're my wife. I'm her friend. She just likes me, that's all. It's easy to talk to her, because—" He hesitated.

"Because what?"

His voice sounded smaller when he answered. "Because she's never disappointed in me."

I sat stunned for a moment. "And I *am*?"

"Yes, Franny," Michael said. He put his hands to his face and slowly rubbed his eyes. "I feel it all the time."

"But I love you!" My words came out more like a protest than a declaration of affection. "All I've wanted is you, the way you are, when you're strong and sure of yourself."

"Maybe I'm not that person." Michael dropped his hands to his sides. He stared at me like he was looking right through me. "Maybe you just made me up."

"I don't understand."

"LeeAnn doesn't have illusions about me."

He said it again, her name again; he kept saying that name.

She'd become the Enemy, an evil presence constantly hovering over my marriage.

"Are you—" The words stuck in my throat, an unformed, unthinkable question taking shape, forcing its way out of my lips and then quickly retreating, as if saying the words, posing the possibility, would be the one step necessary to make it true. "Michael—are you involved with LeeAnn?"

"Involved?" Michael seemed to be surveying his fingers with intense interest. He looked up and said, "You mean, like sexually?"

"Yes!" I said, taken aback at my own sudden fury. "*Involved*. Like *fucking*! And don't tell me I'm insane and imagining things. Just answer the question."

"No," Michael said simply, arching an eyebrow as he studied my face, apparently gauging my reaction. For a moment I thought he meant, no, he wouldn't answer my question, but then he said, "No. It's not like that at all. Not sexually. You shouldn't think like that." I could feel my heart sighing with relief. I felt like I'd been handed a reprieve.

"Okay. Fine. I just wanted to know, had to know," I said. "I know it was a stupid question. It just was odd, your behavior, the way you've been seeing her or at least talking about her so much, that I didn't know what to think. But at least I asked and we've cleared it up and we don't have to discuss the matter any further."

"That's a good idea. Let's drop it," Michael said. "I won't mention her again. She's not important."

We sat in silence, avoiding eye contact.

"Why don't you believe me that I love you?" I asked. "I hate it that you don't know that. You should know that, because I do. There are lots of things I want to tell you. I need you, too. I hate feeling lonely and separate from you. I hate feeling that there's this *thing* between us, that we don't talk enough. I don't have illusions about you. I know you. I love you."

Michael stood up and walked around the coffee table and sat next to me on the sofa again. He slipped his arm around my shoulders and held me, at first tentatively, and then more firmly.

He said, "We'll go to the movies when you get back from New York."

❧ *Chapter 15* ❧

Michael and I had a routine.

Saturday mornings I watered the plants and he wound the wall clock. Michael never let me wind the wall clock. He said I did it incorrectly.

"I think it's going to be okay," I said, while drowning a philodendron artfully positioned on the windowsill. The sidewalks below were virtually abandoned. The year, 1982, had been inaugurated with an icy January rainstorm followed by a nasty blizzard.

"What's going to be okay?" Michael stepped back to admire his perfectly balanced pendulum ticking away like a frantic Ping-Pong game.

"I miss working with Holly, but I like working on hamburgers. So I think the new agency's going to be fine."

"Good." Michael walked around the living room to make sure I'd watered the plants correctly.

"I just hope I don't have to work with this one art director all the time."

"You missed the Swedish ivy."

"I'm getting to it." I'd forgotten it, but I wasn't going to admit that.

Michael pounded the back cushions on the sofa. He would have claimed he was fluffing them, but he was really pounding them.

"And guess what," I said.

"What?"

"My period is late. I was supposed to get it the day before yesterday, but I didn't."

"You *mean* it?" Michael turned toward me with a hopeful, joyous smile spreading across his face. He balled his hands into two fists and began pacing around the room with a bouncing, eager energy. "We'll have a baby!"

"Can you believe it?" I picked at a dead leaf. "The timing is *terrible*. I just started my new job."

"So you're only *two* days late? Maybe you should go check again. When's the last time you were in the bathroom? Maybe you should call the doctor and have a test."

"Michael, there's nothing to check. I forgot to take my birth control pills along when I went to L.A. for that three-day trip. So that probably messed my schedule up and I just haven't gotten my period yet. I should be starting my new month of pills on Monday, but I don't know if I start my pills and then I find out I *am* pregnant, if the pills and all the hormones in them will be bad for the pregnancy."

"Don't do anything!" Michael cried. "Don't take any medicine! Don't do anything that could hurt the baby. You have to call your doctor before you do a thing. This is too important to do anything wrong. I hate those stupid pills. You should have never been taking them in the first place. Who knows what those chemicals are doing to your body?!''

"Yeah. Sure. What about all that crap they dumped into your lungs in Vietnam? If I *am* pregnant, I'll probably have to take a test to make sure the kid doesn't have a defect.''

Michael looked like I had slapped him across the face. "There is nothing wrong with my health!'' he retorted. "I take much better care of me than you ever take of you with all your cookies and cakes and never getting any decent exercise. Don't go thinking you can get away with your rotten habits now. It's not fair. It won't be fair. You can't do that to my baby.''

"Quit acting like you own my body! I don't even know if this is real yet, and you're already mad at me for screwing up. You aren't supposed to care more about a baby than you care about *me*. I don't want to have kids if you love the kids but you're always mad at me.''

"What are you talking about?''

"I don't know, Michael. I don't know,'' I said. "I guess I'm just nervous. We might be *pregnant*!''

"Jesus,'' he said wondrously. "Do you think it's possible?''

Michael insisted on driving me to the Walgreen's immediately, so I could purchase one of those home pregnancy tests. We walked up and down the aisles, holding hands, looking for the section filled with douches, Kotex, and boxes of E.P.T.

"I didn't mean to blurt it out,'' I told him. "I wanted to surprise you. I was going to find out if I was really pregnant and send a singing telegram or something to the bank.''

"So how long have you suspected?'' Michael asked, point-

ing me down an aisle beneath a sign that said: PAPER GOODS,
BATTERIES, FEMININE HYGIENE.

"Maybe two or three days."

Michael stopped and turned to me, looking incredulous.
"And you didn't *say* anything?"

"No. I told you. I wanted to surprise you."

I didn't know how I felt about having a baby. I'd have
wild swings of emotion, barreling back and forth between
fantasy and excitement, and horror at the thought that the
timing was all wrong; I wasn't ready yet; what about work
and my life? What if I couldn't be good at it and Michael
ended up disappointed in me for ruining our children? *What
if he ended up loving me less?* Before I told him, I wanted
to make sure I was happy.

There were two brands of pregnancy tests, and Michael
carefully read the labels on both, trying to decide which would
be the best choice, and making sure we didn't have any
important questions to ask the pharmacist before we left.

"Oh, no," he said, his eyes flooding with disappointment.
"We have to wait. You have to use your morning urine. We
have to wait until *morning.*"

He set the alarm for 6:00 A.M. "Get up! Get up!" he told
me excitedly. "Don't you have to go to the bathroom?"

Like two laboratory scientists, adding the contents of the
water vial into the glass test tube with the dry powder; then
using an eye dropper to add two small drops of morning
urine; we balanced the glass tube in the plastic holder, making
sure it was perfectly steady. Then we set the alarm for two
hours later and waited to see if a doughnut appeared.

"Yes!" Michael cried. "Oh my God!" Michael cried.
"We did it!"

"Oh my," I said, far more quietly. "We did it."

I spent the week fantasizing about redecorating the den
into a nursery and what to buy; and would it be hard to

find a nanny who would work late and cook dinners? All I could see was babies—babies in strollers and on buses and bundled up on elevators with red noses and rosebud smiles. I had the next nine months of my life planned out. And I was terrified.

"I want a little girl to take care of," Michael told me. "With your curls and your dark eyes." He'd pat my stomach and talk to it, as though he already knew the person who would emerge from there. "And the next baby can be a son. There won't be any more Wedlans unless we have a son." At night Michael held me and whispered in my hair. "I thought it was never going to happen to me," he'd say. "I thought I was never going to be this happy." Then he added, almost dreamily, "It's scary to want something so much, isn't it?" But I didn't answer him, because I didn't know quite what he meant.

The following Saturday afternoon, when Michael was at the grocery, the bleeding began. I felt a dull ache, then a sharp cramp, and clutched my stomach protectively; and then there was the blood. My first thought was: *I'm getting my period.* And then I thought, *Wait! I can't get my period. I'm* pregnant!

I sat in the bathroom as the cramps grew worse and the bleeding grew heavier, afraid to look between my legs, half-expecting to see a pair of tiny accusing eyes staring up at me from the toilet. And then I saw the clumps of blood and the tiny red fuzzy pit, and I knew there'd be no baby.

I phoned the doctor's office and pulled out the family medical book Michael had insisted we own, and while waiting for Dr. Gepperman to return my call, I looked up the information under miscarriages. Had I done something *wrong*? Maybe there was something wrong with my body. It had failed me. Failed *us*. Was it that glass of wine I drank to celebrate? Was I sitting in a room filled with smoke? Was it

Michael's Vietnam chemicals? And the one question, the horrible, guilty, painful question, that kept looming up inside my head: Had I secretly wished it?

The telephone rang and I raced for it, grateful that it was the doctor calling and not somebody else. "Were there clumps?" Dr. Gepperman asked, his voice professional and detached.

"Clumps?" *Oh, God*, I wanted to cry. I was thinking babies and he was talking clumps. He said words about one in four pregnancies and spontaneous abortions and mother nature's selective process; this doesn't reflect on future pregnancies; a lot of women miscarry the first time; and of course, there will be another time. Words like that. But all I could feel was failure. And that a highly anticipated party had just been called off.

"It's normal to mourn," Dr. Gepperman said before hanging up. "Feel free."

I was sitting in the middle of the living-room floor with my knees tucked under my chin and my arms wrapped around my legs, when Michael opened the door with his arms filled with grocery bags. A bouquet of flowers rested on top of one of the bags. "How's our little mama?" he asked cheerfully, happily.

My voice seemed to come from another place, a quiet, sadder place. "Michael, there's no more baby," I said. "I lost our baby."

At night we lay separately. I couldn't bear to touch Michael or hear his cries muffled into his pillow. He mourned the baby. And a small part of me began to mourn our marriage.

❦ *Chapter 16* ❦

Christopher Brodwolf drew cartoons for me during boring meetings. We'd be sitting in a half-darkened room through some endless slide presentation on the hamburger-purchasing habits of the American public, and Christopher would be scribbling caricatures of himself dozing off, or pictures of Ronald McDonald hiding under the conference table jotting down the Hobo Hamburger Corporation's deepest darkest secrets.

The first time we tried working together, Christopher Brodwolf rewrote my copy, followed by my telling him to stick to his drawing pencils. He responded by *insisting* we work together as partners. I speculated if that meant something about him preferring abusive women, but I said sure, okay. I was intrigued by the man. He was the most self-effacing know-it-all I ever met. But I honestly wasn't sure if his bossiness was false bravado, or if his constant poking fun at himself was false modesty. I leaned toward the false modesty theory, on account of his being a hunk.

I'd sit in his office trying to think about cheeseburgers, when—throughly appalled at myself—all I could concentrate on was Christopher's sandy-colored hair, Christopher's blue eyes, Christopher's dimples. He wasn't particularly tall, maybe only an inch or two taller than me, but he was *solid*. His daily wardrobe selection alternated between navy Land's End pullover sweaters and dark gray Land's End pullover sweaters, beneath which I could decipher the outline of one hell of a chest and some major contender biceps. He caught me staring at his arms one day, and quickly informed me he did three hundred push-ups and three hundred sit-ups every morning. Christopher loved being admired.

He began working at Watts, Watts, Ross and Malinick a few weeks before I did. Andy Hodgeman, our group creative director, teamed us together sensing deep down in his executive gut that the creative chemistry between Christopher and me would be explosive. That and the fact that I needed an art director and Christopher needed a writer and nobody else was available.

Christopher had grown up in the Chicago suburb next to the Chicago suburb my family lived in, but for the past five years he'd been living in some ski town in Colorado, trying to run a small local newspaper until he got run out of business by a large local newspaper. After that he spent a year as an illustrator; then, bored with starving to death, he returned to Chicago in search of a big bucks advertising job, like the job he left before moving to Colorado. Life was coming full circle for Christopher Brodwolf. With one notable exception. His last go-round in town he'd rented an apartment in the city. But this time he was "bunking" at his parents' house until he decided if he wanted to buy a place or opt for a lease.

Christopher was the only ladies' man I knew who was living with his mother and father.

He conducted his social life out of his office, calling and receiving calls from former girlfriends, reinstating himself into their lives. I wondered about all those women who apparently had found nothing or nobody better to spend their time with since Christopher had moved away five years earlier.

"One of them's been married and divorced in the past five

years, two others just got out of long-term relationships, and the other one's been dating around," Christopher explained.

"You're disgusting," I said. But he knew I was impressed.

For Valentine's Day he called a florist and ordered four dozen roses to be delivered. One dozen per girl.

"I don't know how you do it," I said, with unabashed admiration for a state-of-the-art sleazeball. "Do you love any of them?"

"No," he said. "I love all of them."

"And what about your girlfriends back in Colorado? You must have had girlfriends back there."

"We'll still be friends."

In between Christopher's social calls, we were up to our ears in hamburgers. In order to compete with the rather steller budgets of a McDonald's or a Burger King, the Hobo Hamburger chain offered "specials." One week free fries. The next week free Cokes. Christopher and I became specialists in the world of free specials.

Andy Hodgeman told us we were doing a great job. We were two of his star players, Andy said, congratulating himself for teaming us together. After that I was permanently stuck working with Christopher Brodwolf and his dimples.

"These are for you," I said, walking into his office one morning carrying a handful of pink phone messages. "Isabelle asked me to give them to you. Aren't I nice?"

"Yeah. Yeah. No. Yeah," Christopher commented while shuffling through the pile. "I don't know when I can do this. I don't know when I can see her. Uh-oh. These two things are on the same night. I just don't get it." He looked up at me with choirboy innocence. "I'm just a dull and boring guy. But women can't keep their hands off me."

"I guess they must go for your poor-little-me egomaniac act."

Christopher looked hurt. "It so happens I'm the most sincere guy you'll ever meet. By the way, you look especially pretty today."

"Thank you, Mr. Sincere. Let's get to work. We've got Buy One Get One Free week coming up."

"It's not my fault women find me irresistible," Christopher continued.

"Oh yeah?" I started picking at some dirt under a fingernail with my teeth. I considered Christopher such a complete jerk, I was totally comfortable with him. "Is that why you're what—thirty-nine years old?—and you've never been married?"

"Are you implying that I've never married because no woman would *have* me?" Christopher said, sounding truly indignant.

"Have you ever even *asked* anyone?"

"Unfortunately you're already taken." He smiled. "Let's get this work done and I'll buy you lunch."

"I can buy my own lunch, thank you," I informed him.

"I know. But it'll be a pleasure and an honor."

Within an hour and a half we'd roughed out three commercials. It was easy working with Christopher. Probably because of our explosive chemistry.

I rewarded him for a morning of excellent creativity by permitting him to buy me lunch.

In March, after more than three years in the customer-service department, balancing passbooks and wooing new accounts from widows, Michael was transferred into the bank's marketing department and elected an officer of the bank, a distinction that resulted in his receiving a free navy tie with little bank logos stitched all over it, and a sizable raise. I was still earning more, but he was earning more than before. As the newly ordained product manager for checking accounts, certificates of deposit, and automated teller machines, which in 1982 the general public still considered newfangled and intimidating, it became Michael's job to motivate customers to use the ATM's, so the bank could then save lots of money by firing tellers. He had long since abandoned his accounting courses. We entered a comfortable Ozzie and Harriet stage of our marriage, with a friendly rhythm and heartbeat all its own, each member performing his assigned marital role according to tradition. He brought me flowers from the train station. I brought him beers from the refrigerator. I loved my husband. My heart was capable of aching with love for my beautiful husband. I just couldn't understand how we'd ever ended up together. We'd grown so incidental within each other's lives.

Without much conversation, the subject arising out of a few random comments, we decided we needed a joint activity, a way to spend more time together. For years, our only real shared interest had been each other. At first that struck me as highly romantic—we've got each other, we'll live on love, and all that. But without coming right out and saying so, we knew we needed something more to talk about than the latest episode of *Lou Grant*. Having eliminated for various reasons—all of them mine—bridge, fishing, cross-country skiing, attending temple, and political activism, we enrolled in a class at the Art Institute, a class that met every Saturday morning for adults with no artistic talent who still wanted to do something artistic. We'd look at Calder mobiles, then go back into the classroom and make our own mobiles out of construction paper. We'd look at Henry Moores, then go back into the classroom and carve our own Henry Moores out of balsa wood. I'd be sitting across from Michael at one of the long working tables covered with oilcloth, playing with my scissors and my construction paper and my pieces of long black string, treating the whole thing like one big artistic joke, whereas he became a man possessed. It's good working with my hands, he told me. I'm tired of only using them for shuffling papers. At night he couldn't wait to come home from work, spread newspapers out on the den carpeting, and dive into his project; sanding and shaping his balsa wood into the shape of a naked woman with a Henry Moore hole in her stomach. I'd watch Michael as he worked, as if he were one of the sculptures we'd studied in the museum—indecipherable but compelling—frenziedly scraping away at his creation while absorbed in a hidden place oblivious to the rest of the world.

I tried to carve a naked man. But I ended up with something that could only be described as abstract.

Christopher Brodwolf kept buying me lunch.

He insisted what with all the money he was saving until he moved out of his parents' house, he needed *some* way to spend his millions. Then he'd pick up the check. He was just a guy I worked with, but he managed to turn our lunches into something that felt mildly like a date.

We usually ate at the Blue Clock, one of those semigeneric Greek-owned restaurants with vinyl booths and fake wood paneling and waiters who spent the first ten minutes of every meal trying to romance the day's specials with words like *charbroiled* and *fresh-frozen*.

I'd been working with Christopher for over two months and we'd already sold and were about to produce *two* Hobo Hamburger campaigns, which was considered some kind of land speed record because Hobo was an impossible client.

"What are all your girlfriends going to do with themselves while we're in L.A. filming burgers?" I asked Christopher in my sweetest snottiest voice. "Maybe you should introduce them to one another. They can all go to the movies together."

Christopher smiled briefly. "What'll your husband do when you're out of town?"

"He watches basketball."

"Smart man."

"So how's the apartment hunting coming?" I asked. "Or the house hunting? Or the whatever hunting? You don't seem to be in any mad rush to move out of your parents' house."

"Why should I be? They don't bother me. I don't bother them. We get along fine."

"Doesn't it bother them that their *grown* son is living at home?"

"No," Christopher said pleasantly. "Most of the time my old man's sleeping in front of *Wagon Train* reruns. He doesn't care who's living there or what's going on. I think my mother's glad to have me around." Christopher flashed me a couple of dimples. "I can be very charming company, you know."

I crumpled my face at him. "How do you have time to be charming company for your mother plus charming company for all the lady friends?"

"I'm not that busy with the ladies. You're just imagining that. I spend most of my time at the office with you."

Lester slapped down two plates of runny eggs Benedict.

"Is this the way this is supposed to come?" I asked Christopher, while picking pieces of black olives off the top of my eggs.

"I'll eat them," he said, reaching over onto my plate.

I watched Christopher eat my black olives.

"Are you close to your father?" I like asking that question. It has a way of making men shift in their seats.

Christopher's face grew somber. "I was when I was a kid. But by the time I got to high school all we did was fight."

"Why? Were you a hoodlum?"

"Worse," Christopher said. "I liked drawing pictures." He picked up the pepper shaker and sprinkled black granules over his eggs. "Dad was hoping for some butch bruiser of a son. And my idea of fun was painting the sets for school plays." Christopher shifted in his seat. "I didn't even join the service, a young man's ultimate rite of passage. I got out using old medical records about having asthma as a kid."

"Typical North Shore boy," I remarked. "At least you didn't go to Vietnam."

"But I *should* have gone." I was caught off guard by the sudden passion in Christopher's voice. "I missed Vietnam and the whole military experience. I feel like I missed something meaningful."

"Michael was over there," I said, using the tines of my fork to make rivulets of egg yolks weave through my hollandaise. "He thought it meant a waste of time."

I mulled the ways Christopher was different from Michael. He wasn't perfect like Michael, as always in control. But in a way I liked that. Christopher talked about things that bothered him and intimidated him. Which made it a lot easier for me to talk about those things. Michael never owned up to any insecurities, and he never quite understood them in me. The more I thought about it, the more I could understand why women loved Christopher. Talking to Christopher was like talking to a girlfriend.

I tore off a hunk of onion bread and dragged it through my plate, sopping up the runny eggs.

"Now there's an attractive sight," he said.

I contemplated fixing Christopher up with Piper, but for some fuzzy reason I resisted the idea.

Lester appeared again. "How was everything?"

"Awful as usual," Christopher said.

"Good," Lester said, as he cleared our plates and disappeared. Half a minute later he zipped back depositing the two junior-size chocolate sundaes included with our house specials. Then he disappeared again. Christopher automatically handed me his maraschino cherry without even knowing how much I love maraschino cherries.

"You know, you could use a wife," I said, for the sheer pleasure of goading him. "Pick one of those girls' names out of a hat and get on with it."

Christopher smiled one of his Hollywood smiles. "Maybe I will get married someday. If I find someone I get along with as well as you."

"Yeah, sure." I swallowed a big mouthful of whipped cream. "You're only saying that because I'm safely married. If I were single, you'd be a nervous wreck around me."

"That's not true. I like talking to you. You have interesting wiring up there. Things come out in strange ways."

"My interesting wiring frustrates the hell out of Michael. He's always mad at me for not being logical enough."

"Well, he's wrong." Christopher reached across the table and tapped my forehead with his index finger. "It's like an electrical pinball machine up there. Fun to listen to." He pulled back his hand. "You know, I hate being in a big agency again. But I look forward to seeing you every day. You're the only reason I'm staying."

I was used to people leaving in spite of me; my father skipping the country, Michael taking off for Alaska. But Christopher was the first person who ever said he *stayed* somewhere because of me. "What a bunch of bullshit," I told him.

But I couldn't stop smiling.

❧ *Chapter 17* ❧

In theory, it was a swell plan.

I invited Christopher for dinner so Michael could get to know him. They'd been introduced before, but they'd never really sat and talked. Michael would like talking to Christopher. They both liked fishing. They could talk about fish.

I arranged everything for a Tuesday after work. The previous night I whipped together a big pot of chili and one of my many questionable Jell-O molds, and walked around the dining table setting out three places.

"You folded the napkins wrong," Michael informed me. "The folded edge is supposed to go on the inside."

I turned the napkins around so the fold went the correct way. "Now they're okay."

"And straighten the forks. You put them back crooked."

I straightened the forks and grinned at Michael in hopes of his approval. "Is something bothering you?" I asked, fancying myself an astute observer of the human condition. Or at least of Michael's condition.

"No, everything's fine," he said. He readjusted the position of the water glasses.

On Tuesday night Christopher and I didn't stop for our usual après-work cocktails. We'd fallen into the routine of stopping for a margarita or a beer after work so we could keep working and talking. But this Tuesday night was the dinner party.

"This will be educational for you," I told Christopher, as I unlocked my front door. "You can experience a taste of domestic life." (I hardly counted living with his parents as domestic life.) We walked into the apartment. Christopher didn't comment on it at all, not on the decorating or anything. I didn't hear the sound of the den television, so I knew Michael wasn't home yet.

"What is it about married people that makes them hate to see anyone else who's not married?" Christopher asked. "Women are attracted to me because I'm a free entity, and the next thing you know, they want to tie me down and sign me up."

"Relax," I said, walking into the kitchen and tossing my purse on the counter. Christopher followed me. "I'm not at all attracted to you."

"I know," Christopher said. "That's what I find so attractive about you."

I opened the refrigerator and pulled out my pot of chili and set it on the stove, lifting the pot cover to observe my creation, a cold bulbous brown lump of beans. "This is what you get to eat."

Christopher peeked into the pot. "Can't wait."

I turned on the burner beneath my chili. "Do you want a beer?"

"Chili and beer? What a great combination!" Christopher put his hand up against his mouth and made a loud blowing noise on it.

"Tell me again how much women like you." I pulled two cans of Coke out of the refrigerator. "You're obnoxious. Only insane and desperate women could like you." I shoved one of the Coke cans into Christopher's hands.

"Don't you want to get out your best crystal?" he asked, popping the tab off the can.

"Not for you." I checked the chili burner one more time.

We walked out of the kitchen, past the dining area into the living room, and both sat down on the couch. Realizing I had sort of landed too close to Christopher, I hunkered down the couch a few inches farther from him.

"Hey, do I smell bad?"

"Quit looking for compliments," I told him as he sipped his soda, taking note of the wildly provocative way he used his tongue along the rim of the can. "Maybe we should talk about our production notes."

"Only if you don't mind me falling asleep on this couch," Christopher said.

The phone rang. I got up and walked to the kitchen, conscious of Christopher staring at my butt the entire way. Michael was calling to say he was stuck in a meeting and to start without him. I checked the chili, stirring it so it would cook faster.

"Who was that?" Christopher asked when I walked back into the living room. "Good news or money?"

"Michael." I sat down again next to Christopher. Close but not too close. "He's not coming."

"How could he not come here? He lives here."

"He will be here, but he'll be here later. He's still in a meeting. He said to go ahead and eat. He knows my cooking well enough to know you probably can't wait a minute longer." I didn't know why, but it suddenly felt uncomfortable that Michael wasn't home.

The chili in the middle of the pot was still lumpy and cold, but the chili around the edges of the pot was warm enough to be almost edible, so we ate the chili from the sides. Christopher was impressed that I'd made a Jell-O mold; Jell-O molds were a lost art, he insisted. He complimented the chili and raved about the slices of Wonder Bread I ended up serving because I forgot to buy French bread. He even admired the way the cloth napkins were folded.

"You two are lucky," he said, sitting across from me at the dining table. "You have a real life. A real home. Jobs you like." Christopher placed his crumpled napkin on the table. "And each other."

"You could have all that."

"No. Not me." Christopher sounded genuinely wistful.

I leaned forward in my chair. "It's nice talking over dinner, isn't it?"

"Who doesn't talk over dinner?"

I sat back. "Do you want any dessert? I've got ice cream and Hershey's sauce. Your favorites."

"No, thanks. I think your chili just hit bottom."

An awkward tension had settled between us. "Should we go sit in the living room again?"

"No. Maybe not," Christopher said. "Maybe I better get out of here. Maybe I shouldn't stay."

"Don't go. You don't have to go. I want you to be friends with Michael."

Christopher stood up and carried his dirty plates to the kitchen. "No. I better go." He walked to the front door with me right behind him, and then he did something I considered very peculiar. He turned and pressed his face against mine, and he kissed me. It was a friendly kiss, but still, it was on the lips. Before I could complain or laugh or think of some appropriate sophisticated response, he left, mumbling something about seeing me in study hall.

I stood in the hallway, momentarily bewildered, then I headed into the kitchen and made quite a production of rinsing the dinner plates and loading the dishwasher. I made myself a chocolate sundae, then sat in the living room shoveling it down my face while waiting for Michael. Fifteen minutes later he walked in, looking handsome and important in his navy pin-striped banker's suit and navy wool overcoat. His confidence, poise, and forthright mannerisms never failed to touch me.

"Hello, spouse!" he said, smiling at me, in obvious good spirits. "Where's your dinner guest?"

"He had to leave," I said, standing up to plant a wifely kiss on my husband's lips.

"Too bad," Michael said pleasantly. "It would have been nice to get to know him."

Michael ate his dinner sitting on the floor of the den, in front of the television. He'd found a basketball game to watch. I sat on the den couch, watching him watch the basketball game.

Despite what had once been considered a rather good head on my shoulders, I wasted hours of work, squandered entire days of productivity, fantasizing what it would be like to submit myself to Christopher Brodwolf. Maybe his biceps weren't all that big. Maybe he just stuffed the arms of his sweaters with Kleenex. Was he concealing a chestload of thick hair under those Land's End sweaters? Michael had hardly any hair on his chest. One night when we were first married, we'd tried to count his hairs, and came up with a grand total of thirty-two. I imagined Christopher's chest to be perfect. Sometimes, without any self-consciousness, standing in a hallway in the middle of a conversation, he'd place his feet together and rotate his hips, rocking from one foot to the other, like he was schussing down a secret mountain, practicing some sexy ski movement. I was mesmerized by those hips. And the way he had of talking to me with his eyes floating over my breasts, inevitably causing my face to flush. No sane reason could possibly explain my being so embarrassingly attracted to such a disgusting skirt chaser. Maybe Michael was right. Maybe I was incapable of logic.

Two weeks after my attempt at a dinner party, Christopher and I flew to Los Angeles to produce our Hobo Hamburger campaigns, and I inadvertently seduced him in my hotel room. At least I think it was me who did the seducing. It was difficult to tell. He was the one who offered to give me a back rub when I complained that my back hurt from sitting in the casting session all day. But I was the one who didn't resist when the back rub turned into a front rub and then turned into an everything rub. He lauded my body, sang dirty limericks. He treated sex like such a delightful, fun, thoroughly entertaining event. With Michael lovemaking was sacred and fragile; with Christopher, it was raucous.

"You have the stamina of a thirty-nine-year-old and the enthusiasm of a seventeen-year-old," I informed him, as I lay flabbergasted on the hotel bed.

He was perched on the end of the bed, massaging my feet, stopping to noisily kiss each individual toe. "You just needed some attention." He scooted up the bed and flopped down next to me, pulling me alongside him. "And as our beloved boss and leader has often made note of, Mrs. Wedlan, you and I have *chemistry*."

Lying with my body pressed against Christopher's seemed a moderately inappropriate time for him to be calling me Mrs. Wedlan, but I didn't complain. I was afraid that if I said anything wrong he might stop holding me.

While trying to force away all thoughts of Michael waiting at home for me, I allowed my conscious mind to acknowledge the deep bewildering truth of how lonely I had been, and how much I craved being held. After that, I stayed with Christopher every night until we went back to Chicago.

It seemed like an absolutely necessary thing to do.

❧ *Chapter 18* ❧

It's no easy task to carry on an affair when one of the participants lives with a husband and the other one lives with his mother and father.

Christopher no longer spoke about his many girlfriends and whom he was currently honoring with the opportunity to date him. I didn't know if his silence was due to his no longer dating the women or if he just wasn't talking anymore. I was jealous even though I had no right to be. After all, I had a husband, and Christopher never seemed jealous or, for that matter, even curious about Michael.

Married life while having an affair didn't seem all that different from married life without an affair. Michael and I did the same things, saw the same friends, watched the same television shows. Only now my thoughts were preoccupied with Christopher. Michael needed so little from me. He didn't seem to *care* that we spent so little time together. I convinced myself that I was magnanimous and all-loving, capable of loving two men and giving each what he needed from me. On some weird level Michael seemed to be giving me his blessing, without acknowledging what was going on. I'd suggest that we see some particular movie and he'd say he didn't want to see that movie, so I'd say maybe I should go see the movie with Christopher, and Michael would say, yes, that sounded like a better idea. I was creating a motherlode of deceptions between Michael and me. But I couldn't switch off my feelings for Christopher. Michael was the only thing preventing me from being where I wanted and with whom I wanted. And yet I knew Michael wasn't doing anything different. He was still Michael. I tried to love him better. I tried to talk myself into refocusing on him. At times I would lower my eyes, averting his scrutiny, feeling positive that if our eyes did meet he would *know*; he would suspect that huge parts of me no longer wanted to be sitting in that room, going through the motions, always pretending. I'd curl up in a corner of the sofa and open a magazine, forcing myself to concentrate on photographs of faceless models, trying not to cry. I'd tell myself: *He doesn't know. He couldn't possibly know. And he seems so content with what little he wants from me.*

In July, Christopher's parents went to Boston for three days for his father's fiftieth reunion from Harvard's business school. With only the slightest hesitation, I informed Michael that I had a last-minute music session in New York, then spent two nights making love in Christopher's twin bed in his knotty pine bedroom with the shelf full of high school yearbooks and the clay ashtray shaped like his hand that he made in fourth grade and his mother refused to let him discard. Christopher drew the line at our using his parents' double bed, protesting that that would be some form of borderline incest. I called home each night, chatting to Michael as if I were in New York, calling him like I always did, wanting to reassure him that everything was fine. Hearing from me he sounded content. When I returned home I told him what a successful business trip I'd had, and how much I'd missed him the entire time; then found myself angry at him for not noticing my lies.

Barry Salzer, Michael's roommate before me, found himself a woman who managed to appreciate his well-hidden charms. After years of mowing his way through the dating population of Chicago, like General Sherman marching through the South burning a fiery trail in his wake, pursuing short-term relationships, one-night stands, and blind dates with a blinding fury, Barry ended up engaged to the insurance adjuster who handled his someone-stole-my-car-stereo claim.

Susan, the future Mrs. Barry, was slim with long straight black hair that fell below her shoulders Pocohantas-style. She was the type of woman who could immediately enhance the image of any man whose arm she graced. Hey, Susan likes Barry? Maybe he's not so bad. That sort of woman. The happy couple had come over so Susan could elegantly dangle her monstrous new engagement ring in our faces. The two of them sat welded together on the sofa, holding hands and tripping over each other's sentences. Michael and I sat on the two chairs opposite the sofa. The four of us ate Junior Mints and drank iced tea while politely conversing about Barry and Susan's good fortune in finding each other. Susan would continually smooth her hair behind her ears with her jeweled hand; whether from nervousness or high energy, I couldn't tell. She'd touch Barry, playing with his hair or stroking his cheek. He'd rub the back of her neck. Their constant pawing got on my nerves.

"You must have robbed a bank," Michael said to Barry, admiring Susan's diamond. "I hope it wasn't my bank."

"When's the big date?" I asked.

"We haven't figured that out yet," Susan said. "I'm more interested in the being married part than in the hoopla part. I just hope things are as good for us as they are for you two."

"Even better," I wished her.

"I'm so phenomenally lucky," she sighed.

"No, I'm who's lucky," Barry insisted. Barry was a better Barry now that he was Susan's Barry. He was more relaxed.

Easier to take in large doses. "I talked her into it," he confided.

"You did not," Susan said, laughing. "I proposed to *you*."

"Who paid for the diamond?" Michael asked, slouched forward in his seat, rummaging through the candy dish holding the Junior Mints.

"He did," Susan said. Then she turned to me. "There's a definite advantage to not finding the right guy until you're almost thirty. The diamonds are bigger. Then again, while I was dating an endless succession of morons and maniacs, you had your husband to curl up with."

"I think Franny deserves a bigger diamond," Michael announced. "If she's a good girl and behaves herself, I'll buy her one for our tenth anniversary next year. I've been thinking about that for quite some time."

I'd had no inkling that Michael intended to buy me a new diamond. I twisted in my seat and avoided his eyes, inwardly cringing and hating myself for being so undeserving.

"It's nice having these men showering us with jewels," Susan said happily to me. "Don't you think?"

"Ten years of marriage. That's practically a lifetime," Barry said, whistling through his teeth. "You can't have too many secrets left after ten years."

"No," Michael said.

"No," I said, forcing myself to smile. "What would be the point?"

The next day, while lunching at the Blue Clock with Christopher, I casually asked when he was planning to move out of his parents' house.

He promptly rallied off a long speech about how he still wanted to save some money, and how he wasn't fully certain just where he wanted to live, and how he hated the hassle of moving, and how he was afraid that if he moved out of home, when he did move out of home, things between us would intensify.

I looked at him. "*Intensify?* I thought they already were intense."

Christopher took a bite of meatloaf, then wiped some dribbled gravy off his mouth with the back of his hand. He reached under the table, surreptitiously squeezed my knee and patted my thigh, then arched his head to one side and grinned; well aware that his boyish charm held a powerful hold on me. "Oh, well, yeah, sure," he said. "Of course they are. They don't get any more intense, right? Yeah! But they could escalate, you know, get too serious. And I'd hate the guilt. You're married to a nice guy. I'm sure he loves you. I don't want to screw things up for you. Maybe I should just move away from Chicago. I could go back to Colorado or get a job some place out West. You're my best friend, Franny. I'd miss you. I'd hate to be without you. I can't talk to any woman the way I talk to you. But I don't want to ruin things for you or make a mess of your marriage."

He's so considerate, I thought. *All his verbal tap dancing about things getting too serious is because he cares so deeply about me.* "Please don't move away from Chicago. I'd hate that," I told him. "I'd be so lonely."

That night, before falling asleep, lying next to Michael on my own absolutely separate side of the bed, the July heat creating a weighty stickiness in the room, I asked, "Why did you marry me?"

"What kind of question is that?"

"A straightforward one. You don't like to talk to me. You don't like to do anything with me. Why did you marry me?"

"I do want to do things with you, Franny, but you don't have any interests. There's nothing you like to do."

"That's not true. I like reading. I like going to the movies."

"Reading is not an activity we can do together. And we go to plenty of movies."

"You don't seem to *like* me," I said, staring into the dark. "So I don't know why you married me."

"I married you because I wanted to. Quit worrying about stupid things," Michael said, impatient now. "This is a stupid conversation about stupid things. Go to sleep." He rolled over with his back to me. I concentrated on a thin crack in the ceiling, trying to think back, rerun the tape, trying to remember why I'd married Michael. And yet it was still unthinkable to me that I might ever *stop* being married to him.

The following Saturday I stopped in my office to check a sheet of hamburger lyrics I needed to fix before Monday, but had neglected to take home on Friday. Michael and I were out running errands. Michael enjoyed visiting Watts, Watts, Ross and Malinick on weekends because he could wander into all the offices, putter around, and examine people's work. Once, late on a Saturday night, back when I was working at Ethan King, we had made love behind my desk on the floor of my office, with most of our clothes still on. But that was a long time ago.

I sat in my office and reworked my lyrics while Michael roamed up and down the hallways, checking out the other offices. When I finally finished I trotted off to the Xerox room to make a copy of my brilliant accomplishment. I walked back into my office and found Michael snooping around. He was studying some of the cartoons Christopher had drawn that I had pinned to my bulletin board. Cartoons of Christopher and me riding hamburgers like flying carpets, and wrangling with gigantic french fries.

"What are you doing?" I asked.

"Just looking. I was curious," Michael said.

"There's nothing to be curious about."

"They're funny cartoons," he said, sounding hurt and confused. "I wanted to read them."

"I'm finished," I said. "Let's get out of here."

Michael was taking a shower. I was brushing my teeth at the sink. We were getting ready to meet Louie and Nadine at a movie.

"Something's wrong," I heard him say over the splashing water.

"What's wrong?" I said back to him, after spitting and rinsing my mouth.

"I don't know. You won't tell me. But something's not right. You don't care about me the way you used to." He was choking on his words. "Something's wrong and I don't know how to fix it, because you won't tell me what it is."

I pulled back the shower curtain just enough to poke my head into the shower without getting wet. Michael looked lean and mangy with his body hair plastered down from the rushing water. He looked like he was drowning.

"Nothing's wrong," I said. "Honest."

❦ *Chapter 19* ❦

Piper guessed in September.

After years of using my psyche to practice the art of picking someone's psyche apart, she guessed my psyche was fooling around. On one of her days off from her recently established private practice specializing in "alcoholics, twins, old people, and thirty-five-year-old women who want babies but don't have boyfriends," we scheduled a long lunch and met in the Executive Woman section at Marshall Field's. Piper had taken to wearing suits to work. She felt that was the least she could do when she was charging people sixty dollars an hour to talk to her.

I, of course, talked to her for free.

"You're seeing someone, aren't you?" she said, shuffling through a rack of silk blouses with bows at the neck.

"What do you mean?" I looked around to make sure there weren't any hovering salesladies or nosy customers listening in on our conversation. For someone who worked in a strictly confidential business, Piper had a way of blurting out observations about my private life in the most public places.

"I know the signs," she said, holding a cream-colored blouse under her chin, and then rejecting it. "Too drab with my blond hair, right?"

"There are signs?" I wondered if everyone else knew the signs. I wondered what the signs were. I didn't think I *looked* any different. "What signs?" I asked, feeling like a case of big red measles had just sprouted across my face.

"It's the guy at the office, right? The one you talk about all the time. Who lives with his mom and dad? Probably some sort of unfinished childhood sexual rivalry with his father, huh? That's what I'd bet. Interesting that you should pick someone so unavailable to you. You must be quite ambivalent about the relationship." Piper headed over to a dress rack, with me trailing her. "Unless it's one of those transitional relationships many people need to help themselves get out of a no-longer-satisfying marriage. Which would make a lot more sense if you weren't married to Michael."

"What's wrong with Michael?"

"From what I can tell, hardly anything." Piper examined a black knit dress that looked like something my mother would wear. "I see a lot of women who were in a real hurry to get out of their marriages and later on end up sorry. And they weren't married to guys half as decent as Michael. There are a lot of jerks out there, Franny."

"I'm not interested in a lot of jerks," I said frostily.

"Just one in particular?" Piper loaded my arms with several suits and dresses. She had recently started dating a podiatrist who she said had both good points and bad points. The good points were he was smart, handsome, loving, and his wife had died of cancer two years earlier, which meant there was no ex-wife hanging around. After Piper's first marriage, no ex-wife was her idea of a major good point. The bad points were the smart, handsome, loving podiatrist's five motherless children. "So how long's it been?" Piper asked. "Since you two started?"

"Since May or June," I admitted. "We don't actually see each other much—you know, sleep with each other much. We just talk a lot."

"Oh. You talk a lot. I see."

"He's a good listener."

Piper shook her head and sighed. "There's something incredibly compelling about a man who's willing to listen."

A gray-haired saleslady in thick-soled shoes walked up and said, "May I help you?" She then marched us into a dressing room like she was leading a parade and we were the floats. I sat on the one chair provided in the tiny pink dressing room, unzipping, unbuttoning, and rehanging, while Piper tried on suits. "You've been married a long time," she said, stepping into the skirt of a sensible little gray gabardine number. "Maybe you just need a little fling, a perk. It happens all the time. More often for wives then men realize."

"It's not that simple. Christopher's different with me. He likes me without wanting to change me. And he touches more than Michael. Plain old affectionate-type touching."

Piper raised an eyebrow. "At the office?"

I ignored that question. "It's a bunch of things. Hard-to-explain things. Christopher let's himself be more of a kid than Michael does."

"I don't necessarily consider that a selling point in a man," Piper said, addressing her reflection in the mirror. She buttoned a white blouse.

I continued defending Christopher. "When you first meet him, he talks like he's a regular Don Juan, but basically he's real shy. He seems to *like* me more than Michael does."

Piper turned and looked directly at me. "Don Juan didn't live with his mother."

"That's temporary. Until he figures things out."

Piper slipped on the gray suit jacket and studied herself once again in the mirror, scowled, and immediately took off the entire suit. "You know, divorce doesn't solve your problems. It just replaces them with a new set of problems. Do you want to divorce Michael and go live with your boyfriend at his parents' house?"

"Don't be mean."

"I'm not being mean. I'm just asking what you want."

"Nothing. I don't want anything. I don't know what I want!" Piper handed me the gray suit to hang up. I handed her a navy suit to try on.

"And how much do you think Michael knows?" she asked.

"He doesn't know," I said firmly.

"You've been in love with another guy for four, five months, and you don't think he's suspicious?" Piper's eyes were filled with amazement.

"Maybe one time he wondered. But now he never says anything. And I certainly don't say anything. I love Michael. I don't want to hurt him."

Piper tugged on the navy jacket. "You should have thought of that back in May."

❦ *Chapter 20* ❦

I dreaded Christmas in Springfield.

For three weeks Michael had been coming home from work carrying little packages and clumsy boxes and closing himself off in the den with scissors and tape and wrapping paper, creating a growing pile of gifts.

"What are all these presents for?" I asked.

"They're surprises. I want you to have surprises," he said.

"So many of them? All for me?"

"I want you to be happy," Michael said.

Two months earlier Norma and Gordon had sold their house

and rented a two-bedroom townhouse. Gordon worked out a plan with everything organized so that the money he stuck in the bank from selling the house paid enough interest to cover the monthly rent. That, along with their Social Security checks and the small salary Gordon received for handling Springfield Central Baptist's monthly bookkeeping, gave the Wedlans enough to live comfortably and take one nice car trip per year.

Norma had been hinting for the past several years, in her unique if-you-people-could-read-between-the-lines-you'd-know-what-I-was-talking-about way, that she wanted to sell the house and move to a place easier to handle. She never came right out and said it, but she feared Gordon would be insensitive enough to die on her someday, leaving her stuck caring for the house all by herself.

Norma considered the new townhouse quite an improvement.

The first floor consisted of a small living–dining room with white walls and carpeting the color of old mustard. All the furniture from the old living and dining rooms was carefully arranged and jammed together surprisingly well. A powder room, and a small but big enough to eat in kitchen with—what luck!—*green* appliances, completed the layout. My favorite part of the kitchen was the dishwasher. Norma *finally* had an automatic dishwasher. Gordon's bookkeeping desk was stored in the cement basement along with the washer and dryer. Upstairs there were two tiny beige bedrooms (with gold carpeting), and a beige tile bathroom (with gold throw rugs). A small patio, garbage cans, and a carport off the alley in back, and it was home.

We arrived just in time for the traditional lamb and mint jelly and Brownberry rolls Christmas Eve dinner. Norma had already set the table with the Santa Claus and his reindeer placemats and the Christmas tree china from Judith and Walter. The pine cone wreath was hanging on the front door. The three cardboard wise men graced the top of the TV. The wooden Swedish stick tree with geegaws and doodads sat on the coffee table. I had stopped insisting on a real tree years ago.

"You seem settled here, like you've always lived here," I said, slicing through a piece of extremely well done roast lamb.

"Yes, it was very clean when we moved in," Norma said. "We only had to replace the toilet seats. You wouldn't believe what Sears charges for a toilet seat. The salesman tried to sell me the most expensive one, the one with the ten-year warranty, but I told him that was ridiculous. Can you imagine me walking into Sears in 1992 carrying a ten-year-old broken toilet seat and demanding my money back?"

"No, Mom, I can't," Michael said.

"Pass the succotash," Gordon said.

Michael and his parents discussed the Cubs. I concentrated on chewing my lamb and wondering what Christopher was doing right that very second. His sister Kimberly and her husband and two children, who lived in Dallas, were flying in for the holidays. Kimberly's husband was a pilot for American Airlines, so they were always flying around the country for free and coming home for Christmas. Christopher said his family made a big fuss over Christmas, singing carols around the piano, stringing popcorn for the tree, baking cookies and making fudge, relatives dropping over for eggnog and punch, and tons of presents. Always tons of presents. I wondered what Christopher had bought me for Christmas. I wondered if he'd like what I'd bought him. I wondered if life was less complicated for girls who were born with the name Kimberly.

"I hope she doesn't sell it," Michael was saying. He was talking about his aunt Vivien's house in Pasadena. "It's a beautiful house. I spent a week there right after I came back from Vietnam.''

Norma disagreed. "She should sell it. Vivien doesn't need such a big house. I can't imagine living in such a big place all alone. I'm much happier in a small crowded place like this with your father.''

"Pass the Potato Buds," Gordon said. Then he asked Michael, "How's the bank?"

"Boring," Michael said.

"It must be Christmas in Switzerland already," Norma said. Michael's sister and brother-in-law were vacationing in Zurich. "I don't know the exact time there because my watch has been acting up, but I bet Judith and Walter are celebrating Christmas right now." Norma's Christmas hints that year were for a new watch. Since September she'd been writing letters with phrases like, "If only my watch weren't so old and rotten.''

"It's the middle of the night there," Gordon said. "They're sleeping right now."

"It must be nice to sleep in Switzerland," Norma sighed.

"It probably feels just like sleeping in Springfield," Gordon said.

"We should go to Switzerland sometime," Michael told me. "Let's plan a trip."

"They have a lot of good watch stores in Switzerland," Norma said. "They're famous for their watch stores. Maybe Judith and Walter will buy me a watch."

"Did you tell them you wanted a watch?" Michael asked.

"Of course not," she said. "That would be rude."

"She told them every Sunday," Gordon said. "Every time they called. She'd tell them they shouldn't talk so long on the phone when it's long distance, not that she could tell how long they'd been talking with a watch as old as hers."

"It was a hint," Norma said. "It's not rude to hint."

"If you want something, Mom, just come right out and say it," Michael told her. "There's nothing wrong with being direct."

"I'm direct," Norma said. "I can be plenty direct."

"Good," Michael said. "Now tell me, Mom. What would you like for Christmas? Are you hoping for a new watch for Christmas?"

"I don't need a new watch," Norma said. "Most of the time my old watch works just fine. And the rest of the time I can ask someone."

I wondered what Christmas carols they were singing at Christopher's house.

After dinner I cleared while Norma rinsed and loaded. Michael and his father sat in the living room watching the *Andy Williams Holiday Special* and reading the newspaper. Then Norma and Gordon left for church. Michael didn't want to go to church. "Let's go to the movies," he said. "You love the movies." We saw *Gandhi* with Benny and his new girlfriend, Kitty, a nurse Benny was living with whom he met in the emergency room of St. John's Hospital after he was bitten while trying to pet a dog tied up to a bicycle rack. Benny had a new career. He was selling refrigerators and garbage disposals, a job he liked a lot more than teaching school in dangerous neighborhoods.

His hair was no longer shoulder-length.

After the movie we found a bar that was actually open and fairly crowded. How depressing, I thought. I felt miserable watching all those people sitting around drinking with apparently nothing better to do on Christmas Eve. People like us. I suppose it could have still turned out to be an okay evening, except that Kitty never talked. I'd ask her a reasonable, straightforward question like, "Kitty, did you like the movie?" and all she'd do was shrug. Michael held my hand while Benny and he discussed passive resistance and the fall of the British empire. Kitty shrugged. And I thought about Christopher.

In the morning Michael and his parents and I went around the living room and took turns opening our gifts.

I gave Michael an I.O.U. for piano lessons. We didn't have a piano. I didn't know where we'd put a piano. And I didn't particularly want a piano. But Michael had been talking about wanting piano lessons. I also gave him a set of wood-carving tools.

"What do you need these tools for?" Gordon asked, examining a chisel.

"I can carve things with them," Michael said appreciatively.

"Great! You can carve the roast!" his father guffawed.

We handed Gordon his annual cardigan.

Michael's parents gave me a subscription to *Good Housekeeping* magazine, three pairs of pantyhose, and a ten-dollar bill.

They gave Michael a wool robe and a twenty-dollar bill.

Norma got three watches. One from Diana and Garry-with-two-r's. One from Gordon. And one from Michael and me. "What if Judith and Walter buy me a watch in Switzerland?" she said, holding up her three new watches and scrutinizing them under the light.

"Don't worry," Michael said. "Maybe they'll just send you a box of chocolates."

I opened my gifts from Michael last.

"The big one in the poinsettia paper is just a little thing, but the little one in the reindeer paper is a bigger thing and the rest are just for fun," he said. "I hope you like them."

"Let's see them, already," his mother said.

First I opened a white lace camisole, followed by a pink cashmere sweater, a tortoiseshell brush and comb set, and an antique silver frame. Michael had put one of our wedding pictures into it, the one where we were walking down the aisle, happily smiling, right after our vows.

"You were so extravagant," I said, feeling somehow sad and perturbed at the same time.

"I'll say," his mother said.

"There are two more," his father said. "You aren't done. Open the others."

"You're my wife," Michael said to me, his face looking both eager and anxious. "I'm allowed to be extravagant."

In one box there was a pearl and diamond drop on a thin gold chain. In the other package were two paperback books: *Having Babies After Thirty*, and *Your Baby's First Twelve Months*.

"Are you trying to tell us something?" Michael's father asked.

"I think he's trying to tell me something." I looked at Michael. He smiled at me, a sad smile, then looked away, busying himself with picking wrapping paper off the carpet.

"Try on the necklace," Norma said. "That's a cute necklace."

"Maybe you can trade it for a watch," her husband said.

I asked Michael to help me on with the necklace. "It's lovely," I told him. "Thank you."

"What time is it?" Norma asked, picking up her watches. "I have to set these things."

"It's time for breakfast," Gordon said. "Enough with Christmas already."

We ate cornflakes and raisin toast with jelly and then Michael and his father went outside to shovel the sidewalk. It had snowed over night. Norma and I cleared away the dishes and sat together in the living room watching television. The news was on, clips of the Pope waving Merry Christmas off his balcony in Rome. Norma was busily knitting a brown sweater vest for Walter's next birthday. Walter was her favorite son-in-law.

"How's your sister's new baby?" Norma asked, her knitting needles clicking. "Walking already?"

She asked the question and then lost interest before I could answer. That's what she always did. She'd ask a question about my family and then her eyes would glaze over before I started to tell her anything.

"Fine," I said. "Joel is fine. Not walking yet, but he's working on it."

"Michael walked at eight months," Norma said. "He was quite gifted."

Now the news was showing Christmas day in Poland, how empty the streets were, how dreary, how disheartened the Poles were.

"Hm! They had snow, too!" Norma said. She pulled at the yarn on her knitting ball, causing it to go bouncing off the sofa and onto the mustard-gold carpet. "Do you think they like Michael at that bank? Is he doing well?"

"He's fine. I'm sure they like him just fine."

"That advertising place was all wrong for him. I knew he'd be unhappy. I knew going back to school was a waste of time for him. And that Alaska business. Never! I could have told him that wouldn't work out." She tugged at her ball of yarn again. "But of course, it wouldn't have been my place to say anything."

I didn't understand why, if Michael's mother was so sure he'd be unhappy, she was so proud of herself for not saying anything. But of course, I didn't say anything.

"He's always had too many interests," Norma continued. "Too many things he's curious about." There was a silence; the only noise in the room the drone of the television and the tapping of Norma's knitting needles. "Even as a boy he was always off by himself trying this or fooling with that!'' Norma suddenly huffed. ''And then the Marines!''

''*What* the Marines? I thought Dad and you thought the service was good for Michael.''

Norma stopped knitting. ''Michael doesn't have a mean bone in his body. What do you think Vietnam did to someone like him?'' She resumed knitting, and before I could ask her what *she* thought, the Wedlan men trooped back into the living room from the back door and the kitchen.

''Hello, television viewers!'' Michael greeted us. His face was all red from the outdoor cold. He was slapping his gloved hands together. ''How's my lovely wife?''

''Okay,'' I said, without much conviction.

''Is there snow on your feet?'' his mother asked. ''Your lovely mother doesn't want snow on her carpet.''

''I was just leaving,'' Michael said.

We spent the afternoon at Wes and Dominique's house. Two years earlier Wes had married a short, chubby, sweet-faced girl he'd met behind a Revlon counter while buying perfume for his grandmother.

Clifford dropped by, and Wes, Dominique, Michael, and Clifford played bridge after I graciously and quickly volunteered to watch.

''I don't want you to be bored,'' Michael said, sounding really concerned.

''You can look through my new lingerie, if you'd like,'' Dominique offered.

''I'm fine,'' I said, making myself smile. ''I'm having a good time.'' I ate half a box of Salerno Christmas cookies.

Clifford had a new job working for the state. He was taking calls on the child-abuse hotline. During the bridge game, in between bidding and finessing, Clifford told stories that made everyone want to throw up.

Afterward, Michael and I wished Clifford, Wes, and Dominique a very Merry Christmas and left.

"Can you believe people can be so awful?" Michael said, while we were driving back to his parents' townhouse.

"They're our friends," I said.

"I mean those people with those children. How could anyone not love a child?"

I stared straight ahead out the windshield. "Maybe not everyone's good at it."

Michael drove into his parents' carport and shut off the engine. We looked at each other. There was a shyness and a tenderness to him when he spoke. "I think motherhood will bring out surprising new parts of you that will be wonderful. That's one of the reasons I want a child. So I can watch you be a mother."

"That's sweet," I said. But making babies with Michael would mean giving up sleeping with Christopher.

There's a drawback to being someone's friend and confidante before you turn into his lover. I knew things about Christopher's former love life I would have preferred not knowing. I knew about Bernadette and her garter belts; Jennie naked in the sleeping bag; Lisa and her abortion. Christopher kept telling me to watch out. He was devious, he told me. He had loved women before and let them down, and he cared much too much about me to ever want to do anything that could hurt me.

How could I not trust a man who was as open and honest as that?

We were exchanging Christmas gifts in Christopher's office with the door closed. He presented me with a handblown perfume bottle, clear crystal except for one thin strand of royal blue swirling through. On the top was a tiny frosted stopper. On the bottom was the artist's signature. I loved it. I planned to tell Michael I'd bought it for myself.

I gave Christopher a burgundy Land's End sweater. Nothing too personal. Nothing his mother would wonder about and start asking questions like: Why is that woman from the office buying you red jockey shorts?

"When you wear this you can pretend it's me hugging you."

"I'd like to be hugging *your* new sweater," Christopher said.

"Thank you." I smiled. I was wearing my new cashmere. The one Michael gave me for Christmas.

"You look great in pink." Christopher stared at me in a manner that could best be described as a warm leer. There was something about how that boy focused on me that made me feel like I was one hot tomato.

"We have a french-fry sale to concentrate on," I said.

"It's hard to concentrate on french fries when you're wearing a sweater like that," Christopher said, still leering.

There was a soft knock at the door.

"Come in!" Christopher called out, hiding his sweater box behind his chair.

"Come in!" I called out, hiding my perfume bottle in my lap between the folds of my skirt and my thighs.

Isabelle, our secretary, slowly opened the door, holding up and waving a tight little fistful of memos and office mail.

"Exchanging gifts?" she asked. Sometimes I wondered what people at the office assumed about Christopher and me. Then I'd tell myself: *Don't be ridiculous.*

Everything about Isabelle was round. She had round arms, round legs, round eyes, and curly hair. She walked into the room and dropped Christopher's mail on his drawing board. "New sweater?" she asked, peeking over Christopher's shoulder. "About time you owned something that wasn't beige or gray." Isabelle turned her back on Christopher and said to me, "Did this gorgeous lout tell you my good news? I'm pregnant! After all this time, one of those buggers finally took."

"I kept volunteering to help!" Christopher said, honoring Isabelle with one of his award-winning smiles.

"That's great news," I told her. "I'm happy for you. I really am."

Everybody on our floor at Watts, Watts, Ross and Malinick knew about Isabelle and her fertility problems, mainly because Isabelle was always sitting out at her desk, right in the middle of everything, surrounded by all our open doors—except for Christopher's or mine now and then—making appointments with her gynecologist, calling her pharmacist, or chatting on the phone with her girlfriends about some new pills she was taking, or some magazine article about low sperm count she was reading, or how if she gets her period again this month she's going to kill herself.

So it was really good news to hear Isabelle was pregnant.

"I was about ready to give up," Isabelle said, rolling her round eyes above her round cheeks. "I'm almost thirty-two years old." (We all knew that.) "I was all set to try and adopt." (We all knew that.) "But Teddy said it just wouldn't be the same if it wasn't really ours." (We'd heard that, too.) "Thank goodness for whatever it was that did the trick."

The next morning I gave Isabelle my copies of *Having Babies Over Thirty* and *Your Baby's First Twelve Months*.

❦ *Chapter 21* ❦

He claimed it was the assignment for the B & V flyer on men's socks that did it. He simply announced one morning that the only thing worse than spending his life not knowing what to do, was spending his life knowing he had to design flyers for men's socks. Then Christopher quit his job. He immediately mailed out business cards letting the advertising world in on the good news that his artistic talents were now available for cartoons and illustrations. And he casually mentioned that he planned to prolong living at home until he established himself as an illustrator, so he wouldn't have to worry about money.

Andy Hodgeman was quick to assure me that the agency would find a new art director for me, someone I'd really like working with, and if I had any suggestions to please be sure and let him know.

I told him I'd prefer working with a woman.

Christopher called at work a few times to inquire if he was as irreplaceable as he hoped. He asked how the men's-socks flyer was going, who got stuck doing it, and by any chance did it call for an illustrator? I called Christopher a couple of times, but both times his mother answered the phone and I felt self-conscious and hung up. Something was terribly wrong with me. I was back in my normal pre-affair married life; I'd get a new art director, maybe even Holly; Christopher said we'd still be friends; and there I was feeling miserable all the time.

I tried talking to Michael while he was washing up for bed one night. Under the circumstances, I was probably asking a lot, but I figured since he didn't know I was asking a lot, it was okay. I sat on the edge of the bathtub wearing a white terrycloth bathrobe embroidered with PLAZA HOTEL. Michael was stationed in front of the mirror over the sink, wearing his new Christmas robe. He turned on the faucet, wetted his face, then briskly rubbed his hands together around a bar of Dial soap.

"I feel bad," I said to him. "I just do. We worked well together and he quit and now I feel bad. Can't you feel bad for me?" Michael never wanted to deal with me when I was in a bad mood. He'd dismiss it; he'd wait for me to snap out of it.

"So he quit! I'd like to quit my job, too." He spread suds over his cheeks and chin and forehead.

"Is something wrong at work?"

"No."

"Do you want to talk about it?" I rested my elbows on my knees and my chin in my hands.

"No," Michael repeated. "There's nothing to talk about." He bent over and splashed his face with the running water. "You'll survive. You thought the world would end when you changed jobs and stopped working with Holly, and you ended up fine. You'll find someone new and you won't care about Christopher anymore." He sounded so calculating.

"Is that what you would do if I got hit by a bus tomorrow?" I sat up straighter. "Run right off and find someone new and not care anymore?"

"Of course not." Michael grabbed a towel off the rod beside the sink. "I would throw myself on the ground and rend my garments. *Then* I'd find someone new." He was joking, but I didn't feel like giving him the satisfaction of my laughter. "I'm kidding," he said, apparently thinking he'd hurt my feelings. He patted his face with the towel.

"Thanks," I said, sincerely. I felt even worse. "I'm sure you're right and things will be fine, but right now I feel bad about it. Don't you want me to tell you everything I'm feeling?"

"Not if you're feeling bad!" I could tell Michael was teasing again, genuinely trying to entertain me and make me smile.

"If we're going to be married, you should feel bad about the things I feel bad about," I persisted.

"What do you mean *if*?" Michael stared at me now. His face was red from all his scrubbing and splashing and patting.

"I didn't mean *if*. I meant *since*. If I'm upset, you should at least be a little upset for me, since we're married."

"You'll snap out of it." He carefully refolded and rehung the towel.

"I'm going to get some ice cream," I said, standing up, wanting to change the subject. "Do you want some butter pecan?"

"What do you need that for?" Michael asked. "You'll make yourself fat."

I frowned at his reflection as I headed toward the kitchen.

I couldn't make things right. I couldn't make myself love him the way I wanted to love him. Or used to love him. I couldn't go on pretending everything was okay and nothing had gone wrong. Things didn't feel bad. They just never felt good. And I didn't want to keep on feeling *not good*.

I began to believe the problem was The Lie. The pretense that everything was business as usual, when I'd just spent the past year in love with somebody else. Maybe if I could stop pretending there'd never been a problem, we would stop having a problem. Maybe our fresh start needed an honest foundation.

At least once a month Ann Landers was convincing some reader that to spill the beans about an affair is selfish. Piper told me that hiding an affair bred dishonesty. Ann maintained that to confess was just a way to unload your guilt and dump it onto your spouse. Piper said it was important to trust the marriage, and each other's commitment to working through the rough times. I knew about the rough times. I worried about my commitment.

I felt both ladies had valid points. But since I hadn't roomed in college with Ann Landers, I decided to listen to Piper and tell Michael the truth. He'd consider the mix-up with Christopher a stupid, unforgivable weakness on my part. And how could Michael understand a stupid, unforgivable weakness when he detested weakness? Oh God. I didn't want to hurt Michael. I was scared of hurting him. But I was more scared of continuing to live like his personal actress, instead of his wife.

There was no good way to do it.

I debated if it would be easier if Michael was in a good mood, in which case he might be more understanding, or if I should tell him when he was in a bad mood anyway, so I wouldn't ruin one of his good moods.

He was sitting on the edge of the bed clipping his toenails. He was in a good mood. And I just willed the words out.

"Honey, there's something I need to talk about." I was standing in the doorway wearing my blue shirtsleeve dress with the black patent belt. I'd even thought about what I should wear. I wanted to look nice, so that maybe Michael wouldn't get as angry at me.

"I think I dropped one of these clippings in the carpet, but

I couldn't find it. We'll have to vacuum extra hard here," he said.

"Yeah. Okay." I nodded in agreement, not really hearing what he'd just said. He was concentrating on his right foot, staring at it. "Michael?"

"Yeah."

"Michael?"

"What!" Now he was looking at me.

"Uh, you know when I said I loved Christopher like a friend?" Michael refocused his attention on his feet. I kept talking. "Well, I kind of loved him more than that."

There was a silence, and then Michael turned his head to me slowly, and after taking a long breath, filled with fear and resignation, he asked, "What do you mean by that?"

"Well, I, uh, cared about him a whole lot." I was backing off. Maybe I didn't want to say any more.

"You were good friends," Michael said. "It's normal to love a good friend, right? You said you were good friends."

I stood in the doorway clasping and unclasping my hands. "Well, it was sort of more than good friends."

Michael stared at me. "I don't get it. What are we talking about?" He didn't want to get it. His face tightening, his eyes narrowing, his face sinking into a horrible comprehension. His voice was very small and quiet when he finally asked: "Was it sexual?"

I could tell he was waiting for me to say, No, of course not. And for the slightest moment I thought, *Okay, fine, tell him no, reassure him, then go about your business, continue with your marriage.* Instead, I answered. "Yes. It was sexual."

Michael directed his next two words at me without actually looking at me. "How long?"

"Not that often. We weren't together all that often. But

for a year now, it started almost over a year. It just happened. It wasn't *supposed* to happen. I didn't mean—''

His voice overrode mine, shivering with outraged horror and stark pain, a panic-stricken expression on his face as he cried. ''Why? Why? How could you *hate* me so much? He's such a weak man!''

''Yes? Well, you perpetually strong men get a little boring!'' I retorted. Michael flung himself off the bed, flung himself toward me. I thought he was going to hit me, and I automatically put my hands up to protect my face, at the same time feeling that I deserved for him to hit me, to hurt me. But he turned from me, looking at me with such hate and confusion, and slammed his arm into the closet door, beating his arm against the closet door, screaming. ''How could you! Why would you? I hate you!''

I didn't know if I should run or what. I was scared. He was so crazed and scary. But he was hurting so much. I didn't want to leave him when he was shaking and screaming and maybe going to hurt himself.

Then he sat down on the bed again and just stared at the floor, his arms hanging at his sides. Then he started crying. There he was, sitting on the corner of the bed in his boxer shorts and his thirty-two hairs on his naked chest, with his face in his hands, crying. I didn't know what to say, so I went and sat quietly in the den, my hands folded in my lap, listening to my husband sobbing in the next room. They seemed to go on forever, those muffled, heaving tears, and finally I crept to the bedroom and stood in the doorway and asked, ''Is there anything I can do?''

''Get out of here!'' Michael erupted. ''Get your fucking face out of here!''

He lunged at the dresser and threw my perfume bottle— the one Christopher had given me but which I'd said I'd bought for myself—threw it across the room at the closet doors. I grabbed my purse and ran out of the apartment, using the stairs instead of the elevator, terror rushing through me as I pounded down all those stairs. Of all things, how had he known to grab that perfume bottle?

❦ *Chapter 22* ❦

Piper made me drink tea. I didn't want any, but she made me drink it.

I was huddled in a corner of her sofa, not sure what I was doing or why I was there. I spilled some tea on my blue dress but I didn't care. I didn't even bother to wipe at it with a napkin.

"Do you want to talk about it?" Piper asked.

"Not really."

"Okay, then don't."

As soon as she said I didn't have to talk, I felt like talking, and everything came out in one big tumbling rush. "He looked so awful. Really awful. I felt terrible. Just terrible. It shouldn't be so hard to love him, or I wouldn't feel so bad, right? I don't know why I don't love him. Things can't have changed so much. Something's wrong with me. Something must be wrong with me."

"Quit feeling like the bad guy," Piper said, sprawled out on the carpet below me. "Maybe you're just more honest than he is. Maybe there's nothing left between you, and you're more willing to face up to that. It happens all the time.

People get out of sync, and one person's ready to face facts before the other is, but someone has to start the ball rolling.''

"I started my ball rolling with another man."

"Well, you're not the first woman in history to do that."

The phone rang late, really late. It had to be after 1:00 A.M. It was Susan. Piper handed me the phone.

"I thought you'd go there," Susan said. "Michael came here."

"Is he okay?" I asked.

"Yeah. Are you okay?"

"I'm okay," I said.

"Okay," Susan said, "talk to you later."

I tried to sleep but I couldn't. I was exhausted, I ached, and I hurt. My heart felt as lumpy as Piper's sofa, so in the morning when the sun was barely up, I went home. I figured I could sneak in and get some clothes while Michael was still at Susan and Barry's. And maybe write him a note. A can-you-ever-forgive-me note.

I slipped my key in the front door and opened the door quietly, even though I fully expected to find the place empty. I walked back to the bedroom just to check, to make sure the coast was clear. Michael was sitting up in bed, in his shorts and a T-shirt and socks, crying. Soft, muffled crying. He looked up at me like he didn't quite know me and said, "Get out of here," his voice barely audible, weak, and pleading.

I went into the living room, unbuttoned my dress and slipped out of it, and I left it in a crumpled pile on the floor. Then I lay down on the sofa, in my underwear, and tried to sleep, trying not to listen to the sad sounds from the bedroom. I must have dozed off. It couldn't have been for very long, though, because it was still quite early when I was half-aware of Michael banging around in the bedroom. Closet doors. Drawers. I heard the faucet running in the bathroom, the toilet flushing. He passed through the living room, looked at me, then headed toward the front door without saying a word, looking handsome in one of his blue pinstripe banker's suits.

Michael, always-in-control Michael, slammed the front door on his way out to work.

I tried to sleep some more, staying on the couch, afraid to go sleep on the bed in case Michael suddenly returned and threw me out. Somehow I thought my being in the bedroom might make him even angrier than he already was. Sometime before ten o'clock I got up, called the office, and told Isabelle I wouldn't be coming in and not to let anyone call me at home with questions about hamburger storyboards or missing B & V radio scripts. Then I went to the bedroom to pick out something clean to wear, and that's when I saw what Michael had done to my clothes. That's when I saw the torn sleeves and the ripped pockets and the split seams and the broken plastic hangers. Everything I thought Michael had wanted to do to my face last night, he did to my clothes.

I found an okay blouse and an okay pair of pants and got dressed. Then I sat in the den and sort of watched the end of Phil Donahue without really paying attention. I had this vague sense that I was waiting for something to happen.

The phone rang.

I said hello. And after a slight hesitation I heard Barry's voice on the other end.

"Oh! . . . Franny," he said. "I thought Michael might be there. He said he wasn't going to work, that he'd be too tired." Barry hesitated again before saying, "What are you doing there?"

"I live here."

"I know. It's just—I know. I'll call Michael at the office."

"Barry?"

"Yeah?"

"We can still talk, you know, you and I."

There was a slight pause again before Barry said, "Yeah. Sure. Let's talk."

"That's okay," I said. "I don't feel like talking."

We both hung up.

After a while—I have no idea how long a while—the phone rang again. This time it was Christopher.

"Oh, good," he said, "it's you. I was going to hang up if it was Michael. Can you talk?"

"How'd you know to call me here?" I asked. Christopher shouldn't have known I wasn't at work, because he wasn't at work anymore.

"You never told me you were going to tell him," Christopher was saying. "It must have been an awful night. He sounded awful. I feel awful. Are you okay? I'm worried about you. Are you going to be all right?"

I was confused. Pieces weren't fitting. "How do you know any of this?" I gripped the phone cord between my fingers.

"I got a call from your husband last night," Christopher said. "A terrible phone call."

"*What* call?" I felt panicky.

"He was right. Everything he said to me was right. He said it was all my fault, and he was right."

"What? What did he say?"

"That you were sweet and naïve and too trusting and you felt sorry for me and I should never have taken advantage of you, that you would never have done such a thing if I hadn't taken advantage of you. He was right. I should never have let it happen. I should never have let things get out of control."

"I can't believe he called you."

"I deserved it," Christopher said. "Afterward, I felt so bad that I sat up and talked to Mom about everything."

"You told your mother?"

"She knew something was wrong, I was so upset. I had to talk to someone."

"What did she say?"

"She felt bad for me about the phone call. And she said, I must really love that girl."

"Oh."

"What can I do? Can I do something? Do you want to meet and talk? Do you want to never talk to me again? I'll do whatever you want."

Christopher sounded so distressed. I wanted to make him feel better. I could tell he needed to talk. "We can meet and talk," I said. "I guess that would be okay."

"I'd better not," he said. "I'll be here if you need me, of course, but I think I'd better stay away."

"I miss you when you're away."

"Work things out with Michael. He loves you. And I never want to feel like I felt last night during that phone call."

"I don't know what's going to happen."

"Things will be good," Christopher said gently. "You deserve good. And you know I love you."

After we hung up I felt tired; exhausted from sadness. But then I started thinking about Michael having called Christopher last night. Michael had practically exonerated me by telling Christopher it was all his fault and that I'd just gone along with it.

I felt oddly insulted that Michael thought I had no mind of my own.

The phone rang again. This time it was Michael.

"The phone's been busy. Who've you been talking to?" His voice was low, level, very controlled. And sad. Very sad.

"Barry called," I said.

"I know," Michael said. "That was earlier. He called me here."

"And I called the office."

"Figures."

"How are you?" I asked.

"I thought I'd come home at lunch," he said. "Will you be there? I thought we should talk."

"Fine," I said. "I'll be here."

"Okay," Michael said.

"Okay," I said.

And we hung up.

I walked around the apartment, not knowing what to do. Michael hadn't wound the wall clock, and it had stopped. But I didn't want to touch it. If I overwound it, he'd have one more thing to be mad at me for. I took a shower. Then I put on a fresh pair of panties—Michael hadn't done anything to my underwear—and I put on the blouse and pants again and waited for him. I sat in the living room, scared and anxious, waiting for Michael to come home and talk.

He looked lovely coming in that front door. My Michael in a business suit. He looked tired. And hesitant. But he still looked handsome.

"Hi," I said, cautiously.

"Hi."

We sounded like schoolkids at a dance.

We sat at opposite ends of the couch, facing each other, not knowing where to start.

"Are you okay?" I finally asked.

"Swell." He looked mean when he said it. I wasn't used to Michael looking mean, but then his face softened a little bit, and he started talking. "I've been thinking all morning about everything. And I don't want us to just give up. I want to try and work things out. We can go to a counselor. We can take a vacation. Whatever it takes. We should at least try." Then he said, his eyes wide and earnest, "I don't want to not be married to you. I love you."

That was the last thing I expected him to say. I'd been so

awful to him and he was telling me he still loved me. That made me feel even more awful. He was just too good.

I scooted down the couch a little closer to Michael, checking his expression to make sure that he didn't mind. I don't know who took the other's hand first, but we ended up holding hands. We weren't sitting up against each other, but we were close enough to hold hands.

"I'm just so sorry about hurting you," I said. "I don't understand how all this happened."

"Well," Michael said, drawing out the word like he was trying to decide if he really wanted to say what he was about to say, "maybe I understand a little. About how these things happen and all. Because, uh, once, this kind of thing, uh, once happened to me." He paused, and stopped looking at me. "About two years ago, a while ago, there was someone at work." He was staring at the wall across the room. "Someone I got involved with."

I dropped his hand and backed away from him. "What!"

"LeeAnn. It was LeeAnn." I just sat and listened. I was frozen into place, so I had no choice but to listen. "You were traveling all the time. And I was lonely. I was always lonely."

"You never *told* me you were lonely. You always sounded fine when I called."

"I hated when you were gone. And you were gone so often. But LeeAnn was there. She would talk to me. And things were so screwy in her life. She needed to talk to me. And one night—it was the night you were so mad at me for coming home late when you were waiting—one night we were on the roof of her apartment, there's a deck up there, and we were alone and talking, and it just happened. We didn't plan it. We didn't mean it. And it only happened a couple of times after that. We both felt too guilty. And she knew I didn't want to mess up my marriage."

I waited to see if Michael was done talking. He was done

talking. And I could hear my self yelling. "You let me feel so terrible and guilty and awful last night, when you had gone and done the same thing!"

"It was different. Mine was different!" Now Michael was angry. Now his voice was loud. He was glaring at me, his eyes cold and narrowed. "And it didn't go on for so long! It didn't go on an *entire* year." That became his point of indignation. That *his* affair was so short, while mine had lasted a year.

"Why didn't you tell me?" I screamed. "You acted so perfect! Like you never did anything wrong! I've felt so unworthy of you, *dirty* at times, because I muddled my way into something I knew you would never have done; no, Michael's too good, too fine and honorable a person to be capable of lies and deceit. But you weren't any better than me! You're just more self-righteous! Piper nailed it. She told me we all believe the things we need to believe—and if reality interferes, we stick our heads in the sand and ignore it. Maybe if you'd told me about LeeAnn, maybe if you had managed to tell me I mattered to you, there would have never been a Christopher; we would have worked out our problems sooner, before they got to this point. You should have told me! I asked you, I confronted you on it, and you *lied*."

"Very creative the way you're turning this guy around, making him sound like *my* fault," Michael snapped. "I didn't want to hurt you, Franny. I saw no reason to tell you. I simply ended it."

"Swell," I said. "And you decided you were lonely for me, and saw no reason to tell me *that*, either. Touching, isn't it, the way we've both gone out of our ways to avoid hurting each other! You don't need *me*, Michael. You've never needed me. Half the time I don't even think you *like* me. You're always mad at me or disappointed in me. You're in love with some sweet, young person or image who has nothing to do with me. And when the real me shows up, you don't know what to do with her. You want to fix her to be more like that image of that perfect person you're so crazy about. You don't even think I'm capable of getting mixed up in an affair on my own. That the only way it could happen is if someone else lured your perfect darling into it.''

"What are you talking about?'' Michael said.

"I talked to Christopher. He called. He said you called him last night and said the whole thing was *his* fault.''

"I did call him. To tell him he's an asshole.''

"No more than LeeAnn is.''

"Plenty more! LeeAnn and I hardly counted. It hardly lasted! I get lonely. You travel. You don't want to do anything with my friends. You never want to do anything with me, either, or try anything new. You think you're the great understanding wife because you *allow* me to go on fishing trips with my buddies. Well, I want to go on fishing trips with my wife, but my wife's never interested, my wife never wants to go with me! I want a wife. I want *you* to be my wife. I want things to be good again.''

We sat without saying anything. We were each shaken, each confused. And I was so tired. I felt like I'd been mangled inside, and I didn't know how to make things stop hurting. Nothing was the way things were supposed to be. Michael and I were never meant to be so unhappy.

"I ought to get back to work,'' he said. "We can talk tonight. Okay?''

"I'll be here.''

"Good,'' Michael said, finally smiling; a wistful smile. "I want you here.'' I nodded and smiled back at him.

After he left I cleaned out my closet. I threw out the broken hangers, sorted out what could be mended, and threw out the things that were too torn up to mend. Then I watched soap operas I knew nothing about.

I realized that there was a part of me that had told Michael about Christopher because I didn't want to try anymore. But another part of me cared too much about Michael to just walk away. I didn't know how to let go of him. Michael said let's try, so how could I not try? We were only six weeks away from our tenth anniversary.

❦ *Chapter 23* ❦

In June I got lucky.

I was lying on the bedspread in my New York hotel room watching an old *I Love Lucy*, when the maid knocked to turn down the bed, and—this is the exciting part—she gave me an entire *handful* of chocolates instead of the standard-issue one or two that go on the pillow. So instead of ordering dinner from room service and facing one of those greasy solicitous men who deliver the trays, I dined on free candy. I suppose I was depressed. But I couldn't think why I should be depressed, so I decided I must be wrong. I wasn't depressed. If I were really depressed, I'd have stopped at the Häägen-Dazs counter in Grand Central Station and treated myself to a tub of rum raisin and a plastic spoon. Instead, I was perfectly content with my foil-wrapped chocolates and a glass of water out of the bathroom.

Despite the fact I really wanted to talk to him, I wouldn't let myself phone Michael. I was practicing how it would feel to live without him; without Christopher; without a *someone*. I had never lived alone. But now the possibility seemed increasingly real. Christopher had all but dematerialized. And Michael still acted like nothing had ever gone wrong. We were following the happy-husband-and-wife script. And it was difficult for me to remember my lines.

Daisy and Dwayne from Sears had been married almost as long as Michael and me, and they never seemed to have problems. And now that Nadine—crazy, ruthless, ambitious Nadine—was married and pregnant, she'd told Louie she wanted to quit her lawyer job and stay home and raise babies and be a regular wife. Even Louie and Nadine seemed happier than Michael and me, and I'd have given *that* marriage one year tops.

In the morning, Saturday, I called Michael.

"Where are you? Where were you?" he demanded. He sounded awful. "You never told me what hotel you were staying in. I kept thinking you were with someone. All night long I kept thinking like that. *Were* you?"

"No, honey. I was at the hotel. The Harley. Alone. I just watched TV all night." The truth was so lame.

Michael's voice grew tighter and tighter. "You didn't call. You always call. You never not call. You were with someone, weren't you? You were!"

"*Nooo*. I wasn't with anyone. I was watching TV. I should have called." I didn't know what to say or how to make him feel okay again. "I was going to shop for a couple of hours before I caught a plane home, but I'll go to the airport and come right now, okay? Everything's okay. I was just watching TV."

"That's okay," Michael said, sounding immediately calmer, like he'd just snapped back into his characteristic self. "I believe you. Do your shopping. I'm okay."

"No, really, I'll be glad to come home early."

"I'm okay!" Michael insisted, defensive now. "You don't have to rush!"

I bought a black cotton blazer on sale and two pairs of sandals, and a photo book on Alaska for Michael. I wasn't sure if I'd give it to him right away or save it for our anniversary. It would depend on his mood that night, on whether he still believed that I'd just stayed in my hotel room watching TV, or if he started up again with a bunch of accusations.

When I got back to Chicago, Michael was fine, like nothing had gone wrong.

"I don't need a new ring. It's a waste of money."

We were discussing our tenth anniversary, our voices loud because we were competing with *Hill Street Blues* on the television set.

"That's what you always wanted! You've been bellyaching about a bigger diamond for years. And that's what I want to get you."

"It's not necessary. We need new carpeting. Besides, it'll help our resale value."

"But we aren't selling the place," Michael protested. "Who cares about new carpeting? That's no anniversary gift."

"I don't need a new ring. This one's fine." Half the time I didn't even bother to wear it anymore. I'd take it off to wash my face and forget and leave it on the bathroom counter all day. Michael once commented on my forgetfulness, but he never said anything again. Maybe he thought I'd stopped wearing my ring because the diamond wasn't big enough.

"Would you rather have one of those diamond bands?" he asked. "One of those anniversary rings? Dwayne says Daisy wants one of those anniversary rings. Would you rather have one like that?"

"I don't need anything. Honest. Thank you." It wouldn't have felt right to let Michael buy me a new ring.

His face brightened. "A car? Would you like a new car? I'll buy you your own car."

"What? What are you talking about!" I said, shaking my head in the palms of my hands. "We don't need a new car. Let's just go to dinner and a movie. We can celebrate at dinner."

Michael made a reservation at the Whitehall.

"We can eat there, and then we can stay the night. I asked for a good room. I told them it's a special occasion."

"Doesn't it seem silly to stay in a hotel when we live right here? We could eat there and come home to sleep."

"Well, that's no fun. Why are you so afraid to try something different?"

"I don't know. It just seems silly to pack when we aren't really going anywhere."

Over dinner Michael said something about maybe interviewing for a new job at the bank, how he was bored with his marketing job there. But that was all he said about it. I told him about Holly Booker and Andy Hodgeman getting into a huge standoff at work and Holly slinking into Andy's office, head bowed, shoulders down, and apologizing. After a great deal of P.R.ing for her on my part, Holly had replaced Christopher as my art director at Watts, Watts, Ross and Malinick. She was constantly disagreeing with Andy and calling him a creative moron behind his back, but that was because she had a crush on him. I vowed not to get involved, having had my fill of office romance.

The Whitehall specialized in that trendy nouvelle cuisine, small portions of strange combinations that cost enormous prices because everything's arranged so nicely on the plate. I'd have been just as happy with a cheeseburger and fries.

Before we'd left for our celebration dinner, I gave Michael his Alaska book. He gave me a dozen long-stemmed roses. "One for each year, and two for good luck!" he'd said.

We chatted. Michael asked me how I liked my salmon. I asked him how he liked his duck. It felt more like our first date than our tenth anniversary. After our meal, we went up to our hotel room and Michael turned on the TV while I examined all the free gifts in the bathroom. Scented soap. Two toothbrushes. A Yardley perfume sampler.

"I like this place," I said. "This was a good idea."

We didn't like the guests on Johnny Carson that night— some animal trainer and a Las Vegas singer—so Michael shut off the TV, closed the curtains, and turned off the lights. We had both forgotten to bring anything to read. The mattress felt too hard. I reached out to feel for Michael, to make sure he was still there, and he started rolling over me.

"It's so dark, I can hardly see you," I said.

"Is it hard to tell your boyfriends apart when you can't see?" Michael asked. I froze beneath him. "I'm the taller one."

"Get off of me!" I cried, pushing against his weight.

"It was just a joke," Michael said, rolling over, but still next to me.

"Real funny." I turned my back to him and hunched over on my side of the bed as far as I could get.

Sometime early in the morning, when the room was just starting to get light, I reached over to Michael and we made love.

"Happy anniversary," he said.

"You, too," I said.

At least we'd made it to ten years.

The following weekend we were supposed to drive to Springfield. Michael had driven down there a couple of times when I was away on business, but I hadn't been there since Christmas. I dreaded seeing the way his parents sat around without talking. It was too much like the way Michael and I sat around without talking.

It was hot. July cornfield hot. And everything looked overcooked. The steaming black tar on I-55. The corn turning brown and parched in the fields. The sickly yellow-gray gunk hanging in the sky. "This has to be the least scenic drive in America," I said, slouched down in the seat with my feet up on the dashboard. "How do people live like this?" We passed a white and grayed decaying farm house.

"They're farmers," Michael said. "They can't imagine how you live the way you live."

I stared out the window. Michael stared at the road. I turned on the radio. There was one station with someone talking about soy beans, and another station with someone talking about God.

"There's nothing on. They don't have any decent radio stations here." I snapped off the dial.

"The signals aren't strong enough," Michael said. "Quit complaining. It'll be better when we get closer to Bloomington."

I stared out the window. Michael stared at the road. I asked if I could drive. Maybe it would be more interesting if I were driving. Michael pulled over to the side of the road, opened his door, and walked around the car while I slid over to the driver's side. Then Michael stared out the window. I stared at the road.

Finally, off in the horizon to our right, was a tiny dome, the state capital. There were five exits off the highway into Springfield. I could never remember which one we took and what to do once we took it. Michael directed me. I felt my stomach getting crazier and crazier, tighter and more nervous, the closer we got to his parents' townhouse. I didn't want to be their good daughter-in-law. I couldn't be their good daughter-in-law. I drove to the front of the townhouse and Michael was telling me to pull around to the carport in back, but I just continued driving straight down the block and didn't stop. I just kept driving.

"I can't," I said. "I can't go in there with your parents. It's too hard."

"What do you want me to do?" Michael said angrily. "They're expecting us. Why can't you go in there?"

From all of my driving and weaving around the streets in his parents' neighborhood, I ended up at Washington Park, a few blocks from where Michael's parents lived. I stopped the car. A fat man in a purple sweatsuit jogged past. A couple of kids were laughing over the creaking sounds of a swingset. It was a major-size park, but most of it was empty. Michael threw open the car door and stomped across the dry grass, and stood in front of a clump of bushes with his hands clamped on his hips, his back to me, looking down at the ground and then around with his head, not really looking at anything. I sat in the car and watched him until I finally got out and, standing about ten feet behind him, unable to see his face, said, "I don't know what I want to do. I just don't want to spend the weekend here."

Michael's shoulders caved in, like a terrible resignation was crushing his entire body. Then he abruptly turned around and walked back to the car, saying to me in a crisp, even voice, "Come on and drive me home. Take me to my parents' house and you can go home. I'll take the train back to Chicago."

We drove back in silence and stopped in front of his parents' townhouse. Michael reached into the backseat for his overnight bag. I saw the front door opening and his mother standing in the front door. I wondered what she'd say when I didn't go in. Michael got out of the car without saying anything. "I'm sorry," I told him. "I shouldn't have come in the first place." He slammed the door and strode toward his mother, his head slightly down. I drove off quickly, before she could wave me into the house or start asking questions. I drove home crying. It had taken us almost four hours to drive there, and it took me longer to drive back. I was tired and miserable and I couldn't stop crying. It would have been fine to be with Michael that weekend. I just couldn't be with his parents. I couldn't pretend things were that okay.

When he got home Sunday night he said he'd had a good time. He'd played bridge with his parents and Clifford and his mother had made a ham. He asked how my weekend was. I said it was fine, that I hadn't done anything or gone anywhere. He acted like nothing had gone wrong.

Three days later I woke up to find Michael clinging to me, his arms thrown around me. My first reaction was that my hair must be tickling him, I should move my head so my hair didn't bother him. When he realized I was awake, he pulled me even tighter. "Don't leave me by myself," he said. "I don't want to be by myself. I'd hate it that way. Please don't do it that way. Help me." He was like a little boy, pleading and scared and so needy. And it horrified me. I felt embarrassed for him, uncomfortable seeing him act like such a little boy. I started to hyperventilate in his arms.

"I can't breathe," I said, pulling myself loose from his hold. "I need to get up and walk around."

I dressed for work in the den, with the TV turned on, while watching Jane Pauley. Soon Michael appeared in the doorway, dressed in a suit, holding his briefcase, ready for work.

"Are you okay?" I asked.

"I'll see you tonight," he said.

It was another month before the conversation on the couch. The let's-get-it-over-with conversation. It was in August, on a rare Chicago August day when the weather was almost tolerable. Holly and I had sold two commercials for men's wallets and galoshes to our B & V client. I was in an oddly peaceful mood, a tranquil and accepting mood. I got home from work and waited for Michael. I knew what to say to Michael.

I asked him to stretch out on the couch with me. He kicked off his wingtips. I kicked off my heels. We were lying on the couch together, him in his banker's suit, me in my going-to-client dress. He was holding me. I had my head on his shoulder, but I wasn't looking at his face. I didn't want to be watching his face.

"We screwed up this marriage," I began. "This marriage is stupid. We should end it. Then, later, if we decide we still want to be together, and I think we will, don't you think we will? I think we probably will. Then, later, we can start new, get married again, a new marriage."

Michael didn't respond right away, but he responded sooner than I'd expected. "Okay," he said. "Okay." We were still holding each other on the couch.

"We'll need a lawyer," I said. "Not Marty or Nadine. Someone we don't know."

"Okay," Michael said.

"We'll find a lawyer and just have him do it," I said, my words rushing forward now, "so then we can start together all new and okay again."

"That's a good plan," Michael said.

I'd said it. We'd said it. We were going to get a divorce. Strictly in the interests of a clean slate.

We couldn't have agreed to it any other way.

I felt like someone had lifted a huge stone off my chest.

❧ *Chapter 24* ❧

It was Michael who moved out. I got to keep the condo.

He, of course, got to keep the stereo.

Men always keep the stereo.

We figured out how much profit we'd make on the condo if we'd sold it that day, divided it by two, threw in a couple of thousand more for furniture, and that's how much I owed Michael.

I, of course, got to keep the furniture.

Women always keep the furniture.

I spent at least half a day and maybe even part of an evening feeling guilty that Michael was moving out without any furniture to live with, but then I told myself I had paid for all the new furniture, against his wishes and with his protests, so it really seemed only fair that I should keep everything.

He rented a one-bedroom apartment in the city in one of those old high-rise buildings along the northern part of Lake Shore Drive, where the average age of the residents is about seventy-five. His apartment had yellow walls and brown carpeting and a cracked mirror on the medicine chest in the bathroom, but the building manager told Michael they'd paint the walls white and tape the mirror until they could order a new one, which never seemed to happen.

I had helped Michael find his apartment. We spent a pleasant afternoon together circling newspaper ads and making phone calls and ringing janitors' doorbells. We had a nicer time apartment hunting together than we'd ever had condo hunting together, back when Michael was so distracted looking for camping tents for his trip to Alaska. Once Michael and I decided we didn't have to be married anymore, we started to get along great. We were much nicer to each other now that we had the option of not being nice to each other.

He rented furniture from some place he found in the Yellow Pages.

He showed up on a Saturday night to pack the last of his books and clothes and records and various sports paraphernalia. We owned two sets of good china from when we first got married. The real good set, and the okay set. Michael was about to take the okay set when I magnanimously offered him the Limoges. I had no intention of throwing dinner parties. Michael spent over an hour carefully wrapping wads of newspaper around each delicate cup and handpainted plate. When he finally finished, writing "Fragile" all over the carton several times, for whose benefit I did not know, I told him I sincerely doubted that his future second wife would be interested in owning his first wife's good china. Michael's face fell and after that I knew he'd be giving my good china to his mother, which made me sorry I'd said he could have it.

I was packing serving pieces. We agreed to divide them up equally. I was secretly giving Michael all the chipped serving pieces.

"Can I take the silver picture frame?" he asked.

"Oh—now we're taking back presents? Should I take back your carved duck?"

"You hate my carved duck."

"That's not the point."

"Okay," Michael said. "You keep the silver frame. I'll keep my duck."

I couldn't believe how strangely normal things felt. I sealed the carton with Michael's chipped serving pieces and shoved it against the living-room wall.

Michael was standing in front of a shelf of books he was sorting through.

"You better not be taking any of my books," I said accusingly.

"Why would I want any of the junk you read?" Michael said, his voice equally accusatory. "But I'll take the pots and pans."

I frowned at him. "*All* the pots and pans? Don't you think that's a bit piggy?"

"Why? You won't touch them. Besides, you got the condo."

"I still have to eat!"

"You've been eating for the past ten years," Michael said, "and I never saw you go near those pots."

"That's not true!"

"Well, it's *close* to true," Michael said. "But I'll leave you one or two of them."

"Half of them," I insisted. "I'll divide them up."

"Okay, half," he agreed. I planned to give him the one with the scorched bottom and the one with the loose handle. "But I don't want the one with the scorched bottom," he added. I'd have to pack it when he wasn't looking.

Michael ceremoniously removed his framed poster with the big trout.

I kept the wall clock.

"It's stupid for you to keep the wall clock," he protested. "You don't know how to wind it right. You'll only ruin it."

"I paid for it. It's my wall clock." Michael glared at me. I glared back at him from across the room. Then I told him the real reason. "The wallpaper's faded behind it. If you take the wall clock, I'll have a weird shape on the wall and I don't want to buy new wallpaper."

"Keep the damn wall clock!" Michael slammed several books into his carton. "What do I care if you break it?" He began wrapping the small wooden box he'd kept on the dresser top for all his military medals and loose change. It had been a gift from his father.

I was dropping some of Michael's jazz albums into a huge old Marshall Field's gift box and broke a fingernail. But I wasn't going to give Michael the pleasure of knowing I'd hurt myself.

"This is just like *Citizen Kane*," I said, sucking on my injured finger. "That scene where they're married but they start sitting further and further apart at the table. It's supposed to show how the marriage was falling apart."

"So how's this like *Citizen Kane*?"

"Well, you're packing over on that side of the room and I'm packing over on this side of the room."

"You're right. This is exactly like *Citizen Kane*." Michael shook his head.

"How come we never had conversations like this when we were married?" I asked.

"We did have conversations like this. That's why we're divorcing." He folded the carton flaps over his books and then pounded down on them because they wouldn't close together, and finally removed two of the books from the overstuffed carton. "Can I stay over here tonight?" he asked.

"We're divorcing," I reminded him. I couldn't remember if the Richie Havens album was his or mine, so I kept it. "Which TV do you want? I paid for the new one, so I should keep the new one, right?"

"I don't want either TV," Michael said. "We watched too damn much TV. I'd rather read."

"Well, you've got to have one TV. What if there's a national disaster? What if the president's shot? What if there's nuclear war? You'll want to know."

"Call me," Michael said. "You can keep both TVs." That made me feel somehow guilty, probably because I *wanted* both TVs, so I insisted he at least take the old one that was going to break down soon anyway. He could always leave it in his closet and not look at it while he was reading books, but at least he'd have it. Michael said fine, okay, whatever. We were both trying our best not to fight. There was an unspoken rule that no one could fight. Of course, Michael and I had always had that rule.

"Yaaakk!" I screamed.

"What? What?" Michael came running over to me.

"I broke another fingernail. I swear, you have no idea what true pain is."

"Try getting kicked in the balls sometimes," Michael said, walking back to his cartons. "Try a year in Vietnam."

"I'm serious. It hurts."

"Do you want me to kiss it and make it better?" he asked in a snotty voice.

"No. I'll live." Michael studied the albums left in the record rack, and without saying a word placed the Richie Havens album in the Marshall Field's box. "Just tell me what we're supposed to do with the wedding pictures," I said.

"Beats me. I don't want them. At least not the ones you're in."

I refused to feel insulted. "Maybe my mother'll want them."

"She's already got ten sets."

"Maybe we should just leave them for now."

"I'm tired," Michael said. "Let's finish in the morning."

"You're going home now?"

"No."

There was an awkward silence, and then I said, "You don't live here anymore."

"I know," Michael said quietly. "Let's get some sleep."

In the morning I drove Michael and his belongings to his new apartment, and then I drove home. I found his housekeys lying abandoned in the middle of the bed. And a terrible realization sunk in: we weren't playing some game. We were actually ending our marriage.

❦ *Chapter 25* ❦

One month later, Holly and I were working on a newspaper ad for men's pajamas when Tracy, our temporary secretary who was there to replace Isabelle, who had recently given birth to a healthy ten-pound-two-ounce boy and had no intention of ever setting foot in an office again, strolled into Holly's office and started talking without noticing that we were in the middle of a heated discussion on stripes versus solids.

Tracy was nineteen years old and oblivious to things like good manners.

"Some messages here," Tracy said. "None too exciting if you ask me. I worked in the administration office of a hospital last month and those messages were much more exciting."

"Yeah, well, not too many people die around here," Holly said.

"Only storyboards," I said.

Our attempts at humor appeared to escape Tracy. "Some guy called for Holly but wouldn't leave his name," she said, reading off the top of her pink slips.

"Oh, good," Holly said. That was Glenn, the Red Roof Inn boyfriend. Glenn never left his name. Holly had decided that continuing her affair with a married man was more practical than starting an affair with her boss.

"There's an important Hobo milkshake meeting in the conference room on seventeen at two-thirty," Tracy continued.

Holly and I both looked at our watches. "Tracy, it's three-fifteen," I said.

"Jesus," Holly said.

"Sorry." Tracy shrugged. "I guess I should have gotten that one to you sooner, huh?"

"We better go!" I said, reaching to grab the message pile from Tracy. "Anything else?"

She kept reading. "One more. Some guy who said he's your husband called." Tracy glanced at the naked ring finger on my left hand. "He got the lawyer. The whole thing'll take about three weeks. Your half is two hundred eight-six dollars." Tracy handed me my message. "Suing someone?" she asked.

"Each other," I said, as Holly and I raced off to our milkshake meeting.

Actually, I didn't get to sue anyone. Only one of us had to do the suing and Michael insisted on being the suer. I got to be the rotten-no-good-lousy-lying-mental-cruelty-inflicter. The state of Illinois had just passed a no-fault divorce law but it wouldn't be enacted for another year, so Michael and I had a fault divorce, and I was the one at fault.

I didn't even have to go to court.

Only the good guy went to court.

The only thing I had to do was decide if I wanted to change my name back from a last name I'd had for ten years to a last name I'd had for seven years after my mother changed the last name I'd had for fifteen years when she married my new father, the one who didn't have the last name of a crook.

My mother clinched my decision.

She addressed a Rosh Hashanah card to Mrs. Franny Wedlan. I called her right away. "Mom, I'm not going to be a Mrs. anymore. Why'd you write Mrs.?"

"That's what's proper," she said. "I'm Mrs. *Paul* Baskin. If I were divorced I'd be Mrs. *Joanne* Baskin. Not that Paul would leave me in a million years."

"Why couldn't you just write Franny Wedlan? What's wrong with that?"

"Nothing's wrong with that. It's just not proper."

"Who cares about proper? It makes me feel like shit."

"Franny, you know I dislike that word. Only the lowest-class people in the army in World War II used that word." My mother had rolled bandages for the Red Cross during World II, so she considered herself somewhat of an expert on armies.

"Mom, we're talking about my name-changing problems," I said, thoroughly frustrated. "I might not keep Wedlan."

"Keep Wedlan," she said plaintively. "At least that way people will know you've been married." Heaven forbid anyone should think Joanne Monroe Steiner Baskin's daughter had hit thirty-two years old and never married. "It's not easy being a divorced woman, Franny. I've been a divorced woman. It stinks."

"I'll manage, Mom. And I'm telling you right up front: *no blind dates*! I don't want you sitting around the pool with your friends in Miami all winter trying to think up what single sons and nephews you all know in Chicago."

"But what if somebody wants to go out with you? I don't want you to be lonely," my mother said.

"You don't want me to be unmarried."

"Same difference." Then Mom proceeded to tell me my sister was pregnant again and the baby was due in eight and a half months. "I think Madelyn called us as soon as she rolled out of bed."

"That's swell," I said, somewhat less than graciously. It was just like Madelyn to go and do something perfect—like getting pregnant—when I was in the middle of humiliating my mother with my divorce.

I could hear Mom sighing into the receiver. "Okay, let him keep Wedlan. You just be sure you keep the furniture."

I called Michael and asked him to ask his lawyer to decree me back into being a Baskin. "Whatever you want," Michael told me, and hung up.

Two and a half weeks later Michael called me at work when I was in the middle of writing an important radio script for B & V control-top pantyhose. "It's over," he said. "You're on your own. The whole thing only took five minutes. I'm glad it's over."

"Oh." I didn't know what to say. It's hard to hang up on a phone conversation when you've just hung up a marriage. "Well, uh, thanks for letting me know. I guess I'll, uh, talk to you soon!"

"Don't count on it," Michael said.

Necessity required that I reseduce Christopher. Or maybe he reseduced me. I could never tell with that guy. Either way, it was quite an adjustment to go to a movie or out for a hamburger like a regular couple and not have it be something sleazy. Suddenly being together lacked a certain drama. We'd been de-soap-opera'd. One of us was no longer an adulteress.

However, the other one of us still lived with his mother and father. Even when Christopher was wiped out in a dead sleep after my seducing him or him seducing me, he would never stay past three or four o'clock in the morning. He'd start hearing his mother's voice luring him back home before she woke up in the morning and noticed he wasn't a virgin.

"Christopher, don't you think this is rather wacko behavior?" I asked him one time, lying in bed watching him pull on his pants before the sun came up. "Did all your millions of other girlfriends put up with this fun-and-run business?"

"I had my own place in Colorado," he reminded me, stuffing his shirt into his waistband.

"Well, why don't you try having your own place in Illinois? I bet even Phil Donahue can't find three other guys your age who live with their mothers."

"It's temporary," Christopher said, zipping his fly.

"*Temporary?*"

"This is all very new to me." Christopher pulled out a pocket comb.

"Sex?"

"No. You and me. As a you-and-me. I still feel bad about you and Michael. Like it was my fault."

"Don't flatter yourself."

"Well, I still feel bad," Christopher said, combing his hair without looking in the mirror.

"I'm sorry I couldn't stay married just to make you more comfortable."

He jammed his pocket comb back in his pocket and leaned over to kiss me goodbye. "You look very warm and pink and inviting lying in that bed," he said.

"Yeah," I said grumpily. "Think about that while you're driving home to your mother."

I changed jobs. Not just so I could start fresh in a place where most people didn't know from Franny Wedlan and only thought of me as Franny Baskin. Mainly I changed for more money, a better title, and new accounts. But starting out without a personal history was a fringe benefit.

My new art director was a man, but fortunately one with three children and a wife he worshipped. His name was Ned Deeb and we worked on an international cigarette account. When I was offered the job, my new boss, Dirk Wimmer, a skinny man with a goatee who looked like a saxophone player, asked if I had any moral qualms about working on cigarettes. No, I told him, I had no qualms about promoting cancer to foreigners. Besides, the job came with a title I'd lusted after for years, a title that felt pretty shallow and meaningless once I acquired it.

My first impulse was to call Michael. He'd put up with ten years of hearing me moan about how much I wanted to be a creative director; it seemed only fair he should know I'd finally gotten to be one. It never occurred to me that he might not give a damn.

He sounded polite on the phone. Told me it was one small step for mankind and all that. Then he hung up.

Pangs of marriage withdrawal snuck up over the silliest things.

I missed hearing boring basketball games playing on the den TV. I missed hearing keys jangling in the front door, knowing somebody was coming home. And sometimes I even missed having fishing poles cluttering up my closets and falling on my head.

Once a month I'd receive a letter from Norma. A loving, chatty, news-filled letter always signed *Love, Mom W.*, and always ignoring the fact that Michael and I were divorced. How's work? We hope to see you soon. Attended a family reunion at Judith and Walter's. Too bad Michael and you weren't there.

That sort of thing.

Michael's mother seemed to like me a lot more now that I was no longer married to her son.

I'd write back neutral letters. I'm fine. The reunion must have been fun. Work's okay. How are you, too?

I never heard from Michael's father and Norma never sent his warm regards or his cold regards or any kind of his regards in her letters. I knew Gordon, who considered divorce unacceptable, now considered me unacceptable.

Michael called in early June. He hated Chicago. He hated his life. He had quit his job at the bank and was moving.

"What are you going to do?" I blurted into the kitchen phone. It was six o'clock on a Friday night and I'd been glaring at a Lean Cuisine, willing it to defrost.

Michael kept talking. "There's a fondue pot and the wok and a wooden salad bowl I know you'll never use, but if you want them you can have them. I've got enough to drag along. I bought all my rental furniture so I'll have to load up a U-Haul, but I can drop these things off on my way out of town tomorrow."

"Tomorrow? You're leaving town tomorrow?" My voice was squeaky like a cartoon character's.

"Yes. I can't wait."

"But your job?"

"I gave them two weeks' notice two weeks ago."

"Nobody told me!"

"Why should anybody tell you?"

"But what about your apartment?" I kept thinking of excuses why he shouldn't move. I didn't know why I was doing that.

"I broke my lease," Michael said. "So, do you want the stuff or not? If you do I'll bring them by. Probably around noon tomorrow."

"Tomorrow. Yes. Sure." I had no interest in the wok or the fondue pot, but I wanted to see Michael.

"Fine. Tomorrow," he said. And the phone went dead before I remembered to ask where he was moving.

* * *

Saturday morning I worried about what to wear. I wanted to look nice so Michael wouldn't move away remembering me as not looking nice. It was easier to worry about my clothes than to think about Michael hating his life and moving away to oceans and mountains with a U-Haul. I chose a gray cotton sleeveless dress that was very slimming. *This is ridiculous*, I told myself. *Michael is simply an ex-husband dropping off a fondue pot. It's not like we're Humphrey Bogart and Ingrid Bergman standing in front of the airplane in* Casablanca.

Humphrey showed up half-past eleven wearing blue jeans and a tan Polo shirt and carrying a grocery-store carton with CHARMIN TOILET PAPER stamped on the outside in navy letters. "Here's your stuff," he said, placing the carton on the front-hall floor. He was wearing a different gold watch than the one I'd given him.

"Where's your watch?" I asked.

"This is my watch." He glanced at his wrist. "I lost the one you bought me. The band must have broken or something. I got this one with the insurance money. It's just as good."

I hated it. He'd probably lost the other one on purpose. "Do you want to sit down a minute?" I asked.

"I shouldn't. I've got the truck downstairs. Maybe just for a minute."

We sat on the living-room sofa, a couple of former spouses, sitting a few inches apart from each other, give or take ten miles.

Michael told me he was moving back to Urbana, starting classes on Monday, and thinking about becoming a geological engineer.

I could hear myself swallow. "You're kidding."

"It might be interesting. I like rocks." He examined the palms of his hands. "And I was happy in college."

I don't know how we started making love. One of us leaned over, one of us brushed forward, somebody touched; and suddenly my dress was being yanked over my head, my brassiere ripped off, Michael's pants pulled down, and body parts flailing everywhere. Right there on the sofa. The sex was hot and horny and angry and *outstanding*.

"What was *that* all about?" I mumbled afterward, still sprawled, lying in submission, half-dressed on the sofa.

"Something to remember me by," Michael said, zipping his fly as he stood to go. Michael sneered at me. "Now it's up to your boyfriend."

He strolled out, slamming the front door behind him.

❦ *Chapter 26* ❦

I convinced myself: *I am so relieved! It's* terrific *having him gone. Much healthier for both of us! Better I shouldn't even think about him.* So naturally there was always some eager informant offering up news about his latest doings. Susan was the worst culprit, the third link in the Michael-to-Barry-to-Susan-to-Franny hotline. Not that I ever told her to shut up.

We were having pedicures in adjoining pink vinyl chairs at Elizabeth Arden; Susan in Helga's station, me in Rosa's. Helga was clucking over Susan's calluses. Two other lady customers were in the pedicure room. They were discussing endometriosis.

"He writes all the time," Susan said, pushing back a strand

of her long dark hair. "Barry can't keep up with him. Usually he just calls Michael. But Michael must write at least three or four letters to every one of Barry's phone calls." Susan puckered her forehead. "He sounds lonely."

"Oh my." It was more painful for me to think of Michael being lonely than to think of me being lonely. He had abandoned his engineering plans, driven out west, and rented an apartment in Portland, Oregon. He was unemployed, living on his savings, and trying to get someone to give him a chance—as an apprentice woodworker.

Susan shrugged and sunk a callused foot into Helga's soaking tub. "He didn't have to run away, Franny. He had friends here."

I was squeezing tomatoes in the produce section of the Shop & Save, trying to remember just what it was I was squeezing for, when I was buttonholed by Dodi, who used to be Michael's secretary at the bank. Michael wrote her weekly, she said, and gosh, didn't Portland sound beautiful? She'd have to write him when she got caught up on her night courses.

Louie informed me that Michael had written him several times from Portland. Michael hadn't made friends yet, and he hadn't found a job yet, but he'd bought two canaries. Louie intended to write Michael one of these days; he'd just been so busy.

Madelyn and Marty received a notecard requesting photographs of their babies.

Aunt Marlene called to see if I wanted to order any lox boxes from her Hadassah group and relayed that Michael had written her twice. "Isn't it nice that he's writing so much to people who aren't his relatives anymore? I hate writing letters. But say hello to him if you ever talk to him again."

My brother Eddie called me late one night to report on his latest Michael letter. Michael wasn't working yet, but he was dating a divorced lady with two young children. Michael spent periods of time camping by himself. And building a dollhouse as a Christmas present for the divorced lady's daughter.

Two days before Christmas I overwound the wall clock— the wall clock Michael never let me wind because he was so sure I'd overwind it.

And on Christmas Eve, Christopher informed me he was moving back to Colorado.

"Don't be upset. You'll come visit me. I'll come visit you. It'll still be the same between us," he told me.

"*What* will be the same between us, Christopher? I don't even know what it is we *are*!" I was sitting on my living-room floor holding the copy of *The History of Advertising* Christopher had just presented me for Christmas.

"We'll be like Dashiell Hammett and Lillian Hellman," he said, sweeping his arm out like he was offering me some golden opportunity. "Two residences. Two different places we can visit and enjoy."

"With a nine-hundred-mile commute between them!" I cried. "You liked it a lot better when I was married, didn't you? Now that there's no husband to put some distance between us, you need Kansas and Nebraska. I don't want someone who's going to love me from afar. I don't need that!"

"I think it's romantic," Christopher said, still attempting to charm me. "We can call each other up on the phone late at night and talk dirty."

The advertising-history book slid off my lap as I flapped my hands through the air in frustration and scowled. "That's probably what you told your Colorado girlfriends when you left there and moved back here. I don't want to play your games!"

Now Christopher was wringing his hands and shaking his

head. Christopher hates when his women aren't cooperative. "Hey! I'm trying to be a nice guy about this! I never promised you anything! I never said I wanted to play cups and saucers with you. I don't want to live here anymore and I think I can make enough of a living now drawing my cartoons while living someplace I'd rather live. I'm sorry I'm upsetting you, but I can't help it. This is something I've got to do!"

"Well, if it's such a great thing to do, you should never have left there in the first place!" I screamed. "What gets me most is that it's going to keep happening again and again. There's always going to be some lady who'll fall for your charm. And you'll continue to rack up a string of married or otherwise unavailable women until you age beautifully and end up preying on lonely widows in Miami!"

Christopher stood up, holding the box with his new sweater. "Maybe I better go," he said. "This isn't getting us anywhere."

"You just love to run away, don't you? I hate your weakness! I thought it meant you needed me, but all it meant was: you're weak."

Christopher headed toward the door. "I'll call you tomorrow," he said. "After my family opens our gifts and all. Maybe we can talk then."

In the interests of avoiding another farewell sex episode on the sofa, when Christopher called I told him not to call me anymore. Not to see me anymore. Not to even *think* of calling or seeing me anymore. Then I was furious at him for taking me at my word and leaving town without calling or seeing me. By March, stupid I-miss-you letters with stupid erotic cartoons began arriving in the mail, none of which I bothered to answer. Instead, I left for England to shoot cigarette commercials.

My partner, Ned, was forever buying souvenirs for his wife and children. Hand-knit sweaters. Charm bracelets dangling little Big Bens and Towers of London. He had a family waiting for him. But me? I had a condo. I wanted somebody to check in with at night; somebody at home waiting for me to come home.

I called Michael from my London hotel room, miscalculating the time difference and waking him up.

"Hi," I said. "It's me. Franny."

"I know your voice," he said, his own heavy with sleep. "Is everything okay? Why are you calling?"

"I don't know. Habit, I guess. I'm traveling. I'm in England." I could picture him with his dark hair mussed and falling in his face. He was probably wearing one of his gray T-shirts and a pair of shorts. I hesitated. "I've missed you, Michael. I've been thinking about you." I braced myself in case my words had angered him. When he didn't say anything, I continued. "I was thinking I have some vacation time coming up, and maybe, if it's okay with you, and something you want, too, maybe I could come out there, for a long weekend or something, just to visit, to see how you're doing."

"Are you sure that's a good idea?"

"It's just a thought."

Silence; the low humming of an overseas phone connection the only sound between us. But he finally spoke, in a quiet, precise voice: "A visit would be fine."

I called one more time after I was back in the States; we picked an agreeable weekend, set up a flight arrival, made arrangements for meeting at the airport; both of us overly concerned with each other's convenience. I hung up the phone thinking there was a slight possibility that I was acting like a total jerk. There Michael was, trying his best to create a new life, and I was all set to hop on a plane and interfere.

But maybe if we saw each other one more time, we could finally close the door.

❧ *Chapter 27* ❧

I walked off the plane and spotted him standing next to a row of pay telephones, across the main aisle, shifting from foot to foot, his arms folded across his chest, his eyes scanning the galleyway. A surge of warmth rushed through me and I vigorously waved hello as we approached each other, but an awkward tentativeness quickly slithered between us. I grinned and shrugged; Michael smiled shyly, and after hesitating for a moment we exchanged a polite, clumsy hug. We didn't kiss.

He was tan, thinner, wearing blue jeans, a crisp pinstripe shirt unbuttoned at the throat, and tortoiseshell eyeglasses. I had to adjust to Michael in glasses. His hair hung over his forehead, longer, shaggier, prebanker length, giving him a boyish look offset by a few distinguishing gray streaks.

"Hi," he said softly.

"Hi."

"I was writing a letter. I almost missed seeing you walk off," he said apologetically, reaching over and gently prying my suitcase out of my hand. "Is this everything?"

I nodded.

There was something wonderfully comforting and familiar

about Michael ambling through the airport with his chin up and his shoulders thrust back as I tagged along behind. He stood to the side and held open an exit door for me, lightly touching my back as I passed him. "I'm glad you wore your hiking boots." He glanced down at my feet. "They still look new."

We walked out into the parking lot and the cool spring air. "Chilly," I said.

"Did you pack a sweater?" he asked. "It's too bad it's night. You won't be able to see Mount Hood well at night, and it's really beautiful."

Michael had purchased a silver Honda Accord with his money from our divorce settlement. "I've got to work tomorrow," he said, as we drove. "I'm sorry. I just found out today. And it took me so long to get this job, I couldn't say no. But I've got maps and bus routes for you and a list of galleries and you can explore the city while I'm at work; then we can go out for a nice dinner."

"Oh. Okay," I said unhappily. I'd been counting on spending the day with him. "Do you like your new job? Is it what you want?" He had finally found work as an apprentice furniture maker earning seven dollars an hour.

"It's a start. I was lucky to get it. I was down to my last nine hundred."

"*Dollars?*"

"No, Franny, millions."

I had no idea where we were driving. It was a scenic view of darkness. "Do you live far from here?" I asked, not knowing where here was.

"Nothing's far around here. I was going hiking this weekend before I knew you were coming; I left a note inviting the two nurses who live upstairs from me, but maybe it blew away, because they never responded." Michael turned down a side street and into a driveway. He braked, shut off the engine, and looked over at me like he was about to divulge an important confidence. "They're very religious."

Michael lived on the first floor of a two-story building built like one of those roadside motels that have outdoor staircases and a walkway running along the second floor. He was proud of the good deal he'd gotten on his apartment, explaining that it was in an area of town where rents were cheap. Plants filled the living room, hanging plants and potted plants, spilling from the windowsills and the two glass end tables flanking the blue sofa he'd purchased from the furniture-rental place. Two pillows, some sheets, and a folded blanket were stacked on the sofa. On the opposite wall of the room was the old TV we'd bought the first year we were married, the one I'd talked him into keeping. A metal bird cage sat on a brown Formica dinette table. "These are my ladies," Michael said, poking his head up against the cage and waving a finger at the two canaries inside. "They're who I talk to." He looked at me. "I have to get up at six. Do you mind if we visit tomorrow when I get home? I really ought to get to sleep. You can have the bedroom."

"Oh, that's silly," I said. "We slept next to each other for ten years. I'm sure we can handle three more nights."

"Whatever you want." Michael didn't seem to care one way or the other. He headed for the bathroom and closed the door behind him. After all our years together he was suddenly Mr. Modest. I heard the shower sputtering to life as I walked into the bedroom and changed into a long virginal white cotton nightgown. The sheets on the bed were the ones we'd bought eight years earlier, which were later retired to our "backup" sheets, and which Michael took when he moved out. Over the bed he had thumbtacked photos of his parents and his sisters' families and several of his own baby pictures with captions handwritten underneath like "Cute kid!" and "What a little devil!"

He walked into the bedroom wearing only his shorts; his chest bare, strong, beautiful. He ran his fingers through his damp hair. "Don't you want to take a shower?" he asked, eyeing me in my nightgown.

"No. I'll do that in the morning. I'll just go brush my teeth."

As I emerged from the bathroom freshly washed, brushed, and combed, Michael handed me a map and a bus schedule. He tried to explain where to walk to catch the bus and the best place to get off the bus and what to see once I did get off the bus and I finally said I was sure I'd find whatever I had to find, and maybe we should just go to bed.

We crawled under the covers and wrapped our legs together. Michael didn't seem concerned with his old shrapnel wound bothering him or my ticklish hair. He draped an arm around me. "You feel good," he said, just before he fell asleep. "It always felt good to hold you."

After having been married to him and divorced from him and all the back and forths with him, it was the lack of intensity between us that saddened me the most.

I woke up Friday morning and checked over my maps while Michael prepared his lunchbox. He was worried about being late to punch in and not being kept on at his job. We kissed goodbye at the door, a warm married-people kind of kiss, and I trotted back to bed. The phone rang at ten o'clock; Michael was calling to see if I'd gone back to bed. "You should get up! There's actually some sun around here today!" He'd be home by four-thirty.

That evening, Michael brought home flowers, just like a husband.

"How was work?" I asked, just like a wife.

"They don't need me until next Tuesday," he said, clearly disappointed. "How was your tour?"

"I can see why you like it here. It's a beautiful city."

"When it's not raining," he said. "When it's raining, it's depressing."

We ate dinner in an Indian restaurant that looked appropriately moody and authentic with its dark madras tablecloths and brass salt and pepper shakers. Over a variety of dishes that all tasted like curry, Michael told me about Lorra, the divorced lady with two kids, who it turned out wasn't divorced, just separated.

"Do you like her?" I asked.

"She's okay." I could tell he was trying to act casual. "I like the kids. But Lorra's trying to work things out with her husband." He trailed his finger along the rim of his plate. "I'm trying to talk her out of it."

"Because you like her?"

"No. Because he used to hit her and make her unhappy," Michael said, with obvious disgust. "But she's scared to not be married."

I was talking to Michael about his love life like I was his sister or a cousin. "Maybe she wants to marry you."

Michael shook his head. "No. She thinks I'm too needy. And I think she's boring."

On Sunday we hiked along a two-mile trail Michael thought I'd enjoy (dirt, trees, and shrubs). Michael kept stopping to point out flowers or identify birds. I just wanted to keep moving. I was a goal-oriented hiker.

When we arrived at the end of our trail, which didn't look a whole lot different from the rest of the trail (more dirt, trees, and shrubs), we sat on a couple of big rocks and Michael began pulling out oranges and chicken sandwiches and travel-size cans of apple juice from his backpack. Stuffed with trail mix, I didn't want to eat. I volunteered to watch Michael eat. The rubber sole of my boot was loose by the toe, and while Michael munched on a chicken sandwich, I kept flapping my boot. He finally told me to quit playing with it, so I stopped and drew squiggly lines in the dirt with a stick.

"I'd like to have my own business in a few years," he told me. "Designing kitchens or custom-made furniture. I don't like not having any money."

"You could work in a bank again. There must be plenty of banks out here."

"Banking bores me." Michael finished his sandwich and stuffed his used napkins and Saran Wrap back into his backpack. "I'll start a business. Buy a small piece of property. Then find a cute wife and a couple of kids to share it with."

"Maybe you'll meet the cute wife first."

"No. Probably not. Ladies don't want to go out with guys who don't have money."

"Are there any women where you work?"

"No one I'd be interested in." He stretched his arms over his head, picked up a stick, and drew his own squiggly lines in the dirt, weaving his lines through my lines. "I'm not the strong man you thought I was, Franny. I can't seem to make any impact. Nobody wants to listen to me. I watch people when I'm talking to them and I can just see them tuning me out." Michael kept focusing on those squiggly lines. "You didn't realize how important it is to me to have one person in the world to count on."

We sat in silence before I said, "I'm not seeing him anymore. You know—Christopher. I haven't for quite a while."

Michael didn't react. I didn't know if it was because he just didn't care, or if he was lost in his own thoughts. "I don't love you anymore," he said, "but it scares me that no one else will ever take care of me the way you did. The first few years you took such good care of me."

I started crying. "I shouldn't have come here. I've just made you sad."

"It's not you," Michael said. "I feel like this a lot of times, even when I'm alone. Things don't seem to work out for me. You were one of the only things I ever really cared about and it didn't work out for me." My nose was running and I wiped the back of my hand under it. Michael handed me a napkin. "Let's head back."

I fell asleep in the car and woke up as Michael was pulling into Fred Meyers, a huge combination grocery-discount-variety store. "I'll buy some glue so I can fix your boots," he said. Once inside, he stopped to check the price on a Weber barbecue. "In a few more paychecks I should be able to buy one of these." I checked the price tag: thirty-nine dollars.

"Why don't I buy this for you as a housewarming gift? I'd really like to do that."

Michael shifted his shoulders. "Okay. That would be nice." For the slightest fraction of a second, I wondered if he had manipulated me into buying him his barbecue, but it was such an awful thought, I immediately squelched it. "We can come back for this," he said. "Let's get some groceries first. I'll buy some hamburger to grill for dinner."

We loaded a cart with corn on the cob, cheddar cheese, ground beef, and a bag of charcoal. Michael bought a small jar of rubber cement. We swung by the Weber display on our way to the cash register. I offered to pay for the groceries. Michael said he'd help. I insisted. He let me pay.

Michael carried the groceries into the kitchen, stopping to call out, "Hello, ladies!" to his birds. I unloaded the bags while he went back to his car for the barbecue. When he returned he was smiling. "I saw one of my upstairs nurses! They *did* get my note but they had to work this weekend. But they'd like to go hiking next weekend." I was glad he'd have something to do.

We prepared dinner together. I sliced the cheese and shucked the corn while Michael formed the meat into patties. I told him all about how I wasn't liking my job. "There I was in England living on expense account and shooting these swell commercials and not caring anymore."

"So what are you going to do?" he asked, stacking his perfectly formed hamburger patties on a plate.

"I don't know."

Michael nodded without saying anything.

During dinner we watched some nature show on TV. "I like this show," Michael said, "but I don't see it too often. I try not to run my TV too much because it's about to die on me and I can't afford a new one right now." I thought about the portable television sitting in my bedroom that I hardly ever used, but I couldn't think of a way to offer to send it. I didn't want Michael to feel like a charity case.

I cleared and washed the dishes while Michael worked on my boot. The phone rang and I heard him answer it in the living room. I was putting the last plate in the cabinet when he walked back into the kitchen. "That was Lorra. I'm going to take her kids out to dinner next weekend and go kite flying."

"That's nice," I said. "I'm tired. That hike was harder than I thought. Maybe I should go to sleep."

"Me, too," Michael said.

We held each other in bed but didn't talk.

In the morning I packed my few belongings and Michael offered me breakfast.

"You know I don't eat breakfast," I said.

"I just thought I'd ask. So many things have changed these days that I don't assume anything." He carried my bag out to the car.

I looked at all the pretty houses and gardens while we drove. "It really is a pretty city," I said. Michael followed the road under an overhead AIRPORT ENTRANCE sign. "When do you think you'll be back to the Midwest? I mean, to see your folks."

"Long time," he said. "Apprentices aren't paid for vacations." He looked at me. "We don't seem to be able to extricate ourselves from each other, do we?"

"I know," I said. "I don't feel like this is the last time I'll see you."

"Good," Michael said. He pulled the car in front of the passenger entrance. "I hope you don't mind if I don't go in."

"No problem." I reached around to hug him. We kissed goodbye. A simple kiss filled with resignation.

❦ *Chapter 28* ❦

Nothing felt like home anymore. Not even home.

I sold my condo and bought another one, downtown, closer to work, one with absolutely no resemblance to my life-as-a-wife condo, one I could walk around without feeling like someone was missing.

It had been seven months since I'd had any contact with Michael, seven months I'd been missing parts of him but not all of him. I seriously debated not even letting him know I moved, but finally mailed one of my announcements. It seemed wrong that two people who'd spent a decade sleeping in the same bed should go off and have entire new lives without any knowledge of each other. There should be a rule, a mandatory part of all divorce decrees: Okay. Go be happy. But send a lousy Christmas card.

I heard nothing from Michael.

Instead I got chatty letters from Norma. I wrote back equally chatty letters. Mainly because I had a great deal of spare time on Saturday nights.

In a fit of insanity, I did something I swore I'd never do. I let my mother fix me up with the son of a friend of a friend of hers.

I returned home suicidal. Not that Howard, my date the dentist, was a psychopath or a jerk. A psychopath would have been interesting. But Howard was generic. A polite nondescript lump of protoplasm who spent most of the evening talking up a storm about overbites. The next morning I called my mother to laud it over her that I'd had an awful time.

"Give him a second chance," she said. "You can't really get to know a person without giving them a little time."

"That's true," I said, miserably. "I never got to hear his opinions on wisdom teeth."

"I'll tell you what the problem is," she said. "You intimidate men. They look at you and think you've already got a boyfriend."

"Mom?"

"Yes?"

"Mom, I don't think that's the problem."

After years of motels, Holly reached the astute conclusion that there was no future with her married Mr. Red Roof Inn. "I used to think half a Casanova was better than none," she moaned, "but maybe not." I could see Holly's eyes darting around as her mind switched to plan B. "Maybe I should have a child out of wedlock."

Piper admitted she was sorry she hadn't married her podiatrist with the five kids. "Someone else snatched him up mighty fast. If my patients knew how screwed up my life is, they'd sue me for malpractice." Then she said, "Maybe I should have a child out of wedlock."

I didn't have a mad urge to have a baby. I kept waiting for my mad urge to kick in. I was almost thirty-five. I was supposed to be desperate to have a baby. But I was no longer married to the only person I had ever wanted babies with.

On that particular person's fortieth birthday I mailed him a card; my parents shipped him oranges from Florida. But they didn't hear from him. And neither did I. Not until a month later, in March, when the phone rang late at night. I fumbled the receiver and I must have sounded sleepy because I had just dozed off.

"Hello," I heard Michael say. "Is this a bad time?"

"It's fine!" I sat up in bed. "I'm glad you called."

"I was wondering how you are," he said softly.

I scrunched back down under my covers and talked to Michael in the dark, the way I longed to talk to him in the dark when we were married, only he always fell asleep too fast.

"Are you still seeing your friend you were seeing?" I asked.

"No. She went back with her husband. I miss the kids more than I miss her."

"Oh. But have you been meeting people? Making some friends?"

"It's difficult. I volunteered to work Saturday nights in the emergency room at one of the hospitals here. It gives me something to do and I thought I could meet some nurses." He hesitated. "But none of the nurses I meet want to go out with me. They're only interested in going out with doctors."

"I know a dentist I could introduce somebody to."

The next time Michael called he'd been laid off. He sounded angry, not drunk, but the angry sort of way a drunk person can sound when a drunk person's angry. "I need some money," he demanded. "Around eight thousand dollars. I want to buy a house with a garage and some tools so I can set up a workshop and start a business. You can loan me the money. You have plenty of money. You owe it to me for fucking up my life."

"You have no right to ask me!" I cried into the phone.

After we hung up, after I'd said no, absolutely no, with Michael yelling that he knew he could never count on me, I felt cheap and mean and rotten and defensive, and didn't know which feeling was okay to be feeling. But it didn't matter, because it was Christmas before I heard from Michael again, and by then I had met Scott.

Piper dragged me to the art opening. She thought it would be good for me to circulate and good for her because maybe she'd meet someone worthy of impregnating her. The exhibit was held for some hot new painter from New York specializing in neo-depresso expressionistic shit. Paintings that don't really look like anything in particular but you just know they're all about death and degradation and they all cost at least ten thousand dollars. I mingled my way through the exhibit. And trampled on Scott's foot.

"Care to dance?" he asked, with a wide beefy grin.

Later, I was amazed that Piper hadn't nailed him first as a potential donor for her unconceived child. Scott was a regular skyscraper, tall enough that I had to look up at him, which made me feel petite and diminutive, no easy task. He was bear-hug bulky, with wide shoulders, and long skinny fingers that looked like they belonged on someone other than the tall bulky man in front of me.

"Are you an artist?" I asked. My conversational skills for meeting men were somewhat rusty.

"Yes," he told me. "I'm a drummer."

What could be sexier? Certainly few things could be noisier.

"I write advertising commercials," I said. "A lot of them have drums in them."

Piper was peeved that I met someone at the gallery party and she went home alone, since going to the party was her idea in the first place, but she did tell me that dating someone was beneficial for me and would no doubt help me out of the depression she kept insisting I was in.

Scott left no surface unturned when it came to knocking out a few tappity-tap-taps. I'd make a joke and Scott would pound out a shaboom on a nearby tabletop in perfect rhythm. He was forever using his thighs like portable bongos or sitting in restaurants clinking out tunes on his water glass with a spoon. I had no regrets when he left for a holiday gig on a cruise ship to Bermuda.

I received a Christmas card from Michael, a card that came from a different Michael than the angry one I last spoke with. He was working again. At a different shop. And sharing a house with one of the guys from the new job, because he hated living alone. On the bottom of the card, scrawled beneath his signature like an afterthought, he wrote: It's going to be very difficult for us to replace each other.

After two years of refusing to tick, I accepted the fact that my wall clock detested me. It liked Michael. It ticked for Michael. But for me, nothing. It was probably furious that it was still hanging around Chicago and not living in some charming, aesthetic place like Portland, Oregon. But I graciously gave it one last chance to redeem itself and perform for me.

I lugged my wall clock into Grandfather Tyme, a tiny storefront shop with walls sagging with cuckoo clocks, Regulator clocks, baby grandfather clocks, each one ticking away in its own rhythm. The stooped-over white-haired man behind the counter talked to his clocks like they were personal friends. After fussing over my wall clock and telling me it was "a fine piece," he told me to come back in one week. When I returned, my erstwhile clock was happily ticking among all its new friends. I feared it would take one look at me and immediately overwind and die, yet I managed to get it home and hang it up and get it going again without any apparent protest on its part. But after two years of silently collecting dust, its constant renewed ticking felt vaguely censorious. I knew it would be happier with Michael. I shipped it to him in a leftover moving carton after including a friendly, noncommittal note. I'd spent half an hour wondering how I should sign my note: "Love," or "Luv," or "Your friend." I decided not to risk offending Michael with any improper interpretation of our current truce, and simply signed "Franny." But he never called to acknowledge the clock. It wasn't like him to be rude and not call when someone sent him something as nice as our clock. So, after considering all the possibilities, I blamed the post office. Apparently, he had never received the clock.

I waited until the phone rates went down at eleven, so it would be cheaper for me to call, but only nine o'clock in Portland. I pulled Michael's phone number out of my nightstand drawer and dialed his number. The roommate's voice answered.

"Hello?" he said.

"Hi. Is Michael home?"

There was a long, awkward hesitation in response. Like he was about to say, Michael *who*?

"This is Franny," I said.

"Franny? Franny his ex-Fra . . ." He cut himself off and said, "Franny in Chicago?"

"Yes," I said impatiently. "Is Michael there?"

"No, he's not home."

"Will you please tell him I called?"

"One moment please," the roommate said. I heard him put down the receiver. I wondered if maybe Michael was really home and the roommate was going to ask him if he wanted to talk to me.

Finally I heard him come back and pick up the phone. "Franny?"

"Yes."

"Franny, Michael's very sick. He's in the hospital, Franny. He has a brain tumor. He's not expected to live."

❧ *Chapter 29* ❧

The first words out of my mouth were, "You're kidding." Then I made him repeat the words. But they didn't sink in. They didn't make sense. They just kept coming at me. "I don't even know your name," I said. "Who are you? What's your name?" How could some stranger be telling me something so awful? None of it made sense.

"Jim," he said. "I'm Michael's roommate, Jim. They didn't want to tell you. No one expected you to call."

"Who didn't want to tell me?"

"Michael's parents. They're here. His whole family's here. His mom. His dad. His sister from Minnesota and her husband. The sister from Spokane left today, but she'll be back."

I couldn't understand how the whole family could be there and not me. I was closer to Michael than any of them.

"I've got to be with him," I said.

"It might not matter," Jim said. "He's pretty confused right now. He was in a coma eleven days and just came out of it a few days ago. Nobody expected him to come out of it."

"Eleven days!" I exploded. "And nobody *told* me? He needs help! I've got to be there!"

"Maybe you could talk to him tomorrow. He might be ready for that. We can see how Michael is tomorrow and I'll call you and we can set things up. But we have to see what Michael wants and what he can handle. He's had some friends visiting the last couple of days, but I don't know how much he understands."

"He does have friends there?" I couldn't stand to think of Michael being alone and in trouble with no friends around. I was crying into the phone, my nose running over my face and onto the mouthpiece.

"Yeah, he does," Jim said. "Not a lot of friends, but he's got people there. Are you going to be all right? Do you have someone there to talk to tonight?"

"I'll be fine," I whispered. My stomach hurt. And I was talking like a robot, a robot saying lines on a TV show she didn't know how she got on. "I have to get to Portland," I repeated.

"Don't do anything until I call you tomorrow. I promise I'll call you tomorrow and maybe you could talk to Michael then."

"But what if he dies first?" I cried, saying the unsayable.

"I'll call you tomorrow," Jim said. "I promise."

Then there didn't seem anything more to say, so we hung up and I sat on the edge of my bed and sobbed into my hands. But I had to do something. I couldn't just wait to get a phone call while Michael might be dying. *Dying!* I hadn't even thought to ask for the name of the hospital, but I wasn't sure Jim would have given it to me anyway. He seemed so certain about me not just calling or showing up until he talked to Michael. But what if I didn't get to talk to Michael? I had to talk to Michael. I had to see Michael. How could he be dying? Michael was the strong one. Nothing bad could happen to Michael.

Jim had said that Diana had gone back to Spokane. I could call Diana. She'd written a letter after Michael and I split up, saying she'd enjoyed being my sister-in-law for a while and was sorry things hadn't worked out.

I hunted down Diana's phone number in an old address book and dialed it, hoping she'd be home and would tell me that Jim was crazy and Michael wasn't all that sick.

The phone rang four times before anyone answered, four long rings, but it was Diana's voice I heard on the other end, Diana, the sister who Michael hardly knew because she'd gone off and gotten married when he was only four years old.

"Hello?" I said. My voice wavered. "This is Franny. Franny Baskin."

"Oh, Franny!" Diana sighed.

"I called Michael tonight," I said. "I talked to his room-mate."

"He told you? You know?"

"I know. I guess. I don't know."

"Oh, Franny!" Diana said again, and then she was crying and talking at the same time. "It's so awful. I'm so sorry. You were just calling Michael—just to talk—and that's how you found out? How awful for you. I wanted you to know, but I was outvoted."

"Outvoted?"

"By my father and sister. Especially my father. He didn't

want you involved. He was adamant. He said if you knew, you'd just come running out there and it wouldn't do any good and it just might confuse or upset Michael even more.''

"I don't know what's going on. I don't understand. I just know it's a brain tumor. They can remove brain tumors. I knew someone at work whose cousin had a brain tumor and it was removed.''

"Not this kind,'' Diana said. "They can't.'' Then she tried to explain. Something about the gliole cells and something about the left parietal lobe and something about a class four and then the parts about malignant and less than a year, but none of it really registered. "I guess he had a headache. Just a headache. But he stayed home from work and it got so bad he got scared and he collapsed and ended up calling the ambulance by himself and went to the hospital. He called my father after the CAT scan and told him they were going to do a biopsy the next day. Dad flew right out to Portland. My mother didn't go right away. I don't know why. But my father sat in intensive care for eleven days waiting for Michael to come out of that coma. He just sat and watched. Judith flew down to Springfield and brought my mother out. Her nursing background's helped a lot. She can really talk to those doctors. I came back home today because there's really nothing I can do right now, but I'm going back on the weekend.''

"So he'll be okay until the weekend? Jim made it sound like he was going to die right away, that he wouldn't be okay. I have to talk to him. I have to see him.''

"No one expected him to come out of the coma. He was in it for so long. One night we thought Michael was going to stroke out; he'd gone into convulsions. But yesterday he came out of it. The nurses were amazed. He was sitting up and talking a little. He would say things when he was in the coma. Bits and pieces of things. Most of them didn't make sense. But he was calling for you. Judith was sitting with him at the time and she said he'd called your name several times.''

He'd been asking for me and no one had told me. I didn't even know he was in trouble. He'd asked for me and I wasn't there for him. I started crying again.

"I'm so sorry you found out this way," Diana said.

I couldn't imagine a good way to find out.

"You should have been called," she said. "But now that you know, now that you found out, I don't think it's wrong for me to give you Michael's number. He was moved out of intensive care and into a regular room yesterday."

I didn't know why Diana, who was almost as old as my mother, was so uncomfortable doing something that might make her father mad, but at least she was willing to give me Michael's number.

"Maybe you could call him," she said. "And maybe you could talk to his friend Wendy. I don't have her phone number yet, but I could get it. She and her husband, Roy, are good friends of Michael's. Roy is Michael's foreman and Wendy's a nurse at Providence, so she's been there a lot. You'd like her. Actually she reminds me a lot of you. The two of you look like you could be sisters.''

"Thank you for talking to me," I said, writing down the name and phone number of the hospital in Portland.

"He was home to see my folks just three weeks before," Diana was saying. "Isn't that something?"

"I'll see you soon," I said. "I'm sure I'll be out there soon."

It was close to ten, Portland time, so they—the "they" who could keep me from Michael—probably wouldn't let me talk to him so late. But maybe they could tell me how he was doing. And maybe I could talk to him first thing in the morning. Once I talked to Michael, I knew he'd assure me that things were fine.

* * *

I was mad at myself for being scared to call the hospital. I wanted to be one of those people who bulldoze their way through a crisis with that clarity of perspective that says, nothing else matters than what I need to do at this moment. But what I needed to do was find out how Michael was doing, and I didn't know how to identify myself and ask the question. They might not give any information to an ex-wife. And if I said, "I'm his *wife*," why should they believe me, when I wasn't *there* with him? But I couldn't say I'm a *friend*, because hospitals have rules against giving out information to friends. Who I was, was so hard to explain. I dialed the hospital's number, figuring I'd just wing it, and was put through to the nurse's station on Michael's floor.

"I'm calling to find out how Michael Wedlan's doing tonight," I said. Good opening. It sounded like I'd known what was going on since day one.

"And may I ask who's calling?" a young-sounding nurse said.

"Uh, I was his wife."

"Oh!" she said, her voice brightening. She must not have taken time to wonder if what I said meant I used to be his wife, or I still was his wife but was so crazed I was talking like Michael had already died. It didn't matter, because the next thing she said was, "Would you like to speak to him?"

"Could I? Is he awake?"

"Oh yes!" she said. "You have to be patient with him and speak slowly. His words come out scrambled sometimes and we aren't sure how much he understands, but he's awake. I'll ask him if he'd like to talk now."

"Thank you," I said. A million thank-yous.

After several long moments while I sat there thinking, *What will I say, what will I say, is he going to be okay?*, I heard some fumbling and then Michael's voice saying hello.

"Michael, it's Franny."

"Hello, Franny."

His voice was soft and distant, like a little boy's. I lost whatever composure I had mustered. "Oh, honey, I'm so glad to talk to you. I'm so scared. I called your house tonight to talk to you. I'd sent you the clock, the wall clock, and I hadn't heard from you, and I called and I talked to your roommate, and Jim told me. I didn't know, nobody told me, I didn't know you'd been so sick. I want to be there. I have to be there. I hate that you're so sick."

"You want to come here?" he asked. His words were measured and very slow, but he knew what I was talking about. I could tell he knew what I meant. The nurse must have been wrong. The tumor must not be that bad. Michael could understand me.

"Of course I want to go there," I said. "I'll make a reservation tonight. I can be there tomorrow."

"It's been a long time since we've seen each other," Michael said. "It might feel strange."

"Do you want me there? Do you want to see me?"

There was a long pause before Michael answered, "Yes."

My words were tumbling out. "Oh, honey, I'm so sorry. This is so bad. I feel so awful. But I'll be there tomorrow. I promise. Okay?"

"Okay."

"You sleep well, honey. You have sweet dreams. And I'll be there tomorrow." I didn't want to keep him up too late. I didn't want anyone mad at me. I had to get to Portland before anyone got mad at me and told me I couldn't go. "Good night, honey," I said.

"Goodbye," Michael said.

I bit my pillowcase while I sobbed so that the neighbors wouldn't hear me wailing through the cheap plasterboard walls between our condos and think I was being attacked, or somebody died, and come knocking on my door. Somebody *was* going to die. And that somebody was Michael. But it didn't have to be that way. He'd sounded fine on the phone. Much better than anyone said he'd sound. They could be wrong. Doctors make mistakes. What did they know?

When I steadied myself and went from a state of hysterics to a dulled state of semihysterics, I called my mother. She said hello and I got as far as saying "Mom?" when she said, "What's wrong?" All I have to do is get one syllable out and my mother has an exact reading of my mood. "Tell me," she said. "Something is wrong." It was after midnight—another good clue that I hadn't called just to chat.

Somehow, from a few key words among my blubbers—Michael, brain tumor, hospital, dying—she figured it out. "Do you want me to drive down to the city and pick you up?" she asked.

"No. I have to pack. I have to go to Portland. I have to get a flight."

I called the various airlines wondering how their telephone girls could be so damn perky when Michael was dying. "Tomorrow?" the United Airlines lady said. "Nonstop?" the American Airlines lady chirped.

My phone rang as soon as I hung up. It was my mother. "Your line was busy. Is there any more news?" she asked.

"No, I was just booking a flight."

"I'll drive you to the airport."

"I can take a taxi."

"I want to help," my mother said.

I had it all planned out in my head. I'd land in Portland, grab a cab, and go straight to the hospital. I could worry about hotels later. But what could I say to Michael to make things okay? I wondered if Michael's parents would be glad

I came or try to keep me from seeing him. The phone rang and I had my answer. It was Michael's father. We hadn't spoken in almost four years.

"Hello. This is Gordon Wedlan."

"Hi. I know. How are you?" A stupid question. How was he *supposed* to be? And he certainly didn't let me off the hook with a gracious answer.

"Not good," he said. "Not at all good. Michael's a very sick boy." Then he said, "And your phone call tonight upset him very much." Gordon was talking to me like he was a school principal and I was a student who deserved to be thrown into detention hall.

"Huh? No, it didn't. He sounded fine. He could understand me. It was fine."

"I had to return to the hospital," Gordon said. "The nurses called me to come back. I'm sure you were upset and didn't stop to think, but your call left him greatly agitated."

"Huh?"

"All he could understand was that you were upset about something and needed help and that he couldn't provide it." Michael had a brain tumor growing in his head and he was worried about *me*. "He was frustrated and confused and it took me almost an hour to calm him down."

"Oh, dear. I was upset. Of course I sounded upset, but I was upset because he's sick. I didn't mean to get Michael upset."

"I guess we should have let you know," Gordon said, "so you would have found out a different way. It's hard to know what's the right thing to do. I had to answer Michael's questions and tell him that the reason you were upset was because of him and not because you were in some sort of trouble."

My stomach felt like a blob of twisted dough. "I've got a flight set up for tomorrow," I said. "I promised Michael I'd be there."

"Absolutely not!" Gordon ordered. "Michael does not want you to come to Portland now."

"Yes, he does. He told me he does!"

"He doesn't know what he's saying. And he is simply not prepared emotionally to deal with your presence."

I bet it was Gordon who wasn't prepared to deal with my presence.

"You have to realize how sick he is," Gordon said. "We're just waiting now until he's well enough to travel, so we can bring him home to Springfield."

They were bringing him home to die.

"I asked him tonight if he would like to have you visit him later, in Springfield, and his reaction was an immediate, 'Oh, yes.' But not now. It's too soon."

"But I promised," I said. "What if there's no *time* later?"

"We have to take these things one day at a time," Gordon said, in a formal, mechanical voice. "Michael will receive x-ray therapy at one of our fine Springfield hospitals. The treatments will proceed for four to six weeks, several times each week on an outpatient basis."

That was the most hopeful thing I'd heard all night. "Oh! So there is something we can do!"

"We're making no plans beyond that," Gordon continued, "until we see how he responds to such treatment and how rapidly—uh—other things develop. We hope Michael will be ready to travel within a week to ten days. Then I'm certain it will take him some time to get adjusted to being back home and the x-ray treatments, but after that, you could come visit and he'll probably be very pleased to see you."

I was trying to piece together everything Gordon was telling me. If Michael didn't get back home for a week and then he had to get adjusted and how long would it take to get used to the treatments—and was Gordon telling me I couldn't see Michael for almost a *month*? But I couldn't get mad at Gordon and fight with him, because it was now clear that Gordon was the one person who could keep me from Michael. What would he do if I just said the hell with it and showed up in Portland tomorrow? Would he have the nurses block me from the room? I was sure he was capable of it.

"So how long will it be before I can see him?" I asked.

"We'll try to keep you fully informed as developments occur," Gordon said. "But the doctors, *family members*—" the words *family members* were said with special emphasis, one that didn't include me—"and all of Michael's friends are in complete agreement. We want only what will serve Michael's best interests."

"Well, I do, too, of course," I said weakly.

"Do you have someone to be with you tonight?" Gordon asked. Was he asking if I had a boyfriend there? "Someone to help you?"

I felt so tired when I answered him. "Yes. Sure. I'll call my mother."

"We do care," Gordon said. "And I know this is hard for you."

Yes. Sure.

"Maybe we're protecting him too much," Gordon said. "But we're trying our best. You will hear from us."

"Can I write him in the meantime?" I asked.

"Yes. Of course. I don't know that he can read by himself, but someone will be sure to read him your letter."

"Okay," I said. "Thank you. Goodbye."

I didn't know what else to say.

I hung up and clutched my pillow against my chest, choking over dry, silent sobs.

If I slept at all it was a weird sleep. A heavy-with-exhaustion but restless sleep. And for the first few moments when I opened my eyes, before my brain refocused, everything was okay again. Then I remembered.

My parents called first and I told my mother about the conversation with Michael's father and how I wouldn't be needing a ride to the airport. She thought it was a good idea that I wait until Michael came back to Springfield. She didn't understand.

"What if he doesn't get back?" I cried.

"He will," she said.

Then my dad got on the phone. And it was Paul who first used the word, that awful word, the word I hadn't associated with any part of anything yet. "It's terrible," he said. "He's so young to have cancer."

"Cancer? It's not cancer," I said. "It's a tumor."

"But it's malignant?"

"Yes."

"That is cancer, honey."

Then it seemed real.

❦ *Chapter 30* ❦

Okay. Act normal. Go to work. Save your vacation time for when Michael gets home. I couldn't let myself think in terms of *if* Michael gets home. My eyes were all red and puffy and swollen, but my partner, Ned, never asked me if anything was wrong; he wasn't one to pry; and I didn't volunteer any information. I spent most of the day in my office with the door closed, calling everyone who knew and cared about Michael. I needed to *talk* about it. I needed to keep saying it to make myself believe it: Michael is dying. Michael is dying.

I called Piper and Holly and Louie and Dodi and my sister, Madelyn, even though I knew my mother would already have called her, and Susan, who said she'd call Barry at work.

"I'll drive down to Springfield with you," Susan said. "To keep you company."

"I won't need company," I said. "Thank you, but—I just want to get there."

It was noon, ten o'clock in Portland, and I had to know how Michael was doing, if he'd slept through the night all right. But I couldn't call his father again—he'd told me to wait until I heard from *them*—and if it was true that Michael had been so confused by my call last night that the nurse had to call his father, *she* wouldn't help me anymore. But Norma would know. Norma would talk to me. She'd been writing me all those chatty letters over the years. Norma liked me. She'd tell me what was going on. I called the nurses' station on Michael's floor in the hospital and asked to speak to Michael Wedlan's mother.

"She's with her son," the nurse said. It was a different nurse from the night before. She didn't ask me to identify myself. "I'll see if she can come to the phone."

"Hello," I heard Norma say. She sounded like a cold dull knife.

"Hello. This is Franny. How are you?" I forgot and asked that stupid question again.

"How do you think I am?" she answered, in that dead voice.

"I just called to see how Michael is today."

"You better not come here," she said in a flat, cold tone. "It won't do any good for you to come here."

"I know. I talked to Dad." The word *Dad* hung in the air, but I'd never called Michael's parents anything else, even after the divorce. Norma still signed her letters "Mom." But right now she wasn't sounding too motherly toward me.

"My husband told you not to come."

"I'm not coming. I told him I wouldn't. I'll wait until Springfield. I just called to find out how Michael was doing today."

"He's sick. He's been throwing up all morning. We'll call when we get home," Norma said. "Goodbye."

And the phone went dead.

By the end of the day Ned finally asked me if something was wrong.

"Go to Portland anyway," Ned advised.

"I can't go," I said. "They don't want me now."

"I guess I kind of screwed things up there with my phone call last night, huh?" I phoned Jim the roommate, timing my call for hopefully right after he got home from work.

"It would have been better if I'd run relay for you first," Jim said. "But if I were you, I'd've probably done the same thing." For the first time I noticed Jim's soothing voice. Talking to him felt like my idea of talking to a priest. "Mr. Wedlan didn't get back here from the hospital until close to midnight."

"Back where?" Then it dawned on me. Of course the Wedlans were staying there.

"They're using Michael's room," Jim said, as if in answer to my thought.

"Do you know how he's doing today?"

"No," Jim said, softly. "I'm going to grab a sandwich and get over there after I stop to see an apartment I'm looking at. But you can call me whenever you want."

"I'm not sure Michael's parents would appreciate that."

"They're usually at the hospital at this time," Jim said, in his soothing priest voice. Then he told me some more about Michael's diagnosis, as I wrote down the medical words so I'd remember them.

"You said you were looking at an apartment. Are you moving?" I asked.

"I can't afford to stay here without a roommate," Jim said. "I've been helping Mr. Wedlan pack up Michael's things."

"To ship?"

"No," Jim said. "To sell."

I called Diana one more time. She was my last link to Michael.

"So, have you had time to accept it yet?" she asked with the control of a true Wedlan.

"*Accept* it?"

"I mean have you had time to get used to it? We've had a couple of weeks. For you it's all new. Are you okay?"

I felt like I'd never be okay again.

"Not yet," I said. "Your father doesn't want me out there now. He wants me to wait."

"I don't know what's wrong with my dad," Diana mused. "He's been like an army guard about this whole thing. I don't even think they should be bringing Michael back to Springfield. Wendy and Roy volunteered to take care of him so he could stay in Portland and be with his friends."

"They did? Jim said Michael didn't have a lot of friends there."

"I don't know what he's talking about! The visitor's lounge was filled with friends. My father wouldn't let them all in. He's afraid it's too much for Michael."

"But he needs his friends now."

"And my mother," Diana continued, "she's been like an iron brick. She hasn't displayed one single emotion." I didn't mention how my phone call to the nurses' station that morning had evoked *anger*. "Judith and I keep expecting her to break down any day now, but so far nothing. In a way it's scary."

"You're going back this weekend, right?"

"Actually, I'm not sure now. Michael has so many other visitors he really doesn't need me there. And I can still get back and see him before my parents take him home."

Somehow, Diana figuring she could *wait* and see Michael later made me feel a little less panicky.

"This must be so awful for you," Diana was saying. "I've never really known my brother. He was so young when I moved away. And I've had to make peace with my own guilt for not making more of an effort to be much of a sister to him. But for you this must be terrible."

I thanked her for not treating me like an outsider.

Piper stopped over after her last appointment. She probably considered *me* her last appointment.

I couldn't make myself sit down. I was pacing around my living room with my arms wrapped around me. Piper sat on the couch with her shoes kicked off and her suit skirt hiked up and her legs folded Indian style beneath her.

"You're just working yourself up even more," she said.

"I can't do anything. No one will let me do anything. I just have to wait. And I can't stand to wait."

"Sometimes that's all you can do."

I finally sat down on the opposite end of the sofa, my fingers gripping the edge of the seat cushion to help me relax.

"These things don't just *happen*," I said. "There has to be a reason!"

"Not always."

Piper scooted down the sofa and leaned over and hugged me. I wasn't used to Piper hugging me, but it was all it took to start me crying.

I talked through the tears. "I keep rerunning the tape in my head, wanting to scream, 'Let's leave Chicago! Let's live by mountains and make babies! Let's be happy so you don't have to get sick and die!' "

Piper sat back, gently removing her arms from me. "Brain tumors don't come from being unhappy."

"Some people think so. Some people think you can make yourself sick."

"I'm a psychologist," Piper said, "and I don't believe anybody would give himself what Michael has."

"What do you mean?"

"You said it's a glioma class four?"

"Yeah. What does that mean?"

Piper put her arms around me again. "It means you better get to Springfield as quick as you can."

I couldn't sleep, so I tried writing Michael a love letter. The first draft of the Magna Carta could not have taken as much time as that letter. And once I wrote it, I rewrote it two more times until my penmanship was perfect. "Dear Michael, I just hate thinking of you ever being sick. Whatever the bond is that keeps me connected to you—it doesn't like having its other end sick."

My letter wasn't nearly as sloppy and loving as I wanted it to be, but anything too intense would not have passed inspection by Gordon, and if it had, it certainly would have sounded weird being read aloud by Norma. Maybe one of the nurses would read it to him. Or maybe by the time he got it he could read it himself. I just didn't know. I knew so little. In the morning I sent the letter by Federal Express so

I wouldn't spend the entire next week wondering if the post office screwed up and my letter ever arrived.

After a few days I wondered, has anybody told Wes? Wes, who was Michael's best friend and had been our best man. Did Clifford know, or Benny? I called Wes and he told me yes, he knew, they all knew; a man who attended the Wedlans' church was buying a garbage disposal from Benny, and somehow the subject came up. Wes was mad that no one had thought to call him, and I was mad that Wes hadn't thought to call me. But I didn't say anything. It didn't matter anymore. We talked about Michael. But we were talking about him like he was already dead. Remember Michael doing this? And remember how he liked to do that? I told Wes about the plan to bring Michael back to Springfield.

"I'm glad his parents are bringing him home," Wes said. "I'll be there everyday. We'll go to movies. Out for burgers. If he can't golf, we'll ride around in the golf carts. It'll be great. It'll be terrific. Everything's gonna be just fine."

I was a slave to my phone, scared I'd miss my call. Gordon's call. Michael's call. *Somebody's* call. Two weeks had gone by. Michael had to be back in Springfield.

I passed the time reading books about death. Cancer books. Dying books. Terminal-illness books. *A Death in Venice*. *Death of a Salesman*. If I stood in Rizzoli's and saw the word *death*, I'd whip out my wallet.

"You're making yourself miserable," my mother said, upon hearing my reading list.

"I'm making myself educated," I corrected her.

"And you're making yourself crazy," my mother said. "Just call down there. Quit standing on ceremony."

I finally made myself crazy enough to take her advice.

And Gordon sounded so glad to hear from me!

"Where've you been, stranger?" he asked, with surprising affection. "We've been trying to reach you."

"At what number? I'm here all the time!"

They'd been home for three days. Gordon had been calling my office number during the evenings. I was never at the office during the evenings. I could barely bring myself to be there during the days. "What a mistake," Gordon said. "Michael would very much like to see you."

"He would! Can I talk to him?"

"It's harder for him to talk on the phone," Gordon said. "When can you come here?"

"Tell him I'll be there tomorrow."

"Do you need directions?" Gordon asked.

"Four hours down I-55, turn right," I said. "I'll get there as early as possible."

"Good," he said.

"Good," I said.

I called Ned and told him I'd finally gotten the go-ahead and wouldn't be back to work for at least a week. I called my mother. I called Piper. I called Holly and asked her to check on my mail. I threw some clothes in a suitcase, washed my hair, and went to sleep early. I was up by 6:00 A.M. and headed for Springfield.

❦ *Chapter 31* ❦

When I was a little girl my mother would take me on obligation visits to my great-grandfather, who was blind and frail, an ancient little man who sat in a chair all day because there was nothing else for him to do.

Michael was sitting on the beige upholstered chair with the rust-colored daisies that was pushed up against the picture window. That's what I first saw of him when I was walking up the front stoop mustering up all my here-goes-nothing courage to ring the doorbell—the back of his little head in that big stuffed chair. Gordon opened the door and I kissed him on the cheek. Norma was sitting with her knitting on the couch. I kissed Norma on the cheek. Then I turned to Michael. Or what looked like a version of Michael.

He was skinny, withered, looking like my great-grand-father, sitting with his hands folded primly in his lap, his right leg shaking. He wore a black eyepatch over one eye, the kind the Arrow Shirt man used to wear, and over that he wore a cheap drugstore-bought-looking pair of eyeglasses. Norma explained—talking about Michael in the third person like he was a piece of furniture—that something, either the operation or the growth of the tumor, was causing Michael to have double vision in each eye. He was seeing four images of everything, and at least with the eyepatch he could cut down the number of images to a more controllable two. Maybe it would get better, she said, clacking away on her knitting needles, who knew? He was wearing a Ban-Lon striped shirt and ill-fitting seersucker pants with brown socks and white tennis shoes all borrowed from his father, who explained that Michael's clothes had not yet arrived in the carton shipped from Portland. His arms were bony and scrawny, and his thick dark hair had been hacked away in the back—like someone had attacked him with a dull hunting knife—except for one patch, one vertical strip two inches above his neck where he'd been opened for the biopsy, that had been shaved away and sported a long thin scar. I didn't allow myself to wince when I spotted the scar. From the front he looked fine—not counting the glasses and the eyepatch and the skinny arms and the two big red *X*'s above the sides of his eyes that were drawn there by the radiologist—but from the side he looked like he used the same barber as Bela Lugosi in *Frankenstein*. He was sitting warily, looking scared and uncomfortable with being the focus of everyone's attention. And the shaking never stopped; his right leg constantly trembled, like all his terror was concentrated right there and he was trying, really trying, but failing to control it.

I had been so terrified that I'd never see him again that for those first few moments, those couple of seconds of taking in all the changes that had happened to him and all the things that had been done to him, I was able to keep smiling. I couldn't let myself look shocked or scared. Not in front of Michael.

He spoke first, his eyes round and sad and warm. He said, "I thought I'd never see you again."

"No such luck." My words were stupid. And inappropriate. But at least I wasn't crying.

There was a small upholstered matching beige daisied footstool next to Michael and I sat down on it and kissed him. I could feel his parents looking away in embarrassment. "I'm so happy to be with you," I said to Michael, keeping my voice low for a semblance of a private conversation.

"Me too," Michael said.

"Is that a new car, Franny?" I heard Norma ask from her perch on the sofa.

"Huh?" I turned to her. Gordon was concentrating on a crossword puzzle.

"Your car. Is it new?" She was straining her neck to see out the picture window but she was still knitting.

"Uh, no, I don't own one anymore. I rented it," I told her. I smiled at Michael; he half-smiled back at me. "You wouldn't believe how fast I drove here," I said to him in my just-between-us voice again. "I couldn't wait to get here."

"Is it air conditioned?" Norma asked.

"Uh, yes," I said. I was rubbing my fingers up and down Michael's skinny arm. "If you weigh less than I do, I'm leaving!" I told him, trying to make him laugh.

Gordon looked up from his crossword puzzle. "Michael hasn't eaten yet," he told me. "Did you say something on the phone about wanting to go to Steak & Shake? You could take Michael to Steak & Shake."

"Why would he want to do that?" Norma asked. "We've got plenty of food in the house."

I couldn't remember talking about Steak & Shake with Gordon on the phone, but getting Michael away from the house sounded like a brilliant suggestion. "Would you like that?" I asked him.

"Sure," he said, not exactly brimming with enthusiasm, but sort of smiling at me with that wan, confused, sad smile that seemed to be the most he could manage. "That would be fine."

"I could make him macaroni and cheese," Norma said to no one in particular.

"Let me help you up," Gordon said, springing out of his chair and over to Michael. "Do you have to go to the bathroom first? You should go to the bathroom. It would be easier than going in the restaurant."

"I don't have to go," Michael said.

"Try," Gordon said.

Michael used both arms to push himself up out of his chair, with Gordon assisting him on one side, me hovering on the other, not knowing what I was supposed to do. Michael's walk was hesitant, like a robot's, one foot catching up with the other in a slow shuffle. I bit my lip to keep from gasping.

Gordon helped his son across the room, then both men went into the bathroom and Gordon closed the door.

Norma kept knitting.

"Those are pretty colors," I said, indicating the big square she was knitting. We should have been talking about Michael, but I didn't want to talk about him like I was talking behind his back. "What are you making?"

"Lap robes," Norma said, not looking up. "For the ladies in the home our church sponsors. They sit in wheelchairs and their laps get cold. If you have any spare balls of yarn at home, you could send them to me."

"I'll ask my mom," I said. "Maybe she has some left from sweaters she's knitted for Madelyn's kids."

"How many children does Madelyn have now?" Norma asked.

"Two," I said.

"That's enough," Norma said. Then she said, shaking her head in what almost seemed like disgust, "He forgets things. His memory's terrible."

Norma had to be the youngest-looking, healthiest, sturdiest eighty-two-year-old on earth. And Gordon was number two. To look at either one of them, you'd think they couldn't be older than their late sixties. Michael came from good stock. He should have been able to live a long time.

The bathroom door was pushed open and Michael and his father emerged. "Hi," he said to me. "You're here." Michael used the dining-room chairs and a wing chair in the living-room to balance himself as he shuffled back toward me, his father running shotgun right behind him. Michael smiled at me, such a sweet smile now. "Shall we go?" he asked.

"Yes," I said, taking his arm in case he needed support, and because I needed to be touching him. Gordon held the front door open.

"Don't be gone too long," Gordon warned. "He needs to nap a lot."

"Okay."

"We'll be fine," Michael said, a touch of irritation creeping into his voice.

"He likes chocolate shakes," Norma called out after us.

Michael and I worked our way to my rental car. It was hot—gruesome, sun-beating hot. I opened Michael's door and helped him into the passenger seat, then leaned down and kissed him on the lips. "Alone at last," I said.

"At last," Michael repeated.

As soon as I got in my side of the car and turned on the engine, I switched on the air-conditioner. I half-expected Michael to tell me I was doing it wrong, that we'd only get hot air until the engine had a chance to run, but he didn't say a thing.

"I hope I can find this place," I said. "I should have asked your dad for directions."

"You'll find it," Michael said, staring out the front window, his hands resting on his lap, like he was studying a place he hadn't been before.

"Do I turn right here?"

"Yes," Michael said. I was so glad he remembered. "I think."

I found it, thanks to a vague memory of its location and because Springfield's not all that big.

We pulled into the driveway and I could see through the big plate-glass windows that the place was packed and people were waiting in line. I didn't know if Michael could handle the line-waiting part and I didn't want him to feel bad or embarrassed that he couldn't, so I suggested plan B. Steak & Shake was the last place I knew of where you could still turn on your car headlights and some eager beaver young man would come running out to take your order for "curbside" service and hook a tray on your car window. "There are too many people in there, and I want to be alone with you," I told Michael. "Let's just eat in the car."

"Okay," he said. "That sounds fine."

"What do you want to eat?"

"Anything you want," Michael said.

"We need to fatten you up."

Even with the air-conditioner blasting, it was too hot to sit in a car in the middle of a tar-covered parking lot, so after we got our food, I suggested we drive around the park.

"That would be nice," Michael said. He was so agreeable and passive. As I headed toward Washington Park I'd reach across and rub the back of his neck and he'd turn and smile at me. His leg had stopped shaking.

"It's so strange," I said. "All this awful stuff is going on, but I'm so happy to see you that I don't think about the awful stuff."

Michael didn't say anything. But his leg started shaking again.

Washington Park is filled with big, beautiful oak trees. Sections of it feel like a forest. Right in the middle of the land of cows and corn appear baseball diamonds, hiking trails, clear streams, and a forty-mile-around lake. I stopped the car under a shady oak along one of the park roads, slipped the transmission into park, and turned the key so I could do that thing that keeps the air-conditioner or the radio on without keeping the engine on. I thought Michael would tell me I was going to wear out the battery, but he didn't comment. I scooted down the seat closer to him and asked, "Can we kiss?"

"That would be nice," he said.

I stroked his face while he let me kiss him. He reached one arm up around me. He was slow and hesitant, like it took a great deal of effort for him, but he seemed to like the kissing.

"You taste like french fries," I laughed.

"You too," he said.

Then we sat and held hands.

"Does the eyepatch feel funny?" I asked.

"Yes. A little bit. But there's nothing I can do about it."

"Oh, honey, this can't be real. They can't be right. I hate all this."

His leg was shaking again. I tried to hug him and calm him, knowing that the one thing I couldn't say, the one thing he needed to hear, was: It's going to be all right. I started rattling away to Michael about dying and not being scared of dying and all the people I'd read about who had died on operating tables only to come back and talk about their relatives waiting at the end of a tunnel. I thought Michael would dismiss what I was saying, but he was nodding and listening and eager to hear what I thought. Religious opinions spewed out of my mouth, all spoken with some previously untapped certainty. Another part of me was vaguely aware I was bullshitting me and bullshitting Michael, because what did I know? But when you want something to be true, and you need something to be true, it begins to start feeling like something that *could* be true.

"I'm so scared," Michael said.

That afternoon two of the Wedlans' friends who apparently had been at our wedding, and who apparently didn't realize that Michael and I were divorced, came to visit. Their names were Fay and Archie Marksdon and they showed up with half a dozen home-grown tomatoes. And that's what we discussed. Tomatoes. But every few minutes Fay would look over at me sitting on the foot stool next to Michael sitting on the beige upholstered chair, the two of us holding hands, and she'd look at us with these big soulful eyes and say, "Such a lovely couple." Then she'd shake her head sadly and go back to talking with Gordon and Norma and Archie about that awful greenish orange color of hothouse tomatoes, or the ridiculous prices of store-bought tomatoes. Michael and I didn't contribute much to the conversation. Actually, Michael didn't say anything. He just sat in his chair and smiled politely. At one point Gordon got up to bring him a glass of water and a couple of pills, which Michael just took without comment. My main offering was to say thank you when Archie remarked on how much they had enjoyed the sweet table at our wedding. After Fay and Archie left, with Fay gazing at us and muttering, "Beautiful, beautiful," on her way out the door, Gordon asked Michael if he needed a nap, and Michael said that sounded like a good idea. His father helped him shuffle up the stairs.

"I'll be here when you wake up," I called after him.

Norma picked up her knitting.

"How long are you planning to stay?" she asked me.

"A week," I said, still sitting on the foot stool.

"A week?" she said, not hiding her surprise. "Franny's planning to stay a week," she told Gordon when he came back down the stairs. Then she asked me: "Where?"

"In a motel," I reassured her. "Which one do you suggest?"

"How would *I* know about motels?" Norma said.

"The Pocahontas would be good," Gordon said, turning a Cubs game on the TV but keeping the volume down and then sitting in his assigned seat. "Their rates are quite reasonable."

"Is that the one where that murder was?" Norma asked.

"It wasn't *in* the motel," Gordon said.

"My parents send their very best wishes," I said to her, trying to make some conversation, trying to refer to what was really going on. "They'll come visit soon. My mother feels so bad for you. She says there's nothing worse than losing a child."

Norma shrugged while she knitted. "Some mothers don't get forty years."

Gordon remarked, "He hasn't been as tired today. Probably because he hasn't had the radiation."

"When did it start?" I asked.

"Friday was the first day," Gordon said. "It seems to make him tired."

"Have the guys been here to visit? Clifford or Wes?"

"Wes was here yesterday morning," Norma said. "Clifford's been here once, and we haven't seen Benny yet."

"And you've been home almost a week?"

"Maybe he's busy with other things," Norma said.

The phone rang and Gordon got up to answer it in the kitchen. I heard him say, "He's napping. You can try again later." Gordon walked back into the room, agitated now. "Those Portland friends," he said, like doesn't-anybody-understand? "They keep calling!"

"That's nice," I said.

Gordon looked at me like *you*-don't-understand. "It's too hard for Michael to talk to them. He can't handle a lot of people now. It's too emotional for him. He doesn't need a lot of emotion. You're his former wife, so I suppose that's different, but too many calls or visits would simply upset him. He has enough to deal with." Subject closed. "I'll drive to the motel and you can follow me in your car. That way you can find it."

"Are you coming back here for dinner?" Norma asked. It was a question more than an invitation.

"Is that okay?" I asked.

"We're having lamb," she said, tossing back a string of yarn.

The Pocahontas was one of those courtyard-type places where the door to your room opens onto the parking lot. It would have been an excellent place for a murder. After Gordon drove off, I asked the girl in the Pocahontas office for directions to the Ramada.

"Have some sliced tomatoes," Norma said to me at the dinner table. "I have to get rid of them."

We were eating in the dining room because it was Sunday. Gordon and Norma were seated on one side of the table, Michael and I on the other. Michael had trouble coordinating his knife and fork, holding them the wrong way or using one instead of the other. He'd woken up from his nap depressed and confused. Norma kept correcting him and telling him he was using the wrong utensil, and finally, out of frustration, he just picked up a slice of lamb with his fingers and took a bite out of it. Then he put it back down on his plate and said he wasn't very hungry.

"Shall I cut your meat for you?" Norma asked. "Gordon, cut his meat."

"I don't want any meat!" Michael said, at first angry and then immediately contrite like a bad little boy who's appalled at himself. "I'm sorry. I'm so bad. I'm here with my parents. And my wife is here. I don't know what's wrong with me. I don't know why I'm like this."

He seemed mad at himself for being depressed.

I wondered if he called me his wife because he felt like I was still his wife, which was nice, or because he couldn't remember I was no longer his wife, which was awful.

"You have nothing to be sorry about," Gordon said.

"Nothing at all. If you don't want to eat, you don't have to. Do you want to go back to bed? You can take your bath and go to bed."

"Maybe that would be good," Michael said.

"I can keep you company while you take it," I said, trying to help, trying to do *something*, wishing I knew what it was I could do.

"Who wants more tomatoes?" Norma asked.

I sat on the closed toilet lid watching Michael undress for his bath and that's when I saw how really skinny he was. His shoulder blades poked through his skin like a couple of coat hangers and his legs, his once beautiful legs, looked like two hairy sticks with his knees protruding. Michael smiled at me and said, "You have such big brown eyes."

I smiled back and said, "You have such skinny legs."

"Yes. Aren't they awful?"

"No. They're just fine."

Gordon kept bustling in and out of the bathroom to check the water level of the bathtub as it filled, then to check the temperature of the water, and to make sure Michael had a towel and to hand Michael his toothbrush after squeezing on the toothpaste. "Someone has to be in here with him," Gordon said. "Otherwise he might fall."

"I'll be here," I said.

"And he's not allowed to shampoo his hair because those red marks can't be washed away. It took the radiologist a long time to measure for those marks." Gordon helped Michael lower himself into the bathtub and then hurried off to find some pajamas.

"You're being well protected," I said to Michael.

"I know," he said. "They treat me like a baby."

Gordon helped Michael on with his pajamas. Michael never used to wear pajamas, and these were old-man pajamas. They must have belonged to Gordon, but Michael looked rather sweet in them.

"Do you want me to rub your back to help you sleep?" Gordon asked, as he guided Michael into bed.

"No. I'm okay."

Gordon said good night and patted Michael on the shoulder. Norma had said good night downstairs. After Gordon left the room, I sat on the edge of Michael's bed and stroked his face. The eyepatch and the glasses were removed, so he looked more like Michael now.

"I wish I could sleep here with you," I said.

"That would be nice."

"I'll see you in the morning, okay?"

"Franny, he needs his rest!" Gordon's voice suddenly called up the stairs.

"I guess that means I'm supposed to leave. You have sweet dreams, okay?"

"Okay."

When I went back downstairs Gordon and Norma were sitting in the living room with the TV on and the volume down low.

"Are you coming for breakfast?" Norma asked.

"Would it be okay? I mean, uh, do you have an extra housekey I could use? That way if I get here before you're up in the morning I won't wake anyone. I can sit in the living room and read the paper."

Nobody seemed to think that was a strange suggestion. "Sure," Gordon said, and got up to find me a key. "Michael has occupational therapy at ten tomorrow and his radiation treatment after that."

"I'll go with," I said.

"Are you going, Norma?" Gordon asked.

"It won't be necessary," she said. "There are enough people going."

I kissed each of them on the cheek and said good night.

And then, finally, when I got back to my room at the Ramada, I let myself cry.

❧ *Chapter 32* ❧

I was up at six and sneaking into the Wedlan house like a crook by six forty-five. The house seemed eerily peaceful for a place mired in subliminal turmoil.

I crept up the stairs hoping they weren't the kind of stairs that creak. Both bedroom doors were open, with only the narrow hallway and bathroom between them. A small table had been placed at the top of the stairs in case Michael woke up and wandered his way to the bathroom in the middle of the night and lost his balance. He was still sleeping, lying on his back in his father's blue pajamas, with a funny smile on his face, like he was dreaming something good. The window over the Wedlans' tiny patio was open; I heard a bird chirping and a car driving down the back alley. I sat in a chair at the foot of the bed and watched Michael sleep. I heard footsteps shuffling in the hallway and caught a glimpse of Gordon heading into the bathroom, but it sounded like he went back to bed afterward. Gordon had to be tired. Michael's pill schedule required Gordon to set an alarm clock for four o'clock every morning, so that he could wake up on time and give his son a glass of water and a pill.

A dog was barking outside in that pleasant early-morning kind of way. Michael's eyes opened and flickered with a touch of confusion as he seemed to refocus on where he was. The goofy sweet smile on his face disappeared, and then, trying to keep my voice as low as possible, I said, "Good morning," and he looked over at me and smiled again. He would have been seeing four images of me, so it's a good thing he was glad to see me.

"Good morning," he said.

I moved out of the chair and around the side of Michael's bed and leaned over and kissed him. He held his hand out and I took it.

"Did you sleep well?" I asked.

"Yes, thank you."

"Would it be okay if I lie down with you?"

"I would like that."

So, lying down on top of the covers, next to Michael, I held him in my arms.

"You feel good," I said.

"So do you."

"Did you have good dreams?"

Michael frowned. "I don't remember."

"Well, you were smiling like you were!" I laughed.

"I was?" He looked pleased.

"Uh-huh. Like it must have been something sexy."

I could see Michael's leg start trembling under the covers, just slightly, but it was definitely shaking.

"You're lucky," I said. "You've always been a good sleeper. I have trouble sleeping at night."

Michael responded like I'd just told him the most tragic news possible. "Oh! That's so unfair! People should be able to sleep."

"It's okay. I'm glad I got up early. I was able to come see you earlier."

"Have you been here a long time?"

"Not too long. But I was watching you, waiting for you to wake up so I could kiss you." I kissed him and he kissed me back. His kiss was tenuous, like he was fifteen years old and kissing a girl for the first time, but he smiled afterward. "Would you like to hold my breast?" I whispered.

"Really?" Michael said, like he was about to have an entirely new experience.

I wanted to draw him away from all thoughts about death. I wanted him to feel like a normal, healthy, fully alive man. I listened to make sure there were no footsteps in the hallway, then pulled up my T-shirt and placed Michael's hand on top of my bra. "Does that feel good?" I asked, grinning at Michael. "I think it feels good."

"You gave me back my sex!" he said, with heartfelt delight.

"Oh, I wish I could make love to you right this second," I whispered.

I heard footsteps shuffling in the hallway again, and taking Michael's hand away in mine, I pulled my top back down. Gordon walked into the bedroom, not acknowledging Michael and I lying on the bed, no doubt embarrassed by Michael and I lying on the bed, and went through what must have been his regular routine, closing the window, opening some drawers and the closet to select some clothes for Michael. I felt kind of funny myself, lying there with Michael's dad walking around, but I told myself that Michael liked having me next to him and what he wanted was what counted. Gordon finally left the room and Michael looked at me, all four of me, and said, "I don't want to die."

"It's okay," I told him. "You'll be okay. You'll still be somewhere. And I know you'll give me a sign you're okay. It'll be okay." Words just came out. Words that were trying to be comforting. Words I also needed to hear.

Gordon walked back into the room carrying a glass of water and a handful of pills. He was dressed now in brown pants and a green knit short-sleeved shirt.

"It's time for your medicine, young man!," he announced. "And time to get up. You have to have breakfast, and we have occupational therapy and your radiation this morning."

Michael sat up and took the pills from his father and gulped them down with no complaint. I sat up and straightened my shirt.

"Would you like to wear these pants today?" Gordon asked, holding up some gray slacks. "I'm afraid they might be a little warm, but you've worn the seersucker pants several days now. It'll be better when some of your cooler things arrive from Portland."

"Does he have any shorts?" I asked, slipping into that talking-about-Michael-in-third-person mode.

"No. He could use some," Gordon said.

"Those will be fine," Michael said, steadying himself against the footboard of the bed as he stood up.

"Do you have to go to the bathroom?" Gordon asked.

"Yes."

I heard Norma going down the stairs.

The two men worked their way to the bathroom, Michael holding his elbows out to balance himself. I supposed I could have gone downstairs to help Norma set the table for breakfast, but I wanted to wait for Michael. So I made his bed. At least I could make the bed. It was hard to come up with things to do for him.

Michael sat on the chair at the foot of the bed while he dressed. I sat on the bed and watched his father helping him. Michael seemed momentarily confused by the buttons on his cotton shirt but slowly, cautiously, was able to button them. He pulled the gray slacks over his skinny legs, needing help from his father to stand and pull them over his butt. He fastened his belt on the very last hole, pulling in the waistband of the pants to hold them up. He pulled on his socks but then hesitated with the laces on his gym shoes, like he was trying to remember just what it was he was supposed to do.

"Do you need help with those?" Gordon asked.

"No," Michael said, then tied his laces and held out his hand for his eyepatch and his glasses.

I heard Norma opening and closing the front door, probably to check for the newspaper.

"Are you ready?" Gordon asked his son.

"Yes."

Gordon walked one step ahead of Michael down the stairs so Michael wouldn't be afraid of falling as he worked his way down, putting his right foot on a step and then his left foot on the same step, regaining his balance, and then aiming for the next step.

"I'm right here behind you," I said. "We've got you covered on both ends."

"Thank you," Michael said.

"Good morning, handsome!" Norma said to her son as we entered the kitchen. "We have sliced peaches today! And cornflakes and toast."

There was a small table pushed against the kitchen window. Michael and I sat next to each other, with Gordon on Michael's other side and Norma on mine.

"How was your hotel last night?" she asked me.

"Fine."

"We had our Ladies of the Church luncheon there last May. It was very nice except the rolls were stale. Michael, do you want some milk?"

"No, thank you." He stared at his silverware, his eyes shifting from the spoon to the fork, and then picked up the fork and dunked it in his cereal bowl.

"No," Norma said, "the other one."

Michael put down the fork and Gordon handed him the spoon.

"I thought I'd make Cheese Dreams for lunch," Norma said. "Michael likes them. When he was home here for his vacation he ate Cheese Dreams several times."

Norma chattered away while Michael ate in silence and Gordon gave polite answers to his wife's questions. We'll be back about noon. I could eat two Cheese Dreams. Do you need me to stop and pick up more milk?

I reached under the table and squeezed Michael's leg, but I was sitting on his side with the eyepatch, so I don't know if he knew what I was doing. Hopefully, he didn't think his mother was squeezing his thigh. His leg was shaking. He was so passive. There was no fight in him. No I'm-gonna-fight-this. He was just letting things happen to him.

"You need a napkin," his mother said, reaching across me and wiping some milk off Michael's chin.

Gordon drove. Michael sat in front. I rode in the backseat sitting behind Michael with a bird's-eye view of his scar. It was hard to believe that raw red slice down the back of his head had been done in the interests of good health.

Gordon pointed out highlights as we drove to St. John's Hospital: the restoration on Abraham Lincoln's home, and the new visitor's center.

"What's that pretty white building with the columns?" I asked.

Michael and Gordon both turned their heads to the right as we passed the sign in front of the pretty white building with the columns: BISCH'S FUNERAL HOME.

"Oh," I said, cringing inside. I hoped Michael hadn't read it. But I couldn't tell. He didn't say anything.

Michael and Gordon turned their heads toward the front.

"Since you're here," Gordon said, "maybe you could wait

for Michael while he's in occupational therapy while I run some errands. Then I'll meet you back at radiation."

"Fine. No problem," I said.

The hospital was gigantic, yellow brick, an entire-block monster with wing after tacked on wing, and more construction going on. I couldn't imagine there could be enough sick people in Springfield to fill up such a thing. Gordon pulled into a driveway marked OUTPATIENT, shifted the car into park, and said, "Wait here," to us, then quickly returned pushing a wheelchair.

I scampered out of the car and stood with Gordon while Michael slid from the car seat to the seat of the wheelchair.

"It's too long a walk for him," Gordon explained to me. Michael didn't question not being allowed to walk.

St. John's Hospital was decorated in Early Hospital: pea green and beige cinderblock walls; a dark-green-and-black checked linoleum floor.

"I'll show you where we're going, and then tomorrow you can find it yourself," Gordon said to me. "To the left is the radiation department. That's where you'll come back to after the occupational therapy. But first we have to go upstairs on the elevator." Gordon pushed the wheelchair. I held on to one of Michael's hands. He looked embarrassed being wheeled around, but he didn't complain.

The waiting area for occupational therapy had a ring of orange vinyl chairs along the walls and two brown Formica end tables with ratty magazines piled on top. Gordon walked over to a reception window and gave the blond lady sitting behind it Michael's name.

A pretty girl in a blue smock appeared and said, "Hello, Michael, how are you today?"

"Fine, thank you."

"And how are you?" she asked Gordon. Then she smiled at me and told me her name was Gail.

Gordon introduced me. Sort of. "Yes, this is, uh, Michael's, uh, this is, uh, Franny."

"Hello, Franny," Gail said. I wondered why girls who worked in hospitals always looked so sweet and pretty. I figured it must come from working in a job where everyone goes around doing-good all day. "We can leave the wheelchair out here," Gail said to Michael, offering her hand to help steady him as he stood up. "We'll be done in about a half-hour," she told Gordon and me. Then Gordon left, after telling me again that he'd meet me in radiation. I sat down on one of the orange vinyl chairs and picked up an old *Redbook* magazine.

I looked up and saw Michael being walked down the hallway with Gail and some other young girl on either side of him. A white leash was strapped around him and Gail was holding the leash. I waved from the waiting room. He smiled at me, a pained, mortified smile. When they were out of my sight again, I tried another magazine. Eventually, Gail came walking out with Michael. He was no longer on the leash.

"We'll see you tomorrow." She smiled as she helped him into his wheelchair.

I wanted to take her by the shoulders and stare her in the eye and say, "Listen! I want you to know something! This isn't just some skinny scrawny dying man in dumb clothes you're working with! He's charming and kind and thoughtful and sexy, only you just can't tell that now because he's sick. He's usually not like this. Two months ago you'd have been thrilled to death if he asked you out on a date. Don't think of him as someone you can walk around on a leash." But instead I just said, "Thank you, Gail. See you tomorrow," and I wheeled Michael off.

"I bet you hated that," I said to him.

"I don't think it's doing any good," he said, as we entered the elevator.

Back on the main floor, I pushed Michael's chair through the double doors under the sign that said RADIATION DEPT. and signed him in at the reception window the way Gordon had instructed. I pushed his wheelchair next to a green chair and sat down alongside a table filled with pamphlets with titles like, "Learning to Live with Cancer," and, "One Day at a Time." A man wearing a stocking cap was sitting across from us and blowing his nose. A pale woman next to him was biting her fingernails. On the wall was taped a Crayola drawing on thick white construction paper with daisies and a round yellow sun and a big tree. "Thank you Dr. Callahan for making me better." And along the bottom, "Love, Bonnie Brickman."

Lucky Bonnie Brickman.

Someone called a name and the man in the cap left.

"Will it hurt?" I asked Michael.

"No. You can't even feel it." We were holding hands. "It just makes me tired. And fries my brains. I forget things. You should hear the noise it makes when it goes."

Someone called another name and the nailbiter left. I felt like we were in a beauty parlor waiting for our turn with the shampoo girl.

"How long's it take?" I asked.

"Not long. Not more than a few minutes."

He was quieter than he'd been the day before. More distant.

Michael's name was called and a young man who introduced himself as Alan, who had the same good-person persona as Gail in occupational therapy, wheeled Michael away.

I tried to picture what Alan was doing to Michael. I knew the red marks on the sides of Michael's head were where they aimed the radiation. But how did they aim it? Was it like having your teeth x-rayed at the dentist's?

Gordon scurried into the waiting room.

"Is he in there?" he asked.

Of course he's in there, I wanted to say. He's not off bowling. But, "Yes," I said. "They just took him." Gordon sat down in a chair next to mine. I wondered if I was going to get a lecture now, some you-abandoned-our-son lecture. Instead, Gordon looked at me. I looked at Gordon. And all of a sudden we were just holding each other, in an awkward half-twisted-around hug, and Gordon was softly crying. After a few moments he sat back and said, his composure snapping into place, "He seems to be enjoying your visit."

"Good. I'm glad."

"When he was in the intensive care unit, he talked about you. It was something painful. He talked about being cruel to you."

"*Cruel* to me? Michael was never cruel to me."

"That's what he said. He wasn't even conscious."

"That doesn't make sense."

Gordon shrugged. "He'll have radiation treatments five days a week for seven weeks. After that they'll do another CAT scan to see if it did any good."

"And if it's working they'll do more?" I asked, my voice filled with hope.

"No," Gordon said. "They can't. Any more would start killing the healthy brain tissue."

"Oh."

"He wants to go back to Portland to see his friends. If he's well enough to go, I told him I'd take him there in October. But we'll see. You need to know exactly what's happening to Michael. And how serious this is."

"I know it's serious."

"You mustn't waste any energy on hope."

"Huh?"

"When Dr. Heydon, his doctor in Portland, first opened Michael up, he said it would be less than a month."

"What would?"

"Before he died." Gordon wasn't looking at me while he spoke. He was looking at his hands. "But with the radiation, he could have three or four—possibly several—good months. With a quality of life that could be worthwhile. Maybe even a year. Almost a year. But probably less than a year. Michael's been told this. He understands it. And he accepts it. And you must accept it also."

"How can they guess things like that?" I demanded. "Less than a month?! Less than a year?! It's already a month! They were wrong. They can't be right about these things!"

"They're doctors," Gordon said, staring at me now.

"But they're not Gods."

"They *know*, Franny. And you're doing both you and Michael a disservice if you try and kid yourself."

"So you don't want him to have any hope?" I said, the words coming out in a whine.

"There's always hope," Gordon said. "You can always pray for a miracle. But in Michael's case there's no point to it. He'll probably end up with symptoms similar to an Alzheimer's patient. More and more confused and forgetful. It's different in each case. Right now he gets flustered by which utensil to use to feed himself, but he has no trouble with his razor or toothbrush. It's funny the things that stick." I didn't understand how Gordon could keep talking and be so calm. "We don't know about his vision," he added. "The double vision in each eye could better itself with the radiation. We don't know if it's caused by the tumor or by the biopsy. And some things could be a reaction to the radiation."

"Wait—what could the biopsy cause?"

"They can't just cut out this type of tumor. When they tried to get at it, some healthy brain tissue was snipped off. That might be where the vision problems are coming from."

"So he was better off *before* the biopsy? How could they screw up like that?"

"Dr. Heydon is one of the finest neurologists in Portland," Gordon said. He was not about to question Michael's doctor. "We expect Michael will eventually go blind. He'll be unable to walk or feed himself, or control his body functions."

"No," I said. "No." I was listening to Gordon but I wasn't really hearing him. The things he was telling me couldn't happen to Michael.

"Unfortunately," Gordon said, not missing a beat, "the rest of him is in excellent physical condition, and his strong heart could keep his body alive long past his brain stops functioning."

I buried my head in the palms of my hands. My head felt so heavy.

"How will Michael die?" I asked, looking up, not wanting to hear the answer. "What will finally kill him?"

Gordon answered in a very controlled voice; his carriage was stoic and somehow graceful. "The pressure from the tumor will probably cut off a major artery. Or one of Michael's body functions will fail and he'll stop breathing or have a heart attack. It shouldn't be painful. Not like a bone cancer or a liver cancer. There are no nerve endings in brain tissue. The headaches may increase, but by then he hopefully won't be aware of what's happening to him." Not painful? What could be more painful than knowing you're going to go insane? "There's nothing anyone could have done. Dr. Heydon said the tumor's probably been growing there for twenty years."

"*Twenty years?* That was all the time we were married! That was when we were in college. That was back to the year Michael was in Vietnam." I stopped to think. "How could we not know?"

"We just have to be strong for his sake." Gordon looked me straight in the eye. "And not show our emotions for his sake."

We all had to pretend that nothing was wrong.

❧ *Chapter 33* ❧

Tuesday morning a different Michael woke up. I was waiting for him, sitting in the bedroom chair. He smiled over at me, then abruptly held his hand to his head.

"Oh," he said, "something's wrong." Like he was surprised.

Gordon supplied the pills and the glass of water, but Michael just lay there on top of the covers, his whole body shaking with terror. "I don't know what's wrong with me. I don't know why I'm so scared. Why am I being such a baby? The only thing wrong with me is a headache."

"Well, it's a little more serious than that," Gordon said, hovering over his son's bed. Michael was mad at himself and kept berating himself; he thought he was ridiculous and kept insisting it was stupid of him to be so upset over a little headache.

I'd seen his capacity for denial in the past, but now, watching Michael shake and tremble and be so determined that nothing was wrong, unnerved me. I realized just what he could do to protect himself from an unacceptable truth.

At the hospital that morning; Gail and the other lady in

occupational therapy who walked Michael around on the leash, asked him who the nice girl was with him, and he couldn't remember my name.

Later, Gordon sat at the kitchen table with a list of phone numbers trying to find a therapist to help Michael, but the few names he had for people who specialized in "terminal illnesses" were all out of town or unreachable. After lunch Michael sat in the middle of the living-room couch, scared and shaking, repeating, "I must have done something very bad. I must have made a terrible mistake." Norma was in the kitchen. Gordon was in the basement working at his desk on some bookkeeping for the church. I was sitting on the floor at Michael's feet. He wouldn't let me hold him or touch him.

"No, you've never been bad. It's not you," I pleaded. "You were sprayed. There were chemicals. It wasn't your fault."

Michael looked at me quizzically.

"It was Vietnam. It wasn't you." I was trying to push the right button, trying to come up with the right thing to say to help him feel better. It had to be the Agent Orange, I told him; that must have been the reason; there *had* to be a reason. At first Michael seemed fascinated with the possibility, and then he dismissed it. What difference did it make, if nobody could fix the problem?

"I must be very bad," he said. "I want to get it over with. I want to lie down and die now."

I tried another tack. "Okay, go upstairs and die."

He started shaking more, his bony shoulders bouncing up and down. "I can't," he said. "I'm too scared. I'm just a big baby."

"No. You aren't. The part you think's the scaredycat part is your survival part. It won't let you go and die."

He liked that. He liked hearing there was a part of him

protecting him. Words kept pouring out of my mouth. They were all hit and miss. Some made him mad. Some seemed to work.

"Do you have to die today?" I asked.

"No."

"Good. Then can we just concentrate on today?" I was asking him to do something I couldn't do myself.

"Okay," Michael said. "That's a good plan."

Norma walked into the living room and checked the *TV Guide* for the starting time of her Cubs game. Michael napped.

We walked after dinner. The two of us. Michael seemed steadier, a little surer of his step. Just moving seemed to keep him going, as if he kept walking, he couldn't be ready to die. He was mad at his mother and mad at himself for feeling mad at someone who was trying so hard to feed him and please him and take care of him.

"All she worries about is silly things!" he'd say, and then immediately follow it with, "I'm so bad. I'm so ungrateful."

"Try to understand her," I said, even though *I* couldn't understand her. "She's just like that."

"But she won't talk about anything important!" Michael blurted. Then just as quickly said, "I don't deserve anyone. I'm no good."

"Do you want to keep walking?"

"I *have* to keep walking."

We stopped at the corner at the end of his block. Gordon was standing in the middle of the sidewalk in front of the townhouse searching for us. The patrol forces were out. Gordon started walking down the block toward us but we kept standing, holding on to each other.

"I don't want to lose you again," Michael said to me.

"You won't," I told him. "You can't. Dying is the only way you could get rid of me."

We started to kiss, but Gordon was standing there insisting it was time to go home.

I sat with Norma while Gordon helped Michael take his bath. "He's very tired tonight," she said. "More tired than he should be. You shouldn't have taken that walk."

I was allowed to go up to Michael's bedroom to say good night.

"Thank you for today," I told Michael. I leaned over to kiss him just as Gordon called from downstairs, "He needs his sleep!"

I was told not to come so early in the morning. "He used to sleep until eight," Norma said.

"I haven't woken him. I've waited in the chair," I said.

"He doesn't want you here so early," Gordon said.

By the time I arrived the next morning, Norma was in the kitchen making toast. When I headed upstairs she grumbled and muttered to convey her displeasure, but she didn't ask me to wait downstairs.

I stood in the bathroom door and half-waved at Michael and his father but there was some sort of confusion going on. Michael didn't seem to know what he should be doing. He had a hard time shaving. He couldn't remember which way to turn the razor. And he had a harder time walking.

We shouldn't have taken that long walk last night. I wore him out. I was afraid it was my fault. And I was afraid Gordon thought so too. His greeting to me was less than warm. "Get his socks," he said.

Michael sat at the breakfast table staring at his food. I couldn't tell if it was because he didn't know what to do with it or if he just didn't want it. The seating arrangements had been changed. "It's too crowded in here with a fourth chair," Norma informed me. I now sat on a stool by the window, with Norma anchored between Michael and me. He wanted to die again. He wanted to give up.

"I have nothing anymore," he said, "nothing of my own. No job. No wife. No home." His eyes flooded with grief. "No time."

The hospital coughed up a social worker who was willing to talk to Michael even though she really didn't work much with "people like Michael." I hated her on sight. She was a fat girl named Lucinda. She talked to him in a little room off the waiting section of the radiation department. The door was open a crack and Gordon and I hovered outside it in the hallway. Gordon's eavesdropping was discreet. Mine was more overt. "So you have this serious illness, huh?" I heard Lucinda say. I couldn't hear Michael's response. "And so they've, uh, told you you're gonna die, huh?" I heard Lucinda say. I couldn't hear Michael's response. "Well, uh, how long did you, uh, think you were going to live?" I heard Lucinda say.

"Did you *hear* that?" I hissed to Gordon. "She's an idiot. We have to get Michael out of there."

"She's a professional," Gordon hissed back.

Michael returned from Lucinda's charge even more suicidal than he'd been before. I could have pulverized Lucinda and all of her fat into the ground.

At home Michael threw up in the bathroom. He couldn't eat. And he wouldn't sleep. He was sitting on the beige upholstered chair in front of the living room picture window, and I was sitting on the beige footstool next to him. Michael would start nodding off, then he'd pull up his head and open his eyes. He obviously wanted to sleep, but he was fighting it off.

"Michael?"

"Yes."

"Michael, are you tired?"

"Yes."

I took a deep breath. "Are you afraid if you go to sleep you'll die?"

"Yes."

"Well, you won't. You're just sleepy now. But you won't die if you take a nap."

"Thank you," he said. "I think I'll lie down now."

❦ *Chapter 34* ❦

There aren't a lot of places to go in Springfield when you're up early and anxious to go to the place you really want to go but you can't go there yet and you're too crazed to pace around a hotel room.

Friday morning I walked up and down the aisles of a twenty-four-hour grocery store. One of those endless food and florist and video and lawn furniture and deli type stores. In the card and gift section I bought Michael a small stuffed red satin heart. In the paperback books section, I bought a book filled with pictures of pills and descriptions of pills and long paragraphs relaying all the terrible things that could go wrong if you swallowed any of the pills. Michael was taking so much medicine, and was so tired and nauseated all the time, I thought, maybe it's because of all those pills. In the bakery section I bought two custard-filled chocolate-covered donuts, which I ate for breakfast standing up in the parking lot before showing up at the Wedlans' house at what I hoped was the respectable time of 9:05. When I arrived, Michael was sitting at the breakfast table with his parents on either side of him, refusing to eat the smallest, tiniest, most incredibly pathetic scrambled egg.

"He couldn't shave himself this morning," Norma told me, talking about Michael in the third person again. "His father had to shave him."

"He needs food. We have to get food into him," Gordon said.

"Is there anything else you want, honey?" I asked Michael, trying to help.

"I want to die," he said.

"How about some cream of wheat?" Norma asked.

Gordon canceled the occupational therapy session, grateful that Michael made it through his radiation treatment. When we got home, he was too tired to climb back up the stairs to sleep. Norma spread some green sheets over the couch, muttering something about an extra load of laundry, and Michael stretched out with his head on one of her green and beige needlepointed pillows. "I'm sorry," he said. I didn't know why he was sorry, but I told him he shouldn't be. Then he slept.

I sat on the floor right next to him, reading my pill book. Gordon sat in the upholstered chair reading the newspaper. Norma left the room to make Jell-O. I heard the radio snap on in the kitchen: a Cubs game. Every few minutes I'd catch Gordon peering over the top of his paper, scrutinizing me, probably to make sure I wasn't crawling on top of Michael and having sex. I found a way to be helpful. "Look," I semisaid, semiwhispered, getting up and going over to Gordon to show him a page in my book. "That medicine Michael's taking, the white one with the red stripe, should be taken with food to avoid nausea!'' I was really proud of myself. Until Gordon snapped at me.

"You think you know as much or more than the doctors, don't you?''

"No, I don't!'' My voice faltered like a hurt child's. "But I think it's important to have all the information you can.''

Michael spoke up from the sofa. I don't know if we woke him or if he'd been half-awake all the time, but there he was, jumping to my defense. "That's rather harsh on Franny,'' he said. "I don't think that's true.''

Gordon read the pill book while I sat by Michael, holding his hand, watching him sleep. I had to keep my back turned and my volume turned low, like one of Norma's Cubs games. I didn't want Gordon to know I was crying. He was sitting there saying things like, "There's the little baby I take!'' and "It's amazing how many of these little fellas give you constipation.''

Norma stood in the doorway of the kitchen, displaying emotion. "Andre Dawson and Mumphrey both hit home runs!'' Then she went back to her Jell-O. The phone rang in the kitchen, and after a short conversation Norma appeared in the doorway again. "Wes is coming over at three after he's done coaching.'' Then she returned to her Jell-O.

Michael had no interest in the pea stew Norma offered him for lunch. He was depressed. Then he was embarrassed that he was depressed. Then he wanted to die and didn't care that he was depressed. He was tired but wouldn't let himself sleep. He was constantly concerned that he was sleeping too much.

When Wes showed up, I kissed him hello. It had been a long time since we'd seen each other.

He was the first person who seemed to know what to say to Michael. Fifteen years of talking to high school students had trained him well.

Mainly what Wes did was not say anything. He just let Michael talk, unlike me, who had a hard time shutting up, who was always trying to fill any void with chatter.

"I can't snap out of it," Michael said. "I know I'm going to die. I know I'm letting down my friends and my parents and being cruel—"

"Cruel?" Wes said.

"Because I want to give up," Michael said.

"Oh, honey, you aren't being cruel," I blurted. "You're wonderful! You're trying. You're never cruel to us. Please don't give up. You can't give up." Chatter. Chatter. Chatter. Wes looked at me. Michael looked at me. And smiled. I smiled back. Then he looked angry.

"Why are you smiling?" he asked.

I quit smiling. And I shut up.

One minute Michael was mad at me. One minute he was oblivious of me. Then the next minute he was telling me he'd be lost without me. It was a lot like our marriage, only condensed into one hellish week on wheels.

"No one's asking you to snap out of it," Wes said to Michael. "If you need to feel bad, go ahead and feel bad."

Then Michael talked about how bad he felt. I wished I were as smart as Wes. I walked with Wes out to his car and told him how glad I was to see him. He told me he'd be back the next day with Clifford.

"Has Benny been around? Has anyone told Benny?" I asked.

"He knows." Wes opened his car door. "He's just not ready to come here yet."

Michael ate grapes and rice for dinner. Gordon picked the grapes off the stem. "He doesn't like when you do that!" Norma admonished her husband.

"Oh, I'm sorry. I'm so sorry," Michael said. "I didn't mean to complain."

After dinner the two of us sat in the living room alone, Michael on the upholstered chair, me on the footstool. I felt like we were getting away with something. We'd had so little time alone.

"What day is it?" Michael asked.

"Friday night."

"You'll be going soon?"

"Yes. But I'll be back."

"I don't want you to go."

"I know. But I think your folks need a break from me." Michael nodded. He understood.

"I'll be back," I said.

Then Michael seemed to drift off, back into his depression. "I'm going to die," he said.

A little while later, Gordon and Norma came in. We were like three court jesters, each trying to say whatever we could to perk Michael up. Gordon immediately motioned me to go sit in the winged chair on the opposite side of the room from Michael.

"You don't have to be scared," Gordon said, standing over Michael with a hand resting on each of Michael's shoulders. At first I couldn't tell if he was trying to comfort Michael or shake him. "We all have to die. I'm eighty-two years old. I'm going to die. Dr. Heydon explained to you that with the radiation treatments you can still have several good months." I winced at the word *months*. I couldn't see Michael's face. "You have a choice to make—to die well, or to do it badly. It's the choice between dying with grace and dignity, or spending what time you have feeling bitter and angry. Your mother and I are both very proud of you. And we'll do everything we can to help you and make you comfortable."

"Do you want some Jell-O?" Norma asked.

I told Michael I'd come up to kiss him good night after

his bath. I was trying my best to follow the new rules. Gordon helped him up the stairs.

So then it was just Norma and me. A couple of soul sisters. I opted for a safe subject.

"You've certainly gotten far on your knitting!" I said, trying to sound pleasantly impressed.

"Of course!" she said, spitting her words at me. "Otherwise I'd go *batty* around here."

I opted for patience and understanding.

"It's hard for you, I'm sure. Are you okay?"

"Of course I'm okay!" Norma said, as if I had just asked her a very stupid question. We heard a loud thump over our heads. It sounded like Michael had slipped in the tub. Norma didn't miss a stitch. She was talking about how they'd had to drop out of all their bridge clubs to take care of Michael. Her resentment was palpable. Something dropped over head. My guess was a bar of soap.

"Goddammit!" Michael yelled out.

Norma's shoulders hunched together and her face tightened with disgust. "He doesn't have to swear," she muttered.

"It's good for him to let out something. He has so much pent up."

"There are other ways to express yourself!" The knitting needles were really flying now. "He wasn't raised like that."

"He's never had cancer before!"

"Well, he's always done it!"

I opted for changing the subject.

"It was nice to see Wes," I said.

"Yes," Norma said. "I, of course, stayed out of the room so they could talk alone."

I wasn't going to let that one pass. "Are you trying to tell me I shouldn't have stayed in the room? If you are, you can be more direct."

"I'm not saying that. I just thought you *would* stay out."

Innuendos were running rampant.

"Well, I'm glad I stayed in there. Wes knows how to talk to Michael." I heard Michael's footsteps shuffling toward the bedroom.

"I'm waiting until Michael *needs* to talk," Norma said. "I don't want to say the wrong thing. Michael's very smart. He know's what's happening." Her eyes scrunched into two angry little slits as she looked at me. "And he doesn't need someone to try to smooth things over."

"Maybe I should go upstairs and say good night," I said, trying to smile through my clenched teeth. I didn't want Gordon to come downstairs to discover his wife and former daughter-in-law clawing at each other's eyeballs. No matter how angry Norma made me, no matter how much I wanted to bind her to a chair and unravel each and every one of her crazy lap robes stitch by stitch in front of her eyes, I couldn't risk the army guards putting down the clamp on my seeing Michael. I hated being nice in a world that didn't deserve it.

I passed Gordon on my way up the stairs.

"Don't linger," he said.

The stuffed heart I'd brought in the morning was no longer hanging on Michael's bedpost. I asked him if someone had taken it away, but he didn't know what I was talking about. I leaned over to kiss him. "I love you."

"I love you, too," he said, with the innocence of a sweet little boy. His fingers were wrapped around the top of his covers. "I'm just sorry we won't have time to try again."

I smiled at him. "I'll see you in the morning." Then I added, "I'm sure you'll be here."

"I've decided to leave a day early."

Michael was sleeping late in honor of not having a radiation treatment on Saturday. I made my announcement to his parents at the breakfast table.

"Today?" Norma said, politely mocking disappointment and dismay.

"I'd just like to have a few minutes alone with Michael to tell him."

"Well, he'll be down soon," she stated. So much for hoping I could go up to his bedroom and talk to him in private.

We ended up in formation B again. Michael lying on the living-room couch, me sitting on the floor by his side, Gordon looming over us reading the newspaper in the upholstered chair, and Norma in the kitchen. Michael and I spoke to each other in half-whispers, but I could just bet Gordon was listening from behind his sports page.

"I'll call you. And you can have your dad get me on the phone. I'll be back next Friday. Can you wait for me until next Friday?"

"I'll try," Michael said.

I put my arm around him in the best hug I could muster and kissed him on the lips. I heard the rustle of a newspaper and then Gordon barked, "Franny! Don't smother him! The poor boy's defenses are down!"

"I'm saying goodbye!" I told Gordon. That must have been acceptable news, because he resumed reading his newspaper.

I kissed Michael one more time. I stuck my tongue in his mouth, which made him laugh.

❦ *Chapter 35* ❦

"What's going *on* in that house? Roy says it sounds like something out of the Bates Motel."

Wendy from Portland, Michael's nursing friend, phoned me the night after I returned to Chicago. She spoke in one long tangle of words.

"Every time we call, Mr. Wedlan gets on the telephone and says Michael's sleeping or tired or too depressed and doesn't want to talk. We write letters but we don't know if they're read to him. We want to fly out there, Roy and I, so we can see Michael, but we can't even talk to him to find out what he wants."

"Michael's parents think too much emotion is bad for him," I said, trying to explain something that didn't make much sense to me. "They don't want anything to upset him."

"The man's dying. I'd call *that* upsetting!" I wondered how much Michael had told his friends about me. Wendy kept chattering like we'd been friends forever. "They cut us off in the hospital, too. They put up a No Visitors sign. But I'm a nurse at Providence, so I just ramrodded my way into Michael's room. Mr. Wedlan didn't want Michael to know that he's terminal, but of course the doctors legally had to tell him on account he's an adult, so Dr. Heydon goes into Michael's room while I'm standing outside with his parents; then Heydon comes out, and you'd think Michael's parents would go rushing on in. I mean, the poor guy had just been told he was going to *die*, right? But neither of them move. So I go running in and Michael's sitting up in bed and he's crying. It was a good ten minutes before his mother came in the room. She started bustling around, examining all the flowers people'd sent. Michael's still crying. And I say, 'Mrs. Wedlan, Michael is despondent now.' And she pauses, then says, 'Oh. Wendy, are you planning to take back this vase you brought?' Later, Mr. Wedlan and I had this horrible fight. He kept trying to give away Michael's possessions; his clothes and furniture and fishing equipment. His sister Diana and I are out there in the hospital hallway yelling at Michael's father: 'But he's not dead yet!' All the stuff finally ended up going into storage. Except for a few things his roommate Jim's still using. Mainly the TV. Have you talked to Jim lately?''

"No. I guess I should call. I'm afraid of being a pest."

"A *pest*? You're our one connection to Michael now! Are you going every weekend? Can you do that?''

"I hope I can. I want to."

"It helps knowing he'll have you there. You know, I believe minds and bodies are all connected. People can think themselves into cancer, and they can use their minds to overcome cancer." I could hear Wendy stopping to catch her breath. "Roy says that if there's one thing that can keep Michael alive, it'll be you."

"Don't be an egomaniac."

Piper was picking at my psyche again. We were shuffling our way through a waiting line at the post office. Piper was between appointments. I was on my standard two-hour lunch. The man in front of us kept heaving his shoulders, rubbing his crotch, and snorting.

"There's rarely a good reason to mingle with the public," Piper whispered to me, but loud enough for the crotch rubber to overhear and hopefully get the hint. He snorted in response.

"I thought psychologists were supposed to like people."

"I do. I love people," Piper said. "The people I already know. It's strangers I detest."

We shuffled forward one more space. A post-office lady with bad teeth and thick fingers was counting out change like she'd never seen American money before.

"If you're bored, you can go check out some of your relatives on the wanted posters," Piper suggested.

"What is this? Dump on Franny Week? You're calling me an egomaniac. You're denigrating my family tree."

"You are an egomaniac. Anyone who thinks she can give someone else cancer has a pretty hefty ego. Thinking something's your fault is a way of thinking you have some sort of *control* in the situation. Well, you're wrong. You don't." A man standing behind us chomping on a bag of taco chips nodded in interest. "If Michael won't eat, or Michael can't walk, you think it's your fault. And it has nothing to do with you." Piper pulled a thread off her I'm-a-professional suit jacket. We shuffled forward one more space, but we still had six people ahead of us.

I kept my voice low so the crotch rubber and the taco chomper wouldn't eavesdrop. "Michael loved me, and I left. And he got lonely and depressed and I wasn't *there* for him and he thought himself into cancer and sickness."

"You can't blame yourself."

"Oh yes I can. It's easy."

"You always loved him, Franny. You just didn't want to be married to him."

"Same difference," I said. "He deserved better."

"Better than you?"

"Better than anything that's ever happened to him."

"We all do," Piper said. The crotch rubber shook his head in agreement.

"I loved him and I screwed up. I didn't know the value of hanging in there! And now his parents are like these border-patrol dogs coming between us."

"Has Michael complained?"

"How can he complain? He's at their mercy."

"At their *mercy*? They're taking care of him."

"But they don't have to put up barriers against his friends," I said. "Or me."

Piper looked like she wanted to shake me by the shoulders. "When everything else is out of control, it's natural for people to control the few things they can."

"I felt so loved by him this week," I continued, talking more to myself than to Piper. "I don't remember in my entire life ever feeling so loved."

"Well, maybe he values you more now, also."

"I *hate* Christopher!" I suddenly cried. "If he were never around maybe Michael and I would have worked things out. Maybe we would have tried harder."

"Franny, you tried for ten years. It didn't work."

Piper was about to step up to the counter. The guy behind it smiled at her, then put up a sign and left for lunch.

Work was just sort of work. I could do it, but I didn't pay much attention to it. And Ned never complained. He had a cousin whose friend's mother had a brain tumor, so he said he understood. I wasn't quite sure what he understood, but I was grateful that he did.

Suddenly it seemed that everybody in the entire Milky Way galaxy had an "I knew somebody with a brain tumor" story they couldn't wait to share with me.

Nadine called me at work between breastfeedings. "I heard," she said. "It's awful. You must feel terribly guilty.

My college roommate's sister's boyfriend died from a brain tumor, but not until after he spent several months as a vegetable. I wanted to send Michael a card, but let's face it, a get-well card simply isn't appropriate for someone who's never going to get well, right?''

"Try a thinking-of-you card," I said.

"But won't he get upset that he can't think of me?''

"He thinks just fine!" I cried. "He gets a little confused, and things are a little harder for him, but he thinks just fine.'' Before hanging up I added, "And I'm sure you're all he thinks about.''

"People are maniacs. No one knows what to say or do. Nobody's had any courses in How to Talk to Dying People.'' I was blubbering to Holly while picking at the niçoise salad she'd made for dinner to cheer me up. She'd even popped for a jar of capers for authenticity.

"I baked cookies," Holly said. She looked at me with such compassion that she made me feel pathetic.

"Thank you," I said lamely. "I have to call Springfield. I figured if I call at six-thirty, maybe I can catch Michael between dinner and sleeping and actually get to talk to him. But I've been scared to call.''

"Scared of bad news?''

"No. Just generic-type scared.''

"Go ahead." Holly smiled at me with encouragement. "Use the phone in my bedroom.''

I sat on Holly's fake fur bedspread and dialed the Wedlans' number. Gordon answered.

"Wedlans," he said stiffly, like he was his own butler.

"Hi. It's Franny. How's my timing? I was hoping to catch Michael after dinner.''

"He didn't eat dinner," Gordon said, a strained angry tension woven through his words. "He's sleeping. The last two days have been *terrible*. We're at our wits' ends. He's given up. It shows in his locomotion. He didn't even go for therapy today. I told him he's got to get to that radiation tomorrow if I have to carry him there myself!'' I could picture skinny Michael being carted off in the arms of his eighty-two-year-old father.

"Should I come right down?"

"That's what the friends in Portland want to do, too."

Now I was one of the "friends."

"Well, would it help?" I implored.

"You might have been the problem!" Gordon blared at me.

"Have you *asked* him?" I said quietly.

"Not for the last two days."

"All I know is he told me he wanted me there." I sounded as desperate as Gordon did. "Can't you ask him?"

"Not tonight! There's nothing you can do for him that we haven't done already. Only professional help will help now. I'm waiting for Dr. Wynne to call back. I called first thing this morning but he hasn't returned my call yet. When the phone rang I was hoping it was him."

"I'll call tomorrow around noon and see if Michael wants me there," I said. There was nothing more to say.

The next day I picked up my office phone three times before I finally mustered the nerve to call Springfield. But it turned out to be a real waste of nerve because nobody answered. I ran through a frantic laundry list of all the possibilities and then called the hospital and asked if they had a Michael Wedlan listed. They did. No calls were being taken. But since I was his sister—as I lied—the nurse at the station on his floor told me Michael had been dehydrated but was now eating and resting much better.

I plotted my next actions. Do I call and ask Gordon and

Norma how Michael's doing? No. Too much potential hostility. Do I keep calling the nurse? No good. She might get nosy and ask *which* sister. Do I just show up uninvited? Sure. Why not? Who's going to throw me out of a hospital? But just to be extra careful and offset the possibility of my being attacked with knitting needles, I brought my parents along, which seemed like a brilliant idea except for sitting through two hundred miles of Paul singing "A Hundred Bottles of Beer on the Wall." My mother sang harmony and kept grilling me about the best restaurants in Springfield.

"We'll take his parents there and give you kids a chance to be alone," she said, always the romantic.

"Where?" I asked, from the backseat of Paul's Cadillac.

"To the best restaurant in Springfield!" my mother said.

"Oh," I said. "You mean the Steak & Shake."

Michael looked a million times better. He was sitting up in his hospital bed—no eyepatch, no eyeglasses, and his hair had been trimmed—devouring an apparently delicious meal of mystery meat parts and Brussels sprouts.

"Hello!" he said, in the very best of spirits. "I hope you don't mind if I keep eating this."

Norma was knitting in a green vinyl chair next to Michael's bed and Gordon scurried into the room about five minutes after we arrived. I tried to decipher the look on his face when he first saw me and then saw my parents. It was a combination of grim and polite and warm with a dash of what-are-you-doing-here? All the moms-and-dads adults perched in chairs. I stood next to Michael's bed and ran my hand through his hair, which turned out not to be such a hot idea because his hair ended up in my hand. "Whoa!" I said. "Instant baldness. Just add radiation."

"Yeah, they said that would happen," Michael said, popping a Brussels sprout into his mouth.

My mother chattered away like she was charming the guests at a B'nai Brith luncheon. Paul hardly said a word, which was quite a change from a guy who had been singing "Row Row Row Your Boat" in the parking lot. As my parents finally squired Gordon and Norma away for a "good meal," I saw my mother lean against Gordon and say, "You were always our favorite in-laws. The other ones are not so good." I momentarily wondered what my brother-in-law, Marty, and his mother would think about that, but I was too preoccupied to care. A frizzy-haired redheaded girl had removed Michael's food tray and then removed herself, and I finally had him all to myself!

"I'm tired," he said. "I think I better take a nap."

"Now?"

"Well, now's when I'm tired."

"Oh." We had so little time together, I hated for him to spend it sleeping. "Okay," I said. "I'll watch." So I watched him sleep. A nurse walked in and checked whatever it is nurses check and Michael kept sleeping. I kept sending subliminal brainwaves to his brainwaves. Don't keep sleeping. Wake up soon. Wake up before our parents get back.

He woke up.

"Hi!" he said, like he was surprised to see me.

I fell all over him, as much as you can fall all over anyone in a hospital bed.

"Oh, honey, are you okay? I missed you all week. I'm so glad to see you," I said, careful not to rub his hair. "I hate not being with you. All that time we were apart, when you were in Oregon and I was in Chicago, I wanted to be with you." Everything I was saying felt like the absolute truth. "I need you," I told him.

"Me, too." Michael was looking right at me with the sweetest expression. "That's why I never chose anyone else." He sat up and held one hand up to the side of his mouth like he was about to share a big secret. I leaned in closer and he lowered his voice. "But I don't think I'm going to live very long, and that's not fair to you."

I took his hand and kissed it. "I'll take whatever time we've got."

Then we had no more time alone together because Clifford showed up and started telling us gross stories from his child-abuse hotline and all about his date the night before and how it didn't work out and he was sorry about it because he'd been celibate for over a year, at which point Michael said *he'd* been celibate for almost three years, and I sat there getting depressed because that meant Michael hadn't made love since I'd been in Portland and I hated thinking of Michael not making love; I became determined that somehow or other I would make love to him, unless of course it would kill him.

Then our parents walked back into the room and there was regular chatting and about-the-restaurant chatting and good-bye-see-you-soon chatting.

It wasn't until halfway back to Chicago that I realized Gordon and I had not spoken to each other.

❧ *Chapter 36* ❧

"I know Barry's being a jerk about this, but you've got to try and understand," Susan pleaded.

She was speeding down I-55 toward Springfield, with her side window open, her long black hair pulled up into a ponytail flapping around her shoulders, and me in the "death seat."

"This ride sure is a snoozer," she said. "How do you *stand* it?"

"I drag along unsuspecting friends to keep me company." I checked my seatbelt for the umpteenth time. "Barry was one of Michael's best friends," I said. "He should be here."

"Not everyone can rally 'round the dying, Franny. Some of us get spooked."

"That's no excuse. Dwayne and Daisy, who used to be our close friends until we got divorced, never even called him or sent him a card."

"Can he even *read* a card?"

"Yes. The radiation's working. It's great! I called Portland. I wrote his sisters. You'll see."

Michael had lost some of his hair, but he wasn't bowlingball bald. His sprinkle of gray hairs had refused to fall out. If you just glanced at him in passing, you might think he was somebody's grandfather, with those just-a-few wispy gray strands of hair, but then your second thought would be: that grandfather sure has a young face. Your third thought would be: why does that grandfather have red Magic Marker arrows drawn on his head? Michael had stopped wearing his eyepatch and his glasses because he hated wearing them, but every time I asked him what his vision was like, I got a different answer. Yet he always asked me to walk on his left side so he could see me better. He could read the newspaper and was starting to read large-print books, and his walking was better. He could get up and down the stairs without climbing both-feet-on-each-step-style.

The first weekend after he got out of the hospital we had sat in the living room and watched a Cubs game with Norma. Michael seemed polite but distant, reminiscent of the Michael I once believed was bored being married to me; and he spent half an hour of my visit talking on the phone to his roommate Jim from Portland. "Oh, yes, my ex-wife is here," I heard him say into the telephone. He spoke slowly and deliberately, as if rethinking each word as he formed it. "It's a new relationship now. It's rather interesting to be starting over again." I drove home that weekend thinking maybe he didn't care if I showed up or not, but I couldn't stand the thought of him spending the rest of his life sitting with his parents in that dark living room watching baseball. And when I called Springfield during the week and was actually permitted to have a genuine conversation with him, just the two of us, with nobody breathing in on the extension, he told me he missed me; and I couldn't wait to drive through those corn-fields again. I packed a picnic. Susan volunteered to drive. And Saturday morning we were speeding toward Michael.

"Michael and you have never been able to separate from each other," Susan was saying. "Every other divorce I've seen is like somebody took an apple and sliced it in half. But with you two, it's like somebody took a piece of taffy and stretched it farther apart. But it's still attached."

As we walked up to the Wedlans' front stoop, I said, "Brace yourself. You're about to enter the Twilight Zone." I could see the back of Michael's nearly bald head above the top of the upholstered chair in the window, like he had nothing else to do than sit and wait.

Susan and I stood and waited for almost five minutes after I rang the doorbell. Michael had heaved himself up and walked to the door to answer it by himself.

"Hello!" he said, delighted. "I was hoping you'd be coming today."

"Did your parents tell you we were coming?" I asked, hugging him.

He bit his lip. "Maybe."

"Hi, stranger, remember me?" Susan asked. Michael smiled at me over Susan's shoulder while she hugged him.

"Of course I do," he said.

"Pretty wild hairdo you've got there," Susan said. "All we need to do is add an earring in one ear and you'll look like a rock star."

"Yes, it is rather strange-looking," Michael said, as Norma walked in from the kitchen.

"Here already?" she chirped. We'd caught Norma in a good mood. She kissed the air next to my cheek, shook Susan's hand, told us Gordon was at the grocery store, and said, "Were you two planning to eat lunch here? I'll have to make more food."

"Actually we've got food in the car," I told her. "We thought we'd take Michael on a picnic in the park."

"He won't like that," Norma decreed.

I turned to Michael. "Would you like to go on a picnic?"

"That would be very nice," he said.

I had gone crazy whipping together my picnic, so anxious that Michael should like what he ate and get pleasure out of it that I went on a cost-be-damned shopping spree at Gourmet to Go. The three of us sat at a wooden picnic table (after Susan spread paper towels over the bird droppings), and devoured pepper cheese bread, wild-rice-and-celery salad, cheesecake, pasta primavera vinaigrette, pasta tomato herb, flourless chocolate cake, red peppers and mushrooms, taffy apples, ratatoullie and cold barbecued chicken. I handed Michael a napkin at one point; he looked at it, seemed to think about it, then stuffed it in his pocket like a handkerchief. "Honey, do you want some of this? Honey, do you want some of that?" I kept shoving food at Michael, feeling desperate that he have fun. I saw Susan mouthing the word *relax* at me. Then I offered Michael some Godiva chocolates. His head was tilted back and he was observing the sky with a peaceful and beatific smile.

"Do you like it here?" I asked.

"Yes," he said, scanning all the trees. "There are lots of legs here."

I smiled at him. "You mean trees?"

"Yes." We were holding hands. Susan was picking at red peppers.

"Well, you're right. They do look like legs." Michael's word associations might come out twisted, but there was always a logic to them.

Susan told Barry stories: Barry burping in the movies; Barry getting drunk and throwing up at a wedding; Barry sticking straws in his nostrils. Michael laughed, but never asked why Barry hadn't called or come to Springfield.

"Do you want the leftovers?" I asked Norma when we returned.

"My refrigerator's overcrowded as it is," she sputtered. "But you can try to make some room."

I headed toward the kitchen with Gordon hot on my heels.

"We need to talk," he said, opening the back door and gesturing me out to the patio. I had a vague impression that I was in hot water. I jammed four plastic containers and a slice of cheesecake into the refrigerator, then followed Gordon outside. I could hear Norma entertaining Michael and Susan with the play-by-play of the first four innings of the Cubs game. Gordon and I sat down at the umbrella table. Then he started in on me. "Young lady, you are not maintaining a realistic sense of reality."

I responded with eloquence. *"Huh?"*

Gordon smoothed his hand over the top of his white hair. "You wrote a letter to Judith this week which sounded completely unrealistic regarding your hopes for Michael. All that business about hoping for a miracle."

"She read you my letter?"

"Yes. She's concerned with your foolish thinking. Michael is going to die. He knows he's going to die. And he accepts it."

"We don't know that. No one ever talks about it around here."

Gordon continued without missing a beat. "Your visits are confusing him. He doesn't understand why after all this time you're showing up so often."

"If it were the other way around, he'd be there for me."

Gordon looked at me with all the warmth he'd convey to a survey taker who knocked on the door at dinnertime. "You're certainly free to think what you want, but do you really believe he'd be there in Chicago all the way from Portland?"

"Yes, I do." I could see it. Michael sitting next to my bed in a hospital room, looking strong and capable, trying to keep my spirits up. "He doesn't seem confused," I added. "He seems glad to see me."

"Well, don't go thinking you're anything special to him. You're no more important than those other friends in Portland. He lumps you all in the same egg basket. And don't go creating fantasies about the outcome of his illness."

"There's nothing wrong with hoping for a miracle," I said, scraping back my chair and heading into the house.

"See!" Norma was saying, "Davis tagged him out at the plate!"

"We better get going," I said.

"So soon?" Norma looked genuinely sorry.

Michael stood up, holding his arms out to the side for balance, then wrapped those skinny arms around me, and we kissed goodbye.

"What was the big talk on the patio about?" Susan asked when we were out the front door.

"Nothing," I said. "Gordon told me Michael doesn't understand what I'm doing here."

❧ *Chapter 37* ❧

"Hello? Jim? Do you remember me? Michael's—This is Franny." I had called Michael's Portland roommate determined to put together the missing pieces of the puzzle.

"Oh! How is he?" Jim asked. "Did you see him this weekend? Wendy said she's talked to you. That you go all the time."

"Well, I skipped this past weekend, but I'll definitely be down there this Saturday." My voice took on a heightened urgency. "Jim, I need to ask you a few questions. Before things changed . . . you know, were there any *signs*? Any clues? I keep thinking that if the doctors are correct, and he had this *thing* growing in his head for twenty years, there should have been signals; I must have been missing signs when we were married, but I can't remember any. He'd been exposed to Agent Orange in Vietnam—we knew that—but he seemed fine."

"Franny, we roomed together, but we didn't spend much time together, so I can't say I know Michael particularly well. Or that I've known him long. Less than a year, in fact. I couldn't tell you what was *normal* behavior for him versus what constituted a personality change, but as I think back, there were some odd occurrences.

"When he got back from Springfield after visiting his folks

in June, right before this happened, he was laid up with a hideous case of poison ivy, followed by several days of nausea and bad headaches. He assumed the symptoms were from the poison ivy. But maybe not. And another time, he was supposed to pick me up at the airport. Everything was all arranged; he had the flight number and arrival time. After hanging around the airport almost an hour, I gave up on him and took a cab. He told me he'd forgotten. He'd simply spaced out. I also remember Roy complaining a few times about Michael forgetting little things at work. And one night Michael came home all excited about a fruit stand he'd discovered. He lugged in bags and bags of oranges and apples and berries—more than anyone could possibly eat. I couldn't understand why he did it, but he didn't seem to think anything was strange about it. And a couple days before anything really happened—before the hospital—I woke up in the middle of the night and I heard this funny shuffling sound, and I went out in the hall and Michael was wandering around the kitchen, all disoriented and confused. In the morning, when I asked him what the hell was going on, he dismissed the whole thing, saying, 'Oh, I must have been sleepwalking.' But I got the distinct feeling that he didn't even know what I was talking about. Then he stayed home from work a few days later. At first he thought he had the flu. He was sick to his stomach and kept getting headaches, but he didn't have a fever. I think that's when he began to suspect he was seriously ill—the part about not having a fever. He went to this doctor and the guy diagnosed him as having herpes and gave him some pills. Michael was visibly relieved. 'Hey! It was only herpes!' he was telling everyone.''

"That must have put a damper on his dating life," I said.

"That's what struck me as odd. Michael didn't have much of a dating life, and I wondered where'd he picked up herpes. I didn't say anything, and Michael didn't question the doctor's diagnosis. He was just relieved. But two days later, the head-aches were so intense he stayed home from the shop again. He called me at work to come home, that he needed help to get to the hospital.''

"So you were with him? I thought he called the ambulance by himself.''

"No, I was there.''

It was belated, pointless comfort, but knowing Michael hadn't been alone somehow helped.

Jim continued. "I hurried home and found Michael on the floor. He was nauseated from trying to stand on his feet; standing caused him to throw up. I called the ambulance and we got him to the hospital. He had a CAT scan right away, then they scheduled the biopsy for the next day. He called his father and told him what was going to happen. He said, 'It looks grim.' ''

He had to call a roommate for help, someone with whom he only split rent. Lying on the floor, too sick to move. I shivered with guilt for not being there. How scary to need help and not be sure anyone would care.

"What should I do with the clock you sent?" Jim asked. "Michael never knew you shipped it here. He was already sick by the time it arrived. Should I send the clock back?''

"No. I don't need it.''

"I'm not sure I can get it to work,'' Jim said.

"It's quixotic,'' I said. "It's like that song about the clock that stopped when the old man died. It only worked for Michael.''

"Not that it's any of my business . . .'' My aunt Marlene had called. "But your mother told me and I agree with her. It's Agent Orange. It's terrible. I see it on the news all the time. Just thank God you never had a houseful of deformed children. Now tell me, what can I do to help?''

"Nothing, Aunt Marlene.''

''Are his parents going to sue somebody? You can sue for Agent Orange. I can get them the name of a good lawyer. Michael's parents should sue the government.''

''They don't want to sue anyone. They're too busy taking care of their son.''

''Then you should do it.''

''*Me?* I'd look like a money-grubbing ex-wife.''

''You can't ignore this,'' Aunt Marlene said. ''Doesn't it make you mad?''

''Yes! And that's good,'' I said. ''It gives me something to blame.''

''It's very admirable, in a questionable way, for you to be spending all this time with your ex-husband, Franny. He was a nice boy. But now there's no future in it.''

''Thank you for pointing that out to me, Aunt Marlene.''

''Sue the government,'' she said. ''You'll feel better.''

Getting Michael out of his parents' house and into a moving, breathing, living-oriented world was one of the few things that did make me feel better.

The other customers at Steak & Shake were never out-and-out rude, they were just never subtle. We'd walk in and be met with curious glances and looks of pity from the corners of narrowed eyes. Okay, fine, so Michael was a bald skinny guy who walked like a robot with a scar up the back of his head and red Magic Marker arrows drawn on his scalp. But he was doing so much *better*. He seemed oblivious to the stares around him, or else he just plain didn't care; he never was one to worry about what other people thought. But I turned into a den lion. I fancied myself with the same killer protective instincts a mother feels for her young child. Hurt my kid and I'll maim you.

I preferred our picnics in Washington Park. Even though they took place among softball leagues, joggers, bikers, dog-walkers, and children on squeaking swings, our picnics felt more private.

"What day is it?" Michael asked, lying on a blanket with his head in my lap. A soft, sweet haze fringed his eyes.

"Saturday," I said.

"Oh. I thought it was Tuesday."

I slapped my right hand against my left forearm. "Aw damn," I said. I held my arm out and wiped at it with a napkin. "I hate swatting a mosquito and actually *catching* it, because then there's this disgusting dead splat of bloody bug on my arm."

"You'll live," Michael said. Then neither of us said anything. I was never certain if I should encourage him to talk about the cancer or distract him from the business of dying.

"Michael? Is it bad to talk about?" I finally asked. "You know. Do you want to talk about it? I don't want you to be scared."

"I am scared." He looked up at me.

"You'll be okay. You have to think about good thoughts. Mountains. And flowers. And brown speckled trout. It won't be scary. There will be something there." It was so much easier to say the words than believe them. I ran my hand over Michael's scalp, ruffling the few strands of gray hair that had refused to fall out. "You know, you once promised me you wouldn't die first. I made you promise me that years ago."

"I know," Michael said, with sad resignation. "I'm sorry."

"You're doing great!" I said, hoping to encourage him. "You're walking great! You're gaining weight!"

"Yes. I should go on a diet."

"No. I mean that's good. You're reading now and you're almost done with your radiation and after that you can go to Portland." Michael's parents refused to plan or even talk about a possible trip to Portland. He needs something to look forward to, I kept telling Norma. If he has hopes, he'll only end up disappointed when nothing good happens, she responded. "If it's okay with your parents, Michael, I want to be the one to take you there."

"I'd like that," he said. "That's what I want, too."

"Can you ask your folks? Would they let you go with me?" He had to be the one to bring it up. If I suggested it, they'd never say yes.

"I don't have to ask them." His eyes seemed focused on a distant place within him. "I can do what I want."

I swatted at a fly that was hovering over Michael's face. "Well, maybe you could ask just to be polite."

"I'll do that." He paused. "What day is it?"

"Saturday."

"Oh."

I gently rubbed his crotch. I felt like a kinky babysitter. "Does that feel nice?"

"Yes," he said politely. "Thank you."

Michael did not resist as I pulled him up so we were both sitting cross-legged on the blanket, facing each other and holding hands.

"I wish we had stayed married," I told him.

Michael looked confused, like he couldn't remember why we *weren't* still married. "I must have made a terrible mistake," he said. And I finally understood why he'd told Gordon he didn't understand why I was visiting so often. Michael didn't believe I could still love him.

I could no longer remember why I'd stopped.

"In Portland we can be alone," I said. "In Portland we can make love."

I called from my office on a Monday night. Norma answered.

"Are you enjoying the VCR?" I asked. I'd bought Michael a VCR so he could watch movies.

"We can't program it," she said. "And it doesn't have a remote control."

When Michael came to the phone he sounded tired and much more childlike. He mentioned that his father would be taking him to Portland three weeks after the radiation was over.

"Well, maybe we can go away alone for our own weekend," I said, trying to hide my disappointment.

"I don't know if I have time." Michael lowered his voice. "I'm going to be getting very sick."

❦ *Chapter 38* ❦

I developed a pathological fear of phones that rang after midnight. So when mine rang late at night, waking me up, I hesitated before answering it.

"And now for Wendy of Portland with the Portland Report!" I heard. "Hi! Did I wake you? I was waiting for the rates to go down. But I knew you'd want to know how it went. They're flying home tomorrow on a six A.M. flight, which I guess is a whole lot cheaper, but can you imagine getting up and flying that early?"

Michael had been in Oregon with his parents for the past nine days.

"Did he have a good time?" I asked.

"He looks great. He was such a zombie when he left here that no one could believe how great he looks now. I threw this big barbecue so Michael could see his friends; I'm practically famous for my barbecues—" I was used to Wendy's conversations being one long continuous sentence, so I just said the occasional uh-huh and let her keep talking. "Mr. Wedlan walked around the whole evening instructing everyone: 'Don't let Michael near any beer. He can't drink alcohol.' Like we were trying to poison the guy or something. But we did have some really good times. Especially the day we drove down to the ocean. I don't know what kept Michael from always living by the ocean. He certainly loves it. But now he's going to need something to look forward to. I hope you can think of something."

It took two of us to seduce him.

I handled the ceremonies at the Ramada. Piper served as the decoy. I figured if she was along I wouldn't rouse any major parental suspicions as to where Michael and I were spending the afternoon—after all, how many times can one visit the state capital? Piper's never been to Springfield, we said; we're taking her on a tour of Springfield. And then Piper sat in the lobby of the Springfield Ramada reading *People* magazines while I lured Michael upstairs.

"Do you live here?" he asked when we walked into the hotel room. It was peach and pink with dark wood Colonial furniture and two twin beds with pink and beige bedspreads.

"No, honey. This is a hotel room. Piper and I are staying

here tonight so we have more time to visit with you. Do you want to sit down?''

''Okay.'' Michael sat on a peach velveteen chair by the window. I sat on the edge of the twin bed directly opposite him, our knees practically touching. I reached for his hand.

''Honey, I thought maybe it would be nice if the two of us made love. Would you like that?''

''Oh. I don't know.'' Michael tugged at his lip. ''I get shy.''

''Well, we don't have to if you don't want to. I just thought it might be nice. But maybe we could just lie down and hold each other. How would that be?''

''That would be nice.''

''Come sit next to me, okay?'' Michael slowly stood up from his chair and sat on the bed. ''You can take off your shoes, okay?'' Michael flopped back on the bed, unhooked his belt, and started pulling off his pants. I wasn't sure if he was confused between the word *belt* and the word *shoes*, or if he was just a typical guy who couldn't keep his pants on once he was in a bed with a girl. But I helped him pull off his shoes and unbutton his shirt and pull down his white underpants. He was skinny but not as skinny as he was when he first got out of the hospital. ''Why don't you get under the covers so you don't get cold,'' I suggested.

''Hey, look!'' he said, pointing to his erection.

''Hang on to that a second while I get undressed.'' I removed my clothes, then mumbled some apology about being a little chunky these days.

Michael looked at me with total amazement. ''I think you're beautiful.''

I dove under the covers.

We wrapped our arms around each other, lying face to face and body to body on our sides. Michael felt like a bag of bones in my arms, but we kissed and licked and squeezed and held each other close.

"What was your favorite time on your visit to Portland?" I asked.

Michael smiled. "The times you were there."

"I didn't go with you, sweetie. But thank you. I missed you, too."

I rolled on my back and pulled Michael on top of me. He didn't complain but he seemed quite curious as to just what it was we were doing. I reached down between us and made the proper adjustments. Michael's face registered boyish delight.

"Wow!" he cried.

"Not bad, huh?"

"It's so good to be inside you!"

Afterward, Michael lay on top of me, beaming, his body limp as a ragdoll.

"I got scared," he said with a sheepish grin. "I forgot what it feels like." I rolled out from under him. "It's been a long time."

Then we kissed each other. His lips were gentle and pliable. I asked, "Do you know how much I love you?"

"Just enough to keep me going," he said.

"Oh, more than that."

Then Michael began crying. "I'm so scared! I don't want to die now."

I held him and stroked his back until he was calm again. When I helped him get dressed, I asked, "Did it feel good to cry?"

"Yes. It did."

"Honey, don't tell your folks, okay? About us making love?" I could just imagine *that* conversation.

"Don't worry," Michael reassured me. "They won't be able to remember."

I rummaged through my overnight bag and pulled out a small square blue box and handed it to Michael. "Here. It's a present."

"But I don't have a present for you."

"That's okay. I don't need one. Open it." I'd bought Michael a Timex watch with easy-to-read numbers and one of those little slots that tell you the day of the week. I clamped the watch around his wrist. The band was at least three links too big for his chicken-bone wrist. "It's very trendy to wear it loose like this," I told him.

"I've never had a watch before!" He sounded like a little boy who'd just gotten a pony for Christmas.

"Yes, you have. I bought you a gold one. But with this one you'll never have to ask what day it is." Michael admired his watch, then asked me to take it off so he could keep it in the box. I straightened the covers on the bed and took Michael's hand as we left the room.

"You live in a nice place," he said.

By the time we got back, Norma had made dinner.

"Are you girls staying to eat?" she asked.

"That would be nice," Piper said.

"Well, I guess we've got enough." Norma scurried back into the kitchen. Piper set the dining-room table.

Piper and I sat on one side of the table. Norma and Michael sat on the other. And Gordon carved the lamb at the head of the table.

"Did Michael have a nice time today?" Norma asked me. She was dumping a spoonful of mashed potatoes onto her plate.

"He's sitting right next to you. Ask him," I said, praying he wouldn't go into details.

"I love lamb!" Piper said, changing the subject. I love Piper.

"Bye, bye, black sheep," Gordon said, flipping another slice onto Piper's plate. Gordon was turning downright larky lately. I looked over and saw Michael trying to cut his meat with two forks. "Here, honey, try this." I handed him his knife.

"Thank you," he said. He put the knife down and continued fussing with the two forks.

"Have you checked into your hotel yet?" Norma asked, scooping some lima beans onto Michael's plate.

"Yes," I said. "We did that before we got here this morning. It's a nice room."

"It certainly is," Michael said, nodding for emphasis.

I looked at him wide-eyed and wary, afraid he was going to say something incriminating. In unison Norma and Gordon both shot me a knowing look, as if to say: *see how confused he is!* I let that one pass.

"How about a roll, Mom?" I asked Norma.

She reacted like I'd just suggested she eat a bowl of phlegm. "With potatoes and lima beans?"

Gordon and Piper laughed. Norma and I sort of laughed. Then Michael saw all the laughing and he laughed, too.

"I love lamb!" Piper said again, like it was the lamb that was making us all punchy. Michael started yawning.

"I don't know why I'm so tired," he said. *Don't speculate,* I thought. He looked at me and asked, "Would you be upset if I went to sleep early?"

"Of course not. We'll be here in the morning."

Piper and I handled backup on clear and wash duties with Norma while Gordon took Michael upstairs for his bath.

"Your home is lovely," Piper said to Norma, while staring into a cupboard and pulling out a slightly-melted-from-the-dishwasher container from the world's largest Tupperware collection. "It always sounded like you had nice Christmases here."

Norma yanked on her Playtex Living Gloves. "Well, I don't think there'll be a Christmas this year."

"What do you mean?" I asked.

"The last CAT scan showed the radiation didn't accomplish what they'd hoped," Norma said, in her I-told-you-so voice.

"But he's doing so well! He's a little more confused and forgetful at times, but he's doing fine." *He can make love!*, I wanted to yell.

"No. I'm not planning on Christmas," Norma said sadly.

Gordon walked into the kitchen swinging his arms with a sense of accomplishment. "He's settled in his bath," he said.

I looked at Piper for strength and support, then asked the question I should have asked about Portland, only now I was asking about Chicago. "I was wondering if I could bring Michael up to Chicago for a visit sometime soon. He's got a lot of friends there, and I know they'd love to see him. It would be a nice change of pace for him."

Norma flapped her gloved hand at me, then turned back to her sinkful of dishes, deferring to her husband. *Here, you handle this*. But Gordon was definitely in a loosening-of-the-reins kind of a mood.

"Where would he stay?" Gordon asked. "He needs his own room, you know. Otherwise he'd never be able to sleep at night."

"Uh, we could go to my sister Madelyn's. She has a big house with lots of bedrooms. Of course, he'd sleep alone," I lied.

"She has little children. They could be noisy."

"Oh no. They never make noise. They're perfect," I said. More lies.

"His doctor would have to approve it. And his medicine schedule can be very complex. I don't know if you can handle it." I realized I had just been insulted, but things were going fine so I refrained from getting indignant. "But maybe we could work something out," Gordon said. "It's not good for Michael to sit here all day long with only two old people for companionship." Norma was splashing around and banging dishes behind us. "He needs to be with his peers, with people who share his interests. So we'll see. Maybe. You can come up and say good night to Michael in about ten minutes." Gordon left the room and I heard him slowly climbing back up the stairs.

"I'll be here in the morning," I whispered to Michael, smoothing the covers under his chin and leaning over to kiss him. He smiled at me. "It was nice to make love today, wasn't it?" Michael kept smiling at me, a polite smile. "You enjoyed it, didn't you, making love? We can do it again real soon." Michael was still smiling. "Michael, you remember, right? That we made love?"

"Oh, yes," he said. "We've done that hundreds of times."

"Drinks for one and all! It's on me!" I announced to the bartender from our table at the Ramada. I wasn't making quite as grand a gesture as one might think. Piper and I were the only customers in the bar.

"I've been thinking that maybe I should try to get pregnant," I said in a grave voice.

"Now there's a bad idea. Do you know how difficult it would be to raise a child alone?"

"I'd manage." I stared her in the eye. "I'd have a piece of Michael that I can hold on to, that I could keep alive."

"Honey, a baby won't keep Michael alive." She reached across the table and patted my hand. "You're too late, Franny. You're trying to rewrite history and fix things you can't fix. It would be awful to have a kid grow up without Michael here to see it."

"No more awful than having nothing!" I took a sip of my

drink. "Having Michael and maybe a baby and a decent job wasn't enough for me. I needed drama, too. So I went and screwed everything up."

"You had your reasons at the time."

"I guess I got what I wanted, huh? What's more dramatic than losing someone you love?"

"Having his baby after he's dead," Piper said. She dunked her hand into a bowl of pretzels, then signaled the bartender for another drink. She said to me, "If you're so sure Michael's cancer is from Agent Orange, what are the odds of having a healthy baby?"

"There are tests I could take."

"You're insane."

"Is that your professional opinion?"

"No, that's your friend's opinion."

"I'm in love with him."

"You're in love with the intensity of losing Michael," Piper said. "And with how much he needs you now."

"No!" I cried. "I want to take care of him and help him! There are all these things I want now that he always wanted. Babies. A home. Things I want with *him* now. Things I want to *give* him."

"Franny," Piper said softly, "your love cannot save him."

In the morning Piper and I each swallowed a couple of Tylenols for breakfast, then drove over to the Wedlans'. When we rang the bell, Gordon opened the door and hugged me good morning and shook Piper's hand. Michael was sitting in the overstuffed chair and looked up at me with surprise.

"I didn't know you were visiting today!"

"Yes, but Piper has to get back to Chicago," I said, leaning down and kissing Michael on the lips. "We can't stay here long."

"Me either," Michael said.

❧ *Chapter 39* ❧

No wreath. No tree. No three cardboard wise men on top of the television. A lot of parents might have said: "It's probably our son's last Christmas. Let's make it memorable." But Norma and Gordon felt any holiday celebrations would be depressing. And Michael never expressed an opinion. Maybe he didn't know it was Christmas.

I, however, had been granted permission to bring him up to Chicago the day before New Year's Eve. My holiday spirits were *ecstatic*. Before Michael and I left for our three-day leave, Gordon handed me a stack of envelopes, each one labeled with a different time of day, each one filled with various combinations of Michael's pills.

"Maybe you can get together with your bridge group and play some cards one evening," I suggested to Norma.

"No," she said, "what we really need is a good night's sleep." Gordon and Norma were finally looking like two people in their eighties. "Have a good time, handsome," Norma said, kissing Michael on the cheek.

The drive to Chicago disoriented him. He kept asking, "Where are we going? Where are we now?" But I-55 often made people feel that way. It was pouring when we approached the gray Chicago skyline with its highrises sprouting up like Emerald City in *The Wizard of Oz*.

"This is exciting!" Michael said. He'd forgotten how much he hated Chicago.

"Do you like the apartment?" I asked, when we finally got home and settled.

Michael surveyed the living room. "I have to get my own apartment soon," he said. We sat at the dining-room table eating chili out of soup bowls. Michael spilled his glass of apple juice onto the floor. He was surprised, horrified, and embarrassed by his clumsiness and immediately went into a scolding tirade against himself. "You're so stupid! You made such a mess!"

"Honey, don't do that to yourself," I pleaded, quickly blotting the carpet to hide the evidence. "It's the illness that makes you drop things. Not you. You're blaming yourself for things you can't help."

"I'm sorry," he said, but I didn't know if he was sorry he'd blamed himself or was apologizing because he'd spilled his juice.

At night we made love. Tender, intense, gentle love. But I could feel the effort it took just for Michael to reach his arm around me and pull me toward him.

"Does it feel good to lie naked together?"

"Very good," he said.

"I love you, Michael."

"Yes," he said.

I rubbed my hand up his shoulder and neck and outlined his face with my finger. "I was always thinking you didn't like me," I said, amazed at the havoc I'd created with my own form of brain fade.

"You didn't like you," Michael said, sounding sure and alert. "I love you."

In the morning we made love again. I was determined to spoil him rotten. "Tonight's New Year's Eve," I said. "You remember New Year's Eve, right? Not that we all don't have a few New Year's Eves we'd like to forget."

Michael smiled at me, lying back on his pillow, his expression polite and eager to please. "I forget a lot of things," he said.

We brushed our teeth standing side by side at the sink, the way we had when we were first married. Michael picked up his toothbrush and dragged it across his cheek like a razor. I had to look away to keep myself from crying. Then I showed him how to use a toothbrush.

Louie and the very-pregnant Nadine showed up towing along little Louie, who was four years old and spent most of the visit trying to smash his mother's stomach, except when Nadine was running him through his little Louie the Super Child paces like he was some kind of prizewinning show dog. "Show 'em how you count to ten, Louie. Do that dance you always do for Grandpa, Louie." We heard the entire alphabet and three rounds of "The Farmer in the Dell." Nadine rewarded her son with a Hostess Twinkie pulled from her pink quilted carry-all, and Louie, Jr., promptly smashed the Twinkie into my carpet.

Susan came over in the afternoon. Barry was a no-show. When I asked Susan about him, she just shrugged. Michael never asked about Barry, either out of forgetfulness or politeness. It was raining again, but it was warm enough for Susan to suggest we cough up a couple of umbrellas and take a walk in the park across the street. Susan likes to organize activities.

"Would you enjoy that, honey?" I asked Michael.

"Oh, sure," he said. Then he waited for us to tell him what to do. Michael wore a knit cap over his bald, scarred head and looked so much like the normal healthy Michael that it was easy to forget he wasn't. He started a conversation with some dough-faced man in the elevator carrying two six-packs of Budweiser. "Hello. How *are* you?" he asked the man, with such sincere interest that the man responded: "Terrible. I hate New Year's Eve. I'm just waiting for the football games to start."

"Me too," Michael said. The elevator doors opened onto the lobby floor. "It's been nice talking to you!"

Susan took one of Michael's hands. I took the other. Michael said hello to two other people in the lobby as we went outdoors. One smiled hesitantly at him. The other said hello in a suspicious do-I-know-you? voice. "Do we need to open the umbrella?" Susan asked. "It's not so bad, is it?"

"It's not so bad," Michael said. We stopped at a red light next to a woman with a dog of undefined origin on a leash. "Now *there's* a fat ugly dog!" Michael informed everyone.

I grimaced, the woman glared, and once out of the public's earshot, Susan said, "Let's be grateful you didn't say that about the woman!"

"Oh, no, she didn't look so bad," Michael said. I envied him spitting out whatever he thought. Michael's thinking might have been skewed, but it was honest.

The ground in the park was damp, the trees were stripped of their leaves, and the sky was gray. But Michael looked around appreciatively like he'd never seen a park before. "So many sticks," he said. I knew he meant trees. I could understand the abstract Michael better than I understood the logical and linear Michael. Observing all the puddles, he declared, "What a muddy quagmire!" Susan and I looked at Michael, looked at each other, then started laughing.

"You forget the word for trees but you remember *quagmire*?" I said, grinning. "Have I ever told you I love you for your mind?"

I threw my arms around him and kissed him. Michael kissed me in return, then looked up at that dreary gray sky and proclaimed, "The joy of horniness!"

New Year's Eve. The end of a year I was glad to see end

and the start of one I knew I'd hate. No champagne. No wild parties. No dancing until dawn. By eight o'clock Michael and I were in bed and lost under the quiet of the covers. And holding on to each other for dear life.

Holly dropped by the next day, bringing Rice Krispie bars. Dodi showed up for a visit and chattered away about her New Year's Eve date. She talked about people from the bank whom I didn't know and Michael didn't remember. No one ever acknowledged what was really going on. I wondered if Michael ever had the urge to say, "Excuse me, but do any of you realize I'm dying?" He listened, but didn't talk beyond uh-huhs and oh-mys. I couldn't tell if he was tired or just distracted. But when Dodi hugged him and said, "Goodbye, I mean, see you soon," he had tears in his eyes.

We made love at night. We made love in the morning.

Two hours before we were to leave for Springfield, my sister, Madelyn, called and announced that she and her two children, Joel and Clint, were coming over for a visit. Her beloved husband was too hung over, so she was making him stay home. Madelyn had not seen Michael since he'd gotten sick.

I was so accustomed to Michael looking the way he now looked that I was always amazed to see the momentary shock and then adjustment passing across the eyes of anyone who was seeing him for the first time since his illness. But after her initial reaction, Madelyn beamed her full set of perfect teeth at Michael and gave him a big noisy kiss, then rubbed at his cheek with the palm of her hand to blot out her lipstick imprint, while Michael clutched at the sleeves of Madelyn's pink silk shirtwaist for balance. For some reason, my sister was dressed like she was going to a matinee.

Joel was only four the last time he'd seen Uncle Michael, and now he was almost seven.

"Hello! Remember me?" Michael said.

"Hello! Remember me?" Joel parroted, not knowing how difficult a question that could be for Michael.

Clint, who'd been named by his father after Clint Eastwood, was almost four. He and his brother stood in front of Michael and grinned. Madelyn had held some preliminary briefings with her sons out of concern for their psychological welfare, and in hopes that neither child would say something insensitive.

"Hello, Uncle Michael," Clint said, looking up at his new out-of-the-blue uncle and sticking out his small greasy hand with his chubby fingers flailed outward. "Give me five."

Michael said, "Certainly," and mashed his hand on top of Clint's. Clint studied Michael with the unabashed, intense curiosity three-year-olds are so expert at.

"Don't stare," his older brother instructed. Then added in a whisper that no one could possibly miss: "He's sick!"

I could see some dire had-to-be-asked question forming on Clint's lips, but he looked at his mother, then clamped his little hand over his mouth.

"Sit, boys," Madelyn commanded.

The boys sat on the sofa like two bookends with Michael in the middle. Having seen much evidence to the contrary, I knew for a fact that my nephews were not perfect Stepford children, but there seemed to be some unspoken communication going on—one that said, *We must be gentle with Uncle Michael.* Joel reached over and took Michael's hand, and then, not to be outdone by his brother, Clint grabbed Michael's other hand, and the three of them sat on that sofa linked together. Clint was biting his lip.

"Honey, what is it?" I asked him.

He looked at Michael, avoided his mother's eyes, looked at me and back at Michael, and blurted out the one thing he obviously had overheard at home and had been warned *not* to say in front of his uncle Michael.

But three is three.

"Are you *dying*?" he asked.

"Clint!" Madelyn cried, her hand flying up to her forehead.

"It's all right," Michael said.

"He doesn't even know what it means," Madelyn said.

"*I* know what it means," Joel said, his voice triumphant. "It means you're going to heaven!"

"I hope so," Michael said.

"Are you coming back?" Clint asked.

"What *made* you sick?" Joel asked. The visit was turning into a press conference.

"I don't know," Michael said.

I believe children deserve honest answers. Especially other people's children. "Uncle Michael was in a war," I told Joel he was sprayed with chemicals and the chemicals made him sick.

Then, with the accusatory voice of a prosecuting attorney, his small face crunched into a frown, Joel asked, "It was the *bad* guys' chemicals, right?"

I answered him. "No, honey. Actually it was our chemicals."

"Why would *our* guys do that?" Joel asked.

"Somebody goofed," Michael answered.

We drove back to Springfield with the radio blaring on one of those golden-oldies stations. Michael never noticed the music; he seemed too mesmerized by the string of empty cornfields we passed. "It's less shallow," he said. I knew he meant there was snow on the ground.

Norma and Gordon fussed over Michael's return. "Did you eat?" Norma asked.

"Of course he ate," Gordon said. "They've been gone three days. Did you take your medicine?"

"Did you have an easy drive?" Norma asked Michael.

"Your parents sent oranges," she told me. Michael sat on the upholstered chair, readjusting to his surroundings. I didn't want to leave him, I felt like I was abandoning him, but I had a long drive back, so I snuck into the kitchen to scarf down a glass of pineapple juice before hitting the road.

"Did you have fun?" I heard Norma asking Michael in the living room.

A long pause hung in the air before I heard Michael speak. "You know, I think Franny was just here!"

I finally stopped thinking maybe things would get better.

❧ *Chapter 40* ❧

On my next trip to Springfield, I took Michael to see a movie, the first scene of which showed a corpse in a funeral home. Michael never flinched. I leaned over and whispered in his ear, "Next time I come down, we'll go to the Ramada. We can make love."

"I'll have an erection!" Michael blurted. Four people in the row ahead of us turned around.

I reached over and squeezed his right leg in the dark. Michael stared down at his lap, then over at me. "I can't feel that anymore."

I rubbed his crotch and whispered, "Can you feel this?"

"Yes." He laughed. "That I can feel."

"It'll probably be the last to go." He laughed throughout the movie. His smile was beautiful. And afterward he stood up and announced, "I didn't understand any of it—but it was fun!" Michael was unsteady on his feet. His leg was sluggish and a strong wind in the parking lot almost blew him over, but he seemed to think that was also pretty funny. He was fascinated with his own failings.

We considered stopping somewhere for ice cream, then I remembered that Michael had to have his medicine at three o'clock.

Gordon greeted us at the door holding a water glass and two white pills.

Norma corraled me into the powder room and said, "Your visits mean a lot to him. He needs the change in his routine. His days are so long. He'll pick up a book but I don't think he knows what he's reading anymore. He'll just open it at any old place and turn the pages. Are you coming next week?" she asked. "It's his birthday, you know."

"I know."

"I'm going to make a brunch. Invite Wes and his wife and Clifford and Benny and his wife. When I called Benny I told him he should get over here more often."

"You did?" I was proud of Norma. She was speaking up. And if she was actually willing to throw Michael a birthday party, there was a slim chance she was feeling somewhat optimistic. "A birthday party for Michael would be lovely," I said. And incredibly sad. I put on some lipstick and Norma and I returned to the living room. I sat down next to Michael. He looked at my mouth and smiled. "Hey! You put on shoe polish!"

❧ *Chapter 41* ❧

Norma told me over the telephone.

"My husband and I were in bed—it was the middle of the night—and we heard this loud thump like someone had fallen."

"What was it?" I asked.

"Michael had fallen. From what we could tell, he had woken up confused and having to go to the bathroom. He urinated in the corner of the bedroom, then wandered around to the other side of the bed and fell face down on the floor, the way his father found him. He's paralyzed all down his right side. His leg's a dead weight, you should see his father pushing and dragging him into the bathroom with his arms wrapped around him from behind. He won't eat, and he keeps holding up his useless right hand in his other hand and staring at it like he can't remember what it's for. We can't let him sleep by himself anymore so we've moved him into our bedroom. And he can't talk at all well. Everything comes out slurred and sluggish."

"Whoa. What does this *mean*?" I asked.

"It means brunch is off."

I drove to Springfield immediately. Norma was playing hostess, setting a dish of peanut brittle on the coffee table. She walked over and gave me a warm hug. "He loves you so much," she said. Wes and his wife, Dominique, were sitting on the sofa, mumbling in those low polite voices people use in hospital hallways. Clifford was pacing and puffing on his pipe. Gordon was in the kitchen talking on the telephone. Norma informed me that Benny and his wife, Kitty, were upstairs talking to Michael. I climbed up the stairs to see Michael. Kitty was on her way down the stairs. She nodded at me.

Michael was lying in his mother's bed in his father's pajamas, crying and talking in his slurred new language. "I'm so confused. I'm so confused." I could see the shape of his still-good leg beneath the covers shaking full throttle. I kissed Benny on the cheek. Benny kissed me on the cheek. Then he continued with the speech he'd apparently been in the middle of making. Within minutes it became clear that Benny had seen one too many deathbed scenes on *Masterpiece Theater*. "I love you," he told Michael. I thought, *Maybe that's why Michael's confused. He's not used to his boyfriends telling him they love him.* "I'll always have memories of our Canadian fishing trips. I don't think I'll ever be able to look at another trout without thinking of you." I would never be able to look at another Three Stooges movie without thinking of Benny. Benny turned to me. "I can't cry! I couldn't cry when my sister died and I can't cry now. I should feel worse but I don't! I wish I could cry!"

"Benny, do you mind giving Michael and me a few minutes alone together? Please."

"Oh, sure," Benny said, and left.

I sat on the edge of the bed and took Michael's limp hand in mine. "And you think *you* have problems," I said to Michael. But there was no making him smile. His eyes darted from side to side like he was trying to escape something but didn't know what that something was. "It's okay," I said. "It's okay to be afraid." I stroked his face and rubbed his shoulders and wished I were smart enough to know what I should be saying.

Wes and Clifford came upstairs to say they'd be back tomorrow. Michael looked at each of them and said what sounded like a thank-you. But as soon as the two guys left the room, Michael's eyes spilled over with tears.

"Are you afraid you won't be here tomorrow?" I asked. Michael nodded.

"I think you will be," I said.

The dining-room table was carted down to the basement and a hospital bed set up in its place. Either Norma or Gordon would sleep on the sofa each night so that Michael wouldn't be alone. A nurse showed up from the St. John's home-nursing program, filled a few vials with Michael's blood, and left. The doctor called on the phone and changed Michael's medicine schedule. The nurse had shown Norma and Gordon how to give Michael a professional sponge bath with his feet soaking in a bucket of water while he was sponged down limb by limb. I knew all this because I called Gordon during the week for the full report. I hated calling. It was scary. I knew I would not get good news. "What's he do all day? If he can't read himself, can someone read to him? Will he listen to music?" I was still trying to fix things.

"There's no point reading to him," Gordon said, talking to me in an impatient tone. "His short-term memory's so bad he can't remember enough to keep track of what he's just heard. He doesn't want the television on. And he won't listen to the radio."

"So what does he do?"

"He sleeps a lot. And he cries a lot." *Oh, Michael. We were on the home stretch.* "His sisters are coming," Gordon said.

About time, I thought. But instead I said, "Oh, well, can I still come down on Saturday?"

"No. Too many people confuse him. I think you'd better wait."

Wait?

I'd lie in bed at night and picture strange vessels exploding in my brain and foreign tissue growing inside my head. If something went wrong in any other part of my body, I could look *down* at it, feel separate from it. Oh, look, there's my spleen. It's on the blink. But something growing in my head would be something growing inside of *me*, who I was, my soul. How much of that sweet man lying in a hospital bed in the middle of his parents' dining room was *Michael* anymore? During the day I'd see street people talking mindlessly to themselves and think, *They're no different from Michael, except he has his parents to care for him.* And I'd think how all the craziness, the doctors, the medicines, the married years and the unmarried years, no longer had anything to do with Michael and me and who we were to each other right now. Despite all the mixed signals and all the years out of sync, Michael and I were meant to be. If I'd met and married someone else in the past few years I wouldn't have been there now; and I was meant to be there now. I finally understood what it meant to feel married.

"This weekend? Can I come down this weekend?" I asked Norma when I called.

"Of course," she said. "You're the best tonic for him." Norma was my ally.

I spoke to him like I was telling a story.

Norma was sitting on the sofa, knitting. Gordon was working on the church bookkeeping at his desk in the basement. The big upholstered chair had been moved next to Michael's hospital bed. For the past week his sister Judith had slept in the chair holding his hand while Diana slept on the sofa. They had returned to their homes and now I was sitting in the chair with the side rail of the hospital bed lowered so I could lean closer to Michael. His head looked frail and childlike peeking over the edge of the blanket wrapped tightly around him like a baby wrapped in bunting. He seemed calm, resigned, adjusted to the latest plateau of his descent. The doctor had prescribed a regimen of painkillers. I kept talking, spouting all the comforting drivel I could muster.

"Let's talk about the scary stuff. The stuff nobody wants to talk about, okay?"

Michael nodded. Norma kept knitting.

"You don't have to be afraid. You won't be alone. You're simply going on an adventure. The tunnel? Remember when I told you about the tunnel where your grandma and your grandpa and maybe some of your friends from when you were in the Marines will be waiting for you? I bet *my* grandma's making some cabbage soup for you right now! It's about time you two met. She plays bridge. You'll like her." Michael was laughing. Not because he believed a word I said, but because he was willing to laugh. "My mom's friend Beryl has been married three times. What's she gonna do when she goes through that tunnel and finds three husbands waiting for her?" Now Norma laughed. That was her idea of a good problem. Michael smiled at me. "There are some good things that have come from your being sick. There really are. You're close to your parents. You know how much they love you. And how many people care about you. And us. I feel so connected to you. At least this brought us back together."

Michael lifted his head from the pillow. His words were sluggish, yet filled with a strength he didn't look capable of. "If not, there would have been no point to it!"

I clutched his hand against my chest. "We've had good times, haven't we?"

"I'm so lucky," Michael sputtered. "I'd have missed *all this*!"

I bit my lip to keep from crying and looked over at Norma. She was sitting with her knitting set aside, her hands resting on her knees, staring out to nowhere. She looked drained and defeated.

I turned to Michael. "I just wish we hadn't wasted that time, those years we were in different places."

I heard Gordon trudging up the stairs and into the kitchen. He reappeared with a handful of pills and a glass of water. "Will you take these please?" he asked Michael in a louder than necessary voice. Michael held out his good hand and took the pills without looking at them. "Do you need to pee?" Gordon asked in his TV announcer voice.

"No," Michael said.

"He hates urinating into a bottle," Gordon told me. "But it's too difficult to move him onto the wheelchair and in and out of the bathroom each time. We'll have to have a catheter inserted."

I smiled at Michael. I decided to point out the bright side. "It's easier for men to be sick because you can pee in those plastic containers. Women can't do that because we don't have penises."

Michael looked like I'd just told him the most amazing piece of information. "It's so unfair!" he said.

"Oh, no, it's a pretty good system," I said. Then I leaned over and whispered something in his ear. He dozed off with a smile on his face.

❦ *Chapter 42* ❦

I had thought that by the time things got as horrid as things got, Michael would be in some whacked-out place and wouldn't know enough to be scared. But he knew. Through all the haze and confusion and mental chaos, he still knew he was dying.

He would switch between two different personas. One moment he'd be gazing at his mother with the longing, innocence, desire, and sexually tinged adoration of a four-year-old. "I love you, Mommy! I love you, Mommy!" Michael would tell her with the intensity of a lover. And then, suddenly, he'd be angry and violent and flailing about, grabbing at his mother with his one strong hand. "You fucking bitch!" he'd cry with a green ugly hatred filling his eyes. Norma would reel back, then Gordon would take over, speaking to Michael like a naughty child. "You must calm down. We cannot take care of you at home unless you calm down." Michael would suddenly be aware that he'd done something wrong, but he couldn't remember what. The tears would roll down his cheeks. Soon he started refusing to take his pills. Gordon would plead with Michael to take his pills. He'd rub Michael's shoulders or stroke his face, looking off in another direction to keep from crying in front of his son. "I tried so hard," Michael said through his tears, clutching at his father's hand. "Things just didn't work out for me."

Gordon looked at his son. "They were working out. You just ran out of time."

We ate dinner in the kitchen. Gordon tied the belt from an old terrycloth bathrobe around Michael and the back of the wheelchair to keep Michael from slumping over. Michael was lost in distant terror, babbling words that didn't make sense but were laden with fear. He wouldn't eat. Finally, Norma and Gordon gave up. I wheeled Michael back into the dining room while Norma walked like a ringbearer carrying the plastic urine-filled bag attached to Michael's catheter, making certain it didn't get caught in the wheels of the chair. As Gordon lifted his son from the chair onto the hospital bed, Michael's face showed his indignation and fear of being hoisted about, but he never complained. He dozed, then woke in an agitated state. "I have to pee, sir! I have to pee!" Gordon tried to explain about the catheter, that Michael wouldn't be wetting the bed, but Michael insisted no one understood. "I have to pee!" he cried.

"Honey, you have a pee machine hooked up to you," I said.

"I do?"

"You don't have to get out of bed."

"He pulled it out the other night," Norma said. "We had to pay a nurse from Jacksonville a hundred dollars to come over and reinsert it."

After taking his pills without protest, Michael fell into a troubled sleep. A night nurse was due at eleven o'clock. I left for the Ramada at nine-thirty. When I arrived back the next morning, Norma opened the door. Michael poked his head up off of his pillow and said "Hiiiiii!" with such delight that for one false hope of a fleeting moment I thought to myself, *He knows me, he's better, he's going to be okay now.* Then Michael sunk back onto his pillow and stared into space.

Norma's shoulders slumped. She was beyond hiding her exhaustion. "The nurse never showed up," she said. "We've been up all night."

"You should have called me at the hotel. I'd've been glad to come stay here with Michael." Glad and grateful.

"We managed." Norma sighed.

I heard a toilet flush and then some water running and Gordon emerged from the bathroom looking every bit like a shriveled old man in his eighties. He kissed me good morning.

"Why don't you two take a nap while I stay with Michael, okay?" I said.

"Maybe," Gordon said. Then they dragged themselves upstairs to their bedroom.

Michael and I played Here Comes the Airplane with a bowl of Rice Krispies in milk. "Open wide, honey. Here comes some more!" He'd take a few bites and say, "Delicious." Then I'd wipe his mouth with a napkin to keep the milk from running down his chin.

"I brought some pictures," I told him, holding up a scrapbook filled with photos of our honeymoon. Michael saluting in front of Treasure Island. The two of us—taken by another tourist—feigning dizziness in front of Lombard Street. "Do you know who this is?" I asked, pointing to a picture of Michael in front of the Golden Gate Bridge.

"No," Michael said, like he was genuinely curious.

"That's you, honey," I told him, then just as quickly I wanted to take back my words. Michael was crying.

"I forgot what I look like," he said faintly.

"Wait! Here you are!" I lunged for my purse, dug out a small mirror, and held it up for Michael. "See! You're very handsome."

Michael stared into the mirror. A few weeks after the radiation treatments stopped, patches of drab brown hair had begun sprouting on Michael's scalp. Michael liked to rub his hand over his head and feel his new hair, but to me that lifeless growth meant that the afterburner effect of his radiation had worn off, and it was all forces go for quickly reproducing cells like hair follicles and brain tumors. He hadn't been shaved yet that day and he had one of those stubbly beards that looks chic on the cover of *GQ* and decrepit anywhere else. "I love your face," I said, as I took the mirror away. Michael did not look convinced.

Gordon came trudging down the stairs. "Did you sleep?" I asked.

"I guess so," he said absently. "Would you like to have your head raised?" he asked Michael, pushing some button on the hospital bed before waiting for a response. Then Gordon gave Michael his pills, after which he brought in a toothbrush with a squirt of toothpaste on it, another glass of water, and a plastic bowl shaped like a kidney bean, apparently designed to hold under the chins of people who have to brush their teeth and spit out the water while sitting in hospital beds. Michael understood the routine and brushed his teeth. Gordon left the room again and reappeared holding a razor, a towel, and a can of Gillette Foamy.

"No," Michael said, shaking his head.

"But that beard must be so scratchy and uncomfortable," Gordon said.

I didn't offer an opinion. I just held Michael's hand. The one he probably couldn't feel anything with. The two men debated for several minutes, with Gordon suggesting an electric shaver or shaving part of Michael's face and leaving a goatee.

"A goatee might be interesting, honey," I volunteered. "You'll look like a clarinet player."

Michael yelled out, his face red with exasperation and frustration from nobody listening to him, his eyes filling with tears. "People! People! I'm *dying*."

Later, I held his hand while he slept. Norma came downstairs and resumed her post on the sofa, the clackety-clack
of her knitting needles the only sound in the room other than
Michael's occasional guttural snores. Gordon went down to
the basement to work on his accounting books for the church.
He could lose himself in those numbers. Michael woke up
after an hour or so and smiled at me. There were footsteps
on the basement stairs, more pills and another glass of water.
Gordon suggested Michael sit in the wheelchair for a while
to avoid bedsores. We went through our routine again, Norma
with the urine bag, Gordon hoisting Michael, me sliding the
wheelchair under Michael's butt. We were a team now, helping Michael die. I wheeled him into the kitchen and he sat
at the table turning the pages of the newspaper. He'd look at
each page without reading it, set each section aside, then pick
up the same sections and repeat the ritual. I was watching
him, with my hands folded in my lap, not knowing what to
say, when he turned to me with a hatred in his eyes that made
him look like those crazed photos I'd seen of Charles Manson.
"You fucking bitch!" Michael spewed at me.

"Yes," I said. "I am."

"Great news!" I heard the voice of Wendy of Portland
blurting into my phone. "Jim rented a video camera so we
could film this little Cecil B. DeMille hi-how-ya-doin' movie
for Michael's VCR."

"Wendy, Michael's not doing too well."

"Oh." There was a silence before Wendy asked in a far
graver voice, "Like he's getting worse and maybe it's time?"

"Yes. There's talk of him going into a hospice." The word
hospice stuck in my throat. I started crying right over the
phone, blubbering to a woman I'd never met. Somehow it
was easier to spill out the grief to that warm, overly optimistic,
disembodied voice. I told Wendy everything, the whole

down-for-the-last-count everything. "I feel like nothing will be good again. Nothing *can* be good again. How do people deal with something like this and get over it?"

"You won't get over it," Wendy said. "You'll just get on with it. My mom died a few years ago. Right after Tyler was born. The grief kept attacking me in these huge waves. It still hurts. But eventually the waves became less frequent and less intense." I nodded into the phone as though Wendy could see me. "You've been there for Michael. He'll die knowing you loved him, Franny. But when he's ready to let go, you must let him go. He may need your *permission* to die."

"What?" I mumbled.

"You'll know what to do."

❦ *Chapter 43* ❦

I'm convinced that hospice workers come from some higher order of Good Souls. They speak softly, look you right in the eye when they're talking to you about subjects others avoid, nod their heads knowingly, and radiate compassion.

Michael's nurse was named Jill; blond, soft, sweet Jill. In a better world, and under different circumstances, he would have asked her for a date. There were only fourteen beds in the St. John's hospice and Michael was considered lucky to get one. His headaches had taken on a life of their own. From here on out it was make him comfortable, keep him drugged.

It was one of those warm, sunny, out-like-a-lamb March

days, when the earth is brown and damp and smelling fresh from the melted snow. I was angry at that beautiful weather for not turning beautiful in time for Michael to spend one more day outdoors.

The hospice was located in a four-story red brick building across the street from St. John's hospital. One floor of the building was an old people's home, two floors were for drug rehabilitation, and the top floor was for dying. Wes and Clifford were sitting vigil in the waiting room. Wes waved. Clifford was flipping through a tattered *National Geographic*. I stopped at the nurses' station. Set on top of the front counter was a needlepoint canvas with that serenity prayer about changing the things you can change and not changing the ones you can't and being smart enough to know the difference. A woman with warm brown eyes, a hushed voice, and a perpetually tremulous smile pointed me toward Michael's room. The hallway was painted a soft blue and decorated with cardboard cutouts of flowers and balloons and Easter bunnies, all those things that are supposed to cheer you up but inevitably depress you because you know the reason they're there is to cheer you up.

Norma was silently sitting in the dark next to her son's bedside, knitting a lap robe. She wore a beige wool skirt and a white blouse with a cameo pinned at the collar. Someone would come in to open the blinds and let in some sunshine, and five minutes later Norma would close them. Michael had been shaved and looked more like himself again. He was sleeping, resting, dozing, floating. The ever-shaking leg was no longer shaking, whether from morphine or resignation I wasn't certain. He looked so *handsome*. I wanted to crawl under the covers with him and hold on to him so tight he couldn't slip away. An IV loomed over the bed, attached to him through a long tube and a needle taped into the skin of his right hand. A glossy white plastic card on the wall over his head said, HELLO! MY NAME IS: and underneath someone had written *Michael Wedlan* in grease pencil. From all the books I'd read the summer before, I expected the "last stage," the acceptance stage, to be a peaceful at-one-with-the-world kind of a place, but it was just an okay, I'm tired of fighting, there's no point, I can't win, let's get on with it place; a teetering limbo.

Norma was in a bitter, worn-out mood. I could feel her impatience. Not with Michael, but with her own knit-one-purl-two life. I kissed her on the cheek, then went and stood on the other side of the bed next to the IV and leaned over Michael and kissed him on the lips. He didn't respond.

"Where's Dad?" I asked Norma. "I saw Wes and Clifford in the waiting room."

"Yes, they come in and out. Dad's at home. I get mornings. He gets afternoons. I'll go home and meet him for lunch and then he'll be coming back here."

"Well, the two of you can have a nice long lunch, because I'll be here." I said that to help out, to give her a change of pace, but Norma reacted like I'd just trampled onto her turf.

"We don't *mind* being here," she said, looking up at me. "We enjoy it." She looked confused by her own words and went back to her knitting.

Nobody wanted Michael to die, and yet his death was what we were waiting for.

I found myself saying the L-word. "It's a nice room. Michael was lucky to get in here."

"Fourteen hundred dollars a week!" Norma huffed.

"There's insurance," I said. "And he has life insurance."

"No," Norma said. "He cashed in his policy when he was out of work." Michael was lying there dying and Norma and I were discussing *money*. The conversation escalated into a discussion of Michael's possessions—who should get the brass floor lamps, and the little wooden box Michael used to keep his loose change and Purple Hearts in on the dresser. I asked if maybe I could have that.

"The box his *father* bought him in Europe!" Norma said.

"Oh—then his father should have it." I felt like an outsider again, clearly out of line. There was more discussion—who should get Michael's TV and microwave, his camera, the barbecue grill in Portland, and his gold watch.

"I bought him that!" I said. *Look*, I wanted to say, *I was good to him. I really was. I'm not some golddigger after a wooden box. I love the man*.

Michael's eyes flickered open. Norma sprung from her chair. She stood on one side of the bed, and I was on the other, each vying for some look of recognition, some you're-the-most-important-person-in-the-world-to-me acknowledgment. I wondered how much Michael had heard and comprehended of our conversation and whether he felt disgust for me now. But he just closed his eyes and dozed into oblivion again.

Suddenly Wes and Clifford appeared in the doorway, peeking over toward the bed but not approaching it. "Hi. He's sleeping," I said. The guys nodded in unison. I walked over and kissed each of them on the cheek. They walked two steps closer to the bed and Wes whispered, "See you tomorrow." Norma shrugged.

As soon as they left, she said, "Maybe Wes will buy Michael's golf clubs." Then she sat down and resumed her knitting. I watched for eyelid flickers.

Jill the nurse walked into the room with a syringe filled with orange glop. When I asked her what it was, she told me, liquid Dilantin. "It's easier for him to get down than a pill."

Jill leaned over close to Michael's ear and said in a strong, firm voice, "Michael? You have to wake up now, Michael!" But Michael resisted her efforts.

"I don't blame him," Norma muttered, her voice ringing with sadness and defeat. "What's the point of waking up when there's nothing to wake up for?"

Michael was still in a half-dazed state when Jill gently forced the tip of the syringe into his mouth and plunged the liquid Dilantin into his mouth. "Michael, you have to swallow," Jill said with a firmness you don't usually hear from someone that blond or sweet-looking. "Swallow, Michael. Swallow." She kept stroking his throat. I found myself involuntarily gulping, practically willing that medicine to go down. Michael was so detached from the process; he was off in that other place, the waiting place. "He did it," Jill suddenly said. She walked around to the other side of the bed and checked his IV bag.

"Do you know how much he understands?" I asked Jill.

"It's hard to tell," she said, opening the blinds to let in some light. "Just remember the hearing's the last to go." Jill left the room while I prayed that Michael's short-term memory problems had already erased the microwave-TV-camera conversation.

Norma checked her watch, stuffed her knitting into her canvas bag, stood up, looked at her son, closed the blinds, and announced she was leaving and her husband would be back for the afternoon shift. "But we're both here after dinner," Norma told me. I could see it. And it hurt to see it. Two old people, one sitting with dignity, the other knitting with dignity, waiting, just waiting, and watching their son die. "Will I see you later?" she asked.

"I'll probably drive home before then," I said, "but I'll be back." Norma shrugged. And then she did something that was totally non-Norma-like. She threw her arms around me —the canvas knitting bag and her purse swung into my back—and gave me a strong hug.

"You've been a big help," she said. Then she left. And

Michael and I were alone. Or I was alone. It was hard to tell where Michael was.

We held hands. I had to do most of the holding, but after a while he started gently rubbing his thumb against my skin. "May I kiss you?" I asked. He nodded slightly, just slightly. His breath was stale and bitter, but his mouth was still soft; it was still Michael's mouth.

His eyes were open now. They didn't seem to be seeing anything, but they were open. I squeezed his hand a little tighter. His thumb moved a little faster. I started talking. "Honey, I know you can't talk to me now and I shouldn't be talking to you now—that you need to separate—to let go—I know. But it's hard for me, because I love you—and I'm going to lose you again. I don't want this to seem like I'm just trying to get in the last word but, honey, oh please don't be scared, please don't please—" The words stopped in my throat. "Oh, Michael, just because you don't think there's anything there—doesn't mean you're *right*!"

His eyes were closed. He was very weak. But he brought my hand to his mouth like a kiss.

I rested my face against his and whispered. "I love you."

I was so certain that I would *know* when he died, that I would *feel* it, even if I wasn't there.

I was blow-drying my hair when the phone rang. "Hello, this is Mr. Wedlan," I heard the voice say. And while I was standing in my bedroom with half a head of wet hair dripping down my back and wondering why Michael's father referred to himself as "Mister," I heard him say: "We lost our boy tonight."

❦ *Chapter 44* ❦

I would have done it differently.

I would have taken Michael's ashes out to Oregon, talked to him as though those ashes were a *him*, then let them flutter away on some mountaintop.

But nobody asked.

He was buried next to his grandparents in an old cemetery on the south side of Chicago, his ashes contained in a white cardboard box. While Dr. Regan droned on about Jesus this and Jesus that, I kept staring at that box. Michael was such a big man. And it was such a small box.

I thought that because I *knew*—because I'd had months to get ready—that once Michael really died, once he was really gone, I'd be prepared.

But it wasn't like that.

I felt a hideous, freeing, form of relief.

I was glad Michael didn't hurt anymore. I was glad he wasn't scared anymore. I was glad he wasn't lying in a hospice anymore.

I was glad he wasn't waiting to die anymore.

Piper had taken a snapshot of us when she was in Springfield. I kept it leaning against the side of the clock-radio on my nightstand. But the day after Michael's funeral, I stuck it beneath a Kleenex box in the drawer.

At night I'd shift under my covers, *furious* at Michael for dying and abandoning me so permanently.

I'd lie in bed at night and talk to him in my head.

And I kept waiting for the phone to ring. I knew that was crazy. But I kept expecting it to ring so I could pick it up and hear that warm, tentative voice saying, Hello, Franny.

I'd wake up in the middle of the night afraid to get out of my bed.

There's a Jewish tradition that when somebody dies, bedsheets are thrown over all the mirrors in the house. My mother's version claims that hiding the mirrors keeps the mourners concentrating on the dead person, instead of on vain things like hairdos. Aunt Rose insists the sheets are there so that the spirit of the dead person won't look in a mirror, see he has no body, and die from the shock, even though he's already dead.

Aunt Rose's theory is somewhat less logical, but still, it spooked me. I'd crawl out of bed to go to the bathroom, but keeping my eyes tightly closed, slapping my hand along the wall until I found the bathroom lightswitch. I couldn't be in a dark room with a mirror.

I was afraid I'd see Michael in the mirror.

I once told him that I felt certain I would get some sort of sign that he was all right. But in a dark bathroom at 4:00 A.M., I didn't want any signs.

I'd tell myself I was being ridiculous. Michael would never do anything to scare me. I told myself I was insane. There *was* no Michael to scare me. Or love me.

I received a newspaper article in the mail about Steak & Shake closing down. There was no note. Just the article. And Gordon's name and return address on the envelope.

Several days later they called.

"When are you coming to visit us?" Norma asked. Her voice sounded smaller, more hesitant. "We're saving the wooden box for you, the one you wanted, the one Michael kept his loose change in. Will you be here soon?"

"Sure," I said. "Soon."

Gordon got on the phone.

"Hello," he said. "How've you been?"

"Okay," I said.

There was silence for a few moments, then Gordon lowered his voice, like he didn't want anyone to hear him, not even me. "We need to get away from this house. I look at the dining room and I still see that hospital bed. I walk into his bedroom and I still see him fallen over on the floor."

"I know," I murmured. "It's difficult to make those thoughts go away."

I'd feel anger at men I saw riding buses, men walking down the streets, mad at men with healthy bodies, men with *futures*. Why does that man in that dumb-looking suit get to be here—and Michael doesn't? I'd be at the office. I'd watch TV. I missed knowing where to go every weekend, what to focus on every day. I missed feeling needed.

I received a letter from Norma. The crocuses were coming up around the patio. They were thinking of planting tomatoes. She ran into Wes's wife, Dominique, at the mall. Dominique was saying how nice it would be if I visited Springfield.

I stuck the letter in a drawer.

I was staring at one of my mother's frozen tuna noodle casseroles, coaxing it to defrost faster, when the telephone rang. "Hello?" Norma said, more like a question than a greeting. She told me the tomato plants refused to turn red because they'd waited too long to plant them. She told me she was running low on yarn for her lap robes. She told me to put my casserole in a pan of boiling water to make it defrost faster. And she told me that whenever she was home alone, when Gordon was out buying milk or busy at the church, she'd go through Michael's old snapshots, or read his letters from Vietnam.

Gordon picked up the extension. Norma hung up.

"Did you know Michael received an honorary journeyman's certificate from his friends in the wood shop?" he asked. "I framed it and hung it in the living room. When my wife's at one of her luncheons or the beauty parlor, I sit and stare at that certificate, and think about him."

"I do that, too," I said. "I think about him."

A month later the wooden box arrived in the mail. There was a note stuck inside, written in Norma's fuzzy handwriting on pale green stationery. "We all did our best," she wrote.

Michael used to keep the wooden box on his dresser top, carefully lining it up in just the right place. He'd come home from work every night and toss his change into the box, along with his keys.

There was something about that wooden box filled with change on a dresser top that made me feel so married.

I had entered marriage with an expectation of permanence, and a longing for the emotional safety I felt certain Michael could give me. Was it too much to hope for someone to fill the empty spaces? I string our finer moments together and ask myself: How did we get off course? I've forgotten the reasons.

I still feel like I need to help him, like he's still somewhere in another city, not really gone, and there's something I'm supposed to be doing.

I set the box on my nightstand, then opened the drawer and took out the photo of Michael and me. He's smiling in the picture. A cap is covering his bald head. I'm standing behind him, my face peeking over his shoulder, my hands resting on his arms, holding him protectively.

He was so beautiful.

I slipped the picture into an antique silver frame Michael had once given me for Christmas and set it next to the wooden box. Then I picked up the telephone and dialed the number in Springfield.

Norma answered.

"Hello, Mom," I said. "I was wondering if you'd like company this weekend."

"Oh yes, of course we would!" Norma said. "I'll make a Jell-O mold."

The rental car was an overheated oven, and even though the air-conditioner made so much noise it *sounded* like it was working, it didn't do much good. Once I was out of the city, I just turned the blower off and lowered the windows. The closest thing I could find to decent music was some sort of jazz. I raised the radio full blast. The fields of corn along the road were tall enough to have a rhythm all their own, waving back and forth, easing me forward. There was something comforting in knowing those crops would be there year after year. I checked the speedometer. Norma would be setting the table with flowered placemats and cloth napkins. Gordon would be outside picking green tomatoes for the salad.

If I hurried, I could get there by noon.